Embrace the Fire

Felice Stevens

Embrace the Fire (Through Hell and Back – Book 3)
March 2017
Copyright © 2017 by Felice Stevens
Second Edition
First released in March 2015
Print Edition

Cover Art by: Reese Dante
www.reesedante.com
Cover Photography by: Varian Krylov of Strangeland Photography
Edited by: Flat Earth Editing
Proofreading by Dianne Thies of Lyrical Lines

Published in the United States of America

Brandon Gilbert has spent years in hiding, but he's finally accomplished his dream of working as a public school teacher. When offered the chance to help bullied children, there was no way he could say no. Not to mention that meeting Dr. Tash Weber, the psychiatrist who helps them, a sad yet sexy older man, ignited a spark inside Brandon he'd never had before.

Though five years have passed since the death of his lover, Dr. Sebastian "Tash" Weber has no interest in relationships or love. But young, enigmatic Brandon awakens his heart and his desire. Despite Tash's best efforts to push him away, Brandon unlocks the passion for life Tash thought he'd lost forever.

Falling in love wasn't part of the plan for either Brandon or Tash, but neither family disapproval nor self-doubts can stop them from embracing the fire that burns between them. And when Brandon returns home to fight for a future he never imagined possible, he and Tash discover that the one thing worth fighting for has been with them all along.

Dedication

This is dedicated to all the teachers who helped and encouraged me. Your guidance and devotion have never been forgotten.

Acknowledgments

Thank you so much to my wonderful editors, Hope and Jess from Flat Earth Editing, and the lovely, Dianne Thies from Lyrical Lines Proofreading. The journey for these men has been an arduous one, but I loved every minute re-reading, and writing more of their stories. And stay tuned....you never know when they might all pop up again. I have a hard time letting go of my characters.

And of course, thank you, the readers for all your emails and messages about Ash and Drew, Jordan and Luke and Brandon and Tash. I'm thrilled you fell in love with them as much as I did.

Join my newsletter to get access to get first looks at WIP, exclusive content, contests, deleted scenes and much more! Never any spam.

Newsletter:
http://eepurl.com/bExIdr

Chapter One

Seven years earlier

IN A FUTILE attempt to shield himself from the pouring rain, Brandon Gilbert lay huddled in a doorway near the Port Authority Bus Terminal in midtown Manhattan. Thoroughly soaked and shivering, he squeezed into the corner of the large, now waterlogged cardboard box. The once-protective box sagged over his head, allowing the cascading water to run like a river down his back. At six feet, Brandon had a hard time finding any place to keep dry, and it seemed at this point, the battle had been lost.

Why he'd thought coming to New York City was a good idea, he couldn't remember. Perhaps it was the anonymity he needed or the fact that he could reinvent himself now that he had papers and a new identity. But nothing had prepared him for the stark loneliness of this huge city; he had no steady source of food or shelter or anyone to talk to day after day.

Brandon shifted in the box, and a fresh torrent of rainwater poured over him. The dank smells of the city coupled with the uncaring stares of people as they rushed by caused unwelcome tears to spring to his eyes. It wasn't supposed to be like this. He and his foster brothers were going to stay together, take care of each other. The three musketeers, that's what they'd laughingly called themselves.

Until Ash unexpectedly disappeared, leaving Brandon and Luke behind, never to be heard from again. Then after a night of frantic upheaval he still didn't understand, Brandon found himself on the road to a new life, ripped away from the only person he knew truly loved him—Luke. Where was Luke? Brandon remembered long ago how his brother had dreamed of coming to New York City to live, so when he first got to the city, he'd foolishly tried to locate him. He went looking for a phone book but couldn't find any. The few times he'd gone to the public library to use their computers, he'd searched for *Luke Carini*, but there were no listings with that name. Discouraged, he'd stopped.

And now he was alone. Not a single person cared about him, plus he could never go home again. Why did he even bother? If he was smart, he'd go to the river and jump in. No one would notice or care.

A tall silhouette holding an umbrella loomed in front of him, cutting off the dim light of the gray, dripping skies. Terrified, Brandon shrank back farther into the dark corner of the doorway.

"Don't be afraid. I'm not here to hurt you." The figure squatted in front of Brandon, and the face of a middle-aged man came into view. His smile radiated warmth and peace, emotions almost alien to Brandon.

"What do you want?" Brandon clutched his thin jacket around him. "I don't have any money or anything." At that moment, a gush of water sluiced down over his face. In his eighteen years, Brandon had never felt so alone and lost.

"I don't want anything from you except your promise to take my help. I'm with an organization that aids runaway youth." The man's calm smile miraculously settled Brandon's racing heart. "You have no place to go; am I right? Let me take you someplace where you'll be safe and secure."

"Who are you?" Although hope flared hot and bright in Brandon's chest, he knew enough to be wary of men offering help.

"My name is Gabriel, Gabriel Heller. I'm a New York City schoolteacher, and I volunteer on the weekends with the Department of Homeless Services." He pulled out an ID and a pamphlet and offered it to Brandon. "Here, see?"

With some trepidation, Brandon took the laminated card and the pamphlet the man offered, after brushing a hank of wet hair out of his eyes. The identification checked out as the man had stated. Gabriel Heller worked for the Department of Education. A teacher. Brandon bit his lip as he read over the mission of the organization and how they planned to help.

"Here." He handed back the items, his thoughts

racing.

All his life, Brandon had wanted to be a teacher; school had been the only outlet he had to escape his home life. Teachers had been his saviors, and until that last, horrible night with his foster father, his plan had always been to go to college and get a job teaching young inner-city children.

"So, have I passed the test? Will you come to the shelter with me?" Gabriel's lips curved in a wry smile. "This isn't a night fit for even a New York City rat to be outside. I'll set you up with a social worker and get you a place to stay. What's your name?"

A yearning Brandon had thought dead burst to life, almost choking him with its intensity. Things like this, good things, never happened to him. "Randy. My name is Randy." Close enough to his real name, Brandon, Randy was the name he'd chosen when he'd run away, making sure no one could find him.

"Okay, Randy, come on. I'll get you out of those wet clothes, give you a hot meal, and a place to sleep." Gabriel stood and held out his hand. "You don't have to figure out the rest of your life tonight."

The force of the pelting rain lessened, and the gray of the sky shifted to a lighter haze. Brandon stood and pulled off the wet strips of cardboard clinging to his hair and body. "I don't have any money to pay, and I don't take charity." Some vestige of pride he'd thought long gone emerged. "I'll work for whatever I have to."

A smile crept over Gabriel's face. "How old are you?"

"Almost nineteen."

Brandon heard Gabriel sigh. "What's wrong?" Was he too old? Now that the chance was in front of him, so close he could reach out and brush it with his fingertips, Brandon wanted it. Desperately.

"I don't suppose you have your high school diploma?"

"Yes, I do." His chin lifted. "I was going to go to college." He slanted a quick look at Gabriel through the wet strands of hair that hung in his eyes. "I wanted to be a teacher too."

They'd reached the van Gabriel had left parked down the block and they climbed inside. Another man waited behind the wheel.

"Antonio, this is Randy."

"Hey, man. No night to be outside. You don't know how lucky you are Gabriel found you. He's a life changer."

Brandon's eyes met Antonio's in the rearview mirror. Something tight loosened in his chest, allowing him to return the smile. "Yeah?"

Antonio nodded. "Yeah. Last year I was in your shoes: no home, no job, and no place to go." He started the engine and put the windshield wipers on to clear the windows. "Today, I got a place to live and a job helping Gabriel getting guys like you off the streets. I'm even going to college now." His voice rang with quiet pride.

Gabriel slid into the front seat next to Antonio, and the van bounced along the street on its journey downtown. Water dripped from his clothes onto the seat and floor of the van.

"I'm glad you came with me, Randy. You have the opportunity now to help yourself and hopefully, help others in the future." He turned around to give Brandon a gentle, reassuring smile. "The first step is the hardest, isn't it? But it's all worth it in the end."

The warmth of the heater finally began to penetrate his wet clothes, yet Brandon shivered. The enormity of the second chance he was being offered overwhelmed him. If these men had faith in him, there was nothing he couldn't accomplish. Could he do it? Could he start over again and achieve his dreams?

As Gabriel spoke, Brandon forgot his wet clothes and empty stomach, and listened.

Present day

MOST PEOPLE LOVED the rain. They waxed poetic about its warmth and how it cleansed them, turning everything fresh and new. Brandon, remembering many nights spent hungry, wet, and miserable, hated it. There was nothing fresh and beautiful about soaking-wet clothes and feet. As he walked outside PS 100, also known as the JFK School of Urban Development, Brandon grimaced, glancing up at the sheets of water pouring from the gray, forbidding sky. It splashed down onto the already streaming streets, creating puddles that made it almost impossible to navigate crossing at each corner.

Brandon pulled his hood over his head and narrowed his eyes, attempting to calculate when the light would change, so he could make a mad dash for the subway station. He hefted his backpack onto his shoulder, wondering why it was so light.

"Damn." A quick glance inside it proved his fear correct. He'd left his laptop in his classroom. Well, he had to go back for it. Even though the rooms were locked, he couldn't leave it there overnight until he returned the next day. He gave a rueful glance up at the dark sky. Maybe by the time he came back out, the rain would be lighter. He trudged up the steps of the school and went back inside.

Look on the bright side, Brandon. That's what you've learned in the past seven years.

Upon re-entering the building, the absolute stillness in the air amazed him. No children's shouts nor laughter echoed off the cement walls; no bells sounded in the hallways. Although the staff attempted to liven up the walls by hanging children's artwork, it couldn't hide the overall institutional atmosphere of the hulking brick-and-cement building.

The swarms of children exiting the school had diminished. A few remained behind for after-school programs and clubs, but most couldn't wait to leave and go home to watch TV, have playdates, and hopefully do their homework. Brandon hadn't been at this school long, only about three months, but already he loved everything about his teaching assignment.

After he graduated college, he'd applied for the NYC Teaching Collaborative program and was accepted. There he was able to partner with a mentor teacher and work as an apprentice in one of the city's highest-need areas. It was a hands-on, practical program that allowed him to work directly with an experienced teacher and the students, and after eight months, he'd received his teaching degree. Paying it forward, helping the ones who needed it so desperately, had been his mantra for the past seven years since Gabriel found him cowering in that doorway. Tears burned behind his eyes as he remembered the man who had changed his life, and how he'd died from a heart attack without any warning.

After Gabriel's death, Brandon had dedicated himself to the single-minded purpose of becoming a teacher. To making Gabriel proud. To proving he could fulfill his lifetime dream.

He loved his sixth graders. They were still eager to learn and able to see beauty in the world around them. Brandon wanted to gather them all in his arms and protect them from what he knew waited to hurt them outside. They deserved everything good the world had to offer. Safety, stability, and hope. Everything he'd never had, Brandon was determined to give his kids.

Brandon took the stairs to his second-floor classroom, praying he'd find his laptop still there. He tested the doorknob, glad to see it hadn't been locked yet, which would have necessitated a trip to the custodian to get the keys. Two students sat in the back of the classroom; they jumped up when he entered the room. A book clattered to the floor between them.

"Hey, guys. What're you two doing here after school?" Brandon knew these two kids, even though they weren't his students. Best friends and equally studious, they had each other's backs and stood up to the taunts and teasing from the other kids who made fun of them for getting good grades and being bookish. The tall boy's name was Wilson; the shorter and more slightly built boy was Dwayne.

"Sorry, Mr. Gilbert." Wilson bent to pick up the book. "We were going over the reading assignment Mrs. Forsch gave us."

Every student should be like these two. "No problem. What are you reading?"

Wilson showed him the book. "*The Three Musketeers.*"

Brandon's stomach twisted. The name Luke and Ash had always called the three of them. "One for all and all for one, huh?"

"Yeah." Dwayne glanced at him. "You all right, Mr. Gilbert? Your face looks kind of funny."

Brandon forced a weak smile. "I'm fine. You guys should go on home."

They grabbed their backpacks and left the classroom.

To his immense relief, his laptop sat in the desk drawer where he'd left it. With his starting salary, he could ill afford to replace it.

For a second he stood at the front of the classroom, thinking about the three musketeers, his mind spinning back in time. Of his oldest brother, Ash, he had only the hazy memory of a tall skinny boy with black hair, silver eyes, and a sad smile. Brandon never understood why one day Ash was there, tucking him in after reading him a bedtime story, and the next he was gone. After several weeks of them both waiting for Ash to return, Luke told him to forget Ash, that he was never coming back, and held Brandon tight as he cried.

It had been over fifteen years since Ash left, and Brandon barely remembered him now. But Luke? Losing Luke crushed him. Brandon had never forgotten that last awful night of screams and chaos. And the next morning, Brandon was gone, speeding off to a new life, with never another mention of the brother he'd left behind. Any questions he'd had about Luke were answered with a backhand to the face or a belt across his back.

Brandon long suspected his foster father had abused Luke somehow; Munson delighted in hitting Brandon on occasion but saved his real violence for Brandon's poor foster mother. Too many nights Brandon had lain awake listening to Munson yelling at her—for a perceived wrong he thought he'd suffered at work that he blamed her for or for something so small as dinner being late. His mother would go silent; then Munson would leave the house, stomping out his fury, and drive away, tires spinning on the gravel.

In the morning, his mother would show up in the

kitchen to give him breakfast, her eyes reddened and face haggard. When he grew older he'd told her he'd report Munson to the authorities for abuse, but she balked and refused to admit to it, claiming she'd hurt herself when he pointed out a fresh bruise that hadn't been there the day before.

Brandon blinked, returning to the present. Another time, another world. He'd long since made peace in his heart that he'd never see his brothers again. And while life was far from perfect, he no longer lived in the blackness that had surrounded him on the fateful night Gabriel found him. In the years since, he'd gone to college, gotten a job, and even had his one and only love affair, so to speak.

A slight smile crossed his lips. Charlie had been goofy and fun, but it was nothing more than two friends coming together to stave off their mutual loneliness. There'd been no grand passion, no thoughts of anything permanent between them. When Charlie told him one night as they lay in bed that he'd accepted a job in Florida, Brandon wished him well and kissed him good-bye, regretting only that he was losing a friend, not a lover.

"Who's in here? Oh hi, Randy." Gage Taylor stuck his head inside. "What're you doing here?"

Brandon switched his easygoing persona back on. *Never let them see how scared you are, how frightened that in an instant, your entire world could go up in flames.*

"I forgot my laptop and came back inside to wait out the rain." Brandon zipped up his backpack and headed toward the door. "I think it's stopped. We can walk out together."

He shut off the lights and closed the door behind him. They walked down the stairs, and as Brandon had predicted, the rain had ceased. Peeks of blue sky appeared from between the heavy clouds. He stood at the corner waiting for the light to change and surveyed the glistening, wet streets.

"Well, see you tomorrow." Brandon stepped off the curb.

"Wait. What are you doing tonight?" Gage put a restraining hand on Brandon's arm, and Brandon froze at his touch. Though Gage had been his mentor teacher at the school, Brandon had kept him at arm's distance, never encouraging the friendship he knew Gage tried to build.

Without noticing Brandon's reaction, Gage continued to speak. "The reason I ask is, I'm going to this meeting at a clinic in Red Hook. They have programs where adults help kids. Mentor them if they need help in school or an ear to listen to their problems. I was wondering if you'd want to come with me tonight. The doctor who runs it is pretty cool." Gage dropped his hand, and they faced each other. "I think you'd be perfect."

Brandon shifted his backpack to the other shoulder. "Why me? Not that it isn't flattering, but we don't know each other outside of school."

Gage's dark eyes pierced through Brandon. "I wanted you to have your own space and not think I was intruding on your ability to run your own classroom.

But I see how you feel about these kids. It's personal with you, like you understand them. You really want to help...they mean something to you."

"Yes, yes they do." Brandon swallowed against the rising lump in his throat. Gage had no idea.

"These kids need a champion. Someone like you who wants to help, judgment-free. If you were in trouble and needed help, wouldn't you want someone there to catch you from falling, or prevent you from getting hurt?"

Those poignant words struck Brandon deep in his heart. Maybe if he'd had someone to talk to, he wouldn't have needed to run away. At the very least, he could have talked to his foster mom and explained. Perhaps Ash and Luke had been forced to do similar things. He hoped not because no one should live with the taste of fear forever on their lips.

"Sure. I'll be there. Give me the information." Brandon took down the address and agreed to meet Gage there at seven that night. As he sat in the swaying subway car, Brandon smiled to himself. He'd finally made it—a dream job and another purpose now, with this mentoring program. As for the aching loneliness? Well, it was a small price to pay for what he'd done, no matter how well deserved.

Brandon had spent years debating his decision, never reaching a satisfying answer. Life stuck you with the choices you made and the consequences that were born from them. And sometimes, you had no choice at all.

Chapter Two

HE MISSED SEX. Dr. Sebastian Weber, "Tash" to his family and friends, came to that startling revelation as he surreptitiously watched the good-looking male waiter in the diner approach his table. And not simply sex for the sake of getting off. That he could find anywhere, with anyone—his own hand included. No, what he missed was hot, sweaty, screaming-down-the-walls sex with a lover who knew better than anyone else what he wanted and needed to feel loved.

He hadn't had that in years.

Refusing to think about that now, he glanced into the dark eyes of the patient man who stood by his table waiting to take his order. "Sorry. I'll have the French toast and scrambled eggs. You can leave the menu. I have someone joining me soon."

The young man smiled. "Certainly, sir. Do you want your coffee now?"

"Yes, please."

The waiter poured and left. Tash stirred in his

milk, staring unseeingly into the swirling caramel depths of the coffee mug.

The diner was practically empty; only a few retirees and moms with young children sat drinking coffee and passing the time. It was off-peak for breakfast, around ten thirty on a Monday morning, and he was meeting his sister for a late breakfast. Her boss's boyfriend had surprised him with a two week-long vacation to Paris, and subsequently, she'd found herself with unexpected time off from her job as his personal assistant. She and Tash tried to see each other at least once a week, but with her long hours and his spur-of-the-moment appointments with patients, their plans often got pushed off to once a month.

But that was as far as he'd let it go. Now that their parents were no longer snowbirds and had permanently moved to Florida, he and Val were each other's only family in New York. And while Val had an active social life that included dates, parties, and a stream of admirers, Tash remained alone. Aside from his two cats, there had been no one to share his evenings with for far too long.

To her credit, Val refused to allow him to wallow in his self-imposed solitude, forcing him to come with her to events he'd rather miss and dinners he'd prefer not to eat. It was at the opening of a local community center that Tash had met her boss, Luke Conover, and his lover, Jordan Peterson. He drank down his coffee, wishing he could have a relationship like Jordan and Luke or Ash and Drew did, fiercely devoted and loving.

Those men had been through hell with each other and had come back stronger than ever to embrace life to the fullest.

When he'd agreed to treat Jordan for a Xanax dependency, he never imagined he'd be inheriting a new social circle instead of a solitary patient undergoing treatment. Jordan came with a group of overprotective, highly involved friends, all of whom had taken Tash on as not only their colleague but as a friend and, he suspected, a group project.

So, against his better judgment and desire to isolate himself from these well-meaning people, their laughter, conversation, and happiness, Tash became swept up into their lives and love affairs. He found himself invited to Friday night dinners, Saturday night movie watching, and Sunday afternoon brunches, complete with subtle and not-so-subtle offers to set him up.

Highly involved was ostensibly also code for nosy and intrusive. They constantly tried to set him up on dates, which he almost always turned down—using work and a busy schedule as his excuse. The mentoring program had become his latest passion, and he preferred to give it all his attention for now.

Tash finished his coffee and checked his watch.

"I'm on time, big brother. You're always early; that's the problem." Valerie slid into the seat across the table from him. Immediately, the waiter reappeared and gave her a big smile and greeting.

Val turned on her lovely smile. "Just scrambled eggs and toast, please. No butter. And milk for the coffee."

The waiter hurried off to do her bidding. Anyone who became caught up in the glow of Val's big brown eyes immediately fell under her spell. Her coffee appeared instantaneously, as well as a small bowl of fruit "on the house for the pretty lady."

She blushed. "Oh, you shouldn't have, but thank you." After tasting a piece of strawberry, she pushed the dish to the middle of the table. "Here, share with me."

He shook his head. "No, thanks. What's up with you? I haven't been able to get ahold of you for ages."

Val drank her coffee and moaned with delight. "God, that's good. Well, with Luke leaving so unexpectedly for Europe, we had a lot of things to settle before he went away. I didn't have the heart not to help him." She drank more coffee, and as soon as she set it down, the waiter was right there to refill it.

"You should've seen him; it's so cute how excited and nervous he was to meet Jordan's parents."

Tash smiled faintly. "I'm glad things worked out for the two of them."

Val's happy face turned sympathetic. "I know you liked Jordan, sweetie. I'm sorry it didn't end up the way you would've wanted." She reached out to take his hand. After a moment's hesitation, he took it, giving a hard squeeze before releasing it.

"It wasn't any big deal, and in the long run it turned out for the best. Jordan loves Luke. They belong together; anyone can see that." The coffee burned an acidic trail down his throat. For the first time in years, he'd been somewhat attracted to another man, but

17

Jordan, recovering from the death of his fiancé, had come out of his yearlong grieving process to fall in love with Luke. "I'm happy I could help them in some small way. It's how it was meant to be."

Him. Alone. If he remained alone, he couldn't have regrets; he already had enough of them to last a lifetime.

A small sound of dismay escaped Val. "Oh, Tash, don't. You sound as though you've given up on everything." She stopped speaking as the waiter approached with their food.

The warm, tantalizing smell of cinnamon and vanilla hit his nose as the waiter placed the plate of French toast before him. He busied himself by dousing the food with maple syrup but stopped when Val placed her hand over his. He shook off her touch. "You can't give up what you don't have. Leave it alone."

"But—"

"Enough." Torn between his love for his sister and the pain he still carried within, Tash knew he'd lash out and say something cutting and mean if he didn't stop the conversation at that moment. He already lived with enough remorse crushing his soul. To hurt Valerie, the person who meant more to him than anyone, would break him. "Please," he gritted out, dangerously close to losing the strict self-control he placed on his emotions. "The past is meant to be left where it is, not reopened and dissected. I made peace with everything long ago."

But Valerie, who loved him, also knew him best. "You're hiding away because of a mistake you believe you made years ago. I never thought of this before, but maybe you need to see someone yourself, to come to terms with what happened with you and Danny."

Tash winced at the sound of Danny's name. He huffed out a strained laugh. "The shrink needs a shrink?" He shoved a piece of French toast into his mouth and chewed, barely tasting it. After swallowing, he patted Val's hand. "I don't think so. I said I'm fine."

Val shot him a disbelieving look through narrowed eyes. "That's why you spend every night alone, you and those cats. I know the guys have tried to set you up and you refuse."

"I'm busy. Between putting together the joint men-toring program with the Clinic, the community center, and the shelter, plus helping Legal Aid with the kid who sold Jordan his drugs, as well as my own patients, I've got a full plate." He drank down his coffee. "I barely have time to eat."

"Then slow down. You're not doing anyone a favor if you get sick." Tash squirmed under her gaze, but she ruthlessly continued. "You look like hell; your eyes are tired, and you've lost weight."

"Gee, nice to see you too. Thanks."

"I'm saying it because I love you. Punishing your-self isn't helping you, and it won't bring Danny back either."

At her simple statement, he lost his breath. For so long he'd worn the guilt of Danny's death like a second skin. He'd been living a shadow life, present and accounted for but never really there in full spirit. He'd lost himself somewhere along the way, and the sad thing was, he didn't see the need to find himself again.

It was like the nursery rhyme: *"All the king's horses and all the king's men, couldn't put Humpty Dumpty together again."*

Tash was broken beyond repair, and he saw no need to gather the shards of his mental wreckage and try to piece himself back together.

"I promise to start eating better. And I think this mentoring program will be great. I always wanted to do something to help kids. If we can give them a support system before the bad outside influences sink their claws into them, they'll have somewhere to turn. Drew's clinic is great, but it steps in *after* the problem. I want to get to them before."

A relieved smile broke across Valerie's face. "Oh, I haven't seen you this passionate about anything in so long." She grasped his hand. "I think it's terrific, and I know it'll be a success."

"Eat your breakfast." He pointed at her plate of eggs and toast. "It's getting cold."

Val wrinkled her nose at him but took a bite of her toast. "There, satisfied?"

He tweaked her nose. Damn, he loved her. They finished their meal, and after he paid the bill, they walked outside and stood on the street waiting for a cab for Val to go back to the city. It was almost lunchtime now, and the nearby courthouse would begin emptying—all the judges, attorneys, and jurors fanning out to the restaurants in the neighborhood. He could see the kids from one of the local schools playing soccer in the park. He and Val hugged and made plans to get together over the weekend and have lunch.

"I love you. Promise me you won't sit in your house with only those cats for company when you don't have patients." She wound her scarf around her neck, then buttoned her jacket.

He rolled his eyes. "God, you make me sound like a pathetic loser. Is that what you think I do?" She opened her mouth, and he put his hand over her lips. "Never mind. Don't answer that. I'll call you about the weekend."

They kissed good-bye, and he hailed an oncoming cab for her. After watching Val get inside the car, he continued his walk down Court Street. Tash enjoyed the bright blue of the brilliant October sky and, as always during this season, welcomed the brisk freshness of the cooler air. Brilliant fall colors of crimson and gold painted the trees arching overhead, as he turned onto Pierrepont Street, walking deeper into the Heights. He loved his little enclave of a neighborhood. Brooklyn Heights was like a small town in the big city, where people knew each other on the streets and local storeowners were friendly and welcoming. Fewer and fewer independent stores remained due to the exorbitant rents, and he mourned that fact as he came to his street, wonderfully named Love Lane.

When he unlocked his front door, his two Siamese cats, Caesar and Cleopatra, ran toward him, yowling like banshees, looking for attention. They'd been returned numerous times to the animal shelter because of their loud meowing, but Tash didn't mind. They were something to break the loneliness and give him love.

"Okay, you two, quiet down." Identical pairs of turquoise-blue eyes regarded him steadily; then with a noise that sounded more machine-gun-like than should come out of any felines, they ran to the back of the carriage house.

At four, he'd be meeting with Connor Halstead, a Legal Aid attorney, and his client Johnny, about Johnny's court-ordered treatment. That case promised to be tough. The young man who'd sold Jordan his Xanax was as mistrustful as they came. Another product of the streets. This time, Tash promised himself, he wouldn't fail.

Johnny would be a perfect candidate for the mentoring program. Both Ash and Luke had agreed to help him; they would speak to the kids and show them that growing up with abuse and grinding poverty didn't have to keep you from accomplishing a dream. It was a great idea to include teachers and other leaders from the community—possibly clergy and politicians. He stretched out on his sofa.

A deep rumbling resonated through his body. When he opened his eyes, a very determined turquoise-blue gaze came into focus, staring straight back at him.

"Meow." Caesar's claws delicately pricked through Tash's shirt as he continued to purr and began to knead Tash's chest.

"Ow, stop." Tash lifted him and placed him gently on the ground, yet the cat still gave him an affronted look as though he couldn't believe Tash had had the nerve to displace him. Tash rubbed his face with his hands and sat up, his back creaking from the uncomfortable position he'd fallen asleep in on his sofa. He scratched his head, then stretched. At thirty-nine, he tried to keep himself in shape, but some days felt considerably more like a losing battle than others.

When he saw the time, he groaned. Damn, he'd never meant to take a three-hour nap. That's what a restless sleep during the night would do, but he hadn't slept properly in years. What all this meant was, now he'd have to haul ass to Drew's clinic. Tash had taken a tour of it with Jordan and Luke and was extremely impressed at what the men had accomplished, and he was thrilled to be able to lend them whatever help he could.

He tied his sneakers and headed out the door. After checking his watch, he saw he had about twenty minutes to make it to Red Hook where the Clinic was located, and Johnny was doing his community service. Tash's therapy session with the young man was to take place there, but first, they'd meet with the Legal Aid attorney. Hopefully, Johnny would open up and let Tash in. From the reports he'd read on the boy, he was a silent, resentful teenager.

As luck would have it, he picked up a cab right away on Henry Street and settled into the back seat as it rattled off down the cobblestones of lower Joralemon

Street, heading toward Red Hook. Sheets of rain now poured from the sky, but even that didn't diminish the sheer strength and enormity of the glass-and-steel skyline interspersed with the late nineteenth-century architecture of lower Manhattan. The cab bounced around as it ran up Van Brunt Street, finally slowing the jostling of his inner organs as it pulled up in front of the Clinic. He made a mad dash between the raindrops to the Clinic's front door.

"Marly. How are you?" He shut the door behind him to keep the miserable weather out of the reception area.

He sensed the energy humming with the doctors and staff as he watched them bustle back and forth in the hallway. These people were so dedicated to their work; many had chosen to give up lucrative careers to help or volunteered after they'd already retired from private practice.

Seeing these kids who lived in the age where supposedly everyone was more enlightened and accepting, and hearing their stories of abandonment, bullying, and outright rejection from their parents and their peers reinforced Tash's belief that he'd made the right choice in his life, at least where work was involved. In his first case working with the Clinic, he'd helped a young man named Stevie, who had struggled with acceptance of his sexuality as well as some residual effects of the bullying and abuse he'd suffered at the hands of the foster brothers he once lived with. Only recently had Stevie begun to blossom and discover all life had to offer. He now excelled in his last year of high school and planned a future working at the Clinic. Tash was thankful he'd been able to help, even in his small way.

"Hi, Dr. Tash." Marly smiled at him. "Dr. Drew is waiting for you with your patient and his lawyer." She handed him a sheet of paper.

"Thanks." He flashed her a smile. "How's everything with you?"

"Great. Did you hear that I got accepted to St. Francis College, so I can still keep working here while I go to school?" She looked nothing like the scrawny, scared teen she'd been over a year ago, now projecting an image of a confident, healthy young woman.

"That's great." He shook her hand, knowing she wouldn't appreciate a congratulatory kiss from him. "You should be proud of yourself."

"I am. If it wasn't for Dr. Drew, I never would've made it." The phone rang. "Excuse me, I have to answer that." She picked up the phone. "Home Away from Home Clinic. How may I help you?"

Tash walked down the hall to the back where the examining rooms were located. He heard the low murmur of voices behind the closed door of Drew's office and knocked.

"Come on in."

When Tash opened the door, he came face-to-face with Dr. Drew Klein. Sitting across the desk from Drew was the attorney, Connor Halstead, and the teen, Johnny Ramatour.

"Tash, great. I was hoping it was you." Drew indicated the empty chair next to Connor. "Have a seat."

"Thanks." He dropped into the chair closest to the wall, next to Connor. He liked the bright Legal Aid attorney who defended his clients with a ferocious intensity. He was a man who believed in what he did, and in turn, Tash had nothing but the utmost respect for him.

Connor bent to retrieve a file from his briefcase. "Now that we're all here, let's get this started. Johnny is doing his community service at the Clinic, and as part of his probation, he's also required to undergo psychiatric evaluation and therapy."

"I still don't think I need no fuckin' shrink. There ain't nothing wrong with me."

Great. Another teenager with an attitude. And this one had no reason to be angry, since he was getting out of jail time, as a result of the goodness of his Legal Aid attorney and the deal he'd worked out with the prosecution. Did the boy know how fucking lucky he was that someone gave a damn? Tash was about to find out.

"You have a problem with the sentence, Johnny?" Tash glared at him. "That's fine with me. I don't give a shit one way or another. Go back to your miserable life—stealing, selling dope, and living on the streets. But know this. This is your big chance. You may not get another one. So if you fuck it up, there's no guarantee you're going to have another Connor or Drew or me to help you get and keep your ass out of jail." He grimaced as he saw Johnny's face grow pale.

"And let me tell you; you have too pretty an ass for the inmates not to notice."

Connor's lips twitched. "So, kid, you've now seen how this is going to play out. Dr. Weber here isn't going to cut you any slack. You're gonna have to work hard and dig deep within yourself to see where you messed up."

Johnny scowled. But behind the sneer, Tash glimpsed fear and uncertainty—a relief to him. It let him know that Johnny remained vulnerable, a child who'd never had a chance to grow up before society gave up on him and threw him away.

But Tash knew not to show him weakness nor cut him any slack. At least at first. And this time he wouldn't fuck up and think the problem solved because he believed what he was told. This time he knew the warning signs.

"Are you up for it, Johnny? Or is that all you want to do with your life—live on the streets like a small-time hustler?" Tash saw he hit home with that point as Johnny's eyes widened. He wasn't surprised when the teen lashed out at him next.

"What the fuck am I supposed to do? Nobody gives a shit about me. And tell me how I'm supposed to live, huh?" He folded his arms across his skinny chest and continued to glare at Tash.

"How old are you?"

"Seventeen," he spat out. "Why?"

Tash turned to Connor. "Can we get him in a home and back in school?"

"Shit, man. I can't go back to school. It's been more than a year since I left home."

There was a knock at the door, and Johnny fell silent but continued shooting daggers at Tash, his animosity a visible presence in the room.

"Come in," Drew called out.

The door opened, and Steve North came in with an armful of files. "Oh, I'm sorry, Dr. Drew. I thought you were by yourself. These are the files for tomorrow's patients."

Drew smiled with affection at the young man. "Thanks. You can put them on the desk."

He smiled back. "Sure." He set them down then looked around, obviously curious, Tash surmised, but too polite to ask any questions. "Well, I'll be going."

Drew held up his hand. "Wait a minute. You know, Connor, Steve lives with a foster family. Maybe he can talk to Johnny and tell him how the experience has been." He looked over at Johnny, who was gazing at Steve with a mixture of mistrust and a little bit of envy.

"What do you think, Johnny? Steve had it really rough the last few years until my partner, Ash, and the rest of us got him the help he needed, right, Steve?"

The young man nodded vigorously, long brown bangs flopping over his eyes. "Yeah, honest. They were all amazing. I'm doing really well in school, and I'll be going to college next year." He straightened up, tall and proud. "I'm going to study to be a medical technician so I can help the doctors here at the Clinic."

A myriad of expressions played out across Johnny's face—envy, disbelief, wonder, and a dawning realization that maybe he too could break out of the cycle of despair. "Steve," Tash said to the young man, "why don't you take Johnny around and show him what he'll be working on. He's going to do some community service here for the next six months or so."

"Sure." Steve beckoned to Johnny, who gave them a cautious smile—no more than a flicker across his lips, but Tash saw it and inwardly cheered. "Come with me; I'll show you the computer system and the files."

Without a backward look, Johnny followed Steve out of the door and down the hallway. Tash could hear Steve chattering to him, and Johnny answered back, at first hesitant, then with increasing enthusiasm.

"Steve will have him sold on this place by the end of the day." Drew leaned back in his chair, a satisfied smile on his face. "He's our number-one champion."

"He's a great young man." The story of Steve's transformation, from bullied teen to model student, was almost a legend at the Clinic. "You did a wonderful job helping him."

Drew leaned forward on his desk, his face bright with excitement. "You and this mentoring program are going to help so many like him; I can't even begin to imagine. It's a great thing you're doing. So many lives are going to be changed by this." He glanced over his shoulder to look out the window. "Even the rain's cooperated and stopped."

What Drew didn't know was how badly Tash

needed this program for his own mental health. It was a way to give back, pay it forward for those who'd been left behind, and to make up for his own past mistakes. In the end, he'd be helped as much by the kids as he'd be helping them.

Chapter Three

A BIT APPREHENSIVE, Brandon waited for Gage on the corner of Van Brunt Street in Red Hook. He was somewhat familiar with the area, having been to the Ikea to buy furniture for his apartment and Fairway to buy food. It had seen a resurgence in the past few years with young people, driven out of Manhattan and other areas of Brooklyn like Williamsburg by high rents, coming to live and work in Red Hook. Still, the overall fog of poverty hung over the hulking projects and this corner of the city like a dark shroud.

The nerves had nothing to do with the area; he'd lived on the streets long enough to remember how to take care of himself in most situations. It was putting himself in a new environment, meeting new people. Exposing himself. The potential for discovery was enormous.

Yet he couldn't refuse Gage. In the back of Brandon's mind, he wondered…if he and his brothers had a place like this when they were growing up, would his family be intact today? As if Luke stood there with him

on that windswept corner, Brandon heard him
promising to always be there and almost felt his
comforting arms hugging him tight. Over ten years had
passed, but Brandon missed his foster brother every day
like crazy.

*Where the hell did you go, Luke? Are you even still
alive?*

He drew his resolve around him like a shield of
armor and promised to do for these kids what society
had failed to do for him and Luke.

Protect and save them.

Darkness spread rapidly, and the streetlights glowed
on, beaming out mellow golden pools of light down the
block. Brandon idly watched a man exit the deli across
the street, hefting a bag. He stood under the streetlight,
and like a beacon, it shone on his waving brown hair
and glinted off his glasses. He must be close to forty,
Brandon mused, taking in the man's long legs, pausing
at his handsome face. Unaccustomed heat flooded
through him.

It had been months since Brandon had thought
about sex or had a physical reaction to any man. Even
when he'd been with Charlie, his emotions remained
muted, the gropings and mutual hand jobs between
them merely a means to an end. The times they'd had
sex had always left him unsettled, edgy, and a bit
depressed, as if some glorious secret, the one everyone
became all dreamy-eyed about when they spoke of their
lovers, remained tantalizingly out of his reach. Brandon
yearned for an intimacy he sensed existed yet he'd never

experienced.

Averting his gaze so the man wouldn't think he was staring, Brandon nevertheless tracked his progress as he crossed the street and entered the Clinic. Perhaps he'd be lucky enough to catch a glimpse of him inside. He was extremely good-looking.

"I hope you haven't been waiting long."

Brandon jumped, knocked out of his reverie by Gage's arrival. "Oh, shit, yeah. Hi." Brandon fumbled his words.

"Did I scare you? Sorry about that." He pointed at the Clinic. "That's where we're going. Why don't we head inside? I can introduce you to Dr. Weber and get you settled."

Brandon shrugged. "Sure. Is anyone else coming from school?" It still disturbed him a bit that Gage had asked him. As if the man had somehow figured out Brandon had a secret and peeled back the layers he hid behind, exposing his core.

"Nope, only you." Gage patted him on the back. "You're my first victim." He laughed, and though Brandon joined him, an uneasy feeling settled in the pit of his stomach.

They entered the low-rise brick building, and Brandon was immediately struck by the vibrant, almost electric energy inside as Gage greeted the young woman at the front desk. This was a place of action where things were accomplished, goals were achieved. Brandon came to a standstill, looking at the pictures on the wall behind the front desk, of all the doctors who worked there, he presumed.

"That's Dr. Drew Klein." Gage pointed to a picture of a dark-haired man in his mid-thirties with a nice smile and light green eyes. "This clinic was his dream, and he started it and brought his two friends in on it. Dr. Jordan Peterson is an orthopedist"—Gage indicated the picture next to Dr. Klein's of a handsome blond-haired man—"and Dr. Mike Levin is the dentist. The three of them run the medical center."

Once again, regret pricked Brandon's heart. *If only...*but past regrets wouldn't help present problems. "They sound like amazing people. Not many doctors would willingly come to a poor area and work with people who most want to forget." He followed Gage down a hallway to the back of the building. They passed examination rooms and offices. Finally, they stopped in front of one of the closed doors marked Conference Room.

"And Dr. Weber, the psychiatrist who is starting this mentoring program, is also a great guy." Gage knocked on the door, then opened it without waiting for an answer. "I have a feeling the two of you will hit it off."

Immediately, Brandon's antennae buzzed. "Why? Not to sound rude or anything but we don't really know each other. Why would you think this man and I would be friends?"

Giving him a funny look, Gage leaned against the doorway. "You're right; we don't know each other, but I'm hoping that'll change. You remind me of someone." His eyes darkened with pain for a moment. "Someone I lost who also kept things to himself until it all became too much for him. I want to be your friend, Randy. That's all."

"I'm sorry. I didn't mean to come off so harsh. I've been on my own a long time."

A tiny smile quirked Gage's lips. "Maybe it's time to end that as well. Tash is a great guy, and I think you two would make a good couple." With those words, Gage walked into the empty room, leaving Brandon standing in the hallway, mystified. He hurried after Gage.

"Wait. Uhh…how did you know I'm gay?"

Gage shrugged. "A feeling. Am I right?" At Brandon's nod, he continued. "My brother was gay, and like I said, you remind me of him."

"Well, I appreciate it, but I'm not looking for a relationship. I have the kids, my job…" He trailed off. "I'm fine as I am."

"No one wants to be alone."

Wanting desperately to change the subject, Brandon glanced around the empty room. "Guess we're a little early." Chairs sat around in a haphazard manner, and the desk in the front was bare of any material.

When Gage checked his watch, he shrugged. "Yeah, only by about ten minutes. Why don't I go tell them we're here?"

Before Brandon had a chance to answer him, Gage left. After wandering around the room, Brandon stood at the window, gazing out over the dark city sky. With

Gage's words still echoing in his mind, Brandon wondered if he could risk it all, go back home, and deal with the consequences. He understood a little better now, with the wisdom coming from a life hard-lived, why his foster mother had become so overprotective of him. Years of being beaten down and weakened by living with a bully and abuser like Munson would make anyone want to believe in a religion that promised salvation. While he didn't understand the religious aspect, he supposed it gave her something to hold on to when her life crashed and burned around her.

The door opened. "Oh, hello. I didn't realize anyone was here yet."

Brandon turned from his contemplation and his eyes widened, recognizing the man he'd seen outside. Once again, his body registered an unusual heated response.

"Yes. I'm here for the mentoring program. I came with Gage Taylor." The man was even better looking close-up. Behind the glasses, his hazel eyes glowed with interesting streaks of gold. The rugged face with its angular bones wasn't classically handsome but rather, arresting, and in Brandon's eyes, so much more memorable.

"Oh, great." The man entered the room, leaving the door ajar behind him. "We were hoping Gage was able to pick up a few volunteers to come tonight." He extended his hand. "I'm Tash. I run the program."

This was who Gage had spoken about? Admittedly, the man had caught his eye from across the street, but realizing he was a doctor set Brandon back a bit. He had little in common with such an accomplished person. Gage must be nuts. Tash would never be interested in a poor nameless schoolteacher. And what the hell was he even thinking about a relationship for?

But at the press of Tash's hand, a shiver rippled through Brandon; Tash's hand felt warm...secure...safe. He wondered if his lips were as soft as they looked. Obviously, that conversation with Gage had set off something in his brain.

No one likes to be alone. But what do you do when all you've known is loneliness? How do you break free?

Confused and disturbed by his battling emotions, Brandon withdrew his hand a little quicker than he normally would and sat in one of the chairs. He clasped his shaking hands together and attempted to make normal conversation, hoping Tash wouldn't notice how strained his voice sounded.

"Uh, Tash. That's an unusual name."

Tash rubbed his chin ruefully. "Would you believe my mother is an avid reader of Regency romances and Sebastian was her favorite name? My sister couldn't pronounce it when she was a baby, and she shortened it to Tash." He chuckled. "I suppose I should be grateful she didn't also add the title she loved the most, or you'd be calling me Duke."

They were still laughing when Gage walked in followed by a group of people, some of whom Brandon recognized from the pictures hanging on the wall.

"Oh good, Randy, you met Tash." Gage dropped

into the chair next to Brandon. "Randy is the teacher I told you guys about. Even though he joined our staff permanently only this year, he's already made a tremendous difference in the lives of the kids he teaches."

Brandon's face colored, and he squirmed under the scrutiny as the attention of everyone in the room shifted to him. "It's no big deal," he muttered. "The kids are awesome and eager to learn."

"My man here is too modest." Gage stretched out his long legs. "Within weeks of the start of the school year, all the kids could talk about was Mr. Gilbert and how much they love him. All the kids want to be in his classroom. He's taken it upon himself to stay late, well after school is over, to work with any of the kids who are struggling, not only the ones in his class."

"Come on, Gage, cut it out. That's not why we're here," Brandon protested, unzipping his jacket. He hung it on the back of his chair. "Don't hold up the meeting. No one wants to hear you talk about me."

"But you're wrong, Randy," Tash cut in. "You're exactly the type of person we need for this program. Someone young the kids can identify with, someone who doesn't look down on them. Someone with empathy for their pain."

Young in years only, Brandon thought bitterly to himself. He'd seen enough in his twenty-five years to last him a lifetime.

"Everyone deserves a chance. I want to make sure they have that opportunity."

Their gazes held, and Brandon's breath grew short in his throat. The rest of the people disappeared; it was as if only he and Tash were present in that small conference room, with Tash whispering the words straight to Brandon's heart.

The familiar trepidation at facing new people vanished; Tash's presence centered Brandon, untangling all the knots the big ball of his hopes and dreams had twisted themselves up into. For the first time in what seemed like forever, Brandon connected with another person. It didn't make sense. He didn't know Tash. And while he might be the nicest person in the world, Brandon couldn't reveal too much.

"You make me sound special. I'm not." It was the truth. All he gave those kids was his time and concern. They craved attention and the knowledge that another person gave a damn about them. Brandon was anything but special. If they knew who he really was, they'd avoid him.

"Everyone is special." The man he recognized as the founder of the Clinic, Dr. Drew Klein, spoke from the front of the room. "That's what we need these kids to understand. Because they're different, either in their looks or their sexual orientation, that doesn't make them weird or bad. Loving someone differently doesn't make you wrong." The doctor smiled at him with a clear, friendly expression.

Gage patted him on the shoulder. "I know Randy can help you since he's already taken it upon himself to tutor the kids after school. He's the newest teacher there, yet he's made the greatest impact on the students." The door opened, and a young man walked in carrying a box of coffee and a bag that smelled like sugar. Gage's eyes lit up. "Oh. I didn't know you were having coffee and snacks."

Tash chuckled and bent over to whisper in Brandon's ear. "If I hadn't seen how dedicated Gage was to these kids, I'd swear he did this for the free coffee and doughnuts."

Brandon snorted, knowing full well his fellow teacher's propensity for caffeine and sweets. "I know. The man should just get an IV of the stuff."

He and Tash shared a smile, and Brandon's heart gave a funny thump. Heat rose in his face and embarrassed, he fidgeted with his watchband then raked a hand through his hair. He couldn't sit still and tore his gaze away from Tash's mesmerizing eyes. After years of keeping his distance, Brandon wasn't used to the close proximity of people, and having Tash so near set off such disturbing thoughts in his head, they left him shaken.

"Maybe we should get started? I'm, ah, kind of interested in seeing what you want me to do." Beneath lowered lashes, he shot a glance at Tash, who, thank God, had turned his attention to talk to the other men in the room.

Though he couldn't remember their names, Brandon recognized the husky blond-haired man, hovering protectively next to a dark-haired young woman, from the picture hanging outside on the wall.

"That's Mike, Dr. Levin, the dentist. He and Drew's sister, Rachel, are dating," Gage murmured between sips of coffee. "She's getting her PhD in child psychology and set up the twenty-four hour hotline at the Clinic. They've really thought of everything."

Once again, regret and pain slammed into Brandon. What dreams could Ash, Luke, and he have accomplished if someone had cared about them? Ash might not have run away, and Luke might've had someone to talk to instead of becoming so sad and withdrawn.

"Hey, Randy, where'd you go?"

Brandon blinked and found Gage's sympathetic, curious gaze trained on him. He swallowed hard and averted his eyes. "Nowhere."

Gage shot him a sharp look but returned to sipping his coffee. As Drew approached, Brandon braced himself for the inevitable onslaught of getting-to-know-you questions. It didn't matter as he had his whole pretend history well rehearsed.

"So, Randy, we've already heard from Gage before today. What do you think we need to do to reach and help as many kids as possible?" Drew sat in the chair next to him.

Brandon instantly placed Drew as a person who rarely passed judgment on people; he was the person you wanted to come home and tell all your problems to.

"I think you need to make sure the kids know first this is a place of trust and security. Also, if they come here to talk, or we talk to them anywhere, we're there to help them work out their own solutions safely."

Rachel's friendly smile encouraged Brandon and increased his confidence. "The most important thing to teach these kids is that they have a chance to break free and be what they want to be."

Drew rubbed his chin, and his eyes clouded. "One thing I have to make clear from the beginning. If we hear of any abuse, we go straight to the police. If there's any bullying, the school and the parents have to know." The smile he wore so easily faded, replaced by an almost trembling frown. "We lost someone very dear to all of us because we held back, and I made the mistake of trying to handle the problem on my own."

Rachel whispered in Mike's ear, and he walked over to Drew and placed a hand on his shoulder. Drew smiled tremulously at him but continued. "The consequences are too enormous and dangerous if we don't bring in the authorities when we know a person is at risk."

The police? Shit. He couldn't be a part of this. For years Brandon had evaded them, deliberately taking every precaution to keep as far away from any contact with the legal system as possible. Now with this project, he'd be putting himself practically in their pockets. Though the mission sounded amazing, he knew he'd have to decline. He couldn't afford the risk.

"Um, I'm not sure if I'm the right person for this." Brandon's fingers shook as he reached for his jacket behind him. The room fell silent as he fumbled and stuttered over his words. "I mean, I'm so new; you really need a person who's more experienced."

He stood and grabbed his backpack. "Uh, I have to go, but I'll let you know if I can do it. Thanks."

"Wait, Randy, please." Tash put himself in between Brandon and the door, but Brandon couldn't let the disappointment and confusion in Tash's handsome face dissuade him from leaving. He circled Tash and wrenched open the door.

"I'm sorry. I gotta go." Cheeks burning, Brandon put his head down and raced through the hallway toward the front of the building. He'd just reached the door when it burst open, and a tall, dark-haired man stood facing the street, shaking out his wet umbrella.

"Excuse me," muttered Brandon, brushing by him, not waiting for a response. He plunged headlong into the foggy drizzle that had begun again, uncaring if he got wet. His long strides ate up the block as he pushed himself farther and farther away from the Clinic. It hurt, walking out so abruptly, but once he got home, he'd call Gage and make up some excuse.

At the intersection, he spotted a cab with its light on, and even though he could barely afford the fare for his monthly subway pass, he hailed it, asking the driver to drop him off at the nearest subway station in Carroll Gardens. He'd find a way to get home to Flatbush somehow.

The farther away he got from the Clinic, the better, yet as he sat back in the cab, he couldn't help recalling the disappointment in Tash's face. But Brandon knew if he stayed, he'd do more than disappoint everyone, and that wasn't a chance he was willing or able to take.

Chapter Four

THE AIR FAIRLY vibrated in the conference room after Brandon flew out the door. Tash stood, utterly confused.

"Does anyone know what that was about?" There were equally perplexed looks on the faces of everyone in the room. He honed in on the one person who might have an answer.

"Gage? You brought him here. Any idea why he freaked out?"

The dark-haired man's expression was as troubled as Tash felt inside. "Not a clue. Honestly, in the months I've known him, he's always been the most easygoing and calm person." He shook his head, meeting Tash's eyes. "I thought he'd be perfect for this program and kind of perfect for you if you want the truth."

Gage's words hit Tash like a fist to the solar plexus. "Tell me you didn't just say that." Dumbfounded, Tash wanted to crawl into a hole at the thought of discussing his personal life in front of everyone. "You of all people know I'm not looking for a relationship."

"I know how alone you've been." Gage's sad eyes held his.

The door opened, and Tash recognized Ash Davis as he walked into the room. He could only imagine how the man, with his dark good looks and commanding presence, held a courtroom captivated, but as usual, Ash had eyes only for his lover, Drew Klein. Ash's eyes glittered, and his mouth curved in a smile as he advanced on Drew, grabbed him around the waist, and planted a kiss on his lips, oblivious to whatever else was happening in the room.

"Hey, baby."

Drew slipped his arm around Ash's waist and hugged him close. "Hi. How was work?"

The two men had a unique connection—a true friendship along with mutual respect, but it was something more. Tash noticed how tightly Ash laced his fingers with Drew's. It was as if he wasn't comfortable unless Drew was touching him, Tash mused.

Knowing a bit of the horrors of both Ash's and Luke's childhoods, Tash wasn't surprised Ash had found love and a home with the Klein family. They were the most accepting group of people he'd been fortunate enough to come across. It almost made up for their constant attempts to set him up all the time. He knew they wanted him to be as happy as they all were.

"Best thing I can say is that the day is done, and it's one step closer to the weekend." Ash tossed his coat onto an empty chair and headed over to the coffee.

"Did the meeting end already?"

"Rather abruptly, I'm afraid. And much sooner than we thought." Gage joined Ash at the coffeepot. "I thought one of my colleagues was interested, but before we had a chance to start, something freaked him out, and he ran out of here like a bat out of hell."

Ash stirred sugar into his coffee. "Must have been the guy who almost ran me over as I was coming in. What could you all have said to set him off like that?"

Tash thought back to the conversation. "Everything was fine until Drew mentioned we'd have to go to the police and the schools if we found abuse."

The smile vanished from Ash's face, and his eyes dimmed. "Yeah, well, that's a definite. We all regret not doing that with Steve. Keith died, and Drew and Jordan's friendship almost blew apart because of it."

From treating Jordan's Xanax addiction, Tash knew Jordan's anxiety issues had stemmed partially from the fact that he'd held back from telling Drew he blamed him somewhat for Keith's death. It took nine months of festering hurt before Jordan's anger and anguish had reached a boiling point, and the two had a heart-to-heart discussion. Fortunately, their thirty-year friendship had survived, but Tash knew they still worked on the aftermath of their shared pain.

"Agreed." Tash directed his attention to Gage. "What do you know of his background? You said Randy is a relatively new teacher at the school, right?" He chose to ignore Gage's earlier remark about Randy being good for him. Aside from Tash not wanting a relationship, the man was too young for him. He looked to be no more than in his mid-twenties.

"He is," admitted Gage. "And he's young enough to have that natural connection with the students. He came from the Department of Education's Teaching Collaborative program, which I know for a fact means he didn't go the traditional route to his teaching career."

"You think he has a past, and that's why he's so tuned into the kids, right?" Ash gazed at Gage with shrewd eyes. That was the lawyer in him, Tash could tell. He knew from talk how quick Ash was in the courtroom. The man never met a challenge he didn't relish taking on headfirst.

"Yeah, no question in my mind."

Having seen Randy's reaction and the absolute fear in his eyes, Tash thought it was more than a past involving personal abuse. He believed Randy was hiding something.

"You won't be able to force him, you know." Tash spoke to not only Ash and Gage but everyone in the room. "If he's this skittish, it might do him more harm and send him running not only from this program but from his job as well."

"No way will he abandon those kids." Gage shook his head, his voice adamant. "He told me the other day about two of the seventh graders he's been tutoring on the side, separately from his own students. How proud he's been of them for standing up to the other kids who tease them for liking school and doing their work."

Gage's jaw set in a hard line. "He cares too much, and even if there is something in his past, I don't give a shit. That man is a born teacher."

"Take it easy, Gage." Tash soothed his friend. "I'm trying to figure out how to reel Randy back in, not find out his past. Believe me, we've all made mistakes we'd like to change if we had a second chance."

"And some of us need to stop beating ourselves up over things that were beyond our control. People need to want help, you know?"

And suddenly, Tash knew they weren't talking about Randy. They were talking about Daniel. He was always there between him and Gage. Danny might have been Tash's lover, but he was also Gage's brother, and his death had devastated Gage.

What started out as a night to help kids with problems had now turned into a project to help the teacher. Hard as Tash fought against it, Randy piqued his interest. Those deep green eyes, so wary and defensive, sent out a message of *Don't touch, hands off.* In Tash's professional opinion, it wasn't a natural fear of the unknown. Randy had looked scared to death. The way he'd bolted from the room at the mention of the authorities only reinforced Tash's belief of Randy's past legal problems.

The man projected an air of loneliness, highlighting his vulnerability and sweetness. It wasn't only Randy's beautiful eyes and aura of pain that drew Tash in; from the first, Tash had a physical reaction to him, an awareness of Randy's presence. Tash had always been a sucker for the wounded, and he itched to help the young man.

"Maybe I should talk to him, alone, away from this environment. He might have socialization issues we aren't aware of and handle one-on-one better."

"Good idea." Ash gazed at him with frank approval. "I know I speak not only for myself but for Luke as well when I say it's intimidating for people with personal problems to be confronted by a group of strangers, even friendly, well-meaning ones." He slid his arm around Drew's shoulders. "I'm lucky to have Drew, who stuck by me and wouldn't let me hide." Those glittering gray eyes held Tash's gaze. "It only takes one person, the right person, to break down the walls you surround yourself with, to force you to see the truth."

"And in your case, the truth set you free?" Tash couldn't help but smile.

Ash's return smile transformed his face. "My truth is Drew. He's the one who freed me."

Drew kissed Ash's cheek. "I love you." Still within the circle of Ash's arms, Drew directed his attention to Tash. "Help Randy, Tash. I know what you did for Jordan. You forced him to face the truth of his addiction, freeing him to love Luke."

"I'll try, but he has to want it. That's the key." This was what he'd been missing lately. Tash's blood ran hot with purpose, and he itched with the desire to work, to help someone so obviously lonely and scared. Jordan had needed Tash for the medical treatment, it was true, but it was Luke who'd helped him emotionally, and in return, Jordan helped Luke find his way back to life and Ash.

"You can do it." Gage squeezed his arm, but the confidence placed in him felt unwarranted, considering how miserably Tash had failed his brother.

"I'll have to move carefully." Tash thought for a moment. Ideally, he'd like to talk to Randy alone.

"When does he finish class tomorrow? Maybe I should stop by the school and talk to him." There was something to be said for a bit of a surprise attack. And if done on Randy's home turf, he might be more willing to talk.

"I think he's done at three thirty or four. That's a great idea to come to him. I'm telling you, I know you two will hit it off." The excitement in Gage's voice both amused and annoyed Tash.

"I'm doing it for Randy and the kids, you know. I'm not looking to get laid."

"Don't know why not," grumbled Gage. "Not like you couldn't use a little action."

"Screw you." Tash's halfhearted attempt at a comeback was met with a grin.

"Sorry, you don't have the parts I like, although you do have a cute ass."

Gage's good humor broke the tension in the room, and the meeting ended on a high note. Tash took down the school's address and left the Clinic for home, for the first time in a long time feeling as though he had a purpose.

THE NEXT AFTERNOON, Tash waited by the entrance of Randy's school. It was easy to spot him in the after-school crowd of students, parents, and other school administrators. At least for Tash it was, as Randy drew the light around him like a golden nimbus. There was true joy in his face as a child showed him a paper she clutched in her hand. It must've been a test with a good score; as Randy gave her a high five, his face lit up with a smile. Not one of those that's-great-now-can-I-leave fake smiles, but one of pure happiness with what he was doing. Tash knew he was seeing a man who truly loved his job and was meant to teach.

Then Randy spotted him, and all that beautiful happiness fled his face. Instantly the fearful, wary look Tash remembered from the night before returned to draw a dark veil over those laughing eyes. As Tash approached Randy, he could almost see the man girding for battle. Randy's shoulders drew together, and he widened his stance, bracing himself.

Tash decided to take the friendly, non-confrontational approach. After all, Randy really didn't know who the hell he was. "Hi." Tash gazed up at the man, who remained at the top of the steps. "I hoped we could talk."

A muscle ticked in Randy's smooth jawline, sending his skin jumping. Tash had a crazy urge to press his mouth to all that soft-looking skin.

"What about? And why you?" Randy's fair brows drew together in confusion. "I was going to tell Gage I don't think I'm the right fit."

"Because it's my program, and I think you're the perfect fit. Let me try and convince you, okay? Have coffee with me? No strings attached. Hear me out, and then if you still don't want to work with us, I'll go away."

Tash held his breath, watching as a myriad of emotions played over Randy's handsome face. "It's not that big of a deal," Tash pressed gently. "It's only coffee."

"All right, I guess." Randy joined him at the foot of the steps. "When, now?" He hefted his backpack on his shoulder.

"Yes. There's a nice, quiet coffee shop near my house where we can talk. Unless..." An idea popped into his head. "Do you like cats?" At Randy's nod, Tash smiled. "Would you mind coming to my house? I need to check on my devils. They're a little overwhelming, and I hate leaving them alone all day. I've been with patients since early this morning and I'm afraid they might tear the house apart if I leave them alone much longer."

"I don't know." Randy hedged, shifting on his feet. Tash feared the man was about to bolt again.

"Come on. I'm a doctor. You can trust me. I promise not to bite."

A blush crept up Randy's neck, and Tash winked at him. He couldn't help it. The guy was adorable—a caring individual and incredibly good-looking. The complete package.

"All right."

"I have my car and can drive you home afterward." Tash indicated the small SUV parked at the corner. "Consider it added incentive."

Randy chuckled, transforming his somber face back into that younger, alive-looking man Tash had seen earlier when Randy stood surrounded by the children. A crazy thought popped into Tash's head.

I like his smile. I'd like to be the one to put a smile on his face and keep it there.

"Sounds good. Thanks."

Tash unlocked the car, and they climbed inside and drove off, bouncing along the ruts in the streets. He decided to hold off on any questions, even though Randy was a trapped audience inside the moving car. Within twenty minutes, he pulled into the garage across the street from his home. Randy hadn't moved since they began the trip to the Heights, remaining silent, white-knuckling the straps on his backpack.

"We're here. Come on." Tash exited the car, Randy trailing behind him.

Carefully opening the door to prevent the cats from slipping out, Tash entered the house, speaking over his shoulder to Randy, who hung back. "I can't leave the door open because these demons might run out. Hurry up."

Randy moved behind him, standing close enough for Tash to sense his body heat. "How many do you have?"

The air stirred around him as Randy's breath drifted past his ear. Tash's body unexpectedly hardened. A delicious frisson rocketed through him. For five years, desire had lain fairly dormant within him, his blood running thick and sluggish in his veins. Somehow, this unassuming man had awakened what he'd thought was gone forever.

"Uh, there are two, although most days it feels like double that. That's Cleopatra, and her brother is Caesar." He pointed to the two lithe bodies stretched out on his sofa, their almond-shaped turquoise eyes daring him to remove them from their throne.

"Great names." Randy grinned, his concentration on the cats.

"They are devils more than royalty, but they keep me company." Tash strode over to the sofa and picked up Caesar, who immediately began to squirm and yowl. "Behave now; we have company," Tash murmured to the cat, fully believing the animal understood.

As if to prove his point, Caesar ceased his howling and stared at Randy, who reached out to pet him with hesitant fingers. To Tash's ultimate shock, Caesar not only accepted the petting but head-butted Randy's hand and began to struggle to get down from Tash's arms. When Tash set him down, the cat wended his way around Randy's legs like a cream-colored snake. Cleo, loathe to miss any action, joined her brother. Tash could only gape at his usually aloof cats as they lavished attention on this stranger.

"Come on and sit down. I can give you that coffee

if you want, but I also have beer and wine." The guy could use a drink. Randy sat stiffly on the sofa, his rigid posture once again betraying his nerves. What the heck was the guy so scared of? Maybe he was in hiding from an ex-lover. Tash's intrigue grew. "Relax. I'm not going to interrogate you."

"Coffee's fine, honest." Randy's husky voice, that suede-over-sandpaper sound, shot straight to Tash's groin. Without even trying, he projected a sexy-yet-vulnerable air. What the hell was going on with him? He'd never had this kind of attraction toward anyone before. But even as he struggled inwardly with his suddenly reawakened libido, Tash imagined what Randy tasted like. Tash made the coffee, a cinnamon blend he loved, and brought a tray with two thick cream-colored mugs, a small carafe of milk, sugar, and a plate of hazelnut biscotti. He was a firm believer that one should never drink coffee without a little something sweet.

"Here. Help yourself." He placed the tray on the coffee table, and they busied themselves with the milk and biscotti. The cats, who had settled themselves on either side around Randy, watched their movements with avid, gleaming eyes.

He and Randy settled back on opposite ends of the sofa. "So," Tash began. Immediately, Randy tensed, his hand gripping the coffee mug tight, but Tash continued, determined to be as direct as possible. "Do you care to tell me why you're scared to death?"

Chapter Five

*D*AMN, *DAMN, DAMN*. Brandon knew he shouldn't have accepted Tash's invitation. Of course, Tash would want to know why Brandon had left the meeting last night, racing through the doors like a bat out of hell. Brandon knew he'd been wrong—his precipitous exit had only made everyone curious, but he couldn't help himself; the mere mention of the police had rattled him so badly he couldn't think straight.

With practice he'd spent years perfecting, he stared straight into Tash's eyes. "I'm sorry. It was wrong for me to bail on all of you. I had a run-in years ago with the police, and I've been wary of them ever since, even though I know they're here to help." A fine sweat broke over his body, and his hand shook. Some coffee slopped over the side, onto his pants.

Tash moved over and handed him a napkin but remained disarmingly near. Having held those around him at bay for years, Tash's proximity overwhelmed Brandon; his normal steady rhythm played out of sync.

"You don't seem the type who'd stay scared forever.

If there's anything I can do to help you, let me." Tash's eyes glowed behind the glint of his glasses. "Can I? Help you, I mean? Won't you tell me what's wrong?" Tash laid a hand on Brandon's shoulder. It remained there, warm and comforting. The air around them swelled with sounds: Brandon's rapidly beating heart, the pulse of blood singing through his veins, Tash's gentle breathing. A yearning welled up inside Brandon, and all he wanted was to be held. The loneliness he'd lived with most of his life had bled his soul dry. He hadn't felt this desperate since the night Luke told him Ash was never coming back.

But as much as Tash tantalized, Brandon could ill afford to open up and let him in. "I-I'm fine, really." His weak grin didn't seem to fool Tash, who gazed back at him with skeptical, knowing eyes. "Honest. Why don't you tell me about the program now? I know I should've stayed and listened instead of bailing. I'm sorry."

Tash patted his shoulder and removed his hand. Immediately Brandon regretted the loss of his touch. "Don't worry about it. I want you to know that I'm here if you ever need to talk, okay?"

"Sure." Nice as Tash seemed, Brandon didn't put much stock into his words. Everyone who'd ever promised to be there for him had let him down in some way or another.

"How about we talk now and I can tell you what I'm planning; you're still interested, right?"

"Of course." Brandon stroked the soft fur of one of

the cats, the rumble of her purring vibrating through his fingers. It was true what they said about animals; they did relieve stress. His racing pulse and frantically beating heart slowed as his fingers slid through Cleo's plush velvet coat. At least he thought that was Cleo. "I don't want you to think I'm not interested. I have several kids I'm concerned about. They get bullied constantly because they do their homework and like school."

"That's not cool for most kids, right?" Tash relaxed back onto the sofa, and the other cat, annoyed at being ignored, stalked over to him, claiming a place of honor on his lap. Brandon couldn't help but watch Tash's long fingers slide over the cat's sinewy frame and wonder how those hands would feel against his own skin.

Guiltily, Brandon's face heated, and he returned from his daydreams to concentrate on the conversation. "It's unfortunate, but you're correct. These two boys I help after school are intelligent and so eager to learn. Their parents have done so much to help them, yet at school they constantly get teased. I'm afraid if they don't have a safe place, they'll give up and fall into the cycle of drugs and violence."

"And you won't let that happen, will you?" The confidence in Tash's voice surprised Brandon.

"No. No, you're right; I won't." He couldn't let those boys be subjected to the constant barrage of criticism and insults he heard some of the other kids whisper in the halls. "I'd never forgive myself if

EMBRACE THE FIRE

anything happened to these kids."

"I have an idea." Tash rubbed his jaw. "You should come with me to the shelter and meet Wanda."

"Who's she?" Brandon couldn't keep up with all the new people he'd met over the past few days. "Was she there last night?"

"No. But she's the heart and soul of another project intimately tied up with this one. She can introduce you to the people from the shelter she runs, as well as take you around the community center. These boys sound like they'd be perfect for the Center if they can come." Tash lifted the cat from his lap and placed him on the floor. Caesar stalked away, his tail sticking straight up like a flagpole. Free to move, Tash took his coffee mug and a biscotti. "When Jordan and Luke come home from Europe I know they'll want to meet everyone involved with the project."

"Jordan's the doctor, right?" His heart gave a funny thump when he heard the name Luke. "Who's Luke?" Hoping against hope, Brandon's voice trembled. There had to be a million Lukes in the world, but maybe…

"Yes. Jordan Peterson and Drew are best friends, along with Mike Levin, the other man you met last night. Luke Conover and Jordan are a couple."

Brandon's frantic heartbeat slowed. Conover, not Carini. Of course it wasn't his Luke. How stupid to think it might be. "Sure, I'd be happy to meet them."

"So, you're in, then? I'm glad. I really do think you're a perfect fit for the group." Tash dunked his biscotti in his coffee. Fascinated, Brandon stared at

Tash's mouth as he chewed, swallowed, then licked his lips. He couldn't ever remember being this turned on by another person. This couldn't happen. Tash was being kind to get him to help with the program. He was an incredibly attractive man with a life and a family. Brandon was probably another project to take on.

"What? Yeah, sure." He wanted to help; it was the reason he became a teacher. And Brandon hadn't survived for this long without keeping his wits about him. If the police needed to be involved, he'd make himself scarce, come up with excuses. As long as the kids needed him, he'd find a way to help. Their welfare was paramount in his mind.

"What had you so worried; will you tell me? Maybe I can help." Once again, Tash moved closer. "Talk to me. I'm not here to judge or hurt you. It's my job to help people." Once again, he placed a hand on Brandon's shoulder, and Brandon shivered. The simple act of Tash's hand on any part of his body sent unfamiliar sparks through Brandon. His mind might not understand, but his body did. And his body wanted Tash.

"I already told you."

Tash shook his head. "You can trust me, you know. I'd never reveal anything you tell me. You may not be a patient of mine, but I would consider anything you told me privileged."

Everyone Brandon had ever trusted had let him down in some way or another, whether by their own fault or outside influences. The last person he'd trusted was Gabriel, and he'd died. Brandon didn't know who to blame in that instance since he'd stopped believing in God years before.

Tash meant well, and Brandon couldn't deny he was incredibly attracted to him, but wanting to kiss someone and trusting them were on two opposite sides of the spectrum.

"I told you; it was silliness on my part. I'll work through it." Changing the subject, he pressed Tash for more information. "Can you tell me what I missed after I ran out of the meeting? I'd love to hear more about your mentoring program and how I can help."

For a moment, Tash stared at him, and Brandon thought he might balk and continue to question him, but instead, he gave him a wry smile.

"You're like me. When you don't want to talk about something you change the subject. I have a good idea."

Brandon watched a light spark in Tash's eyes and girded himself for whatever he was about to suggest. "Ok, tell me."

"Well," he began, stroking the cat who'd once again jumped into his lap looking for attention. "Everyone goes to Drew's grandmother's house on Sunday for dinner. The guys keep a very close watch on her."

"Not understanding what this has to do with me but that's nice." Brandon took a sip of his coffee, waiting for Tash to finish speaking and make a connection.

"Yeah. Anyway, that leaves the help lines at the Clinic pretty sparsely manned. We got lucky and a doctor joined us, a relationship psychologist named Noah Strauss. Don't know if you've ever heard of him but he's got a radio show Sunday evenings. Would you want to come with me and man the lines?"

"A chance to help questioning kids or someone asking for help? That sounds exactly like what I'd be interested in."

A smile lit up Tash's face. "Perfect. I can meet you there at ten a.m. on Sunday. I bring bagels, and there's coffee, so we'll be all set."

Seeing the lengthening shadows on the wall, Brandon knew it was getting late and time for him to go back home to his dreary studio. From the pictures on the table and fireplace mantel Brandon viewed Tash's past: him laughing with a group of friends and also his family. A typical life but one he'd never known. What would it be like to have people who cared about you? The only memories he had were of Luke holding him tight, telling him not to be afraid, or his foster mother's tear-stained face giving him a hug before bed after escaping his foster father's rage.

Not all memories were pleasant, and sometimes they deserved to be forgotten.

Chapter Six

EVEN THOUGH RANDY sounded enthusiastic about the project, by Sunday morning, as Tash drove to the Clinic in Red Hook, he still had his doubts the man would show. The enigmatic Randy Gilbert had remained in his thoughts over the weekend; his nervousness whenever Tash came near and his refusal to discuss the real cause behind his running away from their nighttime meeting made no sense and proved further to Tash that Randy hid a secret.

Turning the corner, he spied Randy, and all doubts melted away. His protective instincts kicked in, and as he pulled up in front to park, he promised himself no matter what, he'd find a way to help Randy. It had nothing to do with the rapid beating of his heart at Randy's welcoming smile and how the early morning sun shot golden sparks through his thick silky hair. *Nothing at all.*

Tash got out and locked the car, anticipation buzzing through his veins at the thought of spending time with Randy. He hoped for a myriad of reasons they wouldn't be too busy today, even though Sundays could often be the most hectic days. People became depressed after a bad Saturday night experience or another long lonely weekend and needed someone to talk to. Noah, who often came early to relieve the overnight person would most likely welcome a break, and Tash beckoned to Randy to follow him.

"Morning. Let's go inside, grab our bagel and coffee, and see what's going on."

"Hi, yeah, sure. I didn't want to knock or try going inside without you..." Randy bit his lip, suddenly looking very young and vulnerable.

"It's okay." Tash unlocked the front door and held it open for Randy to pass by. He caught his fresh warm scent and steeled himself against the attraction bubbling up inside of him. Tash had never been one to think with his dick instead of his brains, and he wasn't about to start now, especially with someone almost fifteen years younger. "They lock the doors on the weekend since technically it's closed, except for the people on the help lines. Hope you're not frozen."

"No." Randy looked around. "I got used to the cold years ago."

His interest quickened; obviously Randy didn't come from the North if he had to get used to the cold, but Tash stored the information away without commenting.

"Follow me to the back, and we'll see what's going on. I don't think you had a chance to see the setup." They walked as he talked. "It's basically one room where we have six phones and several computers. People can call in to talk with a live person, but sometimes they might be scared, so Rachel set up a chat room where people can message a counselor one-on-one." He opened the door and caught sight of Dr. Noah Strauss, a hand buried in his dark hair, earnestly talking to someone on the phone.

"That's Noah," he whispered to Randy. "He's been invaluable, helping us. Come, let's get something to eat, and I'll set you up next to me."

Standing with Randy next to the coffee machine, it occurred to Tash he hadn't been part of a couple in so long, he wouldn't even know what to do or say on a date. The unforgiving world raced by him while he sat and mourned a doomed relationship.

"He looks so intense." Randy sipped his coffee.

"Noah's like you; he gets personally involved with the people he helps."

"I don't know that I'm personally involved; I think I care about the kids and know how bad it gets out there if they don't have support."

"It was rough for you?"

"Yeah." His eyes darted frantically from side to side. "I mean...um." He drained his cup.

Looking for an escape, thought Tash. He felt bad for the guy, who obviously hadn't worked through his painful past.

"I'm sorry. I'm not digging, honest. You seem like you need a friend is all. I know how it is. Life can get really lonely sometimes."

Disbelief replaced fear in Randy's eyes. "Oh, come on. I've seen your house, full of pictures, and met your friends. You have no idea what it really means to be alone."

"I've only known these men for about six months. Why do you think I have two cats? I need something alive to welcome me when I come home at night." Tash stopped, mortified by his outburst. "I'm sorry; I didn't mean to snap at you." He gestured to Noah, who'd finished his conversation and sat making notes on the pad in front of him. "Let me introduce you." He walked away from Randy, wanting to put some distance between them.

"Noah. How's it going? I brought someone to help us."

Noah Strauss, former underwear model, now psychologist, put down his pen and flashed a brilliant smile. "So I see." He stood and stuck out a hand. "Nice to meet you; I'm Noah Strauss."

Randy returned the handshake with a hesitant smile. "Uh hi, I'm Randy Gilbert. I'm a schoolteacher. This setup looks pretty amazing."

"It is. I was talking to someone right now who is getting bullied in high school. He's so desperate that he's on the verge of running away."

"Oh, wow." Randy let his backpack slide from his shoulder to the ground, and he took the seat next to Noah. "What did you say? I'm so afraid hearing that."

Watching Randy listen to Noah, an ache rose in Tash's chest. A few years past thirty, gay and single,

Noah Strauss would be the ideal man for Randy.

"Hey, Tash, why the sad face?" Noah gestured to the phone. "I worked it out; the kid is going to come to my office tomorrow, and I'll help him. You know that."

A smile curved his lips. "You're one of the good guys; I know. That's why I thought you and Randy would hit it off."

Noah's bright smile faltered to a weak grin. "Uh, hit it off? Who are you; my mother?" He gave an apologetic glance to Randy. "No offense, but I'm not interested in dating anyone."

"None taken and neither am I." Randy shot Tash a frown. "I'm here to help."

"I didn't mean it like that. You people are touchy. I meant that Noah could show you the ropes since he does this more frequently than I do."

Relief flooded through Noah's face. "Okay, good, 'cause I get enough crap from my mother about dating. I don't need it from my friends." He nudged Randy's foot. "Overinvolved family members. You know how it is. They always think they know best."

"Yeah." Randy slipped on a headset. "How about you let me take a call?"

But Tash wasn't fooled by that forced smile. He knew Randy had little to no family and also knew the man wouldn't appreciate any further conversation.

"Sure. Here's how it works. We get a call in and the line lights up. You take it and announce who you are and that everything they say is confidential. You're a natural from what I can tell. I know you'll be able to help."

That hesitant, wistful smile on Randy's lips slayed Tash; what secrets did this young man hold so tight to live such a solitary life?

Why did it matter so much to him?

A button lit up and Randy jumped a bit. "Should I?" His finger hovered over the button as he looked at Tash.

"Go ahead."

He watched as Randy took the call, and in his soft voice, introduced himself, telling the person on the other end, "I'm here for you. Would you like to talk?"

He and Noah left Randy to take the call and walked to the next table to sit and chat.

"How'd you meet him?" Noah nudged his shoulder.

"Gage works with him. He's a sixth-grade teacher in Bushwick—came through the New York City Teaching Collaborative."

Randy's gentle voice rose and fell, his face alight with a fire Tash hadn't seen before but recognized. That passion once belonged to him...before everything went to shit.

"He's a natural. I'm glad he's here."

"Yeah. Me too."

"I can see that."

Noah's teasing tone startled Tash, and he frowned. "Remember what you said about your mother? Don't start that with me."

"The thing is," Noah leaned back in his chair and smirked, "I mean it. But the way you're looking at him, you don't." His tone turned gentle. "You like him. A lot."

"Don't be ridiculous." The words tasted bitter on his lips. "We barely know each other."

"Pffft." Noah brushed off his protests. "I'm not talking about love. The guy's hot as hell and seems like a great person. There's nothing wrong with a little flirtation and fun."

Fun? Tash hadn't known fun for years; he barely remembered what it felt like to let go for pure enjoyment. Pain and lies? Now that he could write a book about.

"I'm too busy. Between my patients, the mentoring work at the Clinic I'm starting, and helping here, my plate is pretty full."

"Don't bullshit a bullshitter." The joking tone had fled Noah's voice, and Tash glanced at him sharply, dismayed by the knowing, yet sympathetic expression in his eyes. "I know exactly what you're doing. The same thing I do."

Noah had confided a little of his story and Tash could relate—at least to the not interested in dating part.

"So why is it good for you and not me? I said I'm not interested in dating, and I meant it."

"Because I know how you struggled with your feelings after Jordan got together with Luke. We talked about it, remember?"

Noah's care and concern grated on Tash's nerves instead of soothing him. It reminded him of everything he'd lost that could never be recovered. "Yeah, we did." He'd confided his tiny spark of interest in Jordan and how it had been snuffed out almost as soon as it arose. "I told you I was happy for them, and nothing's changed."

"Then leave yourself open to it again. It'll find you when you least expect it, and you want to be ready to embrace it." Noah stopped and took a breath, giving Tash a chance to get a word in.

"Are you finished lecturing me? 'Cause you aren't saying anything my sister and parents haven't said for years. I don't want what I once had; it almost ruined me. I'm not interested in flings or having fun. I'm almost forty years old, Noah. I'm done with this shit."

Pushing away from him on his swivel chair, Noah held his hands up in surrender. "Okay, I hear you loud and clear. I'll shut up."

"Thanks."

"For now. Hey, look at Randy; he's a natural at this." Noah pointed to him and Tash watched as Randy, with a big smile on his face, pushed the button to disconnect the call and slumped back in his seat.

"How'd it go?" Happy to leave Noah the Nosy, Tash walked over and sat next to Randy. "Want to talk about it?"

"Yeah. I'm still recovering. It was amazing." The excitement in his face electrified Tash. Something about this man...his passion, sincerity, and the innate sweetness behind the cautious exterior drew Tash in, despite his remarks to Noah only moments ago about keeping his distance.

"Tell me."

"This boy—he said his name was Chacôn—well, he's gay and femme. Like *very* femme. He's in high school and just started experimenting with makeup."

Tash could only imagine. "Is he getting grief from the kids? Or are the teachers keeping them in line?"

"When school started, he got bullied every day. They teased him and called him all kinds of names, wrote stuff on his locker...all the shit kids do." There was a faraway quality to Randy's voice as he spoke. Like he too remembered a scene out of his past. "He can't talk to his parents, and won't tell the teachers 'cause he didn't want to be a snitch and get beaten up for that. If he got bruises he'd cover them with makeup."

"This needs to be reported. He can't get abused at school and let them get away with it." Tash didn't know who to be angry with first: the kids who bullied this boy, the teachers who turned a blind eye or the parents who made their child feel less than a whole person. He trembled, his hands curling into fists.

"Hey, I haven't finished the story." Randy raked back the hair that fell over his brow and into his eyes. "So, he said he was getting more and more depressed every day, and he even thought about killing himself."

"That's why he called?" Breaking into Randy's story, anger flared hot in Tash's chest. "Jesus, you should've let one of us handle it."

"Tash, please, will you let me finish?" Lines of annoyance deepened around Randy's mouth.

"Sorry," he said, chastened by Randy's tone.

"He went to the school psychologist to talk. And in the waiting room, he saw a guy from the football team—a big guy, and Chacôn said he was too intimidated to say anything, but the guy started talking to him."

His interest piqued, Tash's brows knitted in confusion. "The football player talked to him?"

"Yeah." Randy nodded with enthusiasm. "The problem is, Chacôn was too nervous and scared to answer him back, so he sat and listened. Seems the guy confided in Chacôn; he thinks he's gay and doesn't know how to tell anyone. He's afraid of being kicked off the team, losing all his friends, and not being popular anymore."

Curiosity got the better of him. "Why did Chacôn call, exactly?"

"Well, he wanted to know if he should try and be friends with this guy; I think he said his name was Travis. Chacôn is afraid; he's attracted to Travis but he won't hide who he is to be liked."

"Sounds like a mature kid for his age." At Randy's nod, Tash asked, "What did you tell him to do?"

"I told him they should take it slow…maybe talk online and get to know each other first. Meet outside of school and hang out."

Tash nodded. "Wise words. The last thing they want to do is rush things. Kids have enough hanging over their heads these days. The pressure they're under is intense."

"I told him he could call anytime, and we'd help him. But that he should be proud of who he is and that he stood up for himself."

"How did you end it?"

A smile curved Randy's lips. "It was cute. Chacôn joked that he'd be the envy of every girl because he might be the one to snag the best-looking player on the football team. It made him feel good that Travis liked him enough to share a life-altering confidence."

"Good work." He and Randy smiled at each other; Tash caught sight of Noah over Randy's shoulder and frowned at the shit eating grin and thumbs-up sign Noah gave him. "I'm glad your first call was a success." The phone buzzed with another incoming call. "Let's grab another cup of coffee; Noah can take that call, right?"

"You betcha." The gleam in Noah's eyes wasn't lost on Tash, but he chose to ignore his annoying friend and turned his back on him.

"Can I ask you something?"

Glancing over his shoulder to make sure Noah had taken his call and wasn't listening, Tash stepped closer to Randy. "Sure. Anything." They reached the table with the coffee urn, a box of doughnuts, and bagels on a tray. "Shoot."

"Would it be all right with you if I came here every Sunday? I don't have much to do on the weekends, and I'd love to help out."

That was the last thing he'd expected to hear. "Uh, I guess, but are you sure? Is that how you want to spend your Sundays—holed up here?"

"I don't see it that way. My Sundays used to be my mother forcing me to sit through services in a church where the pastor screamed how gay people would burn in hellfire and only true Christians would be saved." Randy stared into his empty cup. "I grew up thinking I was a terrible person, and no one would love me if they knew I was gay. I don't want other kids to feel like I did."

Shuddering, Tash sipped his coffee, thankful his parents had never cared much about religion. "That sounds awful. Where did you grow up?"

He'd meant it as an innocuous question, but Randy's hand shook so much he spilled the hot coffee pouring out of the urn, burning his hand.

"Ow, shit."

Immediately, Tash took Randy's hand in his, blotting off the wetness with a napkin. Watching the red welt spread across the fair skin of Randy's hand, Tash led him out of the room to the small bathroom next door where he washed his hand and applied a healing ointment.

"Better now?" He ran the pad of his thumb gently over the bandaged area.

A surprised light flared in Randy's deep green eyes and Tash glanced down, unaware he'd been caressing Randy's hand.

"Uh, yeah, thanks." With a self-conscious smile,

Randy pulled his hand back and shook it. "That was dumb of me. I don't know how that happened. I guess we should go back and see if Noah needs any help, huh?"

Without waiting for his response, Randy hurried out of the bathroom, leaving Tash more befuddled and confused than ever—not only about Randy's response but his own. Maybe Noah was right, and he and Randy could have a casual, no-strings relationship like people did now. But with his heart pounding and his skin burning where he touched Randy, Tash trudged back to the help room, knowing the desire coursing through his body for Randy was anything but casual.

Chapter Seven

THREE WEEKS HAD passed, and Brandon finally believed he'd found what he'd been missing in his life. Speaking with the people who called in on the help line and tutoring his kids at school gave him a purpose, and for all his dislike of religion, Brandon believed Gabriel looked down upon him and would be proud of what he'd done.

Tash had been so busy with his patients that they hadn't met again about the mentoring project at the Clinic, but had spoken often. In their conversation several days ago, Tash had said he'd drawn up a new plan and wanted Brandon to take a look at it. Every time Tash called him "Randy," Brandon winced, hating that he lied to Tash but not yet ready to tell the truth.

The familiar brick building rose before his eyes as he turned the corner after hopping off the bus. A chill wind bit through him, and he shivered and pulled his scarf tighter around his face. The flu had been going around school and the last thing he needed was to get sick. Brandon increased his pace and unlocked the door with the key Noah had given him last Sunday, sighing with relief as warmth enveloped him.

Hurrying to the back, Brandon shed his coat and gloves, then unwound his scarf, leaving it hanging around his neck. When he entered the room, he was surprised to see only Noah sitting at the desk.

"Hey, how's it going? Where's Tash?" He helped himself to a cup of coffee from the ever-present urn.

Noah swiveled around in his chair. "I don't know. I was hoping you guys were coming in together." He frowned. "I haven't heard from him. He didn't call you?"

A tiny niggle of alarm shot through Brandon. "No. I spoke to him a few days ago, but nothing seemed out of the ordinary. Maybe he had an emergency?" He took a seat next to Noah and slipped on his headset. "I know his sister went down to Florida to see their parents last week. I hope everything's okay."

Shrugging, Noah rolled his chair closer. "Yeah. But he would've called. That's why it's strange."

The phone line lit up and Brandon, his finger poised to take the call, said, "I can stop by his house to check on my way home after my shift."

Relief lit Noah's eyes and his tense features relaxed. "Great. We'll be able to get off early. Rachel has a bunch of grad students coming in about an hour to do a shift. I'll stay until they get here, but if you want to go…"

"Let me take this call and see." He hit the button. "Good morning, this is the Home Away from Home hotline. You're talking to Randy. How are you doing this morning?"

It took all his effort to concentrate on the voice over the phone and not the panicked beating of his heart at the thought of something happening to Tash.

"Hi, I'm Jaime. I'm seventeen and I want a boyfriend, but I don't know how to find anyone. Like, I can't just like go up to another guy and get punched in the face for hitting on him."

Recalling how he'd felt in high school, knowing he could never talk to anyone about his sexuality, Brandon found himself nodding as they spoke.

"Yeah, I know. How about volunteering at LGBTQ centers around you? Do you live in the city?" He reached for the sheet of resources laying on the desk. "I can give you some names and numbers. Lots of people volunteer, and it's a great way to help and meet people. There're also clubs that have social nights specifically for teens to get together."

He gave Jaime the numbers and names of some clubs and chatted with him for several more minutes. After the call ended, he pulled off the headset. Noah was on another call, and Brandon checked his cell phone to see if he'd heard from Tash. *Nothing. No missed call and no text.* His fingers flew over the keyboard to send Tash a message.

Everything ok? Where are you?

It sent but didn't show as being read, even as Brandon stared at the screen until it swam before his eyes, frustration growing with every passing second.

"Nothing?"

Startled at Noah's voice, Brandon jumped. "No." He raked a hand through his hair. "It doesn't make any sense; Tash is the most conscientious person I know."

"Yeah." Usually lighthearted and smiling, Noah's brow furrowed with concern. "Why don't you go check on him now? The others will be here soon."

The sound of footsteps tramping in the hall reached his ears. "There, see? Go on. Let me know."

"I will. Thanks." Brandon grabbed his jacket and raced past the people coming in, giving them perfunctory greetings. He had no time for niceties. Not if Tash was in trouble.

Throwing aside cost, he ran down Van Brunt street and hoped for the best in finding a cab. Luck was with him for once as one happened to be discharging its passengers a bit down the block. With the wind cutting through him, Brandon raced toward it, his hand outstretched. He hadn't even bothered to zip his coat, he realized, as he slid into the back seat and shut the door. The penetrating warmth soaked through him and he shuddered.

"I gotcha. Don' worry 'bout it."

Huffing to catch his breath, Brandon nodded. "Love Lane and Henry Street."

"No problem," the cabbie said and drove off.

Not ten minutes later, Brandon paid the fare and exited the cab in front of Tash's pretty carriage house.

He raced up the steps and knocked on the door, then rang the bell over and over again. He could hear the chimes reverberating inside, and he made out the unmistakable sounds of the cats meowing loudly, but no voice shushing them to be quiet.

Tash had mentioned in one of their conversations that he left a key outside in case of an emergency, but there was no doormat, and Brandon had no clue where to find it. He descended the steps and began looking in the front garden, picking up various rocks. One felt a bit different than the others, and triumph surged through him as he noticed it was a fake rock with a button on the bottom. He pushed it, and two keys fell into his palm.

Brandon pocketed the rock and took the stairs two at a time back to the front door. He unlocked and opened the door, keeping his body in front so the cats didn't run through his legs. An eerie silence filled the air, and Brandon wondered if he'd made the right decision to invade Tash's home without any reason other than his—and Noah's for that matter—unease when he heard coughing from the living room.

"Who is it? Val?"

Unmistakably, it sounded like Tash, only weak and hoarse. After hesitating a moment, Brandon walked into the living room, greeted by the sight of an unshaven Tash laying on the sofa. His pallor and glittering, feverish eyes left no doubt he was ill.

"Randy?" He scrubbed his face with his hands. "Are you here, or am I hallucinating with fever?"

"No, it's me. What's wrong? I mean, I see you're sick. Why didn't you let anyone know?"

"My phone died, and I don't have the strength to climb the stairs to get the charger. The only thing I've managed to do for the past day is feed the cats." His weak laugh led to another bout of coughing.

"Don't you need medicine? You're a doctor. Here." Brandon pulled out his cell phone. "Call the pharmacy and get a prescription. I'll pick it up for you."

He handed his phone to Tash, but he was too weak to hold it himself. Brandon curved his palm around Tash's and held his slightly trembling hand while he called in the prescription. As if that simple effort expended all his remaining energy, Tash fell back onto the sofa pillows with a groan.

"I feel like shit."

"You look like it too. We were worried when you didn't show up today, and neither Noah nor I could reach you. Oh, damn. Let me tell Noah you're not dead. He was concerned." He pulled out his phone and sent Noah a quick text.

A wry smile touched Tash's lips for a second. "I've been doing nothing but sleeping on and off for the past two days. I totally forgot it was Sunday today." His expression softened. "Thank you for coming to check on me. I'll be okay. You found the key I left outside?"

Brandon nodded. "You shouldn't be alone; you could get pneumonia. When did you last eat anything?" Brandon surveyed the coffee table which had nothing but a tissue box and a bottle of aspirin on top of it. "I make a mean chicken soup."

Tash gazed back at him with a sober expression. "Don't be silly. You have better things to do than play nursemaid to me. I'll be okay." His voice caught, and he began that throaty cough again, leaving him sweating and gasping for air.

"I know you will. Because I'm going to stay and make sure. I have nothing to do that's more important."

Their eyes met, and Brandon managed to keep his expression steely and hard until he saw the surrender in Tash's gaze.

"Fine. I'm sure once I get the medicine, I'll be better—most likely by tomorrow."

He took off his jacket and tossed it onto the club chair. "Do I need to go shopping? Is it okay if I look in your fridge?"

"Have at it." Tash waved a hand but didn't make an attempt to get up.

Brandon walked into the kitchen, the two cats running back and forth. When he pulled open the refrigerator door, Brandon winced at the sorry sight inside. Tash's refrigerator was almost as bad as his own. He made a mental list of everything he needed and headed back to the living room, but not before checking the cats' dishes to make sure they had, in fact, been fed, and Tash wasn't dreaming.

"When I go to pick up your medicine, I'll pick up some stuff at the supermarket and make you chicken soup."

"Who knew you were such a chef?" His eyes remained closed, but he smiled and Brandon was able to study his face, wincing at the dark circles under his eyes.

"I'm going to go now. Why don't you try and get some sleep? Do you want me to get you your cell phone charger? I will if you tell me where it is."

Without opening his eyes, Tash responded. "Yeah, if you wouldn't mind. It's upstairs next to my bed. Second door on the left."

"Sure." Brandon took the stairs to the second level and entered Tash's room. It was so personal to enter someone's bedroom without them being present. He spotted the cord next to the huge king-sized bed and rapidly scanned the room, eyeing the fireplace and the mantel with more family pictures. It was a beautiful, cozy retreat. Brandon sighed and left, shutting the door quietly behind him.

"Here. I can plug it in for you." Brandon plugged it into the charging hub on the table next to the sofa. "I'm going to run out now and get everything. Just rest and I'll be back in a little while."

Tash nodded, his eyelids fluttering with fatigue.

As promised, Brandon sped through the supermarket and picked up Tash's prescription, making it back to Tash's within an hour. Entering the carriage house, he spied Tash, now sleeping in the same position, the two cats lying beside him like sentinels. *What would it be like to come home to this every day?* Brandon walked into the kitchen to start cooking. He wondered why a man like Tash, one of the nicest people he'd met, and successful, wasn't with someone. He never even mentioned dating.

Bemused, he set the bags down on the marble countertop and quietly, so not to disturb Tash, took out a big pot he found and proceeded to heat the water, then set about chopping the vegetables while waiting for the water to boil. When that commenced, he slid the chicken into the pot and turned the flame down to a simmer. He'd learned to cook as a young teenager while his foster mother was gone at her innumerable church meetings. He'd found it soothing and a way to forget about his problems, even if only for a little while, but living alone for so long meant he rarely had a chance to indulge.

Once everything was in the pot, he went back out to the living room and stretched out in the club chair and picked up a magazine. To his surprise, Tash opened his eyes.

"Hi."

"Oh. I thought you were asleep."

"I was, then I started to smell something wonderful." Stretching, he arched his back. "God that feels good."

"That's the chicken soup. Here, I have the medicine." He jumped out of his chair, fished the bag from his pocket, and got Tash a glass of water. Brandon handed the pill to Tash and helped him hold the glass while he took a sip. Their fingers brushed, and Brandon's face heated at the warm sparks of gold in

Tash's eyes.

"Um. How do you feel?"

"Like shit. I hope the meds kick in; I have a busy week ahead."

"Uh, I don't think so, doctor. You're going to need to stay in bed for at least another few days. It's cold as hell out there, and you need the time to recover after you start feeling better."

"Listen. My mother lives in Florida; I don't need another one." Tash joked as he struggled to sit up. Brandon helped him by propping the pillow behind him. "And if you're volunteering to be my nurse, you could try dressing up in a cute outfit. That might make me feel better."

"Obviously, your illness has made you delirious." Brandon tucked the throw around Tash so his chest wouldn't be exposed. "The soup will be finished in about an hour."

"Sounds good." Tash coughed again and Brandon wondered how he would be able to leave him alone that night and the next day as well. "Seriously. Thanks for stopping by. I appreciate you caring enough."

The sweet, sad smile tore at Brandon's heart.

"Of course, I care. You're my friend." And Brandon realized it was true. For the first time, he had a real friend. Over the past few weeks, between spending time with him at the Center and sharing his vision for the mentoring program, which Tash not only encouraged but insisted upon, Brandon had grown to look forward to their daily conversations and Sundays spent at the call center.

"How about I make some tea?"

At Tash's nod, Brandon went into the kitchen and put the kettle up to boil. He rummaged around and found a large selection of herbal tea bags.

"What kind do you want?" he called out. "You have a million varieties."

"I don't care; surprise me."

At Tash's voice, right over his shoulder, Brandon almost jumped out of his skin. "Oh, shit. You scared me. What are you doing up?"

"I have to pee." Tash shuffled past him toward the powder room next to the kitchen.

Brandon watched him sway on his feet and stop to brace himself on the counter. Immediately, Brandon turned down the boiling water and raced over to Tash's side to slip a bracing arm around his shoulder.

"Here. Lean on me."

"I can do it."

Tash tried to shake him off, but Brandon held firm.

"Don't be stupid. It's not showing weakness. You're sick. Let me help you."

With Tash leaning heavily on his shoulder, Brandon walked him to the powder room then returned to the stove to make Tash his tea. He heard the water running, and after about five minutes, Tash reappeared, face freshly washed, his eyes clearer, and he seemed somewhat less tired and worn out.

"Feeling better?" Pointing to the mug of tea, Brandon kept his voice neutral. "I made you a cup of tea. Be careful. It's still hot."

His bare feet made no sound on the tile floor as he walked to the large table and sat heavily in the wooden chair. "Thanks. I'm sorry I snapped at you before. You've been really great to me, and I was stupid. I've been by myself so long I forgot how to act."

Curious as to Tash's past, Brandon didn't feel like spoiling the moment to question him about it. "Don't worry. Are you feeling better?"

Cradling the cup in his hands, he took a sip before answering. "A bit. At least my head is spinning less."

Brandon liked Tash's kitchen with the wide counters and gleaming oak table. The chairs had pin-tucked cushions in a brightly checked yellow-and-blue pattern tied to the back with matching placemats at each setting on the tabletop. A basket filled with eucalyptus rested in the center and was the source of the fresh scent perfuming the air.

"If you feel like a nap, I can wait on the soup. The longer it sits, the better it tastes."

"No, God. I've been doing nothing for two days but sleeping. My brain is so fuzzy I feel like I have a sock over my head." His eyes shone with appreciation. "Besides, it smells so damn good in here I can't wait to have it."

Brandon lifted the lid on the pot and stirred the soup then dipped in a spoon to taste.

"It's done. Let it cool a bit and then I'll give you a bowl. Do you like carrots and celery in it?"

"Anything. I haven't eaten since..." He hesitated

for a moment to think. "Huh. I can't remember. Well, I'm hungry. So that's a good sign."

"Yep. Where are your soup bowls?"

Tash pointed to a glass-front cabinet over the counter with the coffeemaker on it. "Over there. Take one for yourself, too. I'm not eating alone."

"I'm not too hungry." That was a lie; he'd had nothing since the bagel in the morning at the Clinic, but he wanted the soup for Tash. "I'll take a little, though."

He ladled the fragrant soup with its carrots and celery into the deep bowls and set them on the table. While Brandon went to get the spoons, Tash pushed one bowl in front of him and took the other for himself. It occurred to Brandon when he returned to join Tash: this was as close to companionship as he'd had in his whole life. Anxiously, he awaited Tash's opinion on the soup.

"Delicious," said Tash and he took another bigger spoonful. "Wow. You're hired. You can cook for me every day."

I wouldn't mind. I wouldn't mind being here all the time.

The unbidden thought popped into his head, shocking Brandon. He finished his soup in silence, and when Tash's bowl was empty, he took their dishes and put them in the dishwasher. Brandon poured the soup into two containers he noticed in the cabinet then put them in the refrigerator and re-joined Tash at the table. The mellow overhead light spilled golden on Tash's hair and glinted off his glasses, but Brandon also noticed the deep lines of fatigue etched in Tash's face and the sleepy look in his eyes.

"How about if I take you upstairs and put you to bed?"

Tash blinked, sleepy-eyed, his body slumped in the chair. "Hmm? Yeah, sure. I gotta take my meds later on. You'll wake me up, right?"

Startled, Brandon thought for a moment. He hadn't planned on staying; he didn't have his clothes or anything for work, but he could make a trip to his studio and back while Tash slept. For at least one night, he could pretend to be a part of this special man's life.

"Sure. I'd be happy to."

With Brandon holding Tash around his waist, they slowly made it up the stairs. He forced himself to ignore the solid muscles pressed against him or the way his body aligned perfectly with Tash's. When they approached the door, Tash turned around and faced Brandon, who at an inch or so shorter, had to tilt his head up to look into his face.

"Thank you for caring. I don't know why you do, but thank you."

Tash bent down and kissed his cheek, the palm of his hand sliding around to the nape of Brandon's neck to hold him close. And for once, Brandon didn't pull away. Standing there in that hallway with Tash, safe and warm in his arms, Brandon had no desire to ever leave him.

Chapter Eight

I T TOOK TASH over a week to kick his cold, and though he hated being sick, there had been one bright spot: having Randy stay with him. One day had merged into two, and before he knew it, Randy had spent almost a whole week, and he had to admit, it felt good to have another person with him. It helped when the person was kind, sweetly generous, and gorgeous.

There was no misunderstanding on his part; Tash knew Randy was staying with him while he recuperated as a sort of payback for Tash introducing him to the help line and the Clinic in general. But for a little while, Tash allowed himself the fantasy of having a lover like Randy, and it enabled him to sleep better at night than he had in years.

On Friday he thought about going back to the Clinic and had texted Noah, who responded immediately.

NO. Stay home. It's cold and you could use the rest.

He laughed to himself.

Yes, mother.

He hadn't told anyone Randy stayed with him this past week; it had become their own personal little refuge from the world. After his work at school had finished for the day, Randy would make dinner, then they'd talk about Tash's program and maybe watch a movie until Tash couldn't stay awake any longer, and he'd drag himself off to bed. Randy slept in one of the spare bedrooms down the hall from him and couldn't know how every evening Tash wanted to invite him into his own bed and hold him all night long.

Coming down the steps, Tash stood and surveyed Randy, standing by the stove, a glass of wine in hand, making them dinner. A painful throb rose in his chest for what he once had and could never have again.

If only this could be real.

Scolding himself for that ridiculous wish, Tash forced a smile on his lips and descended the last two steps.

"Good afternoon, or should I say evening? I don't think I've slept as much in years as I have this past week."

Looking up from the stove, Randy waved his spatula. "Hi. Yeah, you were sleeping like the dead, so I didn't want to wake you. I went out, got the newspaper and some fresh juice for you. I'm making an early dinner; pasta with chicken and vegetables. I figured you missed lunch so you wouldn't mind. Is that okay?"

Almost choking on his laughter, Tash joined Randy at the stove and gave an appreciative sniff. "Is that okay? You're asking a man who subsists on milk with a past-due expiration date and cheese that waves hello when you open the fridge. This?" He pointed to the pan. "This is paradise."

A flush of pleasure crept up Randy's neck. Maybe he was wrong to think Randy had a secret in his past or something to hide because it had been years since he'd seen a man blush at praise. For the moment, Tash wished he could be as young and innocent as Randy.

The yearning in Randy's clear green eyes drew Tash closer, and he wondered if his soft lips tasted as sweet as they looked. Randy's golden lashes swept down against his cheek, and it took every bit of Tash's self-control to not grab him and kiss him. No matter what Noah said, he had nothing to offer a man with the world spread out before him.

Reflectively, Randy sipped his glass of wine, a faraway look in his eyes. "I've been on my own for so long, I'd forgotten how nice it is to have someone to talk to in the evenings."

The loneliness in Randy's soft voice struck Tash; he wondered why a man who appeared to have everything seemed so alone and lost. Most likely it had to do with whatever had happened in his past that made him so jumpy and hesitant around strangers.

They ate their pasta, and Tash finished every scrap of food, including half a loaf of crusty Italian bread. It wasn't until he was on his second cup of coffee that he'd formulated what he wanted to say. "That was delicious. Remind me when the weather changes; I owe you a good dinner. I mean, I owe you a hell of a lot more. Thank you. Thank you for being my friend and caring."

"You don't owe me anything. I'm the one who should be thanking you."

"Well," said Tash, draining his coffee cup, "we can start a mutual admiration society for each other. And the last thing I want you to do is think I'm kicking you out. I'm going to take it easy and later on go to see Wanda."

"Wanda? The woman who runs that shelter you talked to me about?" He stood and began to gather the detritus from their dinner.

Unwilling to let Randy act like his housekeeper now that he felt better, Tash stacked the dishes closest to him, and together they cleaned up the kitchen. He hardly coughed at all anymore, and Tash knew he'd passed the worst of it. He also knew it was only because Randy had stayed by him, made sure he took his medicine and ate properly, that he recovered as quickly as he did without having it turn into bronchitis or pneumonia.

"Yeah. Let's go sit in the living room. Want a beer or something?"

"Nah. I'm good, thanks."

With the cats on their heels, he and Randy headed into the wide living area, and he flopped down onto the sofa, stretching out. Randy took the overstuffed club chair, bracing himself for Cleo to jump in his lap. To Tash's amazement, Cleopatra had attached herself like glue to Randy, even forsaking her brother's company to sleep in Randy's bed with him. Tash wondered what damage she'd inflict on him once Randy left. An overwhelming pit of sadness loomed before him, and he dreaded going back to his dark, one-dimensional days. Having Randy with him here made the world brighter, a place where life unfolded around every corner, waiting with new opportunities.

Randy chased away his darkness, and that's why Tash knew he had to let him go.

"Tell me about Wanda and the shelter."

Tash gave himself a mental shake from his daydream.

Get your act together.

"She's a fighter and stands up for those people like no one ever has. Everyone should have an advocate like her. I know you'll love her."

"She sounds wonderful. I'm sure I will, and I can't wait to meet her."

They sat in comfortable silence for a little while, Randy murmuring to Cleo on his lap. This scenario was all Tash ever wished for; he had no use for the nightlife waiting across the river in the clubs and bars. He closed his eyes.

"Tash? Hey, Tash?"

He blinked awake, finding himself in the semi-darkness. How long had he slept? Randy kneeled beside him, a serene smile on his face.

"I kinda passed out, huh?"

"You still need your sleep."

What I need is you.

Frustrated, he swung his legs over the side of the sofa and sat for a moment with his head bowed. This attraction had to stop; Randy was simply being kind. It was his nature to care about others.

"I'm all right. What time is it, anyway?"

Randy checked his watch. "Almost six-thirty."

"Good. We can go see Wanda tonight, help with the dinner service if you'd like." His mouth suddenly parched, Tash headed to the kitchen for a drink without saying another word.

"Tash, what's wrong? You seem angry."

He was. Angry with himself for being attracted to a man who was wrong for him. Angry for letting it happen despite all the warning signals he himself put up then chose to ignore. Randy had that same sweet, irrepressible spirit as Danny...before drugs distorted him and took him away from the people he loved and who loved him back.

"I'm fine."

But Randy, as he'd learned this past week, was a persistent man and didn't back down so easily.

"You don't look fine. You look upset. Did I do something? I haven't lived with anyone really ever, so I don't know. If I overstepped any boundaries, I'm sorry."

By this time, Randy had followed him into the

kitchen, and Tash had to turn away. He didn't want to see Randy's worried face, his fair brows pinched together as he tried to figure out the cause of Tash's anger.

"It isn't you….it's me. I'm a fool." He wrenched open the refrigerator and pulled out a bottle of water, but before he could open it, Randy took it from his hands and held him by the shoulders, forcing their eyes to meet.

"The last thing I'd ever call you is a fool."

The close proximity of their bodies proved too much for him; for a week now, he'd been lusting after this guy—his dreams had been nothing short of erotic and after his prolonged abstinence, what little self-control he'd been holding onto shattered.

It started out as a sweet kiss of comfort, their soft lips barely touching. Then Tash's long-dormant desire flared hot and deep; holding himself together while Randy ministered to him would do that to any man. He crushed his mouth over Randy's, the softness of his lips as sweet as he'd imagined, yet the reality so much more intense and beautiful. Tash ran his hands over Randy's arms, their muscles flexing as Randy slipped his arms around Tash's neck, pressing their bodies together. The unmistakable bulge of Randy's cock nudged his thigh, hot and hard against the thin sweats he'd taken to wearing since he'd been sick.

Feeding off the hunger that had built up inside him, Tash licked along the seam of Randy's mouth and slid his tongue inside, loving the heat and velvet touch of Randy's tongue as they met. Their teeth clashed and their breaths mingled, sending him reeling—the pleasure-pain centering on the ache in his dick and balls, the liquid fire slowly burning through his veins.

His life had spiraled down to become a blank, meaningless existence. Unremarkable and forgettable until now.

This was the magic he'd been missing.

Incapable of stopping, his lips trailed hot and wet along Randy's jaw to suck at his neck, only to return to once again capture Randy's mouth. Randy sank into his embrace, breathing heavily against the curve of his neck.

"I've wanted to kiss you all week, but I was afraid." His warm mouth moved against Tash's skin and he trembled. "I'm glad you made the first move, or I might've never gotten up the nerve."

Like a bucket of cold water dashed over him, Tash was brought back to reality. For a wild moment, the loneliness had blinded him, and he'd remembered how it was to feel happy and whole. For the past week, his house had been an actual home again, and though he wanted that more than anything, he couldn't shake the thought that Randy was too young for him and deserved so much more.

"I'm sorry. I shouldn't have lost control like that. It shouldn't have happened." Lame as the excuse sounded, Tash knew it was for the best. He touched his burning cheek, the feel of Randy's scruff still hot against his fingertips, and took a step back.

But Randy persisted, confusion clouding his eyes. "Why not? We're both adults. You aren't seeing anyone, right?"

"No, obviously not, but you can see how this isn't right." Keeping his distance, Tash circled around Randy and took a seat at the table. "I know almost nothing about you but that I'm almost fifteen years older than you are. And that right there is enough. You should be out with people your own age having fun. I'm not into that." Much as it hurt, Tash had to say it. "What's the saying? There's no fool like an old fool?" How pathetic did he sound? "I'm not the right person for you."

Randy took the chair opposite him and braced his elbows on the table, his mouth hard and jaw set in a challenging line. "So, admittedly you know nothing about me, but you think you can and should decide who I kiss?"

"I know that you're incredibly attractive, smart, and young. Three deadly sins for an older man like me."

Irritation flashed across Randy's face. "You make yourself out like you're an old man, not simply a man who's a few years older. For Christ's sake, stop being so stuck on this point. I couldn't sit around and listen to a bunch of jocks talking about football, or guys in suits talking about the stock market. I'd be bored to death." He hitched his chair around, closer to Tash. "I may only be twenty-five, but trust me when I say I've lived a lifetime already."

Tash had no idea what to think. Wanting Randy

was easy. But trusting himself not to make mistakes could prove the hardest thing of all.

"It's not only the age difference. I was reminded of someone I used to know and mistakes I made. Mistakes that led to the most horrific consequences. And even though it happened years ago, I can't forget. It's colored my whole outlook on life and drives me in everything I do."

"Was it someone you loved?"

He raised his gaze to meet Randy's. "Yeah. But it forced me to realize I wasn't as good a judge of people or as good a doctor as I thought. He hid everything from me—his addiction, his cheating..." The bile rose in his throat. "His disease."

Randy's face whitened. "He was positive?"

"He was. Without me ever knowing, he'd become hooked on heroin while we were together, and it took over his life until he ran away. And until the hospital called us because he OD'd, we had no idea. By then it was too late."

"I—I've seen people suffering in some of the shelters I volunteered at. It broke my heart knowing how alone they must've felt." Randy bit his lip and looked down at the table as if unable to meet his gaze.

Tash knew what he wanted to ask but was too afraid or maybe didn't think he had the right to.

"Hey. I'm not positive if that's what has you looking so concerned. Danny and I hadn't been together for almost two years before we found him. Of course, I had myself tested anyway. We were just thrilled to be able to be there with him in the end."

"Who's we?"

It occurred to Tash that Randy knew as little about his life as he did about Randy's.

"Gage."

"Gage?" Randy blinked in confusion. "What did he have to do with it?"

"Danny was Gage's brother."

Leaving Randy slumped in his chair to digest all this information, Tash walked away.

Once Randy went home and life went back to normal, he'd see Tash was right. "I think we've had enough true confessions for the evening. Let's go to the shelter and you can meet Wanda."

Randy's face brightened a bit, but he still looked uncertain. "Sure. But we can finish this conversation later, right?"

"I'm going to get dressed. Be down in a minute." He mounted the steps while Randy followed behind him but remained below.

"I see what you're doing," Randy called up to him. "You can only run from it for so long."

"I could say the same to you."

Chuckling to himself, Tash ascended the stairs, leaving Randy standing speechless.

Chapter Nine

IT WAS EASIER to take a cab to the Lower East Side than for Tash to take his car and look for parking. They found one easily enough and settled into the back seat. Randy sat, silent, probably processing all the information Tash had dumped on him, so Tash kept quiet, his own thoughts a mass of confusion as well.

What had possessed him to talk about Danny, to tell Randy about him? Tash knew he was kidding himself. For a brief moment, Tash had allowed his grief to overcome his good sense. Although Randy and Danny were nothing alike, it was the joy of sharing his life with someone, having another person around to talk to and do the mundane, everyday things with that brought the ache of Tash's loneliness to the surface. How many nights before Danny had left him did they spend together, joking around, cooking, and cleaning up, then retiring to their bedroom to make sweet and passionate love?

In the year after Danny died, Tash saw him around every corner in the apartment they'd shared, so he'd bought his little carriage house in the quiet neighbor-hood of Brooklyn Heights. It became his sanctuary; a perfect place to hide away from life. Although the hurt of Danny's betrayal had passed, Tash still mourned a life lost so senselessly.

After that shattering kiss he and Randy had shared, Tash wanted nothing more than to rip the man's clothes off and bend him over the counter right there in the kitchen. Instead, he'd done the mature thing and pulled away before he'd lost his head. Who was he kidding anyway? The guy was young and gorgeous. The last thing Randy needed was an almost forty-year-old man with a head full of baggage. Randy had reacted like any young man full of hormones. "Hooking up," they called it these days—sex without strings or expectations. Foolish, dangerous, and definitely not for him.

After about half an hour, thanks to the usual stop-and-go traffic on the Manhattan Bridge—no matter the time of day or night—the cab pulled up in front of the shelter. Tash paid the driver, and they got out. It looked like the depressing place it was on the outside: dark brick, graffiti on the cement wall, and garbage pails stacked along the sidewalk. Unreal to think that around the corner, real estate developers were gobbling up properties and converting them to million-dollar apartments. Tash couldn't imagine living here.

"Come, let's go inside; it's getting colder as we stand here."

Randy nodded and followed him as they entered

the shelter's warmth. Tash greeted the security guard at the front desk. "Hey, Vic. How's it going tonight?" He shook the big man's hand. Victor had been here for years, and they were all thankful Wanda had someone around like him, who made sure everyone behaved and didn't act up.

"Good, Doc. Can't complain. Wanda's in the back. She's getting ready for the dinner service, I think."

"Excellent. Thanks. This is Randy. He's going to be helping on some projects with me and the other guys."

Randy stuck out his hand. "Hi, Vic. Nice to meet you."

Vic shook his hand, and Tash could see Vic taking Randy's measure, checking him out. "Nice to meet you too."

"Randy's a sixth-grade teacher in Brooklyn."

Vic raised a brow. "One of those fancy private schools?"

Randy laughed out loud. "Hardly. My school's in Bushwick."

"Well, all right, then." Vic nodded with obvious approval.

They said their good-byes and headed down the hallway to the back. Tash pointed out various rooms to Randy before they came to a door marked OFFICE. He stopped and knocked.

"Come on in."

Tash grinned at a nervous Randy who stood bouncing on the balls of his feet. "Don't worry. You'll love her."

He pushed open the door and found Wanda on the telephone. Her hair was in its usual tight braids against her head, and her eyes rolled with frustration at whomever she argued with. When she saw him, however, her face brightened, even as she continued to lambaste whoever was on the opposite side of the phone.

"Listen. I don't care what they say. I'm telling you; every can they sent me was banged up and damaged. Just 'cause these people are in a shelter don't mean they gotta eat bad food. Now send me a new shipment, or I'll call the news on you and run your name all over the television." She slammed the phone down with obvious relish. "Ha! That'll get 'em moving." She stood up and circled around from behind the desk.

"Dr. Tash. How are you?" They hugged, and he kissed her warm lavender-scented cheek.

"I told you to call me Tash. No need for titles here."

She patted his cheek. "And who do we have here?" She turned to Randy, her eyes gleaming with approval. "Is this fine-looking man a friend of yours?" Without waiting for an answer, she stuck out her hand. "I'm Wanda, honey. What's your name?"

"Randy, ma'am. I'm here to help Tash with the mentoring program." He took her hand and shook it.

Her dark eyes flickered between the two of them. "Well, lookie here. You're a Southern boy, aren't you? Where are you from?"

"No, ma'am. I-I'm from Pennsylvania."

Tash knew Randy enough by now to see the alarm flaring in his eyes, and decided to change the course of the conversation before Wanda started her usual third degree. "Randy's a sixth-grade teacher in Bushwick."

Respect and admiration dawned in Wanda's eyes. "You are? That's wonderful. Ain't many young men like you willing to put themselves out for the kids these days. Most of them go to Wall Street where all the money is." She shook her head. "Like my poor Luke. They work my boy half to death over there."

She turned to Tash. "I got a few texts from the two of them. They had such a good time; I'm so glad Luke got to meet Jordan's parents, and they had some time for themselves as well. I can't wait to see them tomorrow. Jordan told me he got me a present from Paris."

"That's great, Wanda. I'm looking forward to hearing about their trip." Tash spoke the truth. He didn't begrudge them anything. The two men had fought long and hard for their relationship. Tash knew, however, that neither Luke nor Ash would ever truly be happy until they found out what had happened to their younger brother, Brandon.

"Randy has agreed to help with the mentoring program we want to start here at the shelter, in conjunction with the community center. He's already taken it upon himself to help kids after school who not only need extra assistance but ones who get teased for liking school and doing well."

Wanda's eyes took on a new light. "You have to be a special young man to want to do that." She took

Randy by the hand and sat him down in the chair in front of her desk, taking the one opposite him. "Tell me, why did you choose to do this? I get the feeling it's kinda personal for you; am I right?"

To his shock, Randy answered her. "Yes. I believe the best way to live your life is paying it forward. All my life, my heroes have always been my teachers. I found my escape in school and books. They helped me through rough times."

Wanda took his hand in hers. "You had some rough times, honey? But you're strong because you didn't let it break you. And you took what you learned, and it made you stronger and now you're helping others."

Tash watched as the older woman and the young man gazed at each other, forging an understanding he knew he couldn't be a part of. He hadn't had a rough life. He'd always had whatever he needed. But that was his reason for giving back. He wanted to give as many people as he could reach the opportunity to climb out of their own personal hells, to make it in the world.

"Tash, you hold tight to this man. He's a keeper."

He chuckled as Randy's face flamed. "Ahh, Wanda, we aren't together. He's here to help. He's a friend." Randy's eyes burned into his with a desire he knew matched the one Tash had in his heart. It was no use, though. The two of them were at different points in their lives, and Tash recognized it, even if Randy didn't. "I knew he'd be perfect for the mentoring program, so I wanted him to meet you, and then I'm going to bring him to the Center tomorrow afternoon. He met Drew last month, and Jordan and Luke need to meet him as well. Luke's been working like a fiend since he came home from Paris and Jordan's recuperating from a cold. They even asked Mike and Rachel to keep Sasha because they didn't feel like they could watch her properly until now. Tomorrow is the first time they'll both be able to go to the Center and Jordan said they'd be over in the afternoon."

"Sasha? Is that their daughter?" Randy asked.

Tash laughed. "No, she's their dog, although they spoil her like a baby."

Wanda slipped her arm through Tash's. "You gonna hang around for dinner? Both of you. It's turkey night with candied yams and cornbread." She shifted her attention to Randy. "Real Southern style."

Tash nodded. "I'll help. How about you, Randy?"

"Of course. Sounds great." His smile wavered slightly as Wanda continued to stare at him. "Is something the matter, Wanda? Did I do something wrong?"

There was a sadness to her smile. "Oh no, honey. I was remembering back to the time when Luke showed up here all hungry and skinny. We were serving turkey dinner that night too, and he ate so much I thought he'd get sick."

Randy said nothing further until they approached the kitchen. "I didn't know Luke had lived in a shelter. I thought he worked on Wall Street and was one of those rich hedge fund guys."

"He works there now but lived in the system for years. He's a real inspiration. I know you two will hit it off." Tash opened the door to the heat and bustle of the enormous kitchen.

Randy shrugged. "I doubt it. I mean, I'm a poor schoolteacher. I don't travel in those kinds of circles or, to be honest, even your circle."

Surprised, Tash stopped short, just inside the doorway. "Don't be ridiculous. There are no circles. You've no reason to think anyone would look down on you or treat you differently because you aren't a doctor or a lawyer or don't make a ton of money. These people aren't like that, and you shouldn't prejudge like you don't want them to do to you."

Randy's face fell, and he kicked the floor with his sneaker. "You're right. It's that I get a little nervous meeting all these new people at once."

Wanda slipped her arm around Randy's waist and gave him a hug. "You've been alone a long time, haven't you?" Her troubled face searched Randy's. "You remind me so much of my Luke when he first came. He was also scared and nervous but so determined." She gave him another hug. "Don't you worry, honey. Everything will work out fine. Let's get something to eat, then serve the others."

She left, barking orders at the kitchen staff. Tash remained with Randy. "She's right, you know. These people will never judge you. They've all been through so much in their lives and will be eternally grateful for your help." A mischievous smile broke out across his face. "Knowing them is like getting sucked into this enormous family of well-intentioned but nosy brothers and sisters. If you're around, maybe they'll get off my back and find someone else to bother."

Randy shuddered as they walked side by side to the table set with trays. "God help me, but no, thanks. I'm happy to meet them and be a part of this project, but that's as far as it's going to go, trust me."

Tash grinned to himself. *That's what you think.* "Let's eat, then serve the others."

AT ONE O'CLOCK the next afternoon, Tash pushed open the door to the Keith Hart Community Center and was greeted with a heartwarming sight. Kids of all ages sat in the library area, ensconced with books, either lying on the sofas or curled up in the armchairs. Teenagers sat at the computers, hopefully doing their homework or studying and not on social media, while in the arts-and-crafts area, little boys and girls played at the tables with some of the adult volunteers, coloring, painting, or simply making an overall mess like they were supposed to do at their age.

Sitting at one of those tables with a little girl on his lap was Dr. Jordan Peterson. It warmed Tash's heart to see the man so well rested and clear-eyed. He'd gained weight and despite his recent bad cold, looked stronger and healthier than he did when he was dependent on Xanax. Gone was the emotional and physical wreck of months earlier. Though he'd be continuing therapy, Tash knew Jordan had passed the most difficult part of his recovery.

At his approach, Jordan looked up, and a smile broke out across his face. "Tash!" He bent down to the little girl and whispered in her ear. She nodded and slipped off his lap and went to sit next to one of the other volunteers. Jordan wiped his hands with a wet wipe and tossed it into the trash before jumping up to give Tash a hug.

"Great to see you. Did you get our e-mails and pictures?"

"Yep. You guys looked like you had a great time."

"We did." He and Jordan continued to walk toward the back where the offices of the Center were located. "Lucas met my parents, and they hit it off. We spent one night in Switzerland; then the rest of the time was in Paris."

"Sounds like a honeymoon." Tash opened the door and turned on the light, then walked to the large wooden desk dominating the back of the office.

"It will be the next time we return. I don't see the point in waiting around for years or even months." The light in his eyes dimmed for a brief moment, then brightened. "I plan on living my life to the fullest every day. Making it count."

"That's a good philosophy."

"Maybe you should take a page from my book. Or at least listen to yourself when you talk to me about moving forward." Jordan leaned a hip against the desk

Tash sat at, those pale blue eyes piercing right through him. "It's hell being alone. It took almost killing myself to understand it, but you deserve so much more than you're willing to allow yourself, and for no reason."

"So you've given up orthopedics and decided to join me in practicing psychiatry now?" Tash ignored Jordan's remarks about moving forward with his life. Simply because they cut too close to home. For one brief moment, he returned to his kitchen and the kiss between him and Randy that nearly stole the breath from his body. Ruthlessly, he squashed the rush of desire that flooded through him at the remembrance of Randy's slick tongue sweeping through his mouth.

Jordan, ever the perceptive bastard, must've seen something in his face, no matter how neutral he sought to keep his expression and pounced. "Son of a bitch, you have met someone." Jordan leaned on the desk, looming over Tash. "Who is he? Come on, tell me."

"Don't be stupid. I haven't met anyone." He fumbled with the keyboard. "What's the damn password to this thing anyway?" He banged a bit harder.

"Liar," said Jordan, his voice annoyingly cheerful. "But I'll find out."

"Shut up. If you don't stop annoying me, I'll call Ash and have him come over." Tash knew that Ash still annoyed Jordan, even though the two of them had basically made their peace once Luke and Ash reconciled.

"Call away; he's already coming over with Drew. We all decided to meet here this afternoon." That smug smile on his face was pure Jordan. "They're even bringing Esther. She missed me."

"Someone has to," Tash grumbled, then caught Jordan's eye. "It's good to see you happy and healthy, my friend."

Jordan's smile grew brilliant. "It's good to feel it. If I haven't said it before, thank you for giving me back my life."

"It wasn't—" Tash's protest was cut short by the door opening.

"Hey. Tash. Good to see you." Luke Conover entered the office, a broad smile on his once usually solemn face. Finding love with Jordan was only a portion of the equation for Luke's happiness. Equal time had to be given to the reconciliation with his foster brother, Ash. Gone was the dark withdrawn man Tash had met who lived behind shadowed eyes. In his place was the man Luke was meant to be: calm, able to enjoy life, and above all, magically in love with Jordan, who loved him back so intensely and with such passion, it was an almost visible force between the two of them.

"Luke." Tash stood and hugged the man. They'd worked through their initial mistrust when Tash believed Luke wouldn't stand behind Jordan because of his addiction, and Luke thought Tash was out to break Jordan and him apart. Both of them wanted only what was best for Jordan, and in this case, it was a life with Luke. "Good to have you back. Both of you."

"Paris was amazing but I've been working so hard since I came back it's like I never left the office." Luke sat, stretching his legs out in front of him. "And I'm stoked to see how well this place is doing." He let out a huge yawn.

"Tash met someone and won't tell me who it is." Jordan stood behind Luke and began to knead his shoulders. Tash watched as Luke closed his eyes and groaned, leaning back against Jordan's stomach. "We're going to have to get it out of him."

"Leave the man alone, Prep School."

"Thanks, Luke, especially since there is no one." After glaring at Jordan, who grinned back and mouthed *liar*, Tash checked his watch. "The guy, Randy, who is going to be working with us on the mentoring program, is going to meet me here in about ten minutes, so I'm glad you're both here."

"Remind me of who he is again?" Jordan finished Luke's massage and went to the coffee machine to make himself a cup.

"A teacher friend of Gage's."

"Oh, right." Jordan filled up the carafe and pushed the button. Instantly, the aroma of cinnamon filled the office. "Damn, that smells good."

"He's a little shy around new people, but I brought him to the shelter last night and he and Wanda hit it off."

"Well, that says enough to let me know he's a good fit." Luke's phone buzzed, and he checked the text message. "That was Ash. He, Drew, and Esther are on their way over. They should be here in about ten minutes, so I guess the new guy will have to learn to be a little less shy." He stood and joined Jordan at the coffee machine.

Maybe shy was a little too broad of a term. Tash pondered this thought as he sipped his own coffee. Even though Randy had a rough start in life, an aura of innocence and sweetness surrounded him. His gentleness with people was assuredly what attracted the children to him.

Tash's phone vibrated.

I'm here, but don't see you.

Tash texted back.

I'll come get you.

"Randy's here. I'll go get him and bring him back here to meet you two."

Luke and Jordan were busy looking at something on Jordan's phone and didn't bother to respond. Tash walked out and immediately spotted Randy, standing off to the side. Not meaning to spy, Tash nevertheless stood and observed the man, enjoying the sight of his lean body in faded jeans and a battered leather jacket. The teacher in Randy showed as he concentrated on the young children in the library, a small smile flickering on his lips. He raked his hand through that marvelous head of hair, which Tash remembered smelled like a combination of lemon and honey.

Once again, Tash was reminded how far out of his league this man was, not only in age but also in looks, and vowed that what had happened in his kitchen would never be repeated. Then Randy spotted him and smiled, visible relief spreading across his handsome face, and Tash's body struggled with his good intentions.

Down boy. He gritted his teeth and willed his traitorous cock to remain neutral. There was only one head he needed to be thinking with right now. The sight of all the young children worked immediately, and he smiled and joined Randy in the center of the room.

"Glad you found it." They smiled at one another, hyperaware of what had happened between the two of them the previous night, but Tash knew if he didn't mention it, Randy most likely wouldn't bring it up.

"Yeah, it wasn't hard. This is a great place. I love what you've created here."

"I had nothing to do with it. It was all Jordan and Luke. They got the volunteers from the shelter, as well as local community help. Follow me." They walked together back to the office. "Luke and Jordan got here a little while ago. I told them all about you, and they're looking forward to meeting you."

Randy stopped. "Are you sure you want me? You guys are all so established, and I'm only a new schoolteacher—"

"With a huge heart and the vision we need." He placed his hand on Randy's arm. "Please don't sell yourself short. You have no idea how much we need someone like you to help these kids." Tash held Randy's confused yet hopeful gaze.

After a moment, those green eyes lit up with a

noticeable fire. Tash held his breath, hoping Randy wouldn't once again bolt like a scared deer.

"Okay, yeah. I'm in." He hefted his backpack onto his shoulders. "Thanks for making me see it's not about me but the kids." He bit his lip and moved closer to Tash. "You've been such a great champion for them and this project. I'm honored."

They stood, their breathing the only sound audible in the narrow hallway. The background noise of the Center faded. Randy's face captivated Tash with his bright and hopeful eyes, and his mouth curved in a sweet smile. Those earlier good intentions flew away as he placed his hand on Randy's shoulder and leaned forward. Randy closed his eyes and moved closer.

The door banged open, and they jumped apart.

"Well, what do we have here?" Jordan's amused voice rang loud in the narrow hallway. "Is this the man we're going to be working with?"

If Jordan's grin grew any wider, it would split his face. Tash personally would like to split his lip. "Yes. Dr. Jordan Peterson, this is Randy Gilbert."

Even though Jordan had changed so much from the arrogant person he knew before, Tash hoped he wouldn't be dismissive of Randy because of his youth and casual appearance. Of course, he needn't have worried, as Jordan was interested in only one thing: Tash's sex life.

"Randy, so nice to meet you. Tash has told us some wonderful things about you. I'm looking forward to getting to know you much better." Jordan extended his hand, and Randy shook it after a brief hesitation.

Bastard. "Jordan, cut it out. Let's go inside the office. He can meet Luke before the others come."

Jordan opened the office door, speaking over his shoulder. "Drew and his boyfriend and Drew's grandmother. Don't worry, Randy. After today you're going to inherit a whole new family."

Tash entered the office first. Predictably, Luke was pouring himself another cup of coffee. "Hey, put that coffee down and come meet Randy. That's probably your fifth cup if I know you." He moved aside and let Randy enter the office.

"I need it. Let me finish pouring this first," said Luke as he glanced up. "What—" He dropped the coffeepot, hot liquid spattering everywhere.

"Lucas, are you all right? What's wrong?" Jordan grabbed some paper towels while Luke stood frozen, shaking and white as death.

It took a few moments before Tash noticed that Luke and Randy couldn't take their eyes off each other. Randy stood rooted to the floor, swaying slightly as if he was going to pass out.

"What's going on, you two? You both look like you've seen a ghost."

Jordan slipped his arms around Luke, but the man shook him off. Mumbling, "*No, no, it can't be,*" he strode across the room to stand before Randy and reached out with a violently trembling hand to touch the other man's face. "Brandon? Is that really you?"

Chapter Ten

HE WAS HALLUCINATING. Or drunk. It had to be one of the two because good things like this didn't happen to him twice in a lifetime. Brandon had thought he'd used up his good wishes the night Gabriel found him in the rain. Perhaps he was wrong. But with Luke real and touching him, life was nothing short of a miracle.

"Luke?" His voice shook so badly he could barely get the name out.

"Brandon," Luke cried. "Oh, my God."

Like stone statues, they stood rooted in place, unable to move. Brandon's mind whirled in confusion. How could this be? His throat closed tightly, and his mouth dried so he could barely speak. "Luke." With shaking legs, he sank into the chair Tash pushed behind him, giving Tash a grateful smile. "I don't understand. They said your name is Conover." He looked to Jordan, then back to Luke. "Have you been here all along?"

"Yeah. I changed my name. I wanted a fresh start."

A pained expression crossed Luke's face. "Once you were gone, there wasn't anything holding me there any longer." He closed his eyes for a brief moment. "I came up north, went to school, and found a job I love."

"And then you met me and your life became complete," Jordan joked, but Brandon watched him squeeze Luke's shoulder in a gesture of comfort.

"You'll discover Jordan is nothing if not humble and modest." Luke rolled his eyes, but his smile flashed brightly when he gazed at his lover.

Brandon couldn't ever remember Luke lighthearted and free. Watching him tease Jordan gave Brandon hope that whatever sadness Luke had carried around with him all those years ago had been exorcised from his soul.

"I looked for you once I was able to, but I never found any trace. Now I know why." *So many wasted years.*

Luke's expression turned somber and he pulled over a chair and sat down. "I'm sorry for that. I wanted no reminders of what I'd left behind."

"Oh." Maybe that included Brandon as well. He pressed the heels of his hands against his eyes to ward off any embarrassing tears that might leak through. "I know we live in different worlds now, but I was kind of hoping we'd get a chance to reconnect."

"Brandon," said Luke gently. "Look at me." He hitched his chair closer.

Uncertain as to what Luke would say, Brandon hesitated a moment. Then he heard Tash's voice murmur in his ear, "Don't worry. It'll be okay."

He looked into Luke's eyes, and his misgivings melted away at the fiery protectiveness burning in their depths.

"You're my brother. Not a day has gone by without me thinking about where you were—if you were alive or safe." Luke leaned forward and gripped Brandon's hands. "I'm still in shock trying to wrap my head around this all, but nothing's going to keep us apart ever again."

Over the years, Brandon had learned to live with disappointment; the terrible loss of Ash and Luke had never strayed far from his mind. To know that Luke had missed him as well released a weight from his chest he wasn't aware existed until he heard those words.

"Are you sure?" His gaze traveled between Jordan and Luke. "I don't really fit in—"

"Don't be stupid," said Jordan, brushing aside his protest. "You're family, and family takes care of each other." Jordan wrapped his arms around Luke. "It's what we do."

"I told you so." Tash's whisper, coupled with the comfort of his hand on Brandon's shoulder, steadied the staccato beating of his heart. As a tentative smile curved his lips, voices could be heard in the hallway.

"Oh shit. I forgot they were coming." A giant smile lit up Luke's face.

"What's going on? Who's coming?" Brandon didn't think he could take any more shocks.

Before anyone had a chance to answer, there was a

knock on the door, and Jordan called out, "Come on in."

Tash took his hand in a tight grip as Brandon rose from his chair and recognized Dr. Drew Klein from that first night he went to the Clinic—the night that started his life in a new direction. A step behind him was an elderly lady, who held the arm of a tall, dark-haired man. His head bent low as he whispered something in her ear that had her laughing.

The smile froze on Brandon's lips as he stood frozen in shock. No, no, this couldn't be happening. And for the second time in the span of minutes, Brandon couldn't breathe. It wasn't possible, was it?

"It's going to be fine," Tash whispered in his ear.

This time he wasn't so sure, as his heart pounded like a jackhammer.

Drew waved. "Jordy, hey. You look like you're feeling better. And Luke." He cocked his head. "You're all hopped up; how much coffee did you have?"

"None."

Drew smiled at Brandon. "Randy, I'm glad to see you again and even happier to hear you reconsidered working on the project."

Unable to answer, Brandon's attention remained fixated on the two other people who'd walked in with Drew. Finally, the dark-haired man straightened up and looked his way. And when their eyes met, Brandon knew their broken circle had been repaired. It might only have been fifteen minutes rather than the fifteen years since they'd been together. He'd recognize those clear, silvery eyes anywhere.

Ash. It was Ash. Both of his brothers, here with him at last. It was almost too much to comprehend. He took a step toward the door, then stopped, once again weighed down by uncertainty and a bit of fear.

No longer a scrawny, scared kid, Ash had grown into an intense, dark man. Intimidating was a good word to best describe him, although the gentle way he held the elderly lady's arm belied his looks.

Ash's laughter drained away, replaced by what Brandon knew his own face mirrored—shock, unbearable joy, and a touch of fear. And also like Brandon, Ash remained rooted to the floor—frozen, white, and shaking.

"Asher, darling, whatever is the matter?" The elderly lady spoke, concern edging her slightly accented voice. "You look like you've seen a ghost."

Luke approached her. "Esther, it's wonderful to see you. You're about to witness one of those miracles you always mentioned yet I refused to believe, at least until now."

"Jordan, do you have any idea what your young man is talking about?" She continued to hover next to Ash, whose gaze remained fixed on Brandon, yet he couldn't seem to move or speak.

"Drew, Esther." Luke's voice cracked as the tears threatened. "Randy, this young man here, is really Brandon." Brandon watched the woman's face transform itself with joy as she placed a hand to her chest and clutched Ash's arm tight.

"Oh, my darling Asher."

Drew immediately went to Ash and took his other hand.

In the depths of Ash's glittering eyes, Brandon witnessed the devastating anguish that lived within his brother's heart. Had none of them escaped unscathed?

"Ash? You, here? How is all of this possible?" Everything seemed to have worked out so perfectly for them. They had loving families and high-paying jobs, while he'd lived on the streets and had to fight for every scrap.

"Brandon, my God, it is you." Ash blinked and swallowed heavily. He let go of Drew and Esther's hands and advanced toward Brandon. Ash had been so much older and bigger than Brandon when he left, now Brandon was shocked to see they were almost the same height.

"Surprise." Brandon attempted a weak laugh.

"Where have you been all this time?" Ash's hands flexed, and it seemed as if he wanted to touch Brandon but was afraid.

And Brandon, who'd longed for this moment for years, didn't know how to react now that it was here. They all seemed like players in a game, circling one another, afraid to get too close or touch for fear they'd disappear.

Tash, however, had put his coat on. "I'm going to leave you all to your reunion. I think it's wonderful you've found each other and can be a true family again." Without waiting for a response, he walked out of the room, shutting the door behind him.

Brandon wanted to run after Tash and drag him back. Why would Tash leave him alone in a roomful of strangers? Even though this was the moment he'd waited years for, it seemed wrong now without Tash beside him to share it. Sadly, he was closer to Tash after only spending the past few weeks together than the two men who were his brothers.

"Go on, sweetheart." Drew's grandmother urged Brandon as she sat down on a chair Ash pulled over for her. "Tell your brothers everything."

Drew's face shone with happiness. "I can't tell you how long we've waited for this moment. Ash has had an investigator looking for you for several years now."

Tell them everything? Never. Alarm cramped Brandon's stomach then died. If Luke or Ash had heard anything, they wouldn't have been so welcoming. So his secret was still safe. "An investigator?" Careful not to sound too nervous and suspicious, he schooled his face to remain pleasantly curious.

After numerous attempts to clear his throat, Ash could finally speak. "Yes. It was how I found Luke. Even though he changed his name, I tracked him down."

"Ash can be a bulldog. I refused to speak to him for months. We had a world of misunderstandings to make up for, and it wasn't easy, but we're in a good place now. Too much hurt and pride made me stubborn and miserable."

"I can attest to that." Jordan smirked. "Lucas was a

miserable person, but I turned him around and made him the charming person he is today."

"Whatever you say, Prep School."

Ash, Brandon sensed, was a different story. Demons still lingered, locked up tight inside his older brother. The eyes told the story of what resided within.

"I always imagined this day," Brandon began in a halting voice; the room grew silent as he spoke. "For years, I lived with the hope that somehow one of you would find me, even though I knew it was impossible. So when that didn't happen, I left on my own when I was seventeen and lived on the streets."

Ash shuddered, and Drew went to sit next to him, taking Ash's hand in his, lacing their fingers together. At Drew's touch, Ash visibly relaxed and threw his lover a grateful smile.

"We're listening. Go on."

The kind face of Drew's grandmother made it easier for Brandon to speak. "I'm sure you've all heard our foster father was a difficult man to live with. He was a drunk and beat our mother and occasionally me." There was no need to get graphic with the elderly woman listening.

Ash met his eyes. "Did he ever touch you? Inappropriately, I mean?" The words came out as a whisper, forced as if it was too difficult for him to say out loud. Obviously, though, everyone in the room knew what Ash was talking about. No one looked shocked or uncomfortable with Ash's question.

"No. He liked taking a belt to my naked butt, but I

think that was more for the pleasure he got beating up someone weaker than himself." A dawning horror raced through him at Ash's grim, unblinking stare. The implications of Brandon's thoughts were too horrifying to say out loud, yet he needed to know. "Did he…? Is that why…?" Unable to put together a coherent sentence, he looked back and forth between Luke and Ash.

Ash's brief, curt nod chilled Brandon's blood. "It was so he wouldn't touch you and Luke, but it became too much for me. I couldn't take it anymore, so I ran." Ash let go of Drew's hand and clenched his own into fists. "I shouldn't have run; I should've stayed and protected you both. I'll never forgive myself for that."

The horror of what Ash had silently endured over those years broke Brandon's heart. "He didn't touch me; I promise. It was never like that. When I was taking courses in child psychology in college, I read up on sexual abusers. I thought it would be good preparation for teaching and what to look for in case one of my students showed up at school with signs of abuse. I learned that sometimes the abuser focuses only on one child and leaves the others alone. Maybe he couldn't touch me because I was so young when I came to live with you all. I guess we'll never know."

Luke let out a shuddering breath. "Maybe he thought he really killed me that night, and he got scared they'd find him and put him jail. I'd kill him myself if I ever saw him again."

Brandon swallowed hard and faced Ash. "You don't

need my forgiveness, Ash. You were too young to have all that responsibility, and with what that man did to you, I'm in awe you stayed as long as you did." The abuse Ash had suffered protecting him and Luke might have killed a lesser man. "You're stronger than I ever imagined."

"Where is he now, still in Pennsylvania?" Luke didn't need to say the name. They all knew whom Luke meant. Brandon couldn't tell them, so he remained ambiguous.

"I-I don't know."

Luke squeezed his hand. "You're safe now. I promise with everything I have, you'll never have to worry about him or anything again." He glanced up at Jordan and smiled. "You've already met Jordan. He and I live together."

Brandon gave a weak smile. "Hi again."

Jordan chuckled. "I know this is overwhelming for you. You don't have to figure out everything now."

Brandon remembered those similar words from Gabriel all those years ago when he sat huddled in a doorway, homeless and alone. "I know. It's only…" He shook his head in disbelief. "How can it be that your entire world can change in a minute? If I hadn't met Gage and he didn't introduce me to Tash, none of this would ever have happened."

The smiles on everyone's faces dimmed at his words.

"Did I say something wrong?"

Jordan's eyes glittered brightly as he answered.

"Not at all. And it's the most wonderful thing that could have happened for Lucas and Ash. We were remembering my fiancé, Keith, who was killed and in whose memory this Center was created." He leaned over and kissed Luke. "The mysteries of the world are best left alone sometimes."

Sometimes dreams did come true. Like a phoenix from the ashes, the wreckage of their family had been pieced together to rise back strong to take its place among the living. Damaged somewhat, and a bit worse for wear, but never broken or destroyed.

From loneliness to abundance, fear to elation, Brandon knew he'd never forget this day or this tiny room. Life with all its untapped promises had seemed impossible at one point in Brandon's life. Now it unfurled like a shining path, stretching endlessly in front of him.

But a certain hollowness lingered with Tash's disappearance. Why would he leave when Brandon needed him most of all? Tash was his support, his steadiness in this flux of emotional chaos that was his life at the moment.

"You see, Asher, darling. It's time you let go of your pain. You have your family, all of us now together." The quiet voice of Esther, Drew's grandmother shook with emotion. She fixed her gaze upon Brandon. "My dear young man, the joy you've brought to us today is hard to put into words. Knowing how Asher has suffered and Lucas as well, I'm so thankful to still be around to see you all reunited." She wiped her tears with a handkerchief. "This day will be a new beginning in all your lives, I'm certain." Her eyes twinkled, and Brandon couldn't help but smile back at her. "And I must be the luckiest woman in New York City to have all these handsome young men around me."

"Nana, you're incorrigible." Drew shook his head as they all laughed.

"Why? I simply speak the truth." Her eyes narrowed. "Brandon, you said you lived on the streets. Where do you live now?"

"That was years ago. I live in a studio in East Flatbush now."

"Don't be ridiculous." Luke looked to Jordan, who nodded. "You'll come live with us. We have a gigantic town house; there's plenty of space."

"We have an extra bedroom in the apartment." Ash's expression was hopefully expectant. "It's all yours."

Destitution to richness. Brandon put up his hands. "Whoa, you guys. Hold on. I don't need to move. I'm fine." The four flights and dingy walls didn't bother him as much as the suffocating loneliness of the nights. Although it was so much more than he'd ever expected, Brandon couldn't help but wish for the home and family his brothers had achieved. Again his thoughts turned to Tash, and shockingly he knew that as amazing as this day had been, he wished he had someone of his own to share his newfound happiness with.

The disappointment over Tash's disappearance

crushed him. Brandon wanted him there as a friend and ally. "I should go." He stood but realized, somewhat disconcertingly, he had nowhere to be; he was supposed to be here with Tash at the Center, helping. But Tash had left him, and his brothers had lovers and lives of their own.

"The reason I asked," Esther continued as if Brandon hadn't said a word "is that Mrs. Delany has been asked by her children to come spend the winter months in Florida. And though she says no, I am sure she wants to go." She fixed Drew with a piercing stare. "*She* has baby grandchildren."

Drew rolled his eyes while Ash hid a smile. "Nana, I've already told you to go bug Rachel and Mike for some great-grandchildren."

Ignoring that remark, she spoke directly to Brandon. "These people have determined I shouldn't live on my own any longer, even if I'm perfectly capable of taking care of myself. Don't you think that's silly?"

"Come now, Esther. You aren't getting into that again, are you? You know what the doctor said." Ash gently scolded her, but Brandon noticed the love in his eyes. The lady was obviously a special person to them all.

"Oh, what do they know?" Esther patted the seat next to her, appealing to Brandon. "Come sit next to me. I have a proposition for you."

Brandon glanced first at Luke, who grinned back at him, then at Ash, who gave him a wink.

"Go on, little brother. One thing you'll learn is it's

useless to say no to Esther."

Bemused, Brandon sat in the chair next to the elderly lady. "You have a proposition? For me?" He couldn't imagine what she wanted.

"Yes. Now since my companion wishes to go to Florida, and I wouldn't dream of keeping her from her family, I propose you come live with me."

He opened his mouth to protest, but she swiftly and neatly cut him off. "Yes, yes, I know, you have your own life and don't want to have to answer to me, but you'd be doing me the favor. I'd never stick my nose into your private affairs."

She stopped to glare at the others in the room, but no one said a word, although Jordan's face was alive with suppressed laughter. "But think of it this way." Here she put her small hand on his arm and fastened her bright blue eyes on his face. "You only just found your brothers. This way you could see them so much more often. They come every Sunday for dinner. Wouldn't it be wonderful to begin to share your lives again?"

Before he could answer, Luke chimed in. "I think it's a great idea. Esther's house is big enough for the both of you, and she's right. It's a chance for us to reconnect and get to know one another again." His voice dropped. "Ash and I never stopped thinking about you, wondering if you were safe or even alive."

Jordan rubbed Luke's back and leaned against him, Brandon surmised, giving support and love. In all their years together before they were torn apart, Brandon hadn't ever remembered Luke's eyes so bright with happiness.

"I thought about you too, hoping you were still alive." Brandon's voice stuck in his throat. "I thought, maybe…" Tears threatened for a moment, then receded. "I'd given up on ever finding either of you. Now to have you both here?" Everything that had happened this afternoon hit him at that moment. "I'm overwhelmed."

At both Ash and Luke's nods, he made his decision. His lease was month to month, so it wouldn't be any trouble leaving. "I'd love to come live with you, Esther, but I intend to pay my way. And I can cook too."

The tension broke in the room, and they all laughed. Esther looked at him, then over to Ash, then Luke.

"Well?" She folded her arms.

"Well, what, Esther?" Ash cocked his head. "What's the matter?"

"As long as I live and as old as I am, I will never understand men." She shook her head and took Ash and Luke by the hand, leading them over to Brandon. "Give each other a hug. After all you've gone through to get to this point, you need to do it to make this day perfect."

They stood for a moment, looking at one another, then grabbed each other tight, holding on, rocking back and forth. The feel of his brothers' arms around him and the warmth of their bodies wasn't a dream any longer. It was real; it was forever. They were home at last. After another moment or two, they broke apart, with Ash returning to Drew's side and Luke to Jordan's. Each of his brothers had found his happiness, and for that Brandon was grateful, knowing now how both had suffered.

The noise level rose around him as Esther planned a big Sunday dinner for them next day, and Jordan argued with Drew about whether the Yankees would ever make the World Series again.

It all was so homey and perfect. And so wrong without Tash there.

Chapter Eleven

TWO IDENTICAL TURQUOISE gazes tracked Tash's movements. Once he opened the refrigerator, the cats hopped off the sofa and padded into the kitchen, winding themselves in between his legs.

"I know you're here, guys." He bent down to pat them, then, with a sigh, closed the refrigerator door. He had no appetite, but that didn't mean his pets had to suffer. After giving them some treats, he sat at the gleaming butcher-block table and stared off into nothingness.

That about summed up his life. Nothingness. While he had a full complement of patients and projects to keep busy professionally, it was the downtime, the absolute solitude of his life sometimes that hit him like a slap in his face. Friends could only offer so much comfort. And even though he'd chosen it, having witnessed Brandon's miraculous reunion with his brothers and seeing how they enveloped him so naturally back into the fold of their family brought his own lonely life into razor-sharp focus.

Five years was a long time to mourn and have regrets. Danny's behavior, his lies, disappearance, and subsequent death had taken so much out of Tash; he'd given up thinking his heart could ever regenerate and heal. He'd forgone finding love and someone who could share his life. Drained and betrayed, he'd chosen to go through the motions of life, since the reality of it was too painful.

Until Brandon showed up and sent him into a tailspin with his giving nature and purity of heart, breaking through Tash's wall of loneliness. Desire, long neglected, had rushed through his bloodstream when they'd kissed the other day. And, this afternoon, if Jordan hadn't interrupted them, he'd have kissed the man again.

Whatever it was that pulled him toward Brandon, it was an invisible force he was fighting against like a riptide in the ocean. He vowed not to get pulled under but to do what was recommended, swim with the tide until the waters cleared. Maybe Brandon had a bit of a crush, and God knew he himself was lonely. Tash refused to listen to his heart and his head, which were speaking to him in concert, telling him Brandon was different, that he could be a man worth getting to know and possibly love.

A loud meow rent the silence, and before he knew it, Cleo jumped into his lap. As he stroked her, he thought about the miraculous events of the day.

Now that Brandon had found his brothers, his life would take a different turn. They'd be able to introduce him to the life he should've had. What Tash still didn't completely understand was why Brandon had run away, lived under an assumed name, and never tried to contact anyone. Although Luke had changed his name, Ash hadn't. Surely Brandon would've looked for his older brother at some point.

The doorbell rang. Caesar stalked off into the depths of the house, and Cleo followed him, jumping off Tash's lap to race behind her brother. He wasn't expecting anyone but figured Valerie was the most likely person. After all, who else would come see him but his sister?

It was a bit of a shock, therefore, when he opened the door and found Brandon on his doorstep. In a calmer state than he had been earlier, Tash hesitated, then leaned his shoulder on the door frame, not offering Brandon entrance into the house. Tash could see Brandon noticed his actions as he'd already taken a step up as if to walk inside, then stopped, an uncertain expression on his face.

"Um, hi?" Confusion reigned in Brandon's eyes.

Tash's stomach tightened with unaccustomed nerves. "Hi. What are you doing here?" Why was Brandon not with his brothers and their family?

"What's wrong? Are you mad at me or something?" Brandon wrapped his arms around his waist as a chill wind blew in from the river. It smelled like autumn: the dampness of the air mixed with the smell of fallen, decayed leaves and the smokiness of people's fireplaces. Tash had yet to light his; it was one of the things he loved about the season.

He knew he'd sounded angry—harsh and more blunt than necessary—but maybe that would keep Brandon at a distance.

You'll thank me for this. I'm doing what's best for the both of us.

"No. I'm surprised to see you is all." The chill was becoming too much for him in his thin clothing and bare feet. With a resigned sigh, he moved away from the entrance and opened the door wider. "Come on in."

Now it was Brandon who hesitated. "Are you sure?"

No. Because if I let you in, I'm going to want to kiss you again, and I know I shouldn't.

"Yeah, come on. I can't let the cats see the door open."

Brandon stepped inside yet made no movement to enter the house, remaining by the front hall. Tash raised a brow.

"Let's go in the kitchen. I was about to make something for dinner."

Without waiting for an answer, he turned and walked away but heard the tread of Brandon's footsteps behind him. The kitchen was safer than the living room, with its wide and comfortable sofa. Nothing sexual would be happening against the cabinets or hard countertops.

"Can I help?" The hesitancy in Brandon's voice saddened Tash.

Help me understand why I can't stop thinking about

you.

"Uh, sure." He indicated the big pot on the stove. "Can you fill it with water?"

"Sure." Brandon hefted the pot and brought it to the sink. "What were you going to make?"

"Just some pasta and sauce." Tash shrugged. "You know I don't really cook, even though I buy all this delicious-looking stuff from the supermarket, intending to try. At the end of the week, I usually have to throw it away. There's still all the things you bought from the supermarket in the refrigerator."

"Would you let me make you something?" Brandon stayed on the far side of the kitchen.

Before he could stop himself, Tash said, "Sure. Knock yourself out."

The smile that broke across Brandon's face would've brought Tash great pleasure if he hadn't already decided to keep away from the man. Still, he warmed to the sight of Brandon busying himself, chopping mushrooms and zucchini and frying them in a pan, then adding a can of crushed tomatoes. Soon the delicious aroma of garlic and onions cooking permeated the air. The comforting sound of the sauce bubbling in the pot mellowed Tash, and he relaxed his guard.

"That smells fantastic." Tash's stomach grumbled, and he laughed. "I don't think I've eaten since breakfast."

"You're still recovering from being so sick; you need to take better care of yourself." Brandon stirred the sauce and tasted it. "Mmm, that's tasting pretty good already." He dipped another spoon into the pot and brought it over to Tash. "Here, try it and tell me if you like it." He held out the spoon.

Tash obediently opened his mouth, and Brandon slid the spoon inside. Flavor exploded inside his mouth, and he moaned around the spoon. "Oh, that's amazing." He licked his lips. "Where in God's name did you learn to cook like this?"

When Brandon failed to answer, Tash glanced up, only to wince at the expression of longing residing in Brandon's eyes. Instead of asking him again, Tash walked to the opposite side of the kitchen, hoping that a little distance between them would cool down the flame of attraction that had been building between them all day.

"Why don't I open a bottle of wine?"

Brandon blinked. "Uh, yeah, sure." He returned to the stove.

Tash picked a bottle of red from the wine rack and opened it, pouring himself a small glass first and drinking it down quickly. He then poured two glasses and brought Brandon's over to him.

"Here you go." Their hands touched briefly, but Brandon merely nodded and placed the glass on the counter. He poured the ziti into the salted, boiling water.

"I'd like the sauce to cook a little longer, but I'll cook the pasta anyway."

"Why are you here?" Even though it may have been abrupt and rude, for the life of him, Tash couldn't understand what a good-looking young man like Brandon was doing spending his Saturday night with him.

"Why did you leave today?" Brandon countered, then took a hasty gulp of wine and wiped his mouth with his hand. "As amazing as finding Luke and Ash was, it kind of dimmed the celebration without you there to share it with me."

"I didn't belong there. I barely know you." Tash returned to the table to sit. He stared into the crimson depths of his wineglass. "It was a time for family. I'm surprised you're not with them all now."

"Luke and Jordan wanted me to come back home with them," admitted Brandon. He joined Tash at the table, and the two sat, sipping their wine until their glasses were empty. Tash poured them each another glass.

"Of course they did. I'm sure Ash and Drew want you with them as well." He sipped the wine, his fingers tightening around the stem. "That's why I don't understand why you're here. With me."

Several moments passed before Brandon answered. "You know, all my life I only wanted to belong, to have people who loved and cared about me. Everyone wants that. I had Ash and Luke, of course, and I was luckier than most in the system." He traced the bottom of his wineglass with his finger. "We were different, 'cause we never knew our parents, and our foster home was less than perfect."

"To say the least," said Tash grimly.

"Finding Luke and Ash today was the culmination of everything I'd hoped for—all the years I spent on the street and at the shelter, it's the only dream I had. All of us together, safe, and happy? I never thought that would happen. But you know what?"

Tash finished his second glass of wine. The warm glow of the kitchen light played off the golden highlights in Brandon's hair. The wine had relaxed Tash to a comfortable mellowness.

"What?" He smiled at Brandon.

"In the back of my mind, it wasn't enough. Something was missing."

"Missing? What could possibly be missing?" Tash couldn't imagine what Brandon meant. He knew how ecstatic Luke and Ash were to finally have their family reunited.

"Not what, who." Brandon grasped Tash by the hand. "I missed you. You shouldn't have left with that lame excuse about intruding on family. In some ways, I know you better than I know them."

"Don't be silly." Tash knew his protest sounded weak, but what could he say when his heart was pounding in his ears and hazy need coursed warm and thick through his body? Even as he struggled against it, a pleasurable ache rolled through him. This couldn't happen; he had to stop it right now.

But Brandon persisted, refusing to back down. "I'm not. You keep fighting this attraction between us, and I don't understand why. That nonsense about our difference in age doesn't cut it with me." Still holding his hand, Brandon stood, pulling Tash up flush against his chest. "I've never felt this way about anyone before. Ever since I met you, I haven't been able to think of anyone else." His breath blew hot against Tash's cheek, smelling sweetly of the tomatoes and wine. Tash's head spun.

"It's so quick, and you could do so much better than me." But even as he spoke, his lips found Brandon's in a scorching kiss. They clung to each other, hungry and desperate, tongues tangling as their mouths slanted across each other, deepening their kisses.

"I don't want anyone else." Brandon gasped, then moaned as he flexed his hips against Tash's, their erections pressing against each other through their pants. "I want you. Please, I really need you tonight. So much about today has been unreal, but not you. You're the only real thing I feel like I have to hold on to right now."

How could he say no to that? Staring into the uncertainty of Brandon's eyes, the years fell away and hope flooded through him, along with a need to hold Brandon in his arms.

"I want you too," admitted Tash, "but—"

"No more buts. I may be confused about my life right now, but the one sure thing in it is you. The way you make me feel and why. You're caring." Here Brandon stopped and kissed Tash on the lips. "Concerned." Another kiss. "And so incredibly handsome."

The kissing didn't stop for a long time then. When

it did, Brandon touched Tash's cheek, his eyes soft with need. "One thing I've learned is that nothing in life is ever certain. When I was little, I thought my brothers and I would always be together. That didn't happen, but I'm all right. Now that I've found them, I don't want them to think they have to be responsible for me."

"You're incredibly mature for your age."

"I'm twenty-five, not ten," Brandon snapped, raking his hand through his hair. "You need to stop focusing so much on our ages. I told you once before I'm not your average twenty-five-year-old."

"I don't think there's anything average about you at all." Tash slipped his hand to grasp Brandon around the nape of the neck. He pulled Brandon close and rested his lips against the soft, warm skin of Brandon's temple. "In fact, what I know is that you're amazing." The atmosphere had changed from casual to intense, heavy with the promise of passion. Tash brushed Brandon's lips with his, then, swept away by the man's immediate response, pressed his lips to Brandon's. Tash leisurely explored Brandon's hot mouth with his tongue, deepening their kiss. The fierce desire he'd suppressed all day rose within Tash; nothing could have stopped him at that moment.

Was there anything better than kissing someone you wanted so badly your body actually hurt from the suppressed tension? It had been so long, too long without the touch of another man. Tash could sense the impending orgasm in his body as a tingling rush seared through his veins. With regret, he pulled away from Brandon's lips and stood stock-still with his eyes squeezed shut, willing his body to cool down.

"If you're going to tell me to stop and leave—"

"No." Tash reached over to brush a hank of that glorious hair off Brandon's forehead. "I need a moment, however. If we keep going, this might be over before it begins."

Sharing a grin, Brandon reached out and traced Tash's jaw with the tips of his fingers. The touch, though tentative, was one Tash longed to sink into.

"Okay. I'd better turn off the pasta water anyway. We don't need to burn the house down."

Tash concentrated on the long lines of Brandon's back, watching the flex of muscles play through his thin Henley shirt as he brought the pot to the sink and drained out the water and wondered if Brandon, young, virile, and obviously experienced, would find him lacking. After Danny died, he'd spent a year mourning what might have been and the life he'd lost. There'd been no need for sex or even friendships with other men. Darkness, solitude, and guilt followed him, making him invisible to the world. After coming out of his self-imposed exile, only because Valerie threatened to call their mother, he decided to rejoin the living. Innumerable nights were spent aching to be touched, to rid himself of the sheer loneliness that clung to him with a talon-like grip.

Well-meaning Valerie had set him up on dates, even forced him into a singles club. He'd had no fight left in him and went simply to keep her happy and off his back. Inevitably he met men and even had a few short-lived flings, but nothing that left any mark on his life. He'd be hard-pressed to remember their names or faces now.

As Brandon walked toward him, an uncertain smile appearing, then disappearing as quickly as it came, Tash knew with certainty he could never forget this man, and though his heart hurt because he knew Brandon's youth would eventually separate them, the promise he'd made earlier to stay away disappeared like late spring snow on the city streets.

Tash was a veteran of the war of love and heart-break. He'd been a prisoner but never yet a victor, and though there wasn't a doubt in his mind he would lose yet again, he kicked the doubting devil off his shoulder. Tash held out his hand to Brandon.

"Come with me."

Chapter Twelve

THERE WAS NOTHING to be nervous about, Brandon decided as he held tight to Tash's hand. From the start, there'd been a connection between the two of them he couldn't explain. He'd read about people who saw one another and instantaneously fell in love and laughed at it, but now he wasn't so sure how funny it was. Tash's hand in his was as real as it could get.

On silent feet, he followed Tash up the staircase to the second floor of the house. There were only three rooms upstairs, but the hallway was wide and gave the appearance of spaciousness. They halted outside of a closed door.

Tash smoothed his hand across Brandon's jaw and drew him in for another toe-curling kiss. He melted against Tash, heart rate kicking up to an almost painful beat as their lips met. He opened his mouth, and Tash's smooth tongue slipped inside to twine with his. A sound echoed in the air, and Brandon recognized that desperate, needy moan had come from him.

Brandon slid his hand up the defined muscles of Tash's chest, the pounding of Tash's heart strong and vibrant beneath his fingers. Their kiss deepened, and he wondered if Tash was as nervous as he was, then forgot about everything else when Tash's arms came around him and cupped his ass.

Brandon's body electrified; if he were a Christmas tree, he would've lit up. He rocked his pelvis into Tash's, needing that hard contact, wanting Tash to keep touching him forever. When Tash pulled him closer and popped the button of his jeans, Brandon moaned with delight.

"I think we can get rid of these; what do you say?" Brandon still had enough of his senses left to hear Tash whisper into his ear. Unable to form a coherent sentence, he simply nodded, allowing Tash to pull down his jeans and boxers. He stepped out of them, slightly embarrassed to be almost naked while Tash remained fully dressed.

A brief smile flickered over Tash's face as he released the string to his own sweats, letting them fall at his feet. After stepping out of them he removed his T-shirt and let it drop to the floor, then he reached over and pulled Brandon's Henley over his head, tossing it to the side, never once taking his eyes off Brandon.

"This is how I've wanted to see you, almost from the moment I met you." Tash massaged Brandon's shoulders; his warm hands were wonderfully strong, and Brandon couldn't help but arch into his touch. "But I never dreamed of it happening."

Before today, Brandon had given up on dreams. Too many years and regrets had passed. "Things change." Brandon gasped at the feel of Tash's hand grasping his cock, which had swelled to almost painful fullness. "Dreams can change."

Their lips met again, and this time it was a harsher, more demanding Tash. Brandon, determined not to disappoint Tash with his obvious inexperience, pulled the man hard up against him and plunged his tongue into Tash's mouth while his hands roamed over the hard planes of Tash's body.

When he and Charlie had been lovers, Brandon had been too scared and not invested enough in the relationship to consider the intimacy of anal sex. But now, with Tash's mouth hot against his neck and his hand wrapped around Brandon's cock, he ached for it. Brandon's body clenched tight, and his insides quivered at the thought, not with fear but rather, with suppressed desire.

"I want you so badly," Brandon whispered against Tash's cheek. "I've never wanted anything as much as I want you."

Tash pulled back, his gaze burning with heat and hunger. "I don't understand why I'm so lucky, but God help me, I want you too. So much so I can't think straight." He cupped Brandon's jaw, a grave expression on his handsome face.

His heart pounding, Brandon waited, holding his breath, wondering if Tash would change his mind. To Brandon's utter relief, the uninhibited smile transformed Tash's somber face, then he opened his bedroom door. "Come."

Exultation spread through Brandon, and he entered the room almost giddy with a combination of happiness and need. With a swiftness Brandon hardly expected, Tash straddled him on the bed, his knees pressing on either side of Brandon's hips.

"Hi." Tash's white teeth gleamed in the dim light of the bedroom. He bent down and gave Brandon a sweet, soft kiss.

"Hi." The air around them fairly sizzled with sex. This was what he'd missed, what he'd waited to feel with a lover. A connection that went deeper than merely the physical. Their gazes locked, and Brandon swore Tash could see down deep into his soul.

Tash began a lazy exploration of Brandon's body with his tongue, beginning with the pulse jumping madly in his neck, that soon had Brandon writhing on the bed for release. He'd read in books where men said their balls ached for their lover and had rolled his eyes in disbelief. Now he understood.

"God, that feels so good." He trembled, the sensations rippling through his body in waves. Tash was being so incredibly loving and tender. Any moment now Brandon might fall apart, and he didn't want that.

He wanted this to last forever. Now he had to make Tash want that too.

The tip of Tash's tongue circled Brandon's belly button, then snaked down to lick the slant of his hip bone, ignoring Brandon's heavy erection. Every whispering touch, each caress, drew Brandon further and further into a deepening haze of pleasure he had no control over, so that without even thinking he spread his legs and opened himself up to Tash.

"Please," he begged, unable to control the emotion he heard in his voice. "Make love to me. Now. Please, Tash. I want you."

An answering smile spread across Tash's handsome face. He removed his glasses and placed them on the nightstand, returning with a few items he'd taken from the drawer. Brandon's quick glance confirmed condoms and a small bottle of lubricant. Instead of fear, hunger spiraled through Brandon, knowing that the man he'd wanted so much it hurt, wanted him as well.

"How long has it been? Do I need to go slow?" Tash braced his arms on either side of Brandon's head and gazed down at him with soft, dark eyes. "I want to make it good for you."

"Uh, it's been a while," said Brandon, keeping his voice steady yet with a note of caution. "So maybe a little slow?" The last thing he wanted was for Tash to know he'd never been with a man.

"That's good because I want to go slow with you." Tash bent over and kissed him till Brandon's head whirled. When they broke apart, Tash murmured in his ear, "I want to taste every part of you, make you beg to come. You deserve perfection."

Brandon found himself unable to answer as Tash began touching him with his mouth and tongue.

Erogenous zones he wasn't aware existed on his body awakened, or perhaps it was the mere touch of Tash's hot, wet mouth sucking his nipples, nuzzling his neck, and finally, thank God, licking the head of his hard cock.

"You taste amazing. Even your cock is beautiful."

When Tash engulfed the head in his mouth, Brandon moaned loud and long, the sound echoing off the bedroom walls. Brandon could feel Tash's lips curve in a smile around his erection, but that didn't stop Tash from continuing the marvelous sucking sensation. God, Brandon didn't ever want him to stop.

A slick, cool finger touched his hole and then entered him. Startled for a moment, Brandon caught his breath and then relaxed, allowing Tash to slide his finger fully inside.

"Damn, you're tighter than I'd imagined," whispered Tash. "You feel amazing. I want your tight ass around my cock." All coherent thought fled Brandon's mind as Tash pushed another finger inside his hole, stretching him, preparing him. The two fingers worked themselves in and out, fluttering and twisting until they touched something deep inside him. Stars exploded behind Brandon's eyes, and he cried out.

"Holy shit." Brandon heaved himself up, almost dislodging them both off the bed. "What the hell?" But he pushed hard against Tash's fingers, needing something, anything to calm this flame of desire.

Tash didn't stop but rather continued to stroke inside him, rendering Brandon writhing and babbling, practically incoherent with need.

"Please, now, now, Tash, I need—I want—oh God!" Brandon wailed as he came, shooting white streams across his stomach, reaching up to his chest.

He should feel embarrassed at the animalistic noises, the begging and pleading sounds emanating from him, but his scrambled brain couldn't come up with a coherent thought. Brandon's hands scrabbled uselessly along the mattress as the tremors rocketed through him. His head thrashed back and forth. "Oh God, Tash," he gasped.

Brandon shuddered, then flattened down against the mattress, his breath coming in quick gasps. It took several minutes before he had the capability to open his eyes. When he did so, Tash sat on his knees between Brandon's legs, a sweet smile resting on his face. He brushed his hand across Brandon's thigh.

"How do you feel, sweetheart?"

Brandon's eyes widened as Tash spoke. He didn't know people talked to one another when they had sex. With Charlie, they'd merely grunted and mumbled about coming as they humped against one another, but that was it. Brandon discovered he liked the sweet talk; it made him feel wanted and special. Something he'd never been with anyone before.

"I feel amazing. How could I not?" He stretched, his body loose yet still humming with desire. "But I still want you." Brandon swallowed against his nerves as he watched the need flare in Tash's eyes. "Inside me."

"Are you sure you don't want to rest for a while?

We have all night," said Tash even as he slid his hands up Brandon's chest so their faces were inches apart. Tash's cock rested on Brandon's stomach, the heat and strength of it sending an ache through Brandon's body. He imagined it inside of him, pushing into him.

Brandon looped his arm around Tash's neck. "I'm planning on a long night, but I want you inside me now."

That need he'd seen in Tash's eyes ignited to a full-fledged firestorm. Tash captured his mouth, and they kissed for several minutes until Brandon once more was vibrating with need.

"Fuck me now."

"Hold on," said Tash. Brandon could hear the rip of a condom package and then the *snap* of the bottle top from the lubricant. "You should be nice and relaxed now."

This was it. He was finally going to have sex and with the man he loved.

His heart lurched as his mouth went dry. *Loved?* He didn't love Tash. He wanted him desperately with every cell of his body, but love? He wouldn't know it if he fell over it.

Tash pushed the head of his cock inside Brandon. The immediate pain shocked him, and without meaning to, Brandon whimpered and tightened up.

Tash stopped, and Brandon, realizing the mistake he'd made, bit down on his cheek and gave a weak smile.

"Go on, don't stop. Like I said, it's been a long

time." Never qualified as a long time in Brandon's mind, so technically he wasn't lying.

Tash shot him an unreadable look but continued, pushing inside him at a slow yet steady slide. The intensity of the pain heightened; Brandon could have cried out from it, but by sheer force of will he made himself relax. The incredible fullness so powerful and intimate Brandon knew he'd been altered forever. He was at his most vulnerable, yet the thought that he could give Tash pleasure made him strong. Accepting a person inside your body had to be one of the most life-changing experiences ever.

He couldn't imagine it with anyone other than Tash.

"How do you feel?" Tash was halfway inside him, and Brandon wanted more. He wanted the whole of Tash, every piece of him he was willing to give.

"Wonderful," he answered honestly. "Don't stop." There was an inevitability about all of this: the man in his arms, the beat of his blood within his veins, and the perfection of their bodies as they meshed together.

Tash resumed his steady thrusts, and Brandon lifted his legs and gripped Tash's biceps, digging his fingers into the muscles of Tash's arms and rocking into Tash's pelvis. This settled Tash deeper inside of him, sparking a wildly passionate response from his taciturn lover.

"Brandon, God." Tash began to stroke inside him, licks of fire heating Brandon's blood. He responded by instinct, pushing up to meet Tash's downward slides, welcoming the incredible fullness of Tash's heavy cock inside him. Brandon's cock began to swell again, his balls aching with need.

Harder and deeper, Tash pounded into him, touching his gland, setting off additional fireworks inside Brandon. Fascinated, Brandon watched Tash's cock enter and reenter his body, wanting to capture the moment when he knew his life had changed forever.

Like everything else he did, there was a quiet intensity about Tash as he made love, his concentration solely on Brandon. With a wicked smile, he leaned over and captured Brandon's lips in a kiss so hard and deep it stole Brandon's breath, leaving him trembling and shaken. The press of Tash's lips and the thrust of his rhythmic strokes inside Brandon grew faster and more punishing as Brandon sensed Tash's imminent orgasm. Their tongues tangled together, and Brandon grabbed on to Tash's shoulders and wrapped one leg around Tash's hip, forcing them harder and closer together. Tash cried out and came, pumping hot and deep inside him.

After a moment, Tash collapsed on top of him, their sweat-slick bodies melding together as neither one had the energy to move. A bit shy but needing to prove to himself how real this was, Brandon ran his hands over Tash's naked back, smoothing over his shoulders, down his rib cage, until he reached the dip of Tash's lower back.

Tash's breathing remained steady, yet Brandon sensed the escalating rhythm of his heart. With a tentative touch, Brandon drew a finger down the crease between Tash's ass cheeks, silently thrilled when Tash hissed his approval and even shifted a bit to give him better access.

"If you want to play some more, let me get rid of the condom first." Tash lifted up on his elbows, his eyes soft and sated. He leaned down to place a gentle kiss at the corner of Brandon's mouth, but Brandon turned his head so that their lips met full on. There was no sense of urgency now, however, as their lovemaking had taken the edge off their previous passion. While Brandon loved the wildness of making love with Tash, he discovered he also loved the quiet aftermath and wound his arms around Tash's neck, wishing he could hold on to him forever and keep the demons at bay.

"Hey, don't worry. I'm not disappearing." Tash drew back and slid out of Brandon's body. "I want to get rid of this and clean up a bit, okay?" Brandon's newly opened passage ached, and he winced and shifted in the bed, hoping Tash wouldn't notice. Lucky for him, Tash was too busy tying off the condom and dropping it into the wastebasket. Tash left to go to the bathroom located in the corner of the bedroom. Brandon heard water running, then as quickly as he was gone, Tash returned with a warm damp washcloth.

"Here, you're all sticky and that can't be comfortable." He swirled the washcloth over Brandon's stomach and chest until all the dried residue of his semen had been removed. Though it was a small gesture, for Brandon, who'd never been completely intimate with a lover, it was a big deal. It showed Tash cared. Their eyes held each other's gaze as Tash continued to wipe him down.

"Thanks," he whispered, unable to voice fully his thoughts and emotions, somewhat overcome by the enormity of what he'd done. He'd known that eventually he'd have sex, but the need for this man above all others was something Brandon hadn't expected.

Though he'd been attracted to a few guys in high school, he'd ruthlessly and swiftly squashed those feelings, unwilling to be the subject of beatings, scorn, and ridicule, which was the standard practice in his small community toward anyone who was different. Certainly it was toward homosexuals, who, as he heard muttered in school hallways and bathrooms, had no business being alive. And when he'd been homeless, he'd rather have starved than sell himself for a few dollars. His health wasn't worth it.

But tonight opened his eyes to what he'd always heard, how magical and beautiful the act of sex could be when it was between two people who cared about one another. And now he also knew that no matter how Tash protested that he didn't want Brandon or that their age difference was too great, Tash cared about him. Whatever help Tash needed to get over his former lover, Brandon would give.

Watching Tash from beneath lowered lids, Brandon didn't know when he'd shifted his outlook and decided to risk everything he'd kept secret all these years. But he did know he'd be making a great mistake if he didn't put aside his own fears and help Tash take a chance at life again.

Brandon wanted to be that chance. Together the two of them would help those kids and help each other.

"What has you so deep in thought, hmm?" Tash lay next to him, and Brandon, enjoying his warmth, turned into his chest. To his delight, Tash slipped his arm around his shoulders to hug him close. Brandon rested his head against Tash.

"Nothing. I was only thinking about stuff."

"Stuff, huh?" said Tash, his amused voice bringing a smile to Brandon's lips. "So it would be all right with you, then, if I interrupted you to ask why you've been lying to me?"

Chapter Thirteen

TASH HATED TO do it this way, especially when he had Brandon all relaxed in his arms. It had been years since he'd held someone after sex, years since he'd experienced the intoxicating pleasure of making love to someone who sent him hurtling off the precipice into a mindless whirlpool of bliss.

He had with Brandon, and it scared him to death. But, as long as it had been since he'd had sex with anyone, he'd recognize a virgin in a moment, and Brandon had been a virgin, of that he had no doubt. When he'd breached Brandon at first, he'd wanted to stop but knew it wasn't the right thing to do. They were so far gone in the moment; Tash couldn't ruin the man's first sexual experience.

And the absolute mind-blowing rush of their love-making scared him with its intensity. He'd never been sucked into a vortex of want and need so deep that the only thing he could think of was this man with his supple young body and trusting eyes urging him on with soft cries.

But now that they'd come down from their emotional, sexual high, Brandon had some explaining to do. And from the way Brandon stiffened in his arms, Tash knew this wouldn't be an easy or quick conversation.

"I don't know what you mean."

But the hesitation and guarded tone in Brandon's voice told Tash everything he needed to know. He removed his arm from underneath Brandon and, with regret, moved away from his heat.

"Come on. Don't lie to me. I can take a lot of things, but not someone lying to me." He stared off into the deepening shadows in the bedroom. "I had that once before and barely made it through, so tell me." He focused back on the bed, his gaze sweeping across Brandon's naked body. Determined to keep his thoughts on the subject at hand, he focused on Brandon's face and sighed. "Why didn't you tell me you were a virgin?"

Was he mistaken, or did a flicker of something like relief flash in Brandon's eyes? With a defiant tilt to his jaw, Brandon glared at him before sitting up in the bed.

"If I'd told you, we wouldn't be sitting here right now." A small smile touched his lips. "I'm not going to apologize for that. It was incredible." Brandon swept his hand across Tash's chest, gliding down to his abdomen.

Heat pooled in Tash's groin, but he refused to allow Brandon to whitewash the issue or play duck and glide. "That isn't the point. Why did you lead me to believe you had experience? Hell." He shook his head and massaged the back of his neck. "How can you of all people—good-looking, young, and so caring and concerned—how can *you* still be a virgin?"

"Well, you took care of that very nicely." Brandon grinned up at Tash, but when Tash didn't smile back, the smile faded. Several moments passed before Brandon got up the courage to answer. "I couldn't come out as gay when I was younger. Maybe if I'd had Luke and Ash with me it would have been different, but that wasn't to be." He fiddled with the edge of the comforter, then continued. "The bullying and homophobia in my religious rural community made it impossible for me to have a relationship. When I ran away, I was too scared to allow anyone to get close to me. By the time I came to New York, I'd been homeless long enough that sex was the furthest thing from my mind when I needed shelter and food. After Gabriel took me to the shelter and set me up with social services, I concentrated solely on going to college and becoming a teacher."

Incredible. Tash was stunned to hear how single-minded and dedicated Brandon was and saddened to hear how cold and lonely his life had been. Considering Tash had never needed to hide his sexuality, it hurt his heart listening to Brandon admit how he'd lived in the closet his whole life, fearful of people discovering who he was, never safe enough to love someone.

"So you've never had a boyfriend?"

Brandon shrugged. "There was a guy while I was in

school, and we fooled around a little." His cheeks stained red as he slanted a look up at Tash, then looked down at the bed.

An unexpected stab of jealousy tore through Tash at the thought of another man touching Brandon. "But nothing serious?"

"No." Brandon slid down in the bed so only his head showed above the covers. "Nothing serious. Charlie and I had fun, but when he moved to Florida, it was no big deal for either one of us to say good-bye." After that statement, he curled away from Tash and hugged the pillow to his chest.

"Hey." Tash slipped under the covers and curved himself around Brandon, kissing him on his naked shoulder. The soft skin jumped under Tash's tongue, tasting sweet and a bit salty. "Leaving you would be a really big deal for me." He stroked the hard planes of Brandon's chest and tweaked his nipples.

"Tash." Brandon sighed into the pillow as he wriggled his ass into Tash's groin.

"Shh. Let me take care of you." His questing hand stroked down Brandon's flat abdomen and brushed against the top of a healthy erection.

God bless the young. They can get it up so easily.

He smoothed the pad of his thumb over the crown of Brandon's cock, smearing the liquid seeping out. At his touch, more fluid leaked from the tip, and he used it to lubricate the slide of his hand up and down Brandon's shaft.

"Yes," Brandon hissed out through clenched teeth.

"Oh God, don't stop."

He couldn't have stopped even if he wanted to. Why would he? With Brandon naked in his arms, his breathy cries and wet, thrusting erection, Tash's heart almost stopped from the sheer beauty of the moment.

With only a few more strokes, Brandon came undone, shuddering against him. "Tash," he sobbed. "Oh God." His cock jerked, and a small amount of liquid trickled out.

Tash held on to Brandon, his lips buried in the thick silk of Brandon's hair. "It's okay; it's going to be okay." Brandon rolled over and buried his face in the curve of Tash's neck while Tash continued to murmur nonsense words into the man's hair, kissing his temple. Eventually, Brandon's breathing evened out, and Tash could tell he'd fallen asleep.

When was the last time he'd held someone close as he slept, his heartbeat in tempo with his own? Unused to such intimacy anymore, Tash cuddled Brandon even closer, adjusting the curves of his body to fit with Brandon's, learning the sounds of the man in his arms.

Contentment, like a sleeping cat in a patch of sunshine, warmed him like sweet honey, his ordinary cold existence unraveling at the seams. Before tonight, before bringing Brandon into his bed, cold sheets and solitude were Tash's constant bed companions. It was meant to be; he'd never looked for sympathy. He'd seen it for what it was—a punishment for his failure to recognize Danny's deception and save him from himself. When trust was lost, hope followed it blindly out the window. For years, he'd lost trust in himself and had given up hope.

But now, with a warm and sleeping Brandon nestled in his arms, his hairy muscled thigh flung over Tash's, perhaps it was time for him to reconsider his isolation. Tash stroked Brandon's cheek, noting the spiky, damp lashes, remembering the tears he'd shed as he came. Somewhere buried deep within this man was a story of broken dreams and pain. It was up to Tash to help Brandon overcome whatever he was hiding and break free, so he could move forward with his life.

"I won't fail you," he whispered, kissing Brandon's cheek. "This time I'll do it right."

Chapter Fourteen

I T WAS THE time right before parent-teacher conferences, and Brandon found himself swamped with reports, meetings, and schedule changes. None of it could dim his mood that Monday as he walked into the teacher's lounge to catch a quick cup of coffee before his next class.

"Randy, hey, come here." Gage waved him over.

With a start, Brandon realized he needed to talk to Gage. Tash had offered to speak to him, but Brandon wanted to tell his friend himself. In a way, he owed the remarkable upheaval in his life all to Gage. He checked his watch, noting with an inward smile, only five more hours until he would meet Tash.

After pouring his cup of coffee, he joined Gage on the worn vinyl sofa. The entire room was decorated in a color scheme they'd jokingly named fifty shades of institutional gray. Brandon normally found it depressing as hell, but after a weekend spent with Tash, nothing could dampen his good mood. He was on top of the world; he'd found his brothers, he loved his job, and he had a man to love.

"Gage. How was your weekend?"

"Good. Watched some baseball, went out on a date. And you?"

Nothing short of amazing. "I had a crazy weekend. Some personal issues I thought would never happen came out of nowhere." As he explained his story and how Dr. Drew Klein's boyfriend was really his brother, as was Dr. Jordan Peterson's, Brandon couldn't help but laugh.

"Gage, man, your eyes look like they're going to fall out of your head."

"Can you blame me?"

They shared a laugh, and then Gage, for the third time in as many minutes, shook his head. "I don't fucking believe it. It's like a movie or something."

"Yeah. So anyway. I wanted you to know that even though my name is really Brandon, you can still call me Randy. I've answered to it for so many years; it's second nature to me now."

"Is Gilbert your real name?" The question wasn't condemning but merely curious. Brandon understood and appreciated Gage treating him not as someone to be pitied but as an equal.

"It was my middle name. My real last name is Kane."

"Will you go back to Kane? Now that you've found your brothers and don't need to hide any longer?"

It wasn't ever going to be safe for him to use Kane again. He was lucky no one had ever asked him too many questions about using his middle name. He'd merely stated he preferred it that way and used it ever since.

"I like Gilbert, and everyone knows me here as that, so I'm keeping it."

"Can I ask you something?"

"Sure." He drained his cup and tossed it in the wastebasket.

"Did you tell Tash?"

Try as he might to keep himself from reacting, that damn blush got him every single time. He ducked his head and hoped his hair hid his flaming cheeks. "Um, yeah."

"He likes you, you know." Gage's soft voice penetrated Brandon's discomfort. "You're the first person he's shown an interest in since Danny. I think you'd be great together."

Brandon thought so too, but things were too fresh and new between him and Tash to talk about. Plus, he wasn't sure if Tash wanted anyone, especially Gage, to know.

"Umm, well, thanks. I'm happy we're friends. That's about all I can say right now."

Gage shot him a look from under raised brows but said nothing.

"I gotta go to class. Are you going to be at the Clinic later?" Brandon stood and picked up his backpack off the floor. "I'm going there around five, five thirty."

"Yeah, I'll see you there." Gage's phone rang.

"See you later." Brandon left him to answer it and headed off to class.

AT A FEW minutes past four thirty, Brandon finished grading the quiz he'd given today in class. After stretching the kinks out of his shoulders, he checked his watch and groaned. Even if he left right now, he'd be late to the Clinic with the way the trains ran. Damn. He'd better text Tash and let him know.

> *Going to be late. Got stuck grading papers. I'll be there ASAP.*

He stood and shoved all the test papers into his backpack, checked to make sure his laptop was inside and zipped it up. Few teachers were about; most preferred to go home right after school ended, and he was usually one of the last to leave the building. Before this weekend, it was because he had no desire to go back to his depressing room in the walk-up he lived in.

Now, everything had changed. He was meeting his lover, and Brandon half hoped Tash would ask him back to his house for the night, even though it would be a pain to get to the school from there. By next week, he was going to move into Esther's house. The lady was so kind; he had no qualms about living with her. After seeing how much both Ash and Luke adored her, he knew he'd be safe there.

He turned out the lights and closed the door behind him. It was always a bit eerie to walk through the silent halls after being there all day, dodging the crush of students and wincing at the roar of so many voices shouting to be heard over one another. Even the security guards had gone. He ran down the steps, eager to be off.

"Going my way?" Tash leaned against his car, arms folded. A wide smile played on his lips.

Happiness surged through Brandon. Without hesitation, he ran up to the man and threw his arms around him. Tash held him tight, and they hugged, then kissed, his warm cheek brushing against the cool, bristly skin of Tash's wind-chilled face.

"Why didn't you tell me you were here? I hope you weren't waiting too long." He hated to let go of Tash and held on to him a moment to draw some of his strength before letting him go.

Tash opened the car door. "Nah. I had already decided to surprise you and pick you up, so I was on my way when I got the text from you."

Brandon slid onto the front seat. A delicious aroma filled the car. He sniffed and waited until Tash settled in next to him before pointing behind him. "I smell something amazing back there. Did you bring food for the meeting?"

"I picked up some food from a little Italian place in Carroll Gardens the guys always go to."

Brandon's stomach growled as he thought of the pathetic peanut butter sandwich he'd eaten around eleven thirty that morning. "Damn, I can't wait."

"I sense you're hungry." A slow smile spread over Tash's face. "Must be all that strenuous activity over the weekend. Maybe I need to feed you more."

At his words, a memory of them naked together in Tash's shower flooded through Brandon's mind. He could almost feel the rush of hot water over his skin again, and the wet suction of Tash's mouth on his cock.

"I think you took care of my needs." They were at a red light at the moment, stuck behind a city bus. Brandon reached over and grabbed at the healthy bulge in Tash's pants. "Remind me later to return the favor." He gave Tash's crotch a nice squeeze. "You deserve attention as well."

Tash's hands gripped the wheel until his knuckles whitened. There was no sound in the car but his heavy breathing as Brandon continued to massage him. He shifted in his seat, a pained look in his eyes as he bit his lip. "Brandon, stop. I can't show up to the Clinic like this."

With a sigh of regret, Brandon gave one last squeeze and withdrew his hand. "Spoilsport. There's so much traffic, I bet no one would even notice if I put my head down and sucked you off."

Tash broke out in a fit of coughing. "Please," he wheezed. "Please tell me you did not say you wanted to give me a blowjob in the car."

Brandon waggled his eyebrows. "Next time I won't say anything; I'll do it, and you'll have no recourse."

Traffic began to move again. "You're determined to be the death of me, aren't you?" Tash's pretense at anger failed when Brandon caught his eye and grinned. They were still laughing about it as he pulled into the parking lot at the Clinic.

He loved seeing Tash laugh. His hazel eyes lit up behind his glasses, and all the tired lines of his face smoothed, rendering him younger and more at peace with himself. "I prefer to think of myself as a life-giving force." Taking advantage of their solitude, knowing Tash might be somewhat uncomfortable displaying affection in front of the others, especially Brandon's brothers, Brandon kissed him. It was a quiet kiss, one that spoke of trust and comfort, respect and friendship.

For Brandon, there were stronger emotions, ones that confused even him, so he kept silent about them. Because Tash was so hyperaware of their age difference, Brandon held off on telling Tash how he felt, preferring to show the man in little ways to make him feel special.

Like after the first time they spent the night together. Brandon had sneaked down to the kitchen and, with the two cats for company, made Tash breakfast in bed—scrambled eggs with maple turkey bacon and homemade cinnamon rolls. They fed each other bites of the food and then fed on each other's bodies. They didn't leave the bedroom until much later that afternoon.

After several minutes of increasingly heated kisses, Brandon broke away. Still caught up in the haze of pleasure, he barely heard Tash's sigh. As he returned to earth and gathered his wits, he sensed something wrong and a quick glance at Tash's sad face validated that feeling.

"Care to tell me what's wrong?" Brandon zipped up

his jacket.

"You don't know? All weekend I've been deluding myself. We were caught up in this bubble we created, but now? Now that I have to come face-to-face with your brothers and Gage." Tash shook his head. "I don't know if I can do this."

Heart beating madly, Brandon swallowed. "Can't do what?" *Don't do this, please; don't hide yourself away.*

"Us. You, me. We're at different places in our lives. You're starting out, and with Ash and Luke, you have a whole new world open to you—places to explore and new people to meet."

Tash unbuckled his seat belt and opened the car door but didn't get out. "I'm the opposite. I'm ready to settle down. I'm not interested in nightlife and the latest scene. I can't and won't ask you to give it all up." Tash climbed out of the car and slammed the door.

The hell he says. If Tash thought he'd simply state his opinions like God and proclaim what Brandon should do with the rest of his life, he was in for a fight. He wrenched open the door. "I'm not giving anything up. I was never into that." Brandon slammed the car door behind him with a vicious thump. "Who do you think you are? You say you don't want to be with me, yet you then get the right to lay out my life in neat little puzzle pieces so it all comes perfectly together as *you* see fit."

Tash had stopped in his tracks but didn't turn around. Hopeful that was a sign he was at least listening, Brandon continued.

"Sure, we were in a bubble; it was wonderful this weekend, beautiful and amazing." He advanced on Tash and stood before him. "Don't think I don't know, maybe better than anyone, how something so perfect and magical can be ripped away with no warning." He put a hand on Tash's shoulder, hoping Tash wouldn't move away from him. "And now the hard stuff begins—reality and all the trouble that comes with it. But aren't you willing to try? See where this journey takes us?"

"Brandon, you're—"

"Don't say it. I'll tell you what I am. I've been homeless and hungry. I've lived on the streets with rats, not knowing where I would sleep at night. Do you think I'm looking for a man whose only interest is a twenty-dollar glass of wine and where the next party is?"

Tash said nothing, and Brandon had no more strength to argue. Besides, they were at the Clinic to do a job. Last time he'd screwed up by running out, and he'd be damned if he'd do it again.

They entered the Clinic in silence. Tash returned to the car to retrieve the food he'd forgotten in the back seat, then went directly to the rear of the Clinic where Brandon presumed there was a kitchen. Three young people were working behind the front desk. Brandon smiled at them as they stared at him, friendly but curious.

"Hi. I'm Brandon."

The reaction was almost comical, in the way their

eyes widened and their mouths formed perfect Os.

Finally, a tall young man with finely etched features and light brown hair stepped forward. "Hi. I'm Steve. I can't tell you how happy I am for you and Ash." His voice dropped. "You're so lucky to have him as a brother. If it wasn't for him and Dr. Drew and the others, I don't know where I'd be."

Pride swelled in his chest at what his brothers had accomplished. Thank God they'd all come through their journeys to get to this point, stronger and able to help. "I'm glad he was able to help."

"They're all great; Dr. Drew didn't know he was inheriting a whole group of kids when he started this place, but we're like a family now." The young woman whose name tag read Marly finished filing her papers and walked over to join them. "Ash was always sad, even when he was trying to cheer me up. I know how hard he, Dr. Drew, and your other brother were trying to find you."

A harsh, resentful voice broke into their conversation. "How come you didn't try to find them?"

Brandon's heart squeezed. Meeting the dark gaze of the angry young man, Brandon recognized that look. He'd seen plenty of young kids like this, like he'd once been. This was a kid from the streets, one who'd lived a truly hard life.

"I did try. But Luke had changed his last name so it was impossible for me to locate him."

"What about Ash?" Steve's brow furrowed. "I'm sure that's his real name."

His throat tightened, and his chest hurt from the tension of holding himself together and not falling apart. "I figured since he left and never came back, never tried to get in touch with Luke or me again, he didn't care. That he forgot about us. Then, when I saw how rich and successful he'd become, with a fancy Park Avenue law practice, why would he want to be bothered with me? I wasn't anything special."

At the sound of footsteps behind him, Brandon turned to see Ash's agonized face. If he'd stabbed himself through the heart with a knife, the pain wouldn't have been as great.

"Is that really what you thought? You knew where I was all along, yet chose to be homeless rather than come to me?"

"Ash, n-no, you don't understand." But in all honesty, it was the truth. He'd done it out of love, to protect Ash, not because he hated him but because he couldn't involve Ash in his ugly problems with Munson. "It wasn't like that."

"What was it like?" asked Ash. "Please tell me."

"I...I thought, you'd become rich and successful, and you wouldn't want someone like me around. I was only going to be a burden and"—he took a deep breath—"a memory of the past you obviously wanted to forget."

"Someone like you? We need to talk." With that, Ash took him by the hand and led him down the hallway, then into an office. His breathing cut sharp and harsh through the air. "Do you know what I did with the first check I got once I joined the law firm? I bought a suit, and I hired a private investigator." Ash's eyes glittered feverishly. "All the years I went to school and lived wherever I could, the only thing I could think of was how I'd failed you and Luke and how, if I made it—*when* I made it—I'd find you both, and we'd be together again and safe."

"Ash, I don't blame you. You and Luke, we all did the best we could to survive."

"I almost didn't."

His heart lurched. "Wha-what do you mean?"

Ash closed his eyes for a moment and took a deep breath before answering. "A year ago, I probably wouldn't have answered you, but after all the therapy I've been through, I need to tell you."

"Ash, please." Brandon moved close enough to his older brother to put his hand on his shoulder. "Tell me."

"For years, I hurt myself and a few times even tried to kill myself. But that's done with now," he added hastily as Brandon, horrified at what he'd heard, stared at his older brother, his eyes filling with tears. "I'm so much stronger now thanks to all that therapy, and I have Drew and everyone else." Ash pulled Brandon down to sit next to him on the sofa.

"Finding you was a reward, the ultimate happiness that could've happened for me. Never doubt that I wanted you, that I want you in my life. No matter what happened before, during, or after we were separated, you always have been and will be my brother. Always."

They hugged each other, unrestrained. This time no one needed to tell them what to do. Tears mixed with laughter as they hugged. A part of Brandon, the one part he'd kept to himself that still believed Ash hadn't wanted him in his life, released the heavy burden anchoring him to the past. "We *can* start again, the three of us. It's all different now. You and Luke are settled, with lives of your own. There's no need to worry about me."

Humor returned to Ash's face. "That's what you think. Since I've been with Drew, I've inherited an entire family who worries." He leaned back, contentment evident in his relaxed body. "I never thought I'd get to a place where I'd feel secure, accepted, and loved."

"Drew seems like a special man. He knows everything you went through? I mean, with Munson?"

The love shining from Ash's bright eyes amazed Brandon. Happiness had been a remote concept growing up in their house, except for those rare times when the three of them managed to steal some time away to spend together.

"He does. It's not an exaggeration when I tell you Drew saved my life. He and Esther both. I'd do anything for that woman." He grinned. "You'll see what I mean. She'll capture your heart and twist you around her finger without you knowing what happened."

"I plan to move in there next week." He'd take what Ash said more as a warning to be on his guard, not reveal too much.

"Good." Ash jumped up. "I think Tash is having his session now with Johnny. We can go to the back and prepare the room for the others, and heat the food up."

"Sounds good to me." He followed Ash. "We brought some Italian food from the place Tash said you guys like."

They walked down the hallway to the back until Ash casually asked, "Is something going on between you and Tash?"

Remembering their earlier conversation, Brandon honestly answered, "I have no idea."

Chapter Fifteen

"SO, JOHNNY, SIT down and tell me what's been happening since our last session." Tash took out a notebook from the desk and looked expectantly at the young man sitting across from him.

To say Johnny had been completely transformed would be a lie, but there was little left of the angry, scraggly-looking teenager Tash had first met. He'd had a haircut, gotten some new clothes, and the sullen look on his face had been replaced by one Tash had seen before in the kids he'd helped in the past—cautious optimism warring with a defensive bravado. These kids were waiting for someone or something to snatch away the elusive happiness they'd only begun to understand existed.

"Nothin' much." But Johnny bit his lip, and his eyes refused to meet Tash's.

Recognizing he needed to take a different tactic, Tash put down his pen. "How do you like the Clinic? It looks like you and the others get along pretty well; am I right?"

"Yeah. They've taught me a lot, and I think they like me."

"I'm hearing a *but* in there. What's the matter?" Tash pressed Johnny gently, not wanting to freak him out. He knew the young man worried about retaliation from his drug-dealing former boss.

"What's gonna happen to me? I ain't in school. I don't have no place to live, really." He dropped his gaze to the floor and kicked the edge of the rug with his sneaker. "I don't wanna go back on the street no more."

Tash's heart went out to this boy. Johnny had never been given a chance to make something of himself. Another runaway kid with big dreams who'd come to learn life in the city wasn't all bright lights. "You won't have to. As long as you keep up with the program and work here, take your GED classes like you have been, you'll be fine. We're working on it. I promise."

"I have been. I did well on the test I took, and my caseworker said she thinks I may even be able to graduate when I was supposed to if I study hard."

"That's great. I'm proud of you. I know your temporary foster family, the Ortegas, reported how hard you've been working."

A rare smile touched Johnny's lips. "I like Mr. and Mrs. Ortega. They've been really nice to me. I felt so bad when they told me how their son had been killed in a drive-by shooting."

Tash sensed Johnny's discomfort as he watched him squirm in his seat. "It's why what the Center does is so important. Every gun they get off the street is one less gun in the hands of a killer. One less innocent death."

"I know," mumbled Johnny. "I still don't believe Dr. Jordan doesn't hate me."

"He doesn't hate you. I happen to know he's proud of you and how you're trying to help yourself; we all are." Tash came around from behind the desk to sit in the chair next to Johnny. "It takes a lot of courage to do what you're doing. You're helping not only yourself but preventing innocent people, children, from getting hurt by drugs and guns. Everyone makes mistakes. The hard thing is admitting it and learning from them."

"I'm *never* gonna go back to selling drugs," Johnny spit out with vehemence. "I don't want no one to die because of me."

"I believe you." And he did. Tash could now send a silent prayer to whoever was listening that this time, a life had been saved, and Tash helped.

"Thanks, Dr. Tash. I don't know why you're so nice to me, but I owe you one. You and Dr. Jordan." They walked out of the office together and headed down the hallway to the front, where Tash heard the familiar voices of his friends.

Everyone had gathered around the front desk and greeted them with broad smiles.

"Tash, come congratulate Mike and Rachel. They're engaged." Drew waved him over, a huge smile almost splitting his face in half.

He said good-bye to Johnny and grabbed hold of Mike to give him a hug. "That's great news. I'm so happy for you both." He leaned down to give Rachel a kiss on the cheek.

Her green eyes glowed, and a smile of happiness lit up her pretty face. "Thanks so much." Her arm was linked with Mike's, but Tash caught a flash of a diamond on her hand. "We stopped by on the way to my grandmother's house."

Drew raised his eyebrows. "You told us before Nana? You are in trouble." He leaned against Ash, who put his arms around him. "I wouldn't tell her you told us first."

They all laughed, and then Mike and Rachel left. Drew checked his watch.

"Okay, gang, time to close up shop. See you tomorrow." The three young people behind the front desk—Marly, Steve, and Johnny, busied themselves with shutting down the computers and locking the drawers. "Marly, honey, do you need a ride home?"

The young woman shook her long dark hair free from the collar of her down jacket. "No, thanks. I have a ride with Javier and Steve." She threw a grateful smile over her shoulder at Steve, who returned it.

Steve checked his phone. "Javier said he'll be here in five minutes. He can drop you off too, Johnny. We'll wait in here until he comes, okay?"

Drew nodded. "Of course. I'll fix the door so it automatically locks behind you when you leave."

As the rest of the men broke into smaller groups, Tash noticed Brandon hadn't left Ash's side. Obviously, the brothers had a heart-to-heart talk that had brought them some type of closure. Even as he watched, Ash pulled out his phone and showed both Brandon and Luke something that caused them to break out into laughter.

"What's so funny?" asked Jordan, who walked over to them after hanging up his coat. "I could use a good laugh after hours of surgery." He flexed his shoulders.

"You're angling for a massage tonight, aren't you, Prep School?" Luke teased, as he placed his hands on Jordan's back. "Hmm, you are one big knot." He massaged Jordan's shoulders and kissed his neck.

Brandon caught his eye, and Tash recalled the massage Brandon had given him yesterday, which ended with a blowjob of such epic proportions it had rendered him weak at the knees. From the intensity of Brandon's stare, it was obvious he remembered it as well.

Shit.

"Need a moment?"

Tash inwardly groaned at Ash's amused voice in his ear. *Don't let him get to you.* "I don't know what you're talking about." He spun back around. "Everyone want to get started? There's food in the back so we can eat while we talk."

He didn't wait for anyone to answer and strode down the hall. To his great relief, he heard everyone follow him, and they streamed into the conference room. After they'd all taken their food and sat around the table making small talk, Tash cleared his throat. Avoiding Brandon's glare, he began to speak.

"In continuation of our discussion last month we here are teaming up with the Center and Wanda at the shelter to bring as many kids and teens together in a safe environment, whether it's to talk to a counselor, like myself or Rachel, work with Brandon on their schoolwork, or simply have a place to go when they think there is no place for them."

"Brandon, you're on board with this now, right?" Gage had finished eating and pushed his plate away as he faced Brandon. "No more freaking out and running?"

"No." Brandon shook his head. "I'm good. Since the last time we met, I've been helping out Noah and Tash with the call center. It's been so incredibly fulfilling. Now as for the Center, I invited the two boys from my school who get bullied constantly. They seemed really eager."

Gage's eye lit up with approval. "Dwayne and Wilson are so excited. I heard them this afternoon planning what books they want to bring with them."

"Yeah," said Brandon. He put down his fork and stopped chewing his baked ziti. "I want to get them into helping some of the kids from the neighborhood around the shelter." He glanced over his shoulder. "That's okay with you, right, Luke?"

Luke had his arm around an exhausted Jordan. "Of course. It's what we envisioned the Center to be, right?" He nudged Jordan, who lay drowsily against his shoulder.

"Hmm?" Jordan yawned and stretched. "Yeah,

exactly. Keep the kids off the streets and out of the way of the people who might hurt them." He drank some water and wiped his mouth. "Say, I meant to ask you. I know you can't give any specifics, but how's the kid, Johnny, doing? Has he been working out?"

"Good news to report on that front." Tash shared a smile with Jordan. "He's following everything we've asked of him and made friends with the others here. I think he enjoys it" Tash's eyes softened. "Honestly, I know how hard it was for you, but it might have been the best thing that ever happened to him to get involved with you. It may have saved his life."

"Well, I'm not saying it was worth it, but it gives me tremendous satisfaction to know that boy is off the streets and getting helped." His pale blue eyes lit up. "I guess you could call me a lifesaver."

Luke groaned and appealed to Tash. "Now why did you have to go do that? You know how big his ego is."

Jordan leaned over and ruffled Luke's curls. "Matches the rest of me."

With that comment, Drew rolled his eyes, Brandon cackled with laughter, and Ash's facial expression was a picture of pained resignation. Luke, accustomed to Jordan's overinflated opinion of himself, ignored him and spoke directly to Tash.

"I'm happy the kid is getting help. I know he'd be going nowhere if he was still with the guy he worked for."

The humor wiped clean from Jordan's face. "In all seriousness, I spoke to Jerry earlier today." He glanced at Tash. "You remember him; he was Keith's partner."

At Tash's nod, Jordan continued. "Jerry said with Johnny's help they were making good progress on nailing down this Donovan bastard, and they hope to make an arrest shortly."

After today's session, he couldn't have received better news. "I know Johnny will be relieved. That kid really wants to make something out of himself."

"And you think he can, don't you?" asked Luke, a thoughtful look on his face.

Tash knew Luke was still somewhat suspicious of Johnny because he'd sold Jordan his drugs. But Johnny wasn't the one who'd beaten Jordan, sending him to the hospital, nor did he control a gun-running, drug-dealing cartel in New York City. The kid was only seventeen, after all.

Before he could answer, to his surprise, Brandon cut him off. "I do. I know kids like him. Hell, I *was* a kid like him." He dragged his hand through his hair. "Not the drug dealing, but the gutting hopelessness of life, when you wake up in the middle of the night wondering why you were even born."

There was no need to wonder anymore, as Tash watched Ash place a comforting hand on Brandon's back and lean over to speak quietly in his ear. The three brothers proved sometimes good things happen. It might've been a journey through hell for them, but through sheer determination and a strong will never to give up, these three men had survived, though each had to go through a very different personal hell to reach the point where they were today.

As young as Brandon was, he seemed to have come out of it the most unscathed. Despite losing two siblings, an abusive father, and life on the streets, he'd risen above it all and become a teacher, untouched by bitterness. It was a remarkable story.

Minutes ticked away as the men continued to talk among themselves. Tash busied himself cleaning up the table when Gage slipped up behind him. "I'm happy for you, man."

Tash faced Gage. Losing a lover was heartbreaking, losing a sibling, inconceivable. For a moment, he thought of Valerie. "I—we..." There was nothing he could say to Gage. The man could always read him. Plus, as Valerie always told him, he was the lousiest liar; every emotion showed on his face.

A weak laugh escaped him. "There isn't much to talk about." Stealing a surreptitious glance over at Brandon, watching him share a laugh with his brothers, so carefree and beautiful, Tash couldn't put into words the music that filled his soul.

Gage pulled him out in the hallway to speak privately.

"There's no need to talk. I know you. You wore your sadness like a dark cloud over your head, no matter where you went. Since you met Brandon, though, it's all different." Gage leaned his hip against the doorframe, effectively blocking them from the group inside. "You've come back to life."

"I'm not sure what I'm doing is right." Gage had

become like a brother to him during those black years and deserved his honesty. "He's so young and starting a whole new life now." Though it hurt him like a physical wound, he had to say it. "I don't want to hold him back. What he thinks he's feeling—"

"Is what he has in his heart." Gage cut him off with earnest desperation. "Don't go there. Don't allow some made-up rules in a society that's disappointed you for years decide who to love. You deserve this." He glanced over his shoulder at Brandon. "You both do." Gage squeezed his shoulder and walked back inside.

Reflecting on what his friend had said, Tash remained deep in thought. If what Gage said was true, and he and Brandon continued their relationship, he wouldn't be able to hide his emotions. Since Danny's death, there'd been no pleasure in his life; one season melded into another, creating an amalgam of grayness.

Gage said he wore a cloud of darkness over him. Perhaps he did.

"Tash?" Brandon stood before him. His honey-colored hair caught the light, and his eyes shone brightly with hope. "Is everything all right? You and Gage looked pretty serious out here."

When he looked into Brandon's face, the clarity of Tash's vision startled him for a moment. It was like driving out of pea-soup-thick fog in a valley to the sharp, wide-open night sky. Blurred lines came into focus, and the tightness of fear, so instinctual he didn't ever realize it was there, relaxed, leaving him almost giddy with relief.

"It won't be easy, you know." He wasn't sure Brandon would understand, but the light that kindled behind those wide green eyes dispelled any doubt. Brandon knew exactly what Tash alluded to.

"I've learned the best things in life are often the hardest won." Brandon took a step closer to him. "Though I wasn't aware we were on opposite sides. I prefer to think we're in this together." He arched a brow. "Are we? Together?"

Tash breathed in Brandon's scent—leather and warm male. How long had it been since he'd hungered to be touched?

Now it wasn't an amorphous person floating around in his head; it was Brandon who filled his mind and his heart. If they were alone, Tash could tell him how close he'd like to be. Fused together, bodies moving in perfect symmetry. Chest to chest, heart to heart.

"Yes." He smiled into the brilliant happiness of Brandon's face. "Yes, we are. Together."

Chapter Sixteen

T HE WEEKEND COULDN'T come fast enough for Brandon. It had been hell not being able to connect with Tash aside from some hurried phone calls. But Wednesday was his first parent-teacher night, and he wanted it to be perfect. He also had lessons to plan, tests to grade, and a couple of classes to sub. By Friday night, he was exhausted, edgy, and ready to rip Tash's clothes off. They were all meeting for dinner at Esther's, and though Brandon looked forward to seeing his brothers again, he couldn't wait to see Tash.

The dinginess of his studio couldn't dampen Brandon's eagerness; Tash had texted him to say he'd be swinging by to pick him up and whatever belongings he had. Tonight Brandon was moving into Drew's grandmother's house. He had no qualms about living with the elderly lady. Tash had assured him she was someone special, and Ash had texted him that Esther had already prepared an entire suite of rooms for him and even sent Brandon pictures of her interior decorating.

After glancing around the room to make sure he'd left nothing personal, Brandon sat down to wait, his attention fixed on the door. He'd leave this room the way he came—with merely two suitcases and his leather jacket. Now he was glad the room he'd rented was furnished so he didn't need to concern himself with selling any furniture, which would have been a major hassle.

His phone buzzed.

Downstairs. Do you need help?

His heart rate accelerated. Damn, he couldn't wait to see Tash.

Nope. I'll be down in a few minutes.

With a final look around, he left the apartment and caught the back of the door with his foot to hook it closed. It slammed with a final hollow thump. As the landlord had asked, Brandon left his key on the table. Never in his imagination had he thought when he'd moved in that he'd leave to move into the home of the grandmother of his brother's boyfriend.

He couldn't wait to see what the future held for him now.

The sight of Tash's car idling at the curb lifted his spirits even higher. As he approached, Tash got out and the hatchback lifted. He walked to the rear of the car, and they each picked up a suitcase and placed it in the trunk. Tash closed the hatch down, then smiled at him.

"Hi." His smile was endearingly crooked, and without thinking, Brandon slipped an arm around Tash's neck and kissed his cheek. He never thought of himself as a particularly demonstrative person, but when he was around Tash, he couldn't seem to keep his hands to himself.

Tash didn't seem to mind and brushed back the hair hanging in Brandon's eyes. "Missed you this week."

"Me too." He touched Tash's face with his fingertips, tracing the jut of his cheekbone. "So much, you have no idea." He leaned in for a kiss, and Tash pressed his mouth to Brandon's, their lips soft and giving.

For a second, they clung to one another; then Tash pulled back, his eyes glowing behind the frame of his glasses. "Oh, I have a pretty good idea." His smile grew broader. "Let's get you moved in. If I know Esther, she's prepared a feast for you, and having eaten her cooking, you do not want to be late."

They drove off into the early evening traffic that for once flowed freely. He and Tash chatted about inconsequential things and before he realized it, they'd reached the quiet, almost suburban-like enclave of a part of Brooklyn he wasn't aware even existed. Tash pulled the car into the narrow driveway and killed the engine but made no move to get out.

Brandon looked at him curiously. "What's the matter?"

With a more serious demeanor than he'd had a moment ago, Tash took his hand. "I know we decided to give this a try. But we still haven't told anyone, so there's time for you to change your mind."

"Tash."

"Hear me out." There was painful hesitancy in Tash's voice. "Once we step out into that group and confirm we're in a relationship, the whole dynamic will change. Ash and Luke will want to protect you, and I can't blame them."

"My brothers will learn I'm a grown man. They might have left when I was a kid, but I'm far from the scared little boy I used to be." With small strokes, he traced circles over Tash's hand with the pad of his thumb. "I can take care of myself. And as for changing my mind"—he stopped speaking and pulled Tash close, their lips barely brushing—"what part of 'not going to happen' don't you understand?" He traced the seam of Tash's lips with his tongue. "I want you so badly I ache from it."

Tash's breath hitched, and Brandon pressed on, nuzzling against Tash's neck.

"I'm so hard right now. All you'd have to do is touch me and I'd come. I won't hide my feelings for you in front of my family or yours." A thought struck him at that moment. "When am I going to meet your sister?"

Tash blinked and cleared his throat as he moved back to his seat. "Probably tomorrow. She's coming to the Center with everyone else." He opened his door, effectively ending the conversation. Brandon got out, and they each took a suitcase from the back of the car and walked up the path to the brightly lit house.

As a child growing up, Brandon had read stories of homes like these; though it was late fall, the yard still maintained an appearance of life, with evergreen bushes dotting the garden beds. Brandon could imagine in the summer there might be a profusion of colorful flowers lining the walkway. The dove-gray paint was fresh looking, and inside, Brandon could see the sheer white curtains draping the sparkling windows.

Unexpected nerves shot up his spine, and his steps faltered.

"Don't be nervous." Tash squeezed his free hand.

Brandon threw him a grateful smile. "Am I that obvious?"

"Nah." Another reassuring squeeze, then Tash dropped his hand. "But I know how I'd feel if it were me. Don't worry, though. Esther will have you thinking you've lived there for years before the evening is finished." He set the suitcase down on the porch and rang the doorbell.

The inner door rattled, and the window curtain parted, revealing Esther's smiling face. Right behind her were Drew and Ash, flanking her like two sentries.

Several locks turned, and then the door opened to a small inner vestibule, paneled in wood, with pretty painted murals on the wall. Ash and Drew stepped back into the house to allow them to enter.

"Oh come in, sweetheart. I'm so glad you're here." Brandon picked up his suitcase as Esther took his free hand and led him into the house.

"I hope you're hungry. Esther always makes a delicious Friday night dinner." Ash sniffed the air in appreciation. "Smell that? It's roast chicken, mashed potatoes, and roasted broccoli. Nothing beats a home-cooked meal by Esther."

For Brandon, who couldn't remember the last time he'd had a home-cooked family meal like this, it smelled like heaven. He and Tash set his suitcases down by the staircase.

"Oh Asher, you're trying to butter me up to get some extra dessert. You don't need to do that, dear." She patted his arm, and the loving look Brandon saw pass between his brother and the elderly lady sent tears rushing to his eyes. Blinking madly, he followed the others to the back of the house, presumably where the kitchen was located.

Esther's huge kitchen bustled with activity. A tall woman stood at the stove, stirring something in a pot, while Jordan lounged at the table. A large dog lay at Jordan's feet. When he entered, the dog sat up and wandered over to him. After sniffing his shoes and giving him an assessing stare from intelligent eyes, she licked his hand and padded back to the table.

Esther beckoned to the woman, who put down the wooden spoon to face Brandon. "This is Louisa. She's the live-in companion my grandchildren were lucky enough to find." Her dark eyes met his, and they shared a smile.

"Hello." Her voice held the lilt of a Jamaican accent.

"Hello, Louisa." Brandon reached out to shake her hand. Her grip felt warm and solid. "Nice to meet you." Something didn't make sense. "I'm sorry, Esther, I thought I was coming to stay here to be with you."

"After I invited you to stay, Drew reminded me I'd need someone here during the day while you're at work and at nights or on weekends while you're out having fun." She patted Louisa's arm with affection, and the woman returned the look. "The boys were lucky enough to find Louisa. She's teaching me how to make Jamaican patties and roti, and I'm giving her my recipes for brisket and apple strudel."

Brandon remained confused. "So why do you need me here?"

The color rose in her face. "Well, I hated the thought of you living in one little room while I have so much space, and this way you'll get to see the others all the time." A defensive note crept into her voice. "I like having the house filled with young people."

Drew kissed his grandmother's cheek. "Congratulations, Brandon, you've become another victim of my grandmother's subtle maneuverings, done so cleverly you never knew what hit you."

"Accept it in the good spirit it was given." Ash chuckled. "There's an entire apartment in the basement with a separate side entrance for you. I'll go put your bags in there."

Luke walked in and greeted him. "Good. We were wondering when you were going to get here." They hugged briefly; then they both sat at the round wooden table. Suddenly ravenous, Brandon reached for a breadstick from the pile wrapped in a linen napkin, inside a narrow wicker basket.

"I had to finish up stuff at school for the weekend and make sure I had everything packed and ready to go when Tash picked me up." He broke the breadstick in two and crunched half of it down. "Damn, I'm so hungry I could eat all of these."

"Don't spoil your appetite," Esther called out from her position at the stove. "Rachel and Mike will be here any minute, and we'll be ready to sit down and eat."

They obediently stopped sneaking bites of all the delicious food on the table. With one last toss of some candied pecans into his mouth, Jordan chewed, then swallowed, and brushed his hands together.

"So…" He grinned at Tash, who'd come to sit next to Luke after stopping to give the dog a scratch on the ears. "You two seem awfully tight these days. Anything you care to share with the rest of us?"

Brandon choked a bit on his breadstick and, with a grateful smile, took a sip of water from the glass Tash handed him. He held his breath, waiting to see if Tash would reveal the extent of their relationship, but Luke spoke first.

"Don't be an idiot."

Brandon's stomach dropped as he stared at Luke, who sat scowling at Jordan.

"I mean, Brandon's a kid. Tash is older than you are. They have nothing in common."

"I'm aware of how old Tash is, and wonder what

that has to do with anything." Jordan's pale eyes gleamed. "Your younger brother certainly doesn't seem like the hard-partying type. I'm five years older than you. Do you think I'm too old for you?"

Ash reentered the kitchen and got himself a bottle of water from the refrigerator. He leaned against the tiled kitchen counter. "What's wrong? You look upset."

Before he had a chance to respond, Luke answered.

"Jordan has this ridiculous idea that Brandon and Tash are a couple."

Ash raised his dark brows, his forehead furrowed. "Uh, what's so ridiculous about it? From what I've seen and heard, Tash is a great guy."

"He's fifteen years older than Brandon. Don't you think—"

"Luke, stop." Brandon stood. "You don't have the right to tell me who to date."

"If you're making a stupid mistake, I do." Luke faced him, his hazel eyes angry. "You should be out having a good time, enjoying yourself. You never had that. Ash and I didn't have the opportunity, but you do."

Ash put his hands on Drew's shoulders, holding him close. "I recall how hurtful it was when Jordan refused to believe I cared for Drew and had changed my lifestyle." He smiled down at Drew, and they shared a knowing look between them. "I think people deserve a chance to show their intentions are for the best, but even if others disagree, no one has the right to tell anyone who to love."

"That was different. I knew Jordan; we already had feelings for each other. Brandon barely knows Tash. He should be spending more time getting reacquainted with us." Luke glowered at them.

"Stop deciding my life for me!" Brandon's voice rang out louder than intended. The dog whined, and Jordan bent down to soothe her.

"I'm not a child, and my personal life isn't an open topic of discussion for you to pass judgment on." He glanced over at Tash, his face a mask of frozen politeness, then back at Luke. His anger escalated at the discomfort and pain Tash most likely was going through. "You barely know me anymore, Luke. I'm not the little kid you left behind. You have no right to dictate my life."

Brandon regretted his harsh words as Luke visibly flinched. The thought that he'd caused his brother pain stripped him raw, but even if he hurt Luke, Brandon owed it to Tash and the tenuous bonds of their relationship to assert himself.

Neither one seemed willing to back down. A gentle hand touched his arm.

"Brandon, sweetheart, come with me for a moment. Let's give Lucas a chance to talk to Jordan and cool down."

He looked down into Esther's kind eyes. There was a hint of steely determination behind the sweet facade. Before he knew what was happening, he found himself being led to a cozy room with comfortable furniture, beautiful paintings on the wall, and a lovely faded floral rug covering much of the shining wood floor.

"Please, sit down." Esther indicated an overstuffed club chair for him to sit in, while she perched on the edge of a straight-backed chair.

He took his seat, a bit nervous. Although Ash and Luke both had a relationship with this woman, he knew very little about her. Out of deference to her age, he'd listen to her but didn't plan on taking her advice. She knew nothing about him.

"Now I know you're thinking, 'What's this old lady want? She doesn't know me well enough to tell me what to do.' And you're right. But I wasn't planning on telling you what to do."

Brandon allowed a little smile to escape. "You weren't?"

"No. I want to tell you instead about your brothers and what fine young men they are. I love Asher as if he were my own child. That man may think my grandson saved him, but I'll tell you he's responsible for bringing the joy back into this house we'd been missing for many years, ever since my dear Max and Audrey died."

"Was that your son?" How sad. He hadn't known her only child had died.

"Yes. And when they died, the children fell apart. I didn't know how to help them. Rachel came out of her wild phase quickly, but Drew..." She shook her head and blew her nose with a handkerchief she'd pulled from her apron pocket. "He retreated into a shell, following his friends around like a lost puppy. It wasn't until Asher appeared that he came alive again."

"I'm glad they found each other. I've never seen Ash happy like this, even when we were young."

"Love will do that to a person. Loving the right person. Now Lucas, he wasn't willing to admit he loved Jordan. And Jordan had suffered such a terrible loss and was in such a black place." Her eyes glimmered wet with unshed tears. "To this day, I say a prayer for our poor sweet Keith every week. I know Lucas rescued Jordan from his terrible tragedy and fell in love with him. I truly despaired that Jordan would ever fall in love again, but he did, and thank God their love is strong and healthy."

Brandon shifted in his chair. "Esther, I hope you don't think I'm rude, but what does this have to do with me?"

"Because against all the odds, your brothers found love. It took many tears and some hurt feelings until the four of them worked it all out. But they never gave up or listened to other people tell them what they should or shouldn't do."

"I see. Thank you for seeing it my way."

"I'm not saying that at all." It was her turn to smile. "It's not my business if you and Sebastian have feelings for one another, but what is my business is your relationship with your brothers. Those boys mean everything to me, all of them. From when I first met Asher, all he spoke about was finding you and Lucas. Lucas too has suffered without you."

Tears prickled behind Brandon's eyes. *Shit.* He'd never cried so much in all his life. Wasn't he supposed to be happy now? He blinked and finally swiped at his eyes with the back of his hand. "I missed them too. So much you have no idea."

"I do, sweetheart; believe me, I do. For every night you missed them, they were missing you as well. You may have taken steps toward each other, but the journey isn't over yet for any of you. The three of you have a special bond and will need one another to lean on and hold as you travel through life."

"But I care for Tash. And Luke doesn't have the right to tell me not to see him."

"Give him the pleasure of being your big brother. Don't dismiss his concerns outright, even if you have no intention of following them."

"You're telling me to humor him."

"I'm suggesting you show him by your maturity that you have made the correct choice. Spend time with Lucas and let him see you aren't the boy he once knew you as, but a strong man who knows what he wants." She tucked the handkerchief back into her pocket.

The front door opened, letting a cool draft of air into the house. From the kitchen, Brandon heard the dog bark and her nails scrabbling on the wood floor as she ran to the front of the house.

Esther's eyes lit up. "That must be Rachel and Michael. Come." She stood and held her hand out.

Without a second thought, he took it and went with her to greet the newcomers. As expected, they were all crowded in the kitchen, even though the dining room was set for dinner. Esther let go of his hand and went to greet Mike and Rachel, and Brandon saw Luke still sitting at the table, stroking the dog's head.

"Mind if I sit down?"

"Feel free."

He sat in the chair Jordan had occupied before. The dog pushed her muzzle into his lap, and he chuckled at her attempt for attention. "She's sweet."

"Sasha's a good dog, aren't you, girl?" Luke smoothed his hand down her back. Her stubby tail wagged furiously.

Brandon took a deep breath. "I'm sorry I yelled at you. It was wrong of me to jump down your throat when I know you're concerned about me."

Luke opened his mouth, but Brandon put up his hand. "Can I finish?" At Luke's nod, he continued. "I'm twenty-five years old. I'm old enough to hold my job, vote, fight in the war. I'm also old enough to decide who to love. And while I always want us to like our respective choices, it's not a requirement. I do expect you to give it a chance."

Luke remained silent. Brandon glanced over his shoulder and found Ash's gaze on them. His brother nodded and gave him a thumbs-up sign, but Brandon desperately wanted Luke's approval as well.

"I was reminded earlier," Luke began, "of how destructive Jordan's disapproval of Ash was to him and Drew and how it almost caused the end of their thirty-year friendship."

Brandon held his breath. Tash stood behind him,

not touching but close enough for Brandon to feel his presence. "That's sad."

Luke agreed. "It would've been sadder had they allowed it to happen. They didn't, and now everyone gets along. I can't help but feel protective of you. Growing up, you were always my first concern. It's hard to break a habit, but I'm going to try." His gaze traveled between Tash and Brandon. "I'm not going to pass judgment. I only want you to be happy. If Tash makes you happy"—Luke shrugged—"I hope it lasts forever."

Brandon stuck out his hand. "So, we're good?" Luke took it and then pulled him close.

"To hell with a handshake." They hugged, and Brandon closed his eyes. A home, his family, and love. It all seemed possible now.

Chapter Seventeen

A T TEN THIRTY the next morning, Tash pushed open the doors to the Center and was greeted by an almost full house. A local librarian had come over to read to the young children in the back, and he could see them all sitting on the floor in a semicircle around her, enthralled as she read from the first Harry Potter book.

The computer section was almost at capacity; Tash recognized several high school and middle school students, their books piled high next to them on the desk. Midterms and tests would be coming soon. Over in the arts-and-crafts area, he had to smile at the profusion of glitter and pipe cleaners that littered the tables as the volunteers helped the little ones make pictures they'd take home later for their parents.

"Dr. Tash."

He turned at the sound of his name and saw Johnny standing at the entrance. An uncertain smile came and went from his face.

"Johnny, great. I'm glad you're here."

The young man looked around. "This place looks pretty awesome." With longing, he gazed at the computers. "Those machines are pretty sweet."

"Do you like computers?"

Johnny's gaze dropped to the floor. "Yeah, I'd love to learn about them, but I dunno…" His voice trailed off as he kicked the floor with his sneaker.

He wouldn't let this kid miss out on his dreams. "I can find you someone who can help you learn the system." After scanning the room, he found who he was looking for.

"Troy." He waved at the big man standing in the doorway of the office. "Can you come here a sec?"

Johnny glanced at Tash as Troy made his way to the front. Tash supposed Johnny might be as intimidated by Troy as Tash was during their first meeting. Troy was a six-four wall of muscle who'd seen and lived the ugly side of the streets of New York. Tash was only thankful Troy hadn't been killed before deciding to turn his life around. The man possessed a quick mind, and Jordan had sung his praises over his handling of the gun buy-back program.

"Dr. Tash." They exchanged a handshake. "What's up?" The man assessed Johnny with his piercing brown eyes. "Who's the kid?"

"Johnny's here as part of his community service by order of the court," explained Tash. "He's been working at the Clinic and taking online high school classes to try and graduate on time." The defeated slump of Johnny's shoulders puzzled him. "What's wrong, Johnny?"

Johnny hesitated, chewing on his lip. "I don't wanna always be known as the kid who sold drugs to Dr. Jordan. I want...shit, I don't know what I want." He tucked his hair behind his ears.

"I know." Troy draped a heavy arm over Johnny. "You wanna matter and show them you're better than some street kid. But you gotta prove it. Show 'em they was wrong about you. And you do that by what you're doing right here, helping with the kids and goin' to school."

A myriad of emotions passed over Johnny's face: fear, determination, and cautious optimism. "I like my classes." He directed his conversation to the floor, perhaps out of embarrassment. Tash caught Troy's quick nod of approval. "I kinda want to learn about computers and stuff, but I don't know." He shrugged.

"Why don't you come help me with something?" Troy led Johnny toward the back. "I need someone to enter information about the guns we collected from Wednesday night's Grins Not Guns drive. I can teach you about using an Excel spreadsheet."

Watching the young man's face light up, Tash prayed Johnny would never be brought back into the horrors of living on the street and dealing drugs, that this program would be the refuge he needed to turn his life around. He made a mental note to tell Jordan and thank him once again for pushing everyone involved to get Johnny the help he needed. As Troy and Johnny continued walking, their conversation grew more animated. A warm feeling of achievement enveloped Tash.

"Hi."

Tash spun around to face Brandon. At the sight of his lover, a different kind of warmth stole through him. His libido, once stalled, now leaped into overdrive every time he set eyes on Brandon. Tash wondered if he'd ever get tired of seeing Brandon's long, rangy body in that battered leather jacket, the hank of soft honey-colored hair perpetually hanging in his eyes. He doubted it.

"Hi."

Brandon leaned forward and brushed their lips together. It surprised Tash how uninhibited Brandon was about his sexuality, but he put it down to their age difference. Most men his age had grown up with little or no tolerance for public displays of affection between gay couples. Brandon's generation was more liberal and accepting.

"I missed being with you last night." Brandon pushed the hair out of his eyes. "I wish you would've stayed."

"No way am I staying over with you in Esther's house. I don't care if you have a whole separate apartment; it would be too weird. Besides"—he winked—"you're lucky you have a boyfriend who owns his own home so you can sleep over anytime you want. Now that Esther has Louisa, you don't need to be as concerned if you come home late."

Brandon took off his jacket and draped it over a

chair. "Yeah. She's great; they both are. When I came upstairs this morning, there were all these bagels and eggs and stuff." He unzipped his backpack. "Here, Esther made me bring you something." He handed over a paper bag.

Tash's mouth watered as he opened the bag. "Oh damn." Inside were two bagels with cream cheese and lox, a chocolate-chip muffin, and two pieces of apple strudel. "This is amazing."

"One of those pieces of strudel is for me."

"The hell it is." Tash's voice came out garbled, his mouth full of bagel. "You'll have to pry it out of my hands."

To his surprise, Brandon grabbed him around the waist. "I like a challenge."

He stuffed another bite of bagel in his mouth. "Bite me. You aren't getting any of my food, no matter how adorable you are." He pretended outrage at Brandon's attempt to steal his food, using it as an excuse to grab Brandon around his neck and yank him closer.

"Tash?"

He peered over Brandon's shoulder to see Valerie standing inside the doorway, a confused look on her face. "Val." He grinned at her and murmured to Brandon as he let him go. "It's my sister; come meet her."

Brandon's hand dropped from Tash's waist. "Oh." The amusement fled from his eyes. "Um, sure." He swallowed hard, uncertainty apparent in the nervousness of his twisting fingers.

He took Brandon's hand and approached Valerie. By her raised eyebrows, he knew she didn't miss his and Brandon's entwined hands. After kissing her cheek, he drew Brandon, who remained half-hidden behind him, to his side. "I'm so glad you came this morning. There's someone I want you to meet."

Val remained silent, but Tash didn't miss her cool assessment of Brandon. "This is Brandon Gilbert. The Brandon who is Luke and Ash's brother."

That got him the reaction he expected. Her big brown eyes widened with shock. "Are you serious? Really?" The beautiful smile he loved bloomed across her face. "Oh my God, when did this happen?"

"It's only been a month since he burst into our lives like a whirlwind, yet now it's as though he's been here forever." He caught Brandon's eye and gave him an affectionate glance. "He's living at Esther's."

Val folded her arms and shot him a pointed look. "Anything else you'd like to tell me?"

Here goes nothing.

"Brandon and I are dating." He reached behind him, and Brandon grabbed hold of his hand, giving it a squeeze.

Surprise flared in her eyes, but she said nothing, her gaze shifting back to Brandon, now raking him with a critical eye. Of one thing Tash was certain: Val would speak her mind and tell him exactly what she thought of him dating Brandon.

"Well, this is quite the shock. I mean, it's been five years since you've dated anyone, and now in a month, you're with Brandon. I assume it's exclusive?"

"Of course it is; what kind of question is that?" he snapped at her.

"A valid one," she shot back. "I mean, I'm sure you've noticed how much younger he is than you, Tash. Most guys his age aren't into dating thirty-nine-year-old men."

Before he swallowed his anger and answered her back, Brandon jumped in. "Valerie, I'm really looking forward to getting to know you better. You're all Tash talks about. And once we do, I guarantee you'll understand when I say I'm not your average twenty-five-year-old guy looking for the next party. I'm in this for the long haul."

"You're only twenty-five?" A shaky laugh escaped her. "Jesus, he's even younger than me." She unzipped her jacket and hung it on the coatrack. "Um, okay. This will take some getting used to on my part." She stood before the two of them fiddling with the strap of her handbag. "You know I only want happiness for you. And if he makes you happy…"

Tash held her gaze, appealing to her loving nature with his eyes. He desperately wanted her approval. Valerie was the one who'd sat up nights with him after Danny's death…when Tash's world rose up so bleak and dark he never dreamed he'd be able to climb out of that void of despair. She'd stayed with him, held him as he cried, and helped him find, then mend the pieces of his shattered life.

"He makes me happy, and somehow, I make him

happy too, though I pushed him away at first."

"Your brother is persistent, but I refused to listen. 'No' isn't a word I respond well to." Still holding Tash's hand, Brandon gave it a firm squeeze.

From the skeptical look in Valerie's eyes, Tash could see she remained unconvinced. "You say you're in it for the long haul. I wonder if you understand exactly what that means. I see you care for my brother. That's all I can hope for." Her smile was sweetly deceptive. "Of course, if you break his heart, I'll come after you with all the wrath of the harpies."

Tash knew how violently overprotective she could be. Brandon swallowed hard. "I only want to make him happy."

"Good. Then we both want the same thing."

"The two of you are standing here discussing me as if I'm a marble statue. This relationship isn't one-sided, you know. I have Luke and Ash watching me like hawks to make sure I don't hurt Brandon as well." He turned to Brandon. "Valerie works for Luke. She's his personal assistant."

"One big happy family," Brandon quipped.

"We are. And I can't imagine how happy Luke is to have you back." Val's caring nature kicked in then. "Where were you for all those years? I know they've been looking forever for you." Her eyes grew misty. "I can't even imagine how you all felt when you first saw each other. It's like a movie. Come get a cup of coffee with me and tell me a little about yourself." She hooked her arm in Brandon's and pulled him away to the back.

Seeing his sister and Brandon chatting together completed a happiness circle that had once seemed impossible. It had nothing to do with the physical, although Brandon had ignited a sexual hunger Tash hadn't known he possessed. It was the joy of togetherness—having someone to share the mundane with, and having it made special simply because it was the two of them. It flowed through him now, unchecked and uninhibited, like the shower of rain from a summer storm.

It didn't hit him like a thunderclap or make him want to shout to the sky. Perhaps age brought wisdom, or maybe it was the cautious knowledge of how easily love and devotion could fade, leaving only the outline of a memory. He held his love for Brandon close, unwilling to share with anyone yet, even Brandon. This had never happened before to him, this instant attraction, this quick journey to love. It startled Tash, forcing him to question himself.

Yet hearing his sister and his lover share a laugh, he knew what was real and began to rebuild the trust in himself to believe what he knew in his heart. It *was* love he felt for Brandon, not lust. It didn't matter what other people thought. He knew what was true. As if he sensed Tash's scrutiny, Brandon caught his eye and winked, giving him a slow smile that set his blood on fire. Tash couldn't wait for tonight when he would hold Brandon in his arms and make love to him.

The front door opened, and Luke and Jordan, along with Ash and Drew, walked in. They hung up their coats and grabbed coffee and headed to the back to greet Valerie and Brandon. With the addition of their presence, the Center hummed with activity. Not for the first time, Tash couldn't help but wonder where he'd be without this group of people. They'd managed to invade his life, bringing with them a happiness he'd never anticipated. His attention gravitated to Brandon, now engaged in a lively discussion about the Yankees with Drew and Luke.

He joined the group, and they headed to the back where the conference room was located. After they were seated around the long table, to his surprise, Brandon was the first to speak.

"I have two students from my school coming today around noon. They're the ones I mentioned before. I wanted them to have a safe environment where they can study and get all the help they need. My plan is to work with them today."

"I have Johnny working with Troy on the gun buy-back program." Tash addressed both Jordan and Drew. "He showed up early and indicated he wanted to learn about computers, and I know Troy is good with them."

Jordan nodded his approval. "Troy is a great choice to work with Johnny. He's been where that kid was and is proof how far someone can go with hard work and dedication."

"These kids need people to have faith in them and show that there is hope." Drew's brows knit together. "I wonder if Troy might want to be the office manager at the Clinic now that Marly and Steve are going to be busy with college starting next September. I know they won't be able to put in as many hours because of schoolwork."

"That's a great idea," said Luke. "I know he's close to finding housing, and this might tip it over the edge for him to get out of the shelter."

Ash finished his coffee. "I have work for him at the office or for anyone else at the shelter who needs a job and can use a computer. I'm certain there are people who once had well-paying jobs who've fallen on hard times."

"I know Wanda said there were several people who recently showed up at the shelter for a meal who used to work at smaller law firms and even Wall Street." Tash made some notes on a pad. "Let's ask her when she shows up, and you can get their info from her."

Jordan's phone rang. "It's Jerry; I'll only be a minute." He stood and went outside.

"They're still very close, aren't they?" Tash addressed Luke.

"Yeah. Jerry and Marie always thought of Jordan and Keith as their sons, since they never had any kids. Now they've taken me in, and we have dinner there once a week. They're great people and love Jordan."

Jordan returned, a look of anticipation on his face. "Jerry's coming right over. He said he had some news on that Donovan guy." He rejoined Luke at the table. "Maybe this is the break they've been waiting for to get that bastard off the streets."

Excited talk rose in the room, but Tash noticed

Brandon said nothing and stared down at the table. He left his seat to sit in the empty chair next to his lover.

"You got so quiet all of a sudden." When he received no answer, he put a hand on Brandon's arm, and the man nearly jumped out of his seat. "Are you all right? What's wrong?"

Brandon looked sick; his face was pale, and sweat dampened his skin. If Tash didn't know any better, he'd say he was scared to death. "Ahh, I need to use the restroom. I'll be right back." Without another word, he pushed away from the table and bolted from the room.

"What's the matter with him?" asked Ash. "He ran out of here like the hounds of hell were at his heels."

"Not a clue. Said he had to use the bathroom. Maybe too much of Esther's good food."

Ash threw his head back and laughed. "Don't ever let her hear you say that."

They joked about it until Brandon returned after several minutes, looking slightly better. At least his color had returned to normal. Tash couldn't figure out why Brandon had gone from happy and relaxed to withdrawn and silent in a heartbeat. They left the conference room and split off; Jordan and Luke went to Troy and Johnny to see how the computer instruction was working out, while Ash and Drew picked out books and gathered some of the children around to read to them.

"Feeling better? Is there anything I can do to help?" Tash grasped Brandon's elbow, holding him back.

With an abashed look, Brandon shook his head.

"No, thanks. I didn't feel well, and it came over me suddenly." A crooked smile crossed his face. "There's Dwayne and Wilson." He left Tash to greet them.

Two boys stood at the door, wearing identical faces of avid curiosity. A tall woman stood behind them, her gaze scanning the room. Recognition dawned in her eyes as Brandon approached.

"Mr. Gilbert, I'm glad to see you. I didn't want to simply drop the boys off and leave without seeing someone I knew first."

Tash watched as Brandon switched into confident-teacher mode, making it hard to believe only moments before he'd been a nervous wreck.

"Mrs. Archer, I'm so glad you came so you can see the wonderful work the Center is accomplishing." He walked her around the Center, pointing out the varied activities and, along the way, introducing her to many of the people working, including his brothers, Drew, and Jordan. By the time they got to him, Tash heard her complimenting their achievements.

"This is exactly what young people need these days to keep off the streets and in school. Dwayne's father and I try so hard, and I know Wilson's mother does as well, doubly hard since she's now a widow."

"We hope to help as many children and young adults as we possibly can." Tash extended his hand. "I'm Dr. Weber. I run the mentoring program that we hope your son and his friend will be a part of."

She took his hand in her firm grasp, her eyes assessing him with a thorough glance. "Nice to meet you.

What will they be doing?"

The two boys had already found two empty computer stations and had logged on. They were both in the process of pulling notebooks and textbooks out of their backpacks.

"Right now, they're doing their homework. We hope they'll be able to study subjects they may not have the time or resources to at home. Plus, they can read to the younger children and maybe help them with their homework." He gave her a friendly smile. "There's no shortage of things to keep them busy."

"Good." She smiled with approval. "It sounds wonderful. I have to go to work, but I'll be back around five to pick them up. Is that okay?"

"Perfect," said Brandon. "Have a good day, and don't worry about them at all."

She left, and he and Brandon stood for a moment, watching the boys at the computers. A stocky older man entered the Center and looked around.

"Jerry." Tash waved him over. "Come over; I'd like you to meet someone."

The detective approached, and Tash watched Brandon withdraw into himself.

"Hello, Tash. Good to see you again. I presume Jordan and Luke are here."

"Yes, they're in the back looking over the gun buy-back statistics with Troy."

"It's working out much better than we could've hoped for. Last Wednesday was our best yet, with over one hundred seventy-five weapons turned in." Jerry smiled with frank approval. He waited expectantly, Tash knew, to be introduced.

"That's great. Jerry, this is Brandon, Luke and Ash's brother. It turns out he's been in the city all along and works as a teacher."

The two men shook hands, and then Brandon quickly excused himself, joining Dwayne and Wilson at the computers.

Jerry stared at Brandon's retreating back. "I'm going to talk to Jordan about what we learned in the Donovan case."

"I'll go get the others. I know they'll be interested." Tash entered the library and waited for Ash to finish reading to the children. He motioned to him and Drew.

"Jerry is here to talk about the Donovan case."

As they walked to the back room, Tash couldn't shake the feeling that something wasn't right, and it all had to do with Brandon.

Chapter Eighteen

I T WAS BOUND to happen sooner rather than later. Brandon had heard how Jordan was beaten up as a warning not to open the Center and knew he'd have to meet the detective who was working on the case. The reality of it was worse than he'd imagined as Jerry was a seasoned professional, and no doubt he saw right through Brandon's weak attempt to escape any questions about himself. Of course, the fear clawing at Brandon's chest, willing him to run, wasn't helping any. He forced himself to remain calm and somehow held his composure together.

After helping Dwayne and Wilson work through a tricky math problem, Brandon joined the group in the back room, where Jerry was explaining what the police had learned about that Donovan person. Brandon slid into a seat next to Luke. Jerry threw him a quick glance but continued to speak.

"We know Donovan was originally from the Pennsylvania area with ties to Philly and Boston, as well as New York. He would get the guns from down South, then have them transported up the I-95 corridor, making stops in DC, Baltimore, and Philly before heading up to New York and Boston." He consulted his notes. "There was never a shortage of people to do his dirty work, whether it was delivering guns or the drugs he happened to be selling. Most often he used drifters in those cities to prevent the police from catching him in a full-scale operation. But we finally got lucky."

"How's that? It would seem impossible if he never had any connection to the people who worked for him." Jordan braced his arms on the table, his chin in his hands. "It's so damn frustrating."

"One of our undercover detectives heard a waitress talking at a bar in the Philly area. She mentioned Donovan had been in the night before, and she's his regular girl when he comes around that way. Seems he's been cheating on her and she's pissed at him." Jerry grinned. "Never underestimate the fury of a scorned woman. She was busy spilling her guts to anyone who'd listen about not only what a lousy lay he is, but what he's going to do when he comes up to New York in a few days."

As the others peppered Jerry with questions, Brandon remained silent, his mind working furiously. When he was younger, he'd done everything short of selling himself to make money, without thinking of the consequences or repercussions to anyone else. It was altogether possible that, when he was living on the streets in Philly all those years ago, he had come across these people and done some work for them, but if he was honest with himself, he couldn't remember. To speak up would add nothing to the investigation, and Jerry might start asking more questions about why he was homeless to begin with.

"Brandon, you lived in Pennsylvania. Did you ever spend any time in Philadelphia after you left home?"

All eyes focused on him at Jerry's question. He slanted a quick look at the detective before gulping down the nerves that were strangling him. "Um, yeah, for a little while. But it was a long time ago. Over seven years."

Jerry studied him, his face a blank slate, revealing nothing. "You were homeless?" His voice was gentle.

No words were necessary as Brandon simply nodded.

"Didn't you try and find your brothers?" Jerry prodded.

Brandon supposed he'd heard the story of their childhood from Luke. "I, um, looked for Luke, but he'd changed his name."

"It's fine, Jerry," said Ash, cutting in. "Brandon and Luke and I have worked it all out."

Brandon threw his brother a grateful look. Neither of them wanted to revisit this painful topic. Jerry, however, wasn't a detective for nothing and continued to ask questions.

"I'm not trying to pry into anything personal. I'm curious as to why you left home and lived on the streets."

"Our foster father was a terrible man, Jerry." Luke scrubbed his face with his hand. "You know my story. Brandon has his own stories, but I don't think he needs to go through them again when it serves no purpose to this investigation."

Like they had when he was a child, his brothers stepped up to protect him. And even though he'd told them he was an adult now and didn't need them to shield him from the horrors of the world, it felt good to have them by his side.

"Brandon's a teacher now and helping us with the mentoring program. He's living at Esther's and is a great role model for the kids." Tash squeezed his arm. "The past is the past, and we don't need to revisit it."

Jerry said nothing, merely flipped his notebook shut. "From the information we received, we expect to make some arrests in the next week or so, when Donovan and his crew arrive in the city. I'll make sure to keep you posted. Before I leave, I want to see Johnny." Shooting Brandon a troubled look, he said his good-byes and left with Drew and Jordan.

A palpable silence descended over the table after Jerry left. Brandon knew Ash and Luke remained curious about the real reason he'd left home, but were trying to respect his privacy. In truth, he was a fucking coward to the core. The comforting presence of Tash fed the excuses he made to himself. He was doing it for all of them, protecting them, the way they did him. He couldn't lose them now.

"I should get back to Dwayne and Wilson." He

stood, and Tash rose with him.

"I need to talk to Valerie; I'll walk out with you."

The two of them walked out to the main room, but Tash stopped him before he walked to the two boys. "I know there's something you aren't telling me and your brothers."

Brandon's stomach clenched. He stared wide-eyed at Tash, unable to speak. Apparently, his silence revealed more than any words he might have spoken.

"I understand how much of an upheaval your life has been in this past month. But if you're keeping something from them, never mind me, you need to reconsider. Those men would give up their lives for you; they'd do anything to help."

Each spoken word jabbed Brandon, like a knife in his chest. He wanted to talk, but he couldn't. As a psychiatrist, Tash must've been used to deception, because he continued, relentless in his attempt to get Brandon to speak.

"Whatever happened, it's eating you up inside. Something's not right when every time your life back in Pennsylvania is mentioned, you either clam up or freak out. To me, that's a sign. And a lack of trust in me and in us as a couple. We should be able to tell each other everything." When Brandon didn't say anything, Tash sighed. "I need to see Val." He began to walk away. With each step, Brandon could see his future trailing away before him like a skein of wool, unraveling his heart.

"Tash?" Brandon's pulse pounded in his ears. He

was unsure if Tash would even stop to listen to him now. When he halted in midstride, Brandon hurried to catch up to where he stood before Tash changed his mind and walked away.

There came a point in life when choices had to be made and the consequences be damned. As a child, he'd lived his whole life with uncertainty, never knowing who his parents were or why they'd given him away. In his subconscious, he'd always believed it was something he'd done, that if he'd been a better boy, they might have loved him.

When Ash left, Brandon thought if he hadn't been such a baby, Ash would've stayed. He remembered crying to Luke, saying he was sorry. Luke had shushed him and said only that it wasn't his fault. Ash would be back. But he never returned.

That last night during the fight with Munson, Luke had screamed at him to get out, once again protecting him. Brandon could do little more than agree to be hustled out of the house, looking back over his shoulder as Luke and Munson came to blows. Munson told him for years afterward that if Luke had wanted to find him, he could've.

When he'd looked for Luke, his dream of seeing his brother again died a bit with each dead end he ran up against. He'd never given Ash the chance, figuring Ash had reached the height of such great achievement in his life, he'd want nothing to do with Brandon. Now, with Tash, Brandon's own dreams and successes seemed attainable. He loved Tash and wanted to spend the rest of his life with him, but couldn't do it without first opening his life up for inspection and putting himself in the spotlight.

"Can we talk tonight? I can make dinner at your house." No more lies, no subterfuge or ducking any questions that might be asked. It was time to act like the grown man he insisted he was. The resigned hesitancy in Tash's eyes distressed him; having seen those beautiful eyes light up with passion, Brandon never wanted to be the cause of Tash's pain. "Please. I need to tell you things. But not here."

After a measured look, Tash gave a shrug. "Fine. Were you planning on spending the day here?"

"Yes. I want to work with the boys and get them started on some projects. I'm hoping to prepare them for the specialized high school exams they'll be taking in the next year or two."

"Good. So we can leave after Dwayne's mother picks them up." Tash didn't smile or give him any indication what he was thinking. Merely a nod and then he walked away to where Johnny, Troy, and several of the others were congregated.

For the rest of the afternoon, as he helped the two boys, Brandon rehearsed what he would say in his mind, but it always ended up badly.

How could he tell Tash he was a murderer?

Tash decided to leave a little earlier with Valerie,

and Brandon wanted to go to the supermarket to pick up some things to make the dinner special. Since Drew had already said he and Ash were going back to Brooklyn to have dinner with Mike and Rachel that night, Brandon asked if they wouldn't mind taking him to the supermarket, then dropping him off at Tash's carriage house since it was along their way.

"Brandon, what's wrong?" Drew hefted one of the grocery bags into the trunk of the car. He slammed the hatch down. "You've barely said a word since we left the Center."

"Hmm? Oh, nothing. I'm wondering if I got everything." The lie slipped so easily through his lips it should've made him feel guilty, but it didn't.

The skeptical look on Drew's face was proof he hadn't fooled him. Drew was one of the most perceptive men he'd ever met. Although Ash was the physically stronger of the two, Brandon had no doubt it was Drew's inner strength their relationship was built upon. He envied the quiet confidence and trust Drew possessed when it came to his feelings for Ash. Brandon could tell their love ran bone-deep, and wanted that for himself and Tash.

The ride to Brooklyn was uneventful, with Drew giving some insight into Mike and Rachel's wedding plans. They were going to be married at Esther's in the springtime to take advantage of her flower-filled back garden.

"I hear Mike could care less as long as he doesn't have to wear a tux." Ash switched lanes on the

Brooklyn Bridge and exited by Cadman Plaza Park. The little restaurants in Brooklyn Heights were beginning to fill up for the evening, and people crowded the streets, deciding where to have dinner.

Drew chuckled. "Can't say I blame him; although you look pretty handsome all dressed up, I have to say." He reached over and squeezed Ash's thigh.

"A wedding is for the bride, period. Except if we ever got married. Then I'd want to see you dressed up too. You're pretty damn hot in your tux, yourself."

The conversation piqued Brandon's curiosity. "Do you guys plan on getting married?"

Ash met his eyes in the rearview mirror and smiled. "No one's asked me yet."

Drew remained silent, a serene look on his face, and Brandon dropped the subject. They pulled up in front of Tash's carriage house, and Brandon hopped out of the car and collected his bags from the trunk.

"Thanks for the ride, guys. See you tomorrow at Esther's."

They drove off, and Brandon steeled himself with a deep breath.

Here goes everything or nothing.

Tash opened the door before Brandon needed to set the bags down on the stoop to knock. His expression remained the same as when Brandon had left the Center earlier—guarded and withdrawn.

"Come on in." He held the door open, and Brandon entered the carriage house. The two cats appeared immediately to twine themselves around his ankles.

After setting the bags down, he knelt to pet them. From his crouched position, he gazed upward at Tash. "I'll start dinner in a little while, but I figured you'd like to talk first, right?"

At Tash's nod, Brandon stood and brushed off his pants. "Let's sit down, okay?" His heart pounded as he walked into the living room. When he sat on the sofa, Cleo jumped in his lap, circled twice, and lay down, purring like a lawn mower. To control the trembling of his fingers, he kept them on the cat's body, stroking her neck and giving little scratches to her chin.

"You know I never meant to drag you into my life. In fact, I ran away from you, if you recall. You pushed me to face my fear and made me open myself up to so much more than I ever thought possible."

Tash said nothing, the light glinting off his eyeglasses.

"But unlike every other person I've met before, I couldn't stop thinking about you and wondering what it would be like to be with you. Now..." Brandon's nerves choked him. "The truth is I haven't been honest or fair with you. You need to know everything to decide whether or not you still want to be with me."

"Don't worry about my reaction. Whatever it is, it's eating you up alive. The worst part is the anticipation of what you think my reaction will be."

Not the worst part by far. Incarceration would be the worst; to be separated from his family and Tash now that he'd found them was inconceivable. But then again, so was looking over his shoulder for the rest of his life, loving Tash and attempting to create a life with him only to worry every second of the day whether it would all be torn away in an instant.

"I'd only graduated high school the week before. The night before I ran away, my foster father was drunk and in one of his usual ugly moods. He often stopped off after work at the bar near the local sheriff's office where he worked and had a few beers before coming home." Brandon stroked Cleo under the chin for a few moments, smoothing her plush, velvety coat. She rubbed her head against his hand and swished her tail back and forth.

"My foster mother hadn't been feeling well, and dinner wasn't ready. That's all he needed to begin the nightly abuse."

"Where were you when all this was happening?" Tash pushed his glasses up on his head and rubbed his eyes, a grim expression etched in hard lines on his face.

"In my room. But when I heard the yelling, I crept down the stairs to see what was happening. Then I watched him hit her and knock her down." It played before his eyes. "He stood over her and laughed. I must've made a sound because he turned around and found me standing on the stairs. I ran out of the house, but he caught up to me at the shed in the back and pinned me against the door."

"What you gonna do, sonny boy?" The stale, beer-laced breath of his foster father blasted over his face, gagging Brandon until he wanted to retch. "No one's gonna believe you, and she ain't gonna say nuthin' if she knows what's

good for her."

The thought of this animal hitting his foster mother again enraged Brandon. "Leave her alone. You're a big fucking bully. You could kill her."

Munson sneered in his face. "Who'd care? Stay out of it unless you want the same." He hitched his pants up and spat on the ground. "She best have gotten herself up off that floor or she won't be able to get up again." He spat again, then went to hit Brandon across the face.

"It was as if something snapped inside me," whispered Brandon, the horror of that night tangible, as if he could reach out and touch Munson or smell his beery, stale breath against his face. "I picked up a loose brick sitting on the windowsill of the shed and hit him over the head with it."

Tash slid next to him, evicting an outraged Cleo from Brandon's lap, and draped his arm around Brandon's shoulders. "Talk it out. Let it go."

"So much blood. There was so much blood, and he fell to the ground." Brandon gulped, tears trickling down his cheeks. "I didn't mean to kill him." He started sobbing, whether from relief at finally telling his story or fear over what would happen next. "I just wanted him to never hit her again. Or me."

"Of course you didn't." Tash gathered Brandon to his chest and soothed him. "So he died and you ran away?"

After gulping down some air, Brandon continued. "I left him lying on the ground. I sneaked back in the house and gathered some clothes. My foster mother was crying in the kitchen as she made dinner." Tash smoothed his hair as Brandon's head lay on his chest. "I was so scared, Tash. I ran out the back door and never went back. I shouldn't have left her but I was too scared at what I'd done to think straight."

They sat for a few minutes. The only sound to be heard was the hush of the occasional car passing by outside. Then Tash sighed and spoke, but there was no condemnation or censure in his voice. "Are you sure he's dead?"

Brandon nodded against the sturdy wall of Tash's chest. Within the circle of Tash's arms, he'd found safety and comfort, but most of all peace. He'd never had someone take him in their arms and hold him until the hurt and pain disappeared.

"Yeah. After I ran, I checked the newspapers a few days later, and there was a small article about Paul Munson being found dead." He pulled away from Tash's arms. "I've spent the last seven and a half years in limbo, looking over my shoulder, waiting for the police to find me and arrest me. I did whatever I could to hide myself."

"By calling yourself Randy? And not contacting Ash because you thought he wouldn't want you?" Tash's gentle fingers combed through his hair in a languid slide. "But now you know how much Ash loves you. He'll take your case and defend you to the death." With a gentle kiss to Brandon's brow, Tash smiled down at him. "You weren't even eighteen, sweetheart. It was an accident, self-defense. I'm sure he can get you off."

Brandon had never thought of asking Ash to be his lawyer. His only thought had been to hide what he'd done and live outside the concrete lines of society. "Will you come with me when I talk to him?" He added in haste, "I mean, you don't have to; I can do it myself." He struggled to sit up and away from Tash. It would be a challenge for him, but he was strong enough.

Instead, Tash held him firm, his muscled arms remaining tight around Brandon's body. "Do you think after everything, I'd walk away from you? Make you handle this on your own?"

"Ash will help me," Brandon replied weakly, trying hard to maintain a semblance of strength. "You're right. I know he will."

With surprising strength, Tash crushed him closer, his lips tasting the curve of Brandon's neck. "But he won't be there to hold you at night and keep you warm like I can. He won't whisper to you that everything will be all right, which I will." Sweet kisses trailed along Brandon's throat, and he moaned, desire running through his body, rich and heavy like a fine, full-bodied wine.

Tash's mouth hovered over his as their eyes locked. "He won't love you like I do."

Chapter Nineteen

T O SAY HE was shocked by Brandon's confession was an understatement. But this was no time to dwell upon it, not when Brandon's mouth opened beneath his, needy, wet, and searching, and his hard body molded itself with Tash's. As their breaths merged and their teeth clashed against one another, they tore at each other's clothes and soon lay naked and entwined on the fluffy rug. Brandon straddled him, his heavy cock warm against Tash's thigh, a solemn look on his face.

"You still want me?"

"I never stopped." Tash hated hearing the anxious uncertainty in Brandon's voice. "I never could." He slid his hand behind Brandon's neck and pulled him in for another deep, searching kiss, leaving both of them breathless and shaking. The taut muscles of Brandon's shoulders rippled under Tash's hands.

"Do you really think—" Brandon began to speak, but Tash cut him off with another dizzying kiss.

"No more thinking for tonight. You've been caught

up in so much pain and fear your entire life, more than anyone should ever have to live through." Tash rolled onto his side, holding Brandon in his arms. "When was the last time you let go and lived in the moment, taking enjoyment only for yourself?"

"I haven't been happy since I was a child. Not till I met you."

Tash found himself smiling. "Then let me make you happy now." He threw his leg over Brandon's hip, forcing their erections up against one another. Brandon's eyes grew wide, then hazy with his burgeoning desire.

"Tonight is a night for feeling, not thinking." Tash sat up and held out his hand. "Come upstairs with me. Tomorrow we'll deal with reality, but right now, forget about everything except you and me and how I'm going to make love to you so hard you won't remember your own name."

Brandon slipped a hand in his, and together they walked up the stairs. The house stood hushed as if holding its breath, waiting for some momentous occurrence to take place. They paused as they reached the top of the stairs, and Brandon put a staying hand on Tash's shoulder.

"You know, you said you loved me downstairs." The luminous expression Brandon now wore had chased the sadness from his eyes. "Yet you didn't ask me how I felt."

"I don't want you to be pressured to respond the same way. You have me for as long as you want me."

Brandon's smile faded. "What? You think I don't have the same feelings for you?"

Being so young, Brandon might mistake his newly awakened desire for love, but it could easily be lust as well. "I know you care for me. I think you're confused and at a crossroads right now. I'm here for you, no matter the outcome." Tash drew Brandon close and kissed him. "I don't want to waste time talking when we could be doing other things." Tash held Brandon around his waist. "I want to do unspeakable things to you."

The fire in the depths of Brandon's eyes spurred Tash to action. "Let's go take a shower." Hand in hand they entered the bedroom and walked through to the connecting bathroom. Tash turned on the tap, sending hot water rushing from the rainfall showerhead. He turned the wall jets on so that there was heated water spraying at them from every direction.

They stood together, the water streaming over their bodies. Tash squirted some liquid soap onto his hand and spread it over Brandon's chest, massaging it until the bubbles sparkled under the water. He smoothed the soap all over himself, then Brandon, briefly massaging the man's back, ass cheeks, and stiff cock. With every swipe of Tash's hand and brush of his fingers, Brandon rocked his hips into Tash's pelvis. His head dropped onto Tash's shoulder.

"God, yeah, that feels amazing," he said, his lips against Tash's neck.

"I've only begun the night." Tash rinsed them both

and turned off the water. "Let's get into bed and warm up. I'll set a fire."

One of the reasons he'd bought the house was the wood-burning fireplace in the bedroom. It cut down on his heating bill, but on a night like this, his only thought was to see the firelight flickering over Brandon's beautiful body.

Brandon had settled under the covers by the time Tash had finished lighting the fire. The delicious smell of the wood drifted through the air. He dived underneath the comforter, relishing Brandon's naked body. As the fire heated the room, he drew back the bedcovers, exposing them both to the rapidly warming air.

"I'm going to make love to you all night until you forget that there's a tomorrow."

Brandon lay still, the absolute trust in his eyes almost breaking Tash's heart. No one had ever looked at him that way. When they kissed, their tongues met, licking and teasing each other. Tash broke away from Brandon's lips, sliding his mouth along the fresh-tasting skin of Brandon's throat. He stroked at the visible pulse pumping at Brandon's neck and sucked at the tender skin beneath Brandon's jaw.

Tash licked a lazy slide down the planes of Brandon's chest and flicked his tongue against Brandon's dark red nipples. He traveled down Brandon's torso to circle his belly button, then nibbled at the edge of Brandon's neatly trimmed groin.

"Tash, please." Brandon moaned, his eyes squeezed tight, his hands twisting at the bedsheets.

Tash licked around the head of Brandon's cock, flicking his tongue in the tiny slit. He loved the warm, clean scent of Brandon's body. "Please what?" The firelight gilded their bodies, the dancing flames flickering and casting shadows on the walls. They were cocooned within their own cave of intimacy.

"Please, more?" He took Brandon into his mouth, engulfing the fully hardened length of him. The taut muscles of Brandon's thighs quivered under his cheeks and fingertips as Tash slid his mouth up and down Brandon's shaft, and swirled his tongue around the head of Brandon's cock. His saliva mingled with the salty-sweet taste of Brandon's precome, and Tash hummed with satisfaction at the delicious taste.

Small sighs and groans from Brandon's kiss-swollen lips spurred Tash on. He reached to cup Brandon's balls, hefting them in his palm, then slid a wet finger behind Brandon's sac, tracing a circle around Brandon's tight hole before teasing the entrance to the tight passage. He remained busy sucking and licking Brandon's cock.

"God, yeah, more." Brandon hissed.

Tash let go of Brandon's cock to kiss a trail down to where his fingers entered Brandon's body.

"Remember, I said I wanted to kiss you all over." He licked and rolled Brandon's balls. "Turn over, sweetheart."

"What?" Brandon blinked, seemingly confused, as he raised himself on one elbow. "Turn over?"

Tash grinned. *Baby, you have no idea how your mind*

is about to explode. "Yeah, go on. I promise; you're going to be fine."

Without further questioning, Brandon lay on his stomach, giving Tash a view of his firm, rounded ass. Tash braced himself over Brandon, kissing the smooth soft skin of his shoulders, tracing his spine with the tip of his tongue from the nape of Brandon's neck to his tailbone.

Twin dimples adorned the top of each buttock. The man's ass was as adorable as his face. After pressing a kiss to each cheek, Tash slid down on the mattress and spread Brandon wide, getting a full view of his perfect little hole. He leaned over and swiped his tongue over the crease of Brandon's ass, coming to settle the point of his tongue in the opening. As he expected, Brandon stiffened.

"What the hell?" His voice shook with shock.

Without any comment or hesitation, Tash slid the tip of his tongue inside Brandon's hole. The tight opening around his mouth quivered, and Tash held on as Brandon, obviously awash in sensations, spread his legs wider, encouraging Tash with his harsh cries. Tash reached deep within Brandon's passage, jabbing in and out, his hands holding on to the globes of Brandon's ass to steady them both. Brandon worked himself on Tash's tongue faster and harder. Tash continued to lap and lick at his opening as Brandon's breathy moans escalated in the darkness.

With one last lick and nibble of Brandon's round ass, Tash lovingly kissed his way up Brandon's back and nuzzled his face in the curve of Brandon's shoulder. Brandon shuddered, and Tash whispered in his ear, "You liked that, sweetheart, huh?" Tash grasped Brandon under the chest and turned Brandon's head toward him. Their mouths met in a clash of lips and tongues, the kiss messy and wild, their mutual desire escalating out of control. This night was for Brandon, to give him the pleasure he'd never enjoyed and show him how important he was to Tash, how much Tash needed and wanted him. "I want you to fuck me."

Brandon stilled and turned over so they faced each other. "You do?" His dark green eyes shone soft and luminous. "I've thought about it, dreamed about what it would feel like to be inside of you."

Tash dipped his head down and pressed his lips to Brandon's. "I like it both ways. You should see if you do too." As he spoke, Tash sank a finger into Brandon's passage, loving the way the suede-silk heat sucked him deep inside, surrounding him in its tight warmth. He added a second finger and began to steadily pump them in and out of Brandon's ass. "You're a beautiful bottom. I love feeling you underneath me, taking me inside your tight body." Tash withdrew his fingers and kissed Brandon. "But I want you deep inside me, becoming part of me. Do you want that too?"

There was no hesitation this time. Brandon nodded, and Tash took the condom and lube he'd placed on the night table and handed them to Brandon. "Here."

Their hands touched as Brandon took the items,

and Tash held on to him for a moment. "Don't overthink it."

A brief smile, then Brandon unsnapped the bottle, and Tash didn't have to wait long. Brandon slid down the bed to sit between Tash's knees.

With a sureness Tash hadn't expected, Brandon's long fingers, cool with liquid, touched him. First one finger slid inside, then two, reaching, stretching him, then hitting that magical spot to send a shower of sparks through Tash, wiping away the sting of the initial entry.

He'd forgotten what it felt like to be touched, to be loved. "Oh God," Tash cried out, tears springing to his eyes. Years. It had been years since he'd experienced the pleasure-pain of lovemaking so intense and soul-deep it choked him.

"Did I hurt you?" Brandon stopped the magic his fingers worked inside of Tash, his voice anxious with concern.

"No," gasped Tash. "Don't stop. Ever." He reached up to grab Brandon close. "Don't stop touching me, please."

"You want more, huh?" Brandon teased and resumed his wicked, twisting fingers.

Tash pushed himself into Brandon's hand, shameless in his need to climb the heights his body so desperately craved. "Yes. Please." He almost didn't recognize his own desperate voice.

Through the haze surrounding his mind, Tash heard Brandon open the condom package, and finally, the marvelously thick head of Brandon's cock pushed inside him.

Never in his life had he been so greedy to claim his lover. He lifted his legs and encouraged Brandon to continue the slide inside; and when he did, the fullness only increased his hunger.

It was life-affirming. Sensation washed over him, rolling through his body in great waves of pleasure, and he reveled in it. "Harder," he begged, afraid Brandon's inexperience and fear that he might be hurting Tash would cause him to be too tentative. "All the way in, sweetheart. You won't hurt me."

Brandon pushed in and withdrew halfway, then plunged back again. They rocked together, harder and faster, and with each slide and thrust, the remnants of Tash's tattered heart knitted back together, creating a new and beautiful mosaic.

"Now, yes." Tash locked his ankles behind Brandon and heaved himself up. The angle shifted, and as Brandon hit his gland over and over again, the slow burn within Tash ignited to a searing flame. His entire body tightened, the ache within his balls grew deep, and his vision narrowed to a pinpoint of black. Tash found it difficult to draw a breath, and he came harder than he ever had before in his life; stream after stream of creamy white shot onto his chest. His entire body trembled and shook as his orgasm rocketed through him.

Brandon continued to pump inside him, gripping Tash's arms so tight his fingers dug into the muscles of

Tash's biceps. He stiffened, then shook and came with a hoarse cry, buried deep inside Tash. Heedless of the sticky mess all over Tash's chest, Brandon rested there, his heart galloping in a crazy beat.

Several moments passed before they picked their heads up and, in unison, smiled at one another. Tash cupped the nape of Brandon's neck and drew him in for a prolonged kiss. They rolled on their sides but still clung together, their kisses leisurely now that the lovemaking had taken the edge off their hunger for one another.

Brandon withdrew, and Tash winced. He waited as Brandon left the bed and went into the bathroom, wondering how Brandon felt. Sated and replete with the most marvelous ache in his body, Tash closed his eyes and stretched.

"You look like one of your cats after they get up from napping in the sun." Brandon grinned down at him, his eyes soft and dark in the firelight.

"Come lie down with me." Tash patted the bed next to him. "Tell me how you feel."

Brandon slid in next to him and lay on his back facing the ceiling. "It's weird, you know? When I lived on the streets, and even in the shelter, I'd never imagined I'd ever be in this position."

"What position is that?" Tash lay on his side, his chin propped in his hand. He reached over to push Brandon's hair out of his face. He frowned at the sight of worry lines etching their way across Brandon's normally smooth forehead and traced them with a fingertip.

"Secure. Happy. And now that it's all within reach, it's like that dream where you're running, and you go to grasp something, but it's either right out of reach or it slips through your fingers." Brandon caught Tash's hand in his and laced their fingers together. "I found you only what seems like moments ago. I don't want to lose what we have." He lifted their joined hands to brush them against his lips. "And I'm not only talking about the sex, even though it's amazing. I don't want to run anymore. I want to stay and put down roots. I want that happily-ever-after life together, the sharing of our days when we get home from work, and having our families all together for the holidays." He slanted a quick look up at Tash.

"What is it?" Tash sensed there was something Brandon wasn't saying. "You have to know I want that too."

"I was thinking about how it would be to really be a family. Maybe someday have kids together."

Stunned, Tash could only stare at Brandon as the clock on the fireplace mantel ticked busily away.

"I understand if you don't. I'm not saying we need to decide right now—"

Tash covered Brandon's mouth with his in a hungry, possessive kiss. The need to touch Brandon had never been so great. "No one's ever loved me enough to want to stay and build a home with me, so I've never talked about it, but children?" He kissed Brandon again. "It would be the dream I never thought I'd get to live. And you'd be an amazing father; I've never seen anyone so good with kids before. It must be because you're so young."

Brandon groaned. "Don't start that again, please. I thought we were past all that." His mouth set in a hard line. "Besides, at this point I have bigger things to think and worry about than our age difference."

"I think you should tell everyone at tomorrow night's dinner at Esther's." Tash pulled Brandon close to hold him. "Ash will be there, and Luke needs to know as well. Everyone will support you. You were young and abused and didn't mean to do it."

That look of trust reentered Brandon's eyes. "I love you, Tash. Thank you for believing me." He laid his head down on Tash's shoulder. "Believing in us."

Tash kissed his cheek. "I love you too. You made me believe in myself again when I doubted everything, sometimes my own reason for living. You gave me back my life and made it so much richer than I ever thought possible." Tash cupped Brandon's face between his hands. "How could I not believe in you?"

Chapter Twenty

ONLY A WOMAN like Esther could bring them all together each week. The love and respect her grandchildren and extended family had for her was never more apparent than at these weekly dinners. There was no doubt she loved having them, evidenced by the care she took in preparing everyone's favorite foods, whether it was the fried chicken cutlets Brandon learned were called schnitzel or the savory stuffed cabbage and delicious brisket.

Her face glowed, her inner joy apparent as she sat at the head of the large mahogany dining room table, flanked on either side by Drew and Rachel. Also present of course were Jordan, Luke, and Mike. Rounding out the lively group today was Tash's sister, Valerie, Gage, and Louisa, who was busy scolding Ash for eating too many meat patties.

"Save some for the others. You have to share." Her eyes twinkled.

"I'm not good at sharing what I love. Ask Drew." He winked at Louisa, and she rolled her eyes.

"Oh my goodness, you are a bad one, aren't you? How do you put up with him, Drew?"

"He has his good points, Louisa." Drew leaned over and kissed Ash on the cheek. "Behave."

"That's like asking a dog not to wag its tail," said Jordan drily.

The entire table broke out into laughter, and even Ash tipped his glass to Jordan. "Point to you, Jordan, but I won't forget you compared me to a dog."

Jordan raised a blond brow, his lips twitching to hold back a grin. "If the shoe fits…"

"You're awfully quiet, Brandon." Luke eyed his plate. "And you barely ate anything. What's wrong?"

Tash squeezed his thigh in a gesture of comfort. Time to face the music. "I need to talk to all of you, to tell you…" He stopped, unsure what to say. Tell them what? That he was a murderer? All the eyes focused on him set his head spinning.

Tash cleared his throat. "Brandon wants to talk to you all about the events that led up to him leaving home when he did. But what we ask is that you let him speak and tell his story straight through. Afterward, you can ask him questions, but understand he may not have all the answers."

Brandon threw Tash a grateful look. God, he loved Tash. It took such a weight off his chest to have someone so strong and steady in his corner. For the first time, Brandon thought he might have a future free of fear.

He took a deep breath and began to speak. As he

relayed the story he'd told Tash the night before, he kept a careful watch on the faces of the people who mattered the most to him in the world: Ash and Luke. Not surprisingly, their expressions registered horror, fear, anguish, and love. Not once, though, did they gaze at him with accusation or anger.

"I didn't know what to do after I left home. I couldn't go back, so I took some money from him." Here he stopped and swallowed, shuddering as he recalled touching the inanimate body of Munson to take some bills from his wallet. "I walked into the city to the bus stop and got on the first bus to Philadelphia. I was seventeen, so the only jobs I could get with no questions asked were as a delivery boy or bagging groceries—I did whatever I could to get a few dollars."

Those days seemed so hazy now, sitting in this comfortable room—warm, fed, and dressed in decent clothing. But that bilious taste of fear never dissipated. "It wasn't enough to live on, though. I could barely eat and slept in parks or in disgusting hotels." There were other more important things he needed to speak of. Things he hadn't even told Tash yet. "I, um, I worked for someone who had me delivering packages, and I would get an envelope in exchange for delivering the package to the person. I didn't know what was inside the packages, but of course I suspected drugs or guns. I only did it a few times, but it made me so nervous I tried to stop. They wouldn't let me and said I had to keep doing what they wanted."

"How did you get away?" Luke's eyes glittered with

pain, and his normally olive complexion shone pale with sweat. Jordan placed a hand on his shoulder for comfort.

Brandon took a deep breath and drank from his glass of water. "One night I got on a bus and went to Atlantic City and stayed there. I could live on the beach in the summer and work around the city. I did that for two months, then came to New York. Luke had always talked of living here, that it was the place to come and reach for the stars. I lived on the streets and did a little begging until six months later when Gabriel found me and changed my life forever."

"Look at you now." Esther gazed upon him with shining eyes. "You went to school, became a teacher, and found your brothers and"—her eyes twinkled—"a very nice young man."

"You're an inspiration, man." Gage gazed at him with respect, not the loathing Brandon had expected.

"I'm a murderer, Gage."

"I don't believe it."

"Brandon." Ash's voice cut in. "I think you should come to my office tomorrow, and we'll talk strategy."

"I think we should stop talking about this unpleasant subject."

Brandon's head snapped up at Esther's voice. There were two pink patches on her cheeks, and her hands trembled. Regret and dismay slammed into Brandon's chest. He immediately left Tash's side to attend to Esther.

"I'm sorry to have brought this on your family. I

can leave and find somewhere else to stay."

"Is that what you think I want?" She turned to Drew and Ash. Drew took his grandmother's hand, and Brandon could see him deftly taking her pulse so unobtrusively she didn't realize it, while Ash left his seat and stood behind Esther, resting his hands on her shoulders.

"Don't get upset, Esther. We're going to help Brandon, but you can't afford to become ill."

"You must help him, Asher. I know he couldn't hurt anyone. Brandon's the sweetest, kindest—"

"Esther. Don't worry. I promise I'm going to do everything possible to help him." Ash held his gaze. "I won't fail you this time; I promise. I'll be by your side every step of the way."

"Not only him but me as well." Luke joined them, giving Brandon a hug. "You'll never have to handle anything alone again."

Grateful as he was for his brothers, their approval was no longer the first thing he looked for. It was Tash whom Brandon sought for comfort. The man who held him in his arms when he cried and passed no judgment on his past sins was his rock and the guidance he listened to. Their eyes met across the table, and the bands holding a tight stranglehold on his chest loosened for the first time in years.

It hit him then. He wasn't alone in this any longer. He could've wept from the enormity of it, but Brandon held himself together, needing to prove to everyone he was the man he said he was and no longer the young boy they'd kept as an image in their minds. It wasn't weakness to accept their help; it showed strength. Damn the consequences. Brandon knew he'd come out of this never-ending journey through hell with his family and his heart intact, stronger than ever before.

"Thank you, Ash."

"There's no need to thank me. It's what families do."

After they hugged and Brandon agreed to come to Ash's office at four o'clock after school ended the next day, he had to apologize to Esther.

"I'm sorry to have brought this to your table and my problems to your life." In the short time he'd spent living there, this house had become more of a home than anywhere else he'd ever lived.

She'd remained silent during his conversation with Ash, but Brandon had no doubt she had some words of advice for him.

"Oh, Brandon." She sniffled into her handkerchief. "You have no idea how wonderful it's been for me to have you here. I'm so happy you have Sebastian to love you and stand by you along with your brothers."

He stood, somewhat frozen. They hadn't yet decided to speak about the seriousness of their relationship. It was so sudden; Brandon didn't want to have to deal with Luke's possible disapproval, especially not now. Brandon thought they'd manage to keep it to themselves. Not with Esther around, it seemed.

"You look shocked, dear, but it's quite obvious to me. The way he looks at you is how my dear Sy used to look at me—so loving and protective." Esther appealed to the others at the table. "You see it, don't you? They are as much in love as you all are."

And when Tash smiled at him, Brandon knew right then it would be fine. It didn't matter if Luke approved or if Ash did either. All that mattered was this man and the glow in his eyes that spoke of a future he now believed in.

"We're taking it one day at a time, Esther," said Tash in all seriousness. "Brandon's focus must be on fighting these charges. He knows how I feel about him."

Brandon left Esther's side to stand by Tash. He reached down and squeezed Tash's hand. "And Tash knows my feelings as well. To have all of you offer your support and understanding is more than I ever thought I'd have."

They all sat back down and finished their meal. Brandon wondered if in the weeks ahead, this might be the last time he'd sit down to an untroubled dinner with his family.

AT A FEW minutes after four, Brandon and Tash were escorted into the library of Ash's impressive midtown law office. Brandon looked around, a little intimidated despite the fact that Ash was his brother. The walls were paneled in a richly grained wood with floor-to-ceiling built-in bookcases containing hundreds of legal books. The table they sat at was polished to a high, dark shine. Brandon could only imagine how daunting it must be for people on the opposite side of a case to be subjected to his brother's lightning-sharp mind.

Tash poured himself a cup of cold water. "Don't worry. I have full confidence Ash will be able to work it out for you."

"Thanks, Tash." Ash entered the room with Luke on his heels. "I'm going to do my best."

Brandon hadn't realized Luke would be there today, but in reality, he should've known. Years spent fending for himself had him braced for disappointment from everyone. But not these men.

"Luke. I'm glad to see you."

From his troubled expression, Brandon sensed Luke wanted to say something but was holding back.

"What's wrong? You look like you have something on your mind." Brandon accepted the cup of coffee Ash handed him.

Looking supremely uncomfortable, Luke drank deeply from his ever-present coffee cup before speaking. "Um, well, last night after we got home, Jerry stopped by."

Brandon's stomach took a nosedive to his knees. "The policeman?"

"Detective," Luke corrected him. "Yeah, and we got to talking, and somehow it slipped out that you had to see Ash today."

"So? I could be seeing him for a lot of different reasons. You didn't tell him anything, did you?"

Luke shook his head. "I swear I didn't and neither did Jordan, but you have to understand, Jerry is a seasoned detective who already had an interest in you because of how you showed up out of the blue."

"What would that have to do with anything?" Brandon knew he was overreacting, and his voice sounded shrill to his ears, but he'd thought his past was confined to the people he'd personally told. To find out the police were now sniffing around terrified him.

"It's fine, Brandon. Don't concern yourself with Jerry. We're here to help you and figure out your next step." Ash's attempt at comfort didn't help much.

Tash rubbed his back. "It's going to work out. You'll see. Your imagination is always worse than actual reality." The warmth of Tash's hand on the nape of Brandon's neck settled his racing pulse. He leaned back onto Tash's arm. "Better?" Tash murmured into his ear.

Miraculously he was. "Yeah, thanks." He smiled into Tash's eyes and saw the love and safety residing there. "Thanks."

The wink he received in return was enough.

"So, let's get started." Ash opened his folder. "Brandon, what was the date you had the fight with Munson?"

"April twenty-second." He swallowed against the sour taste that rose in his throat. "Around six in the evening."

Ash wrote on his pad as he continued to fire off question after question. Did he ever tell anyone about

Munson's abuse of their mother or himself? Were there any physical scars from previous fights? Where did the fight start? Did their foster mother see him leave the house? Did he hear or see anyone after he left the house for good?

As he answered all the questions, Brandon recognized the defense Ash was building for him. "You're going for self-defense? Or the fact that I was abused my whole life and I snapped at last?"

Ash's answering smile confirmed his statement. "Right now, yes. I looked at the newspaper report you mentioned you read, and it was very brief, only a few lines about his death. That was reported"—Ash checked his notes—"on April twenty-eighth. They gave the approximate date of death at around seventy-two hours earlier." His brow furrowed as he checked the article again. "Hmm, that's the twenty-fifth, three days after you said you hit him and left him in the woods."

Brandon shrugged. "So, it's off by a few days."

"Can I see the newspaper article?" Tash took the folder from Ash, and opened it, pulling out the newspaper. Brandon watched Tash scan the short article. When he'd finished, Tash turned to him a huge smile on his face.

"Brandon, I think you're innocent. I don't believe you killed your foster father at all."

Chapter Twenty-One

THREE ASTONISHED FACES stared at him. If it wasn't such a serious situation, Tash might have found it comical. The only one who counted, though, Brandon, seemed far more agitated than happy with his news.

"What are you talking about? I left him bleeding from the head. He wasn't moving." Brandon pushed back from the table, and Tash sat, helpless as he watched his lover fall apart.

"Why are you giving me false hope? For years, I dreamed I hadn't hit him and ran away, instead leaving him on his feet, laughing after me." Brandon wiped at the tears streaking his cheeks, and Tash hurt at Brandon's obvious raw pain. "But I didn't. He went down and didn't move. Didn't make a sound. There was blood coming from his head. I took the brick I used and threw it in the creek down the road, making sure all the blood soaked away." The desolation in Brandon's eyes mirrored that of patients Tash had treated after a family tragedy, wounded and lost.

Ash and Luke tried to calm him down, but Brandon pulled away from them. Tash recognized the basis of his defensive behavior. After all, Brandon had spent almost half his life dealing with whatever life threw his way, alone. Naturally, he didn't know how to take advice from anyone trying to help, his brothers or lover included. Mistrustful as a wild creature and just as nervous, Brandon had to learn to have faith in the people around him.

"Brandon." It took several moments before Brandon focused back on him. "Come back and sit down, and I'll tell you why I said what I did. I know what I'm talking about."

After grabbing everyone's attention with that statement, Tash opened the folder with the newspaper reports again. "It says here that Munson was found dead on April twenty-fifth." He adjusted his glasses to read the tiny print. Damn, he might need to adjust his prescription. Tash cleared his throat, then began reading again. "You, Brandon, told us the fight occurred on the twenty-second. That's a full three days earlier. Forensic science may not be perfect, but we can narrow the times of death to a pretty close proximity."

On raising his gaze from the papers in his hand, he focused on Brandon, only to see the confusion on the man's face. It was obvious to Tash that Brandon hadn't yet understood the significance of the dates. "Sweetheart. Too many days elapsed between when you say you hit and killed him, to the date they said he died. In my opinion, something or someone else caused his death."

Before he finished speaking, Brandon was shaking his head. "No. That's not true. They must've been off with their dates. Either that or you're simply trying to be kind to me and cover up."

"Don't be foolish." Ash scowled at Brandon across the table. "What's the harm in exploring Tash's theory? The man's a doctor; I think he knows better than you how to read a medical report."

Brandon flushed but held his ground. "It was still cool in the evenings there. The body probably lay in the chill. Or something." His voice grew slightly desperate. "You want me to be innocent, so you'll see what you hope to be true, but I know what happened that afternoon."

Tash understood Brandon's hesitancy. After living so many years under a cloud of fear and hiding, it must be a shock to be sprung from the darkness into the light. Fixing his most reassuring smile firmly in place, Tash spoke directly to Brandon, who, from his flushed face and tight fists, looked to be on the verge of a breakdown.

"Calm down. What I'm saying is this. The dates don't seem to coincide. But I agree more research and investigation needs to be done." He turned to Ash. "Why don't we arrange a visit to Pennsylvania, and we can look at the medical records? Surely, Ash, as Brandon's lawyer, you have the right to view them?"

Ash grimaced. "I'm not admitted to the bar in Pennsylvania, so I couldn't represent him unless I made a motion to the court to let me appear. We'd ultimately have to hire someone."

The wheels were turning in the man's mind, Tash could see. His fingers drummed on the table. "I'd hate to go to the authorities, raise suspicions about an old murder investigation, and then back off. There's nothing the police like more than a fresh lead on a cold case."

"So, I'm screwed. And I'm dragging you all into a murder investigation for no reason." Brandon turned his back on everyone at the table.

"We have every reason. You're our brother." But the worry in Ash's eyes told a different story, Tash saw. For the first time, Ash didn't seem as in control and sure of himself.

Tash couldn't stand to see the defeat in Brandon's eyes. He needed to hold Brandon almost as much for himself as for Brandon's sake and didn't give a damn what Ash and Luke thought. Without a word, he walked around the conference table and put his arms around the special man who'd come to mean so much to him in such a short time. They stood for a moment, holding on to one another, drawing a sense of peace in each other's arms. If only Brandon could believe everything would turn out all right. Strength flooded through Tash, remembering the vow he'd made to himself. He wouldn't fail this time. He would help Brandon.

"I won't drag you and all your families into my problems." To Tash's dismay, Brandon pulled away from him to stand alone. "Even you, Tash. You can't fight my battles for me. Maybe the right thing to do is go back to Pennsylvania, turn myself in, and hope for the best."

Pride warred with fear in Tash's chest. He remembered what Brandon had said when the two of them met, and it didn't make sense until now. Brandon Gilbert was no ordinary twenty-five-year-old. He had more maturity than some men twice his age.

"I don't think any decision has to be made this moment. Why don't we have dinner and sleep on it?" Ash checked his watch. "Drew is finishing up right now, and we can all go together."

Before Brandon could answer, Tash decided to speak for the both of them. He wanted to spend time alone with Brandon and let him know how much he loved him and that he would be there for him, no matter what. "Thanks for the invitation, but I think we'd like to spend a quiet evening together. Maybe talk things out?" He looked to Brandon for confirmation and was gratified to see an answering smile.

"Yeah, sorry, Ash. Can we take a rain check?" He reached down and squeezed Tash's hand, and Tash gave him an answering squeeze. "I'm kind of wiped and wouldn't be the best company anyway."

Understanding gleamed in Ash's silvery eyes. "Yeah, of course."

Tash caught the tail end of an annoyed expression on Luke's face. Although Luke hadn't mentioned that blowup about Tash and Brandon dating, Tash knew he still harbored a lingering resentment. One thing Tash knew was not to let problems in a family fester and grow out of hand.

"Something wrong, Luke?"

"Yeah. I'd like to see Brandon more, but he's always with you. I think the least you could do is let him have some time with us. It took years to find him, but since we discovered who he is, we haven't spent more than a few days together." Luke glowered at him.

While Tash was willing to make some concessions to Brandon's brothers, he wasn't about to be treated as a scapegoat for the lack of time they spent with him. Brandon had the right to choose who he wanted to be with, and Ash didn't seem to have a problem with it. Only Luke, right from the start, had issues with the relationship.

"What's the problem, Luke?" Brandon braced his hands on the table. "Don't tell me you still have a problem with Tash and me?"

"You've only known each other a short time and already Tash is the one making decisions with you about the rest of your life. I think you're moving too fast."

"What bothers you so much about it? I'm not cutting you and Ash out of my life; I'm making my own choices, finding my way."

Luke couldn't face Brandon and spoke to the floor. "You used to look up to me, ask me for help when you had a problem."

Tash stood silent, watching the family drama unfold before him. While Ash had easily accepted the transition of Brandon back into his life, Luke seemed to be having a harder time of it. Perhaps it was the extra years spent looking after Brandon as a young boy that had Luke believing he needed to remain Brandon's protector.

But Brandon was his own man. "I told you before; I'm no longer a child. If we haven't spent enough time with each other, I'm sorry. I promise to make more of an effort. But I'm not making apologies for being with Tash. He's the best thing to ever happen to me."

Their eyes met, and Tash found it hard to swallow. Damn, he loved this guy so much. To have come out of his torpor and sorrow to discover the joy of loving a man like Brandon was an unexpected gift. Was it only a little over a month ago he'd told Valerie he was better off alone? Remembering how he'd woken up this morning, wrapped around the naked body of this man standing before him, a flush swept through him. He could never go back to that frozen, lonely life.

"Leave them alone, Luke." Ash nudged his brother's shoulder. "Whatever bug up your ass you have about Tash, it's obvious he and Brandon care about each other."

"It wasn't too long ago he thought he cared about Jordan."

Heat rose in Tash's face as Brandon gaped at him. "You and Jordan?"

"No, no." Tash glared at Luke, who returned his look with a set jaw. "What the hell, Luke? That was like, for five minutes, when I first met Jordan." Tash paced the room, running his hand through his hair. "Jordan's my patient, for God's sake. It would be completely unprofessional of me to treat him if I had feelings for him"—he glared at Luke—"which I don't." He folded his arms. "I thought we had that worked out by now."

"I need to make sure you don't hit on every gay guy you meet."

Tash shot back. "No worries there, Luke. You never interested me in the least."

Luke had the grace to flush. "I'm only looking out for my brother."

"By cutting me down and making me look like some kind of predator?"

Luke still held his ground. "What do you want me to think? I thought it was all okay between us too, yet as soon as my brother shows up, you're all over him."

Tash could not believe Luke was serious, yet the pugnacious tilt of his jaw was irrefutable. Brandon appeared at Tash's side, taking his hand in a show of support.

"No one was all over me. What's wrong with you?"

"There's nothing wrong with me. I'm not the one who's falling for someone he barely knows."

"Are we back to that again? If I recall, Luke, you fell for Jordan, and he kept some pretty serious things from you." Ash leaned against the table and spoke calmly, yet never once took his gaze off Luke. "So couldn't we ask you, how well did you really know Jordan?"

Luke shifted under Ash's probing, and Tash could see why Ash was so effective in court. He cut right to the point.

"It's not even the age thing anymore. It's that it happened so fast." Luke sat back in his chair. "It sounds like one of those stories Wanda loves to read about where the guy meets the girl and *wham*, they're in love. That's bullshit as far as I know."

"My parents were married within three months of their first date." Tash raised a brow at the surprised look on all their faces. "Forty-two years later they're still in love. Why is time the determining factor in knowing when something is right? People can be together for years and fall out of love and end up hating each other." He lifted his and Brandon's enjoined hands. "Each of us knows, I think, the fleeting joy of happiness and love. It's like the spark of a match that flares upon striking. You want to capture it before it blows out." He squeezed Brandon's hand tight. "Brandon has lit up my life in ways I thought were dead to me. I may not have been looking for it, but now that I have him, I'm not letting you or anyone else take him from me."

He held Luke's gaze, unwilling to back down an inch. From the corner of his eye, he could see a faint smile playing around Ash's lips. Finally, Luke broke the stare-off.

"I only want Brandon happy. After all he's been through, he deserves it."

"Then we're on the same page." Tash stuck out his hand. "Come on, Luke. It's me." He held his friend's dark gaze. "You don't really think I'll hurt him, do you?"

With only a moment's hesitation, Luke took his hand. "He means everything to me."

"Me as well."

Ash clapped Tash on the back but left his hand resting on Tash's shoulder. "I'm glad you and Luke worked this out. Don't take what I said earlier as a lack of concern. I love my brothers more than anything. If you do hurt Brandon?" Ash's silver eyes glittered like a feral wolf ready to attack. "Look over your shoulder, 'cause I'll be coming for you."

"I NEVER KNEW your brothers moonlighted as assassins," Tash half joked as he and Brandon entered the carriage house. Brandon held the pizza, and he carried the bag with the makings of ice cream sundaes. They headed to the kitchen, Cleo and Caesar racing ahead of them. While he put the ice cream in the freezer and the chocolate sauce and whipped cream in the refrigerator, Brandon took out the plates and set the pizza box on the table.

"Never mind them. Want me to open some wine?" Brandon held up a bottle of Malbec.

"Sounds perfect." Tash smiled, enjoying the sight of Brandon rummaging around in the cabinet for the wineglasses. Happy for the moment, Tash whistled a tune under his breath as he opened the bottle of wine.

He loved that Brandon felt comfortable in his house. When Brandon came back with the two glasses, Tash poured them each some and held Brandon's gaze over the rim of their glasses as they each took a sip.

"Come on." He put his glass on the table and took Brandon's out of his hand, setting it next to his. "Leave the pizza for later."

"Oh yeah?" Brandon licked his lips, his eyes darkening with his rising excitement. "What if I'm hungry now?"

An idea rose in Tash's mind. He brushed a kiss over Brandon's lips. "Hold on a sec," he said, a bit breathless. Brandon clung to him, plunging his tongue into Tash's mouth and holding him close. If they didn't stop kissing now, they'd end up naked on the cold kitchen floor, and Tash had bigger plans. "Let me get something; then we'll go upstairs." He put the ice cream, chocolate syrup, and whipped cream in a bag and threw in a couple of spoons.

"Let's go. We can start with dessert." Laughing as they ran up the stairs, Tash recalled how only a month or so earlier he'd sat in the diner with Valerie, asking her to leave him alone and let him wallow in his misery. Tonight, the thought of Brandon's smooth naked body, now so familiar, had become like an addiction to Tash. It would kill him to give Brandon up.

"Now you're talking." Brandon shed his clothes as he entered the bedroom, taking only a minute before he stood in front of Tash, completely naked and aroused. "Why don't you light a fire?"

Tash, completely caught up in the sight of Brandon's cock pointing straight at him, swallowed hard. "Yeah, good idea." It took only a few minutes to get the fire started, and when he turned around, his mouth went dry. Brandon sat naked and cross-legged in the club chair, the pint of ice cream in one hand and a spoonful in the other. He stripped in no time, Brandon's eyes never leaving his face.

"Come get your sugar." Brandon wiggled the spoon at him.

That Southern twang, a hold over from his childhood in Georgia, crept into Brandon's velvety suede voice, making Tash so achingly hard, he couldn't think. He watched Brandon slide the spoon inside his mouth and lick it clean. In two strides Tash joined Brandon on the chair and plucked the spoon from his hand. "Let me feed you."

The firelight playing shadows off Brandon's golden skin, coupled with the erotic sight of his glistening mouth, spun Tash's nerves into a frenzy. Tash dug into the container and slipped the spoonful of creamy ice cream into Brandon's mouth. With a hum of appreciation, Tash dipped his head in for a kiss, the taste of the sweet chocolate and coffee ice cream bursting on his tongue.

Brandon took the spoon from his hand. "My turn." Being as they were so close to the fire the ice cream had melted a bit and it dripped onto Tash's lips and chin.

"Mmm, let me." With long sweeps of his tongue, Brandon lapped at Tash's face, then kissed his lips.

When Tash's face was clean, to his surprise, Brandon kept spooning more ice cream into Tash's mouth, dribbling it over his chin and neck and licking it up until Tash became dizzy with pleasure and lust.

"Stay right there," whispered Tash. He hurried to the nightstand to get the lube and a condom, then returned to the chair. "On your knees and face the chair, sweetheart."

Without questioning him, Brandon did as he asked, and soon Tash was faced with the long lines of Brandon's beautiful naked back and ass. Knowing how sensitive Brandon's neck was, Tash spent time seducing him by placing teasing licks all over Brandon's throat and sucking his skin. He loved hearing Brandon moan, the breath hitching in his throat as he writhed beneath Tash.

Brandon's hard cock proved too enticing, and Tash encircled its length with his hand and began to stroke. Brandon arched into his touch and bit out between gritted teeth, "Now, goddamn it."

Laughing softly, Tash ripped open the condom packet, and after rolling it on, he slicked himself with the lube. "Patience, sweetheart, and brace yourself."

Brandon said nothing but grabbed the high-backed chair and spread himself wider for Tash.

"Oh God, that's hot," groaned Tash, smoothing his hands over the mounds of Brandon's ass, trailing his fingers in the crease. He sank a finger inside Brandon's hole and heard a sigh escape Brandon's lips. "You like that, huh?" A second finger joined the first.

The rich, sweet scent of the ice cream, along with the noises Brandon made underneath him, excited Tash to a fever pitch. Unable to wait any longer, Tash planted one foot on the ground and a knee on the chair seat for leverage; then he pushed inside Brandon, loving the way he sank inside as if drawn in deep by an invisible force. He wrapped one arm around Brandon's chest, and as he pumped inside Brandon's body, he fisted Brandon's cock with his slick hand.

"Come for me, sweetheart." Tash planted a wet, messy kiss at the corner of Brandon's mouth as he plunged inside him. He continued to stroke Brandon until Brandon shuddered and shot into his hand. Muscles tightened around Tash's cock, still deeply buried within Brandon, and he sensed that familiar rush of blood to his head and groin. Before he could gather his thoughts to think straight, Tash's orgasm hit him; the force of it was so strong the fire rose to a golden haze and the walls of his bedroom wavered in front of him.

Heedless of the mess on his chair, he slumped on top of Brandon for a moment, their harsh breathing the only sound in the room. At this moment, no words were needed; the press of their heated bodies was enough. Tash's lips were buried in Brandon's hair, and his arm remained locked around Brandon's chest. Tremors rippled underneath Brandon's skin.

Several minutes passed before Tash could move. "Let's get cleaned up and go eat." He stood, pulling Brandon up with him.

Brandon's heavy-lidded gaze fixed on the bed. "Mmm. I think we should start a new tradition. Dinner in bed." He kissed Tash's neck.

Tash shook his head and laughed. "You'd want every meal in bed." He kissed Brandon back. "Give me a minute to clean up here." After retrieving a towel from the bathroom, along with a damp washcloth, he wiped the two of them up as well as the chair.

"Why don't you get into bed, and I'll bring up the pizza and wine."

Brandon slid under the covers and lay propped up on one elbow. "Yeah. I think the ice cream already served its purpose. Hurry, 'cause I'm hungry."

"What else is new?" Tash shot back but left the bedroom to race down the stairs. He was no dope. There was nothing better than a naked and happy Brandon in his bed. When he got to the kitchen, he stopped short and burst out laughing. On the tabletop were Cleo and Caesar, their heads in the pizza box. When they heard his steps, they sat up abruptly and scrambled off the table, racing to points unknown.

With a shake of his head, Tash reached for the menus by the phone and headed upstairs. Looked like they'd have to get dressed for the deliveryman.

Chapter Twenty-Two

A T THREE FORTY-FIVE the next afternoon, Brandon sat in his deserted classroom, waiting for Dwayne and Wilson to show up. The boys were usually on time, so when he checked his watch and saw they were fifteen minutes late, he became somewhat concerned.

He opened the door and stuck his head outside to see if they were coming. Students still walked through the halls, either on their way to other after-school programs or finishing up late classes. It was hard to keep track of everyone with so many children jammed into these aging buildings.

Brandon left the room, closed the door behind him, and walked around the corner. A tall eighth grader, whom Brandon knew to be a troublemaker, had Dwayne crowded up against the wall of lockers. Another heavyset kid had a beefy arm draped across Wilson's shoulders, effectively preventing him from moving.

"My brother told me you little faggots love kissing the teacher's ass in class, huh?" Brandon watched as the tall boy pushed his face into Dwayne's. "And then you spending all that time with Mr. Gilbert. What you think that's gonna get you? He don't give a shit about you. He's just another white-boy do-gooder. And when he leaves, you'll still be stuck here with the rest of us."

Dwayne pushed up his glasses. "Well, I don't think so. Mr. Gilbert's really nice."

Brandon's heart swelled at the thought of the two kids standing up for him.

"And," Dwayne continued, "just 'cause you don't wanna go to college doesn't mean none of us do. Leave us alone."

"You're a fucking little loser like your little friend here. All you two do is read. You suck at gym, and you run like pussies."

Enough was enough. "What's going on, guys?" Brandon sauntered over to the group, and the two older boys sprang away from the younger ones. "Is there a problem?"

"Nah, Mr. Gilbert, uh, we were just talking." Wilson spoke fast, but Brandon caught the silent communication between him and Dwayne.

"Looked to me like more than talking was going on." He directed his gaze at the two older boys. "Are you supposed to be here after school?"

When the boys hesitated, Brandon snapped. "From what I know, you both could benefit from some extra study time, but if you don't belong here, I suggest you leave now." He turned to Dwayne and Wilson. "Let's go to my classroom."

He let the boys pass in front of him, and then when he saw that the two older ones remained where they stood, he glared at them, summoning up all his anger. "Didn't I say to leave?"

Mumbling under their breaths, they picked up their backpacks from where they'd left them strewn on the floor and hurried down the hallway. Brandon made sure they disappeared from sight before turning back to the two students. "Ready, guys?"

They stood before him, both of their faces a mirror of disbelief. "Wow, Mr. Gilbert, you really told them. They're always calling us names, and their brother also teases us." Wilson's eyes reflected admiration as well.

They reached the classroom, and when they'd settled into their seats, Brandon wanted a bit more information.

"Are you two being bullied by only them, or are there others as well?"

Again they shot each other looks.

"Come on, guys"—Brandon came from around the desk to sit in a chair across from them—"I can't help you if you won't tell me the whole story. I know you've had problems." He hoped they trusted him enough by now to open up and tell him everything. "I'm glad you're going to be coming regularly to the after-school center. But I'd like more information on what's happening in school. Are they the only ones bullying you, or are there others who give you trouble?"

"They're the worst ones." Wilson spoke to the floor. "They're always calling us names like 'wimp' and 'faggot' to our faces."

"Yeah," said Dwayne. "And other stuff."

"So why didn't you boys say anything to me or anyone else?" Brandon kept his tone gentle. He knew about peer pressure. It hadn't been that long since he'd been in a classroom as a student, and he remembered the derisive sneer of students when they found someone to pick on. Back in his small town, the guys had always looked at him as strange for never dating or showing interest in any of the girls they went to school with.

Each boy shrugged, and Dwayne spoke. "Well, we figured it's only gonna be like one more year until we can get out maybe and go to a different place for high school, so we didn't want to make any waves."

"I thought they'd leave us alone by now," said Wilson, his sneakered toe drawing a circle on the floor. "I mean, we never said anything to them. Why do they have to pick on us?"

An age-old question and one Brandon had no answer to. "Let's not concentrate on them now." Brandon knew he'd have to report it to the school, and he wanted to talk to their parents as well. "I printed out copies of practice tests from the previous specialized high school standardized tests and made each of you copies." He handed the packets over to the two boys. "I figured we'd start by going over how the test is set up and study models for each section."

He spent the next two hours explaining the different sections of the test and going over the first set of questions. Both boys picked up the format very quickly, and they were working out a geometry question when Brandon caught sight of the time.

"Oh wow, guys, it's almost six o'clock." They'd only planned to be there until five. "Call your parents right away and tell them you're with me, and I'll walk you home." While they made their calls, he packed up his laptop and checked his phone. By the time he was finished, they'd finished their calls.

"My mom was worried," said Wilson. "I hope she's not mad at you, Mr. Gilbert."

"It's okay; this was my fault. She should be mad at me." Brandon shepherded them out of the room in front of him, and they quickly left the school and stepped out into the chilly autumn night. "How far do you guys live from here?"

"Only a few blocks." They began to walk and within fifteen minutes, the dark shapes of the collection of apartment buildings that made up the project where the boys lived loomed up in front of him.

"This is it; you don't have to take us up. It's okay." Dwayne hefted his backpack on his shoulder, and he and Wilson took off before Brandon had a chance to respond. Walking back toward the train station, Brandon figured the last thing the kids would want was to be seen hanging around with their teacher.

He texted Tash that he was on his way to the carriage house. Feeling a little guilty he'd been spending so much time away, he'd told Esther he would take her and Louisa out to dinner the next night when he knew Tash would be working late.

His phone pinged a response.

Patient with a crisis. Home late. Wait for me for dinner.

At least he wasn't late. He decided to stop at the supermarket on the way home and make something nice for dinner. He grinned to himself as he ran down the steps to the subway, hoping to catch the incoming train. It had been hard to sit down today, with how sore his ass was after he and Tash had been up half the night. Tash had proved to be an insatiable lover, and Brandon was happy to reciprocate, kiss for kiss and stroke for stroke.

The sway of the train made it tempting to close his eyes and sleep, but Brandon knew the danger of that. He fought the pull and finally got off at his stop. It only took half an hour to pick out a roast for dinner and the ingredients for mashed potatoes that he knew Tash would love. With a start, he realized how domesticated this all was and how much he enjoyed it.

The night air was redolent with the woodsy scent of fireplaces from the brownstones, and the leaves still had a nice crunch as he walked home from. It was a beautiful autumn evening. Brandon enjoyed the brief walk to revive him from the overheated supermarket. He passed by their neighbor's house and admired the colorful collection of gourds on their front stoop, and thought about how in the spring, he'd love Tash to get flower boxes for the front of the carriage house.

Then he remembered he might not be here in the spring if he was in jail.

Shaking off the negative thoughts, he entered the house and greeted the two cats. "Hey, guys. Miss me?" They answered him with head butts and loud staccato noises, twining in between his legs. Brandon loved the cats; his mother hadn't ever even let him feed the strays outside the house as she thought the cats brought the devil and forbade him to have anything to do with them. Tash was still shocked at how they'd taken to him.

He prepared the roast and put it in the oven and then boiled the potatoes, setting them aside to cool. The tantalizing aroma of roasting beef and garlic teased the air and Brandon's stomach growled, but he knew it would be almost two hours before the meat was done. He caramelized some onions to add to the mashed potatoes.

All this took about an hour. Surprised Tash wasn't home yet, he checked his phone but saw no message. Brandon decided nothing sounded better than a hot shower, so he turned down the roast and then went upstairs. The bed was still messed up from when he left Tash in it this morning, sleeping with a sweet smile on his face. As Brandon soaped and rinsed himself, he wondered, was Luke right? Did he jump into a relationship with Tash too fast? He stayed under the heated spray, the water hissing over him.

Dismissing any doubts hiding in the corners of his mind, Brandon knew Luke was wrong. Long ago when he'd thought about relationships, he'd never pictured hooking up with random guys to have sex. He knew it was silly and most likely an improbable thing, but all he'd ever wanted was a home. Someplace safe to live, with a man waiting who was as eager to see Brandon as Brandon was him. There was something about Tash, from the moment Brandon saw him, that exuded trust, peace, and love.

How could Brandon not have fallen for him? Tash's gentleness and decency were the cornerstones of his personality. It's what made him such a wonderful psychiatrist. Just looking at him, a person knew they could unburden themselves to him without being judged.

What lay underneath the man was for Brandon alone. Tash had proved to be an inventive, passionate lover, spurring Brandon to explore his untapped sexuality. His stomach clenched, remembering Tash's tongue entering him, licking him, and driving him off the cliff to oblivion. Brandon wanted to do the same for Tash.

The water had cooled, and he turned it off and pulled a towel around him. He dried himself, his mood pensive as he slipped on a pair of Tash's sweats and a long-sleeved tee. Brandon's hoodie still lay on the floor from the night before, and he slipped it on as the house was still a little chilly after his shower. The bed looked too inviting, and a wave of exhaustion rolled over him. He set the alarm for forty-five minutes and slid under the covers.

The loud beeping woke him from such a deep sleep he didn't know where he was at first. He rolled over and smelling Tash's scent on the sheet, that cool rainwater smell he loved, Brandon smiled. A sound from downstairs caught his attention. Tash must've come home while he was napping. Slipping out of bed, Brandon decided to sneak up on his lover and surprise him with a kiss. Brandon crept noiselessly to the door and turned the doorknob so it made no sound. To his surprise, he heard two voices, a man's and a woman's.

Valerie must've stopped by. Maybe she'll stay for dinner.

The socks on his feet not only kept them warm but silenced his footsteps as he headed to the top of the stairs. He was about to descend when he heard his name mentioned. He knew he shouldn't listen, that it was wrong to eavesdrop, but he couldn't help himself. From the start, Valerie had seemed suspicious of him, and it bothered Brandon. He wanted to be friends with her like he wanted Tash and Luke to return to their easy friendship before Brandon had arrived.

So instead of doing the right thing, going downstairs and joining the conversation, against his better judgment he stayed at the top of the stairs and listened to her and Tash. He leaned forward to hear.

"I see Brandon is very comfortable here." Valerie sounded curious. "Is he living with you already?"

"No. But I gave him the key so he can come and go. Our schedules are so different—"

"You gave him a key, yet when I asked you for one,

you said no? What happened to you?" Valerie's incredulous voice rose in the air. "I'm your sister, your *family*. He's a stranger; someone you've known little more than a month."

Brandon felt sick to his stomach. He gripped the railing, his fingernails digging into the wood.

"Val, stop getting so upset."

Tash's soothing voice relaxed Brandon. He was confident Tash could calm Valerie down to listen to reason.

"How could I not be upset? Here you sat in virtual mourning for years after Danny died. All it took was a look from a hot young guy and suddenly everything's better? You've never been reckless before. I don't understand."

"Why do you have to understand?" Tash's exasperated voice pained Brandon. "It happened. I can't explain it. From the first, there was something about Brandon I couldn't resist. He was like an overwhelming force to me. I couldn't stay away. I didn't want to, and even now when I'm with him, it only gets better every time I see him."

"It sounds like lust to me, not love."

"You're being ridiculous," said Tash, annoyance creeping into his voice for the first time.

"I'm being ridiculous?" The disbelief in Valerie's voice hung in the air. "You're thirty-nine, almost forty and he's twenty-five. From what Luke's said, Brandon had a miserable childhood and has probably never even been with another man. What does he know about love, relationships, any of it? I'm afraid for you."

"Afraid for me? Why?"

Brandon leaned forward to catch her words.

"I'm afraid he's experimenting, trying to find his way, and who could blame him? I don't doubt that he cares about you; you're a wonderful man. But he sees you as a father figure—someone to look up to for advice and comfort. And you, because you've been so hurt and lonely, mistook his attention and spun it into a love story. Maybe he doesn't want to hurt your feelings."

That's not true. Brandon wanted to run down the stairs and confront Valerie, but hung back, holding his breath and waiting to hear what Tash would say.

"That's not the way it is between us. We love each other."

Brandon cheered inside.

"I'm sure you think you love him, but you barely know each other. And…" She paused, and Brandon, already sick to his stomach, wondered what else she could say to tear his heart to pieces. "How well does he know himself? He's a nice guy, of course. I'm not saying he isn't. But he's coming off a horrible situation for years and finding his brothers. I'm sure he's confused and looking for someone to cling to."

"So you think that's what I am? A security blanket?"

A trickle of fear ran through Brandon's blood as he listened to the resigned tone in Tash's voice. Now Brandon knew why people shouldn't eavesdrop. Acid churned in his stomach, and he had a sickening suspicion his entire world was about to come crashing down.

"What I think is that he's looking for a place for himself and needs someone to guide him. I don't doubt he has feelings for you, and you, because you're so lonely and kind, mistook them for more than they are."

Brandon waited for a response from Tash, an emphatic denial. He wanted Tash to tell his sister in no uncertain terms that he loved Brandon, and Brandon loved him.

"Do you really think so?"

"I do. I'm not saying it to be mean. I'm being realistic. And don't forget all his legal troubles. The last thing the man needs is to think about a relationship right now if he could be going to jail."

Brandon held his breath.

"Maybe you're right, and I've been the fool all along."

Nauseated, Brandon fled from the top of the stairs back to the bedroom. He had trouble catching his breath. Was this happening? How could Tash have so little faith in him? In the two of them?

Maybe he was wrong not to go downstairs and confront them, but Brandon didn't have the strength, not if he had to convince not only Valerie that he loved Tash but Tash as well. All he wanted to do was curl up and lick his wounds. He laced up his sneakers and returned to the stairs. Neither Valerie nor Tash were in the front room. On silent feet, he made his way down the steps and took his jacket from the hook by the front door and picked up his backpack. He turned and scanned the interior of the house, his gaze stopping briefly on the two cats stretched out on the sofa before he turned the knob and opened the door. Brandon closed it quietly behind him and walked into the darkness.

Chapter Twenty-Three

T ASH HAD COME home, expecting to find Brandon waiting, and hoped to spend a nice evening curled up on the sofa together watching a movie. Instead, Valerie had stopped by his office as his last patient was leaving, insisting she wanted to talk to him.

Tired as he was, he couldn't refuse her. They hadn't seen much of each other in the past weeks, and he knew that was his fault, so he invited her home with him. He had the idea for the three of them to spend more time together, reinforcing the relationship he and Brandon had forged in front of Valerie. Then maybe she'd see how happy Brandon made him.

Coming home to a house warm and fragrant with the smells of something delicious in the oven made him think of the future. A future where he and Brandon lived here together, making a life together. Perhaps, if he allowed himself to imagine it, they might one day get married and have a family. Brandon would make an amazing father.

But now, Valerie was acting so out of character he

didn't understand. She'd always been the constant in his life, the one person he could always trust to stand by and support him. Seeing her standing in front of him with her lips pressed in a tight, angry line, he almost didn't recognize her. Displeasure rolled over her in visible waves.

"I must be crazy to let you mess with my mind." He couldn't wait for Brandon to wake up from his nap. When Tash had peeked in earlier and seen Brandon curled up in the middle of the bed with a peaceful smile on his face, he'd wished Valerie wasn't waiting downstairs so he could climb into bed and hold Brandon close. "You're wrong about Brandon, and you're certainly wrong about me."

"I don't think I am. He's—"

"Stop telling me who he is." He slammed his hand down on the wooden table so hard the plates Brandon had set out for them earlier rattled. "You met him how many times? Once? Twice? And you'd already formed an opinion based on what Luke told you, that I was too old for him. You don't know anything about him. You've never seen how caring he is, and how he thinks of everyone before himself. How he spends his time helping his students or at the Center with the kids."

He stopped breathing hard, his gaze locked with Valerie's. "You have no idea how he makes me feel."

"How?" Valerie put her hand on his arm. "How does he make you feel?"

"Wanted. Needed. Alive." The taste of Brandon remained on Tash's tongue long after they'd kissed, and the press of his lips and touch of his hand lingered warm and vital. "It's never been like this before. Even with Danny."

He put his hands on Valerie's shoulders. "I love him, Val. I can't explain why or how it happened like a flash bang of fireworks. But trust me." He pulled her close, and she clung to him. "It's the real thing. For both of us. I want you to love him like another brother."

"I don't want to lose you again. I love you so much it almost killed me the way you withdrew from everyone after Danny died." Her voice was muffled in his chest, but he understood. Val had always been a mother hen, the one who worried about everyone else.

"I promise you won't. And I think it's high time you stop thinking of my life and find yourself a guy to worry about."

She let out a gasp. "Oh God!"

"What's wrong?" He opened the refrigerator and took out a bottle of water.

"I forgot I have a date, and if I don't leave now, I'll be even later than normal." She spoke over her shoulder, already hurrying out of the kitchen to the front hall to get her coat.

"So are we good?" He had to ask. She was his little sister but also his friend. It wasn't only a promise he'd made to his parents to always look after Valerie; it was one to himself.

Valerie flung her arms around him. "I'm sorry for what I said." She hugged him hard and pulled back to speak to him face-to-face. "I watch your eyes and how, when you speak of Brandon, there's a glow there I've never seen before. So if you're happy, then so am I." Her lips curved up in a mischievous smile. "I always wanted a little brother."

"Brat." He pulled her to him and kissed the top of her head. "Now go be nice to the poor guy you've kept waiting."

"Oh, he's been waiting for years for me to come around. He'll wait a little longer." She swung her purse over her shoulder and opened the door.

"Who is he? Do I know him?" Tash frowned. "You never tell me who you're dating anymore."

"Gotta go. Bye." She blew him a kiss and closed the door in his face.

Hmm. Why did it seem as though she was deliberately hiding who she was dating? Cleo wound herself around his ankles, looking for some attention. "What do you say, girl, if we go upstairs and wake that lazy guy?"

"Meorw." Cleo ran down the hallway.

Tash shook his head at his cat's strange behavior as he mounted the steps. His heart rate quickened when he reached the top of the stairs, anticipating crawling into bed with Brandon. To hell with the roast. He'd gladly suffer another night of pizza if it meant a few extra hours in bed with his lover.

"Hey, Sleeping Beauty." His voice died in his throat when he saw the bed was empty. The air rested quiet, without any scent or sound, as if it had been empty for a long time. The light in the bathroom was off, and the room was dark.

"Brandon? Where are you?" Panic rose in his chest. Where could he have gone? It had only been around half an hour since he'd come up here and seen him sleeping. He glanced around the room but didn't see a note.

"What the hell?" Frantic with worry now, he pulled out his phone and called Brandon's cell, but it went straight to voice mail. He texted him.

Where are you? What happened? Call me.

He waited for an answering ping back but nothing. Tash ran down the stairs, searching through the carriage house, but the empty rooms mocked his solitude. Futilely, he kept looking at his phone, willing it to ring, but it remained stubbornly mute.

His pacing continued in the front hall where the cats sat on the stairs, regarding him with their unblinking blue stares. It was then he noticed Brandon's backpack was missing from the floor.

What the fuck?

AFTER A NIGHT waking up every hour or so, at seven a.m. Tash figured there was no sleep left in his bed. The first thing he did was check his phone, but there was no message, no voice mail. Nothing. He took a shower and got dressed, then, after checking his silent phone again, fed the cats and made his coffee. With panic tasting bitter in his mouth, he picked up the phone and dialed Ash's number.

"Tash? What's the matter? Did something happen to Brandon?"

"That's what I'd like to know." He quickly outlined what happened last night, leaving out the content of his conversation with Valerie.

"So you haven't heard from him even though you texted him?" Ash sounded more curious than worried. "Hold on while I text him, and I'll see if he answers me."

Several moments passed by.

"Anything?" Tash asked.

"No. Shit," Ash bit out.

"I'm going to go to his school and try to catch him this morning. I'll keep you posted." He hung up before Ash could answer. Shoving his keys in his pocket, he sent up a silent prayer for everything to be all right. He rushed out of the house to the garage like the hounds of hell were nipping at his heels.

Without traffic, it would take about half an hour to get to Brandon's school; Tash pushed through many yellow lights and skirted the line on some red ones, but he didn't give a shit. Brandon's first class started at eight thirty-five a.m., and he pulled up to the front of the school at eight thirty. For the first time in years, he used the power of his MD license plate and parked in a No Standing zone. Knowing his luck, he'd probably get a ticket anyway.

He headed up the steps of the school with the kids who were rushing so as not to be late for the first period. At the front door, a bored-looking security guard stopped him.

"Can I help you?"

"I have to get a message to one of the teachers. Randy Gilbert?" Tash tapped his foot on the step. "It's a family emergency."

The guard leveled an assessing stare up and down his body, then jerked a nod. "Go on in."

Tash huffed out a quick thank-you and raced up the stairs, then skidded to a stop as he entered the main hallway. The cacophony of noise from all the students walking to class was overwhelming. Tash realized he had no idea where to go; he'd never visited Brandon inside the school. He stopped an older man who looked as though he worked there.

"Do you know where Randy Gilbert's classroom is, please?"

The man peered over his half-moon glasses. "Second floor, fourth classroom on the left."

"Thanks." Tash spoke over his shoulder, then cut in and out between the students going up the wide first-floor staircase. The smell of disinfectant, chalk dust, and the faint scent of whatever was being served for lunch in the cafeteria hung in the air. He passed by endless rows of lockers, then counted down the doors until he reached the fourth one.

Disappointment flooded through him when he

peeked in through the narrow glass window of the door. An older woman stood in front of the classroom. He looked back down the hall to make sure he was standing before the right door, but then he felt a tap on his shoulder.

"Tash? What the hell are you doing here?"

Tash spun around to face Gage. "Hey, I'm really glad to see you. Do you know where Brandon's classroom is?"

Gage gestured with his chin. "It's this one, but he called in sick this morning and said he wasn't going to be in for the next few days."

Tash's stomach sank. His face must've displayed his distress, because Gage stared hard at him and took him by the arm, led him down the hall, and opened a small door marked Private. The room, used as some kind of office, was empty save for a desk and several chairs. There was a credenza piled high with files and books along the back wall.

"What's going on?" Gage leaned against the door, which he had closed and locked behind him. "I haven't seen or heard from either of you in days."

Tash debated how much to tell Gage. Although Gage might be happy that Tash and Brandon were lovers and had pushed for the two of them to get together, the reality of it had to be bittersweet.

"We're fine. I mean, I thought we were until last night. I came home, and Valerie and I had a talk. Brandon had gotten home earlier than me and started dinner and was taking a nap. After she left, I went upstairs to wake him, and he was gone." He ran his hand through his hair. "I haven't seen or heard from him since."

"Hmm." Gage tapped his chin with a finger. "You definitely saw him there, right? And you spoke to him yesterday? Everything was fine between the two of you?"

Tash hesitated. "Are you really okay with this? I know we haven't spoken recently, but I didn't want things being awkward between us. I haven't been a good friend by shutting you out."

Gage dropped into the chair next to Tash. "First and foremost, you'll always be my friend. But remember I thought you and Brandon would be good together. In a strange way, he reminds me of Danny a little—the way he finds joy in life and sees the good in everyone." Pain flickered in his eyes for a brief moment. "It hurt me more to think you were wasting your life mourning my brother who'd treated you so badly."

"It wasn't all bad, only in the end when the drugs and sickness took over." Tash swallowed hard. "We had some good years together."

"But he chose the drugs over both of us. I loved him more than anything, but it wasn't enough. He always needed something more than what he had right in front of him."

"It should've been obvious to me what he was doing, but I loved him too much to think he would lie to me, to both of us." Tash sprang out of his chair to pace the small room. Gage remained seated, watching him with hollow, dark eyes.

"I'm the professional, and yet I let him blind me to his drug abuse. I failed him, with the most horrible consequences."

"It wasn't your fault. Stop blaming yourself. Danny was my brother, but I knew his faults, and one of them was that he was a master manipulator. If he didn't want you to know something, he'd turn on the charm and you forgot what it was you were concerned about."

"I always wondered how you forgave me. I was a psychiatrist, trained to see through things like that, yet I missed all the warning signals in the most important person in my life."

"Because if I couldn't forgive you, how could I forgive myself?" Gage leaned back in his chair and closed his eyes yet kept speaking. His fists clenched tightly in his lap. "I was his brother. I loved him more than anything. Who knew him better than me, the person he grew up with?" He opened his eyes and pinned Tash with his dark, grief-riddled eyes. "But it seemed neither of us really knew him. And that's what you have to understand. The problems he had were kept so well hidden even he didn't know how to escape from them once the drugs took over. And my God." Gage swallowed and shook his head. "Even after two years, when he came back, you went to him in the hospital, no questions asked, sick as he was, and cared for him until he died. How many other people would do that?"

"I loved him and couldn't bear the thought of him dying alone. He didn't deserve that, no matter how much he'd hurt me."

Gage nodded. "I know it and appreciate everything you did for the both of us. But that's why you needed to start living again. You were doing penance for something that wasn't your fault. And selfish as Danny was, I know he would never have wanted you to spend the rest of your life mourning him. Life to him was for living to its fullest."

"So you have no problem with Brandon and me as a couple?" Tash needed this validation from Gage. It was the final step in him cutting the ties that bound him to the past and the darkness he so desperately wanted to leave behind.

"Problem with it? I'm thrilled about it. It bugged the shit out of me to know you spent every night holed up in your house with those damn cats."

Tash grinned. "That's because they don't like you."

"They're hellcats." Gage smiled back at him, and Tash's heart felt infinitely lighter; the weight of his years of sadness and self-flagellation lifted.

"Now about Brandon."

Tash's heart sank. "I don't understand it. Everything was perfect. I know he was a little freaked out about the whole investigation, but he and his brothers had a long talk, and we were all standing by him. We were going to fight to prove he was subjected to so much abuse over his lifetime, he snapped."

Gage looked at him strangely. "I don't think that's

what his disappearance is about at all."

Now Tash was thoroughly confused. "You don't? Then I'm at a loss. He was there last night. I spoke to him before, and everything was fine. The food was cooking in the oven. He simply disappeared."

"Is it possible he overheard what you and Valerie talked about and got upset?"

Tash recalled the conversation with his sister, and coldness swept through him. He remembered how he'd almost allowed Val to persuade him that Brandon was merely experimenting with him. Even worse, that they didn't really love each other, but each was using the other in their own way.

"Shit. I didn't even think of that. I mean Valerie even had me agreeing at one point that maybe I didn't really love him."

"But you two straightened it out; she understands now how much you and Brandon care for each other, right?"

Gage's words barely penetrated. "What, yeah, but what if he heard me saying she was right, that he was too young? I thought he'd fight back, but he ran instead." Once again, Tash's lover had left him, but for an entirely different reason. This time was purely Tash's fault. He should've stood up to Valerie from the start and told her he loved Brandon and to leave him alone about it.

"I can't blame him for being insecure. His whole life is collapsing around him. He's worried about going to jail, and the one person he thought would be with him, me, he thinks is wavering and having second thoughts." Panic rose in his chest. "Do you have any idea where he could've gone? I called Ash, and he's waiting for me to tell him something."

Gage unlocked the door. "Let's go to the office and see if he left any information with the secretary."

They walked through the silent halls. "Don't you have a class to teach now?" Tash didn't want Gage to get in trouble.

"Not until nine thirty." He checked his watch. "I still have half an hour, so I'm good." They reached a door marked OFFICE, and Gage entered first and headed to the desk. "Hi, Pearl."

"Hello, Gage, what can I do for you? Is this gentleman with you?" Pearl was one of the throwbacks to the 1980s. She was a robust elderly lady with gray hair set in waves around her lined face and glasses on a pince-nez that Tash hadn't seen since the last time he visited his parents down in Florida at the senior citizen community.

"He is. I'm trying to find out if Randy Gilbert left any information when he called in this morning."

"He didn't. I spoke with him personally. Poor young man sounded sad, so I assumed it was a personal issue he was dealing with."

Damn. Tash's hopes crashed. "Do you know how many days he said he needed to take?"

Pearl checked her calendar. "Definitely the rest of the week. That's all he told me. He has the time." She glared at him over her glasses. "You aren't from the

Special Investigator's Office, are you? Because he has a right to use his personal time. We didn't do anything wrong in giving him the week off if that's what you're thinking."

Gage chuckled. "No, Pearl. Dr. Weber is a personal friend of mine and Randy's, and we're both a little worried about him." He turned to Tash. "Pearl's like everyone's mother here and is very protective of us."

Somewhat mollified, she took off her glasses and polished them. "Well, he's so young and sweet. I hate to see a teacher like that with so much potential become beaten down and cynical because of the system. Plus he told me all about finding his brothers. The young teachers all confide in me. He even told me his real name was Brandon but he used Randy as a nickname."

Surprised at this, Tash smiled at her. "I'm glad he has people like you he feels comfortable with enough to confide in. Thank you."

They left the office and he and Gage walked silently through the hall when a thought hit him. "Wait a second. How did you know what Valerie and I spoke about last night?" He stopped and grabbed Gage's arm. "I never said what it was about, yet you knew already."

The slight smile Gage wore faded, and he couldn't hold Tash's gaze. "Uh, I gotta go to class."

"Oh no, you don't." Like a dousing of ice-cold water, Tash woke up as if from a fog. "Holy shit. It was you." A grin broke across his face as he continued to grasp Gage's arm. "You were the guy Val was on a date with last night. You're dating my sister?"

He watched the emotions play across Gage's face and waited for him to speak.

"Yeah. Val and I, we've been seeing each other for a while now." The look on Gage's face as he peered up at Tash through his lashes spoke of guilt and hesitancy. "We were going to tell you, but..." His voice trailed away, and he shifted on his feet.

"But what?" Tash pressed, a little hurt that his sister and friend had been keeping this from him.

"You were in such a deep, black place, Val didn't want to upset you and have you think she was going to abandon you. Now that you and Brandon are together, I told her the time had come to tell you. We have nothing to hide." Gage's frankness was one of the things Tash loved about the guy.

Val and Gage. Why not? Delight spread through Tash. "I'm happy for you guys. I couldn't think of a better man for my sister."

His phone buzzed in his pocket, and all other thoughts fled when he saw it was from Ash. "Yeah, what is it? I'm at his school, but they don't know anything."

"Come to my office. Together we'll try to figure out where he went." Ash's grim voice shook Tash. "I won't let him run out of our lives."

Chapter Twenty-Four

AFTER ALL THESE years, Brandon couldn't believe he was going home. He'd opted to take the bus to Pennsylvania from Port Authority since it was cheapest and it would leave him in the center of Reading. From there he could take a cab.

He gave the driver his ticket and settled into his window seat, staring out of the glass as they began the two-and-a-half-hour ride back to where he'd sworn he'd never return. Soon the traffic of midtown Manhattan was behind him, and they lumbered onto the NJ Turnpike. His thoughts turned inward.

Was Valerie right? Going over his relationship with Tash from the first kiss in the kitchen to the night of ice cream and the incredible lovemaking that had followed, Brandon didn't think so. From his very first glimpse of Tash, before he knew who he was, Brandon's body had a visceral reaction to him—an indefinable tug to discover who he was. Brandon shivered in his seat, the memory of Tash's strong arms holding him down, his cock pushing inside Brandon, forever marking him, making Brandon one with Tash.

It went beyond the physical. If his time with Tash had taught him anything, it was that Brandon was not the long-ago little boy his brothers, especially Luke, tried to protect and shelter. Tash treated him like a man. Before he could move ahead and show Tash how he was willing to fight for their relationship, Brandon had to be able to live in the open and not be afraid of who might be following him for the rest of his life.

It wasn't only about him now. He was letting not only Tash down, but the kids at his school. He'd left word that he needed the rest of the week off and called Dwayne's parents and Wilson's mother to say their after-school sessions would have to be postponed this week. Hopefully, he'd be coming back.

After he'd fled Tash's house, he'd gone home to lick his wounds. The comfortable apartment Esther had created in her basement was the perfect refuge; she'd given him two rooms, both large and airy. They were freshly painted in a pale yellow, with a large sectional sofa upholstered in some kind of soft, velvety fabric. There was a flat-screen television in the wall unit and bookshelves Esther told him to fill up with his books, as Drew had taken all of his when he'd moved. There were also two leather recliners, a little cracked with age but so damn comfortable to curl up in and read. His bedroom had a queen-sized mattress and another television set as well. Of course there was no kitchen, as Esther insisted he join her and Louisa for meals if he wanted to. The way those two women cooked, he'd be crazy not to.

Now he understood why everyone treated her as they did, and especially why Ash loved her so fiercely. She was one special lady. Even last night, though it was late by the time he'd gotten home, she had saved him something to eat, *"in case you were hungry,"* she'd said after he'd opened the door to her knock, to find her standing there with a plateful of food.

"PLEASE COME IN." He held the door open for her and took the plate from her hands. He'd left his appetite back at the carriage house but didn't want to seem impolite, so he set the food on the coffee table. "Why don't you sit down, and we can have a talk? I'm sorry I've been so absent lately. I don't want you to think I'm ignoring you."

Brandon watched Esther lower herself into the chair. He was as protective of her as his other brothers and vowed to stay at the house more often and help her and Louisa. A lump swelled in his throat. If he was still able to be around.

"What's wrong, Brandon?" Her gaze, sharp as always, searched his face. "Not that I don't want you here; of course, I'm delighted to have you home. I thought you'd be spending all your time with Sebastian and was surprised to see you come in."

He should've known someone as astute as Esther would see right through him. Instead of responding, he answered her with a question of his own. "Why don't you call him Tash, like everyone else?"

She settled herself more comfortably on the chair. "I call all the boys by their full names because their parents chose those names; they have some underlying meaning. None of them ever try to correct me anymore. It's one of the little perks of getting old," she said, her voice tinged with humor. "I can say almost anything I want and get away with it."

Despite his unhappiness, Brandon couldn't help but smile at her.

"Now, you haven't answered my question. Why are you here and not with your young man?"

Fresh pain sliced through him. "He doesn't believe in us. His sister thinks I'm using him to find myself and latched onto him as a security blanket." The memory of listening to those painful words hurt as acutely now as they did when he'd first heard them. Brandon squashed the black thoughts he'd had about Tash's sister. He hadn't meant to unburden himself to Esther, but she was so damn easy to talk to. His eyes burned, but pride wouldn't allow him to cry.

Her knowing eyes held his, but when she spoke, it was with the softness of love. "You know, family thinks they have a right no one else does because they want to protect the ones they love from getting hurt. That means they might say or do things that to an outsider may strike them as being mean. In their heart, that person believes they are doing the right thing." Esther's kind smile only made Brandon's guilt rise at the hateful feelings he'd had only moments before for Tash's sister.

"I'm going to tell you a story. Drew's sister and Jordan both had reservations about his relationship with Ash. You see, when your brother met my grandson, Drew was coming off a divorce from a woman none of us liked. None of his friends or even Rachel understood the attraction Drew had for Asher." Her lips curved up in a smile. "Plus, Asher didn't have the best reputation, if you know what I mean."

He'd heard about Ash's reputation, but as for Drew, Brandon was stunned. He didn't know Drew had been married before, to a woman. He and Ash were so much in love it was impossible to think of one of them without the other. "I had no idea."

Esther nodded. "Rachel spoke to Drew about it, and he assured her he loved Asher and knew his own feelings. Jordan, on the other hand, had a much harder time of it, and that, plus the death of Keith, Jordan's fiancé, destroyed their friendship for almost a year."

"But Drew stood up to his family and didn't allow them to minimize what he believed in. He trusted himself, Ash, and the love they had." Brandon leaned forward in his seat and hugged himself around the waist—as if to hold back all the pain threatening to burst from his body. God, he hurt so bad. It took several minutes before he could find his voice to speak again. "I'm afraid Tash still has reservations that I'm too young for him, and his sister played on those insecurities."

A sigh escaped Esther's lips. "I've seen so much

hatred and loss in this world. I sometimes wonder why people still believe they have the right to control other people's lives." She leaned forward and placed her small hand on his knee. "You must prove her wrong, prove them all wrong, all the doubters. I see what you feel for Sebastian, and it's mirrored in his eyes. Don't let age or time hold you back. When it's the right person, you know. You feel it"—she tapped her chest with her other hand—"here, where it counts."

"I also have that legal problem to contend with."

She nodded and stood up. He stood as well. "I know. But Asher is a wonderful lawyer, the best. If he can't help you, he'll find the person who can and spare no expense." She took his hands in hers. "To have found you has given him back his life. Even Drew wasn't able to give him complete joy."

He squeezed her hand gently. "I never thought to have a family. Thank you for including me in yours."

"Darling boy." She patted his cheek. "There is no yours or mine. There's only ours. You are as dear to me as Asher, Drew, and all my family. You are part of us." After wiping her eyes with her handkerchief, she continued. "Asher will take care of you."

After kissing her good-bye, he put the food in the little refrigerator, having no appetite to even look at it. He stretched out on his bed and made a decision. No one but himself would be in control of his future—not Ash, not Luke or even Tash. Before he fell asleep, he knew what he had to do.

BY THE TIME they reached the first rest stop in Hellertown, his stomach was in knots at the simple sight of the familiar blue, white, and yellow license plates on the cars whizzing by on the highway. When a state trooper vehicle drove by, he almost changed his mind about going back home and confronting his past. The resolve hit him, though, to deal with his problems head-on and face the day. He checked his phone and listened to the messages from Tash, begging him to call. Brandon's heart squeezed in his chest at the thought of causing Tash pain, but he knew this final hurdle to overcome would be either the beginning of their lives or the end. There were other messages from Ash and Luke and even one from Gage. All pleading with him to call them and let them know where he was.

And though he deleted the calls, it wasn't without a sense of wonder that only a month or so ago he'd had no one who cared: no family, no real friends, no love. Finding Luke and Ash had brought closure to their circle and a sense of completeness. And falling in love with Tash had given him a life he'd only thought possible in movies. No one could replace him, and he deserved a man who could be there for him, free and unencumbered. Brandon wanted to give that to him.

The bus revved up and pulled back onto I-78. Though the morning sky was a bright crisp blue with high white clouds hanging about, there were no gloriously colored trees flashing their autumnal foliage. Past rains had stripped the trees bare, and the rolling hills in the background were that flat dull brown that spoke of a winter yet to come. He closed his eyes and tried to sleep.

He was awakened by the ringing of his phone. Without thinking, he hit Answer.

"Brandon, is that you? Are you all right?" The anxiety in Ash's voice muted its normal hard tone to one full of pain. "Please, tell me where you are; don't run away from us."

"I'm sorry, but I need to do this on my own. You all can't protect me forever." Brandon pushed the button and muted it, then shoved it in his coat pocket. It vibrated a few more times, but he ignored it, choosing to look out of the window and watch the cars and trucks speed by. He loved them all so much but refused to drag them deeper into the sordid mess he'd made of his life. If he kept them at a distance, perhaps it would be easier for them to forget him if he had to go to jail. He pressed his cheek into the rough fabric of the seat, wetting it with his tears.

Another half hour passed, and they pulled into Allentown. He got off the bus to stretch his legs. The bus depot was next to an old-fashioned diner, and Brandon suddenly realized how hungry he was, having skipped both dinner the night before and breakfast that morning. He approached the driver who stood in the chilly air, catching a quick smoke outside.

"Do I have time to run in and get something to

eat?"

The driver exhaled a long gust of smoke to the side and checked his watch. "You got ten minutes. I don't wait, neither."

With a nod, Brandon ran into the diner. The surprisingly comforting smell of hamburger grease and french fries hit him. The place looked like it hadn't been updated since the 1970s; white walls were covered with a grayish film, and framed album covers from the 1950s and '60s hung in no particular arrangement. The booths were upholstered in a once-sparkly vinyl that had long since cracked and grown dull with age and years of bodies sliding in and out of the seats. There were the requisite mini jukeboxes on each table that Brandon bet, had he checked, wouldn't have a song newer than when Bill Clinton was president.

He ordered a turkey sandwich from the desultory waitress standing behind the horseshoe-shaped front counter and grabbed a bag of chips from the rack. She assured him with a snap of her gum that it wouldn't take long, so he sat in one of the spinny chairs at the counter.

"Brandon? Is that you, man?" A voice he hadn't heard in years called out from the pass-through of the open-air kitchen that ran the length of the front of the restaurant.

Brandon whirled around and stared in shock as a guy he'd gone to high school with, Jacob Zimmerman, came out from behind the swinging doors, wiping his hands on his apron.

"Ahh, hey, yeah. Jacob, wow." Brandon was at a loss for words.

"Holy shit, where did you disappear to? Like one day you were there and the next you weren't." Jacob's round face was screwed up as if the thought process was hard for him to continue.

"I, um, went to New York and became a teacher."

"Cool. Are you back here to live or to see your mom?" A sympathetic look crossed his face. "Sorry about your dad."

"S'okay." He craned his neck to see the waitress walking toward him with a bag he hoped contained his sandwich. "Um, I came back to take care of some things." He paid for the sandwich and chips and turned back to Jacob, who still stood waiting as if they were going to have a long conversation. "Sorry, Jacob, but I can't stay; my bus is getting ready to leave."

With a shrug, Jacob began to walk away, then stopped. "Good seeing you, Brandon. Don't be a stranger." He walked back to the kitchen.

Brandon pondered what Jacob had said as the bus started up again. Did Jacob mean it when he said not to be a stranger? Was it possible not everyone in high school had hated him? Perhaps the misery he'd suffered at home had twisted his outlook on everyone he knew. He'd trusted no one then, and that had continued into his adult life. Now he wasn't sure he even trusted himself.

The miles rolled by as he munched his sandwich. Familiar sights sped past him on the road: rolling farmland, all brown and withered now, but in his mind, he knew come the spring the farmers would be out there with their tractors or, if they were Amish, with their teams of mules, churning up the dirt, the scent of manure hanging heavy in the air. So different from the concrete streets of the city, the sidewalks jammed all day with people hurrying, racing to catch up to a life they never stopped to savor.

The careers his brothers had chosen, law and finance, held no interest for him. He respected them for their accomplishments, but to him, nothing was more important than feeding a child's mind. That moment when a child's face lit up with understanding was the greatest of his achievements. Even now he missed the classroom and his students. Guilt washed over him at the thought of disappointing Dwayne and Wilson.

The bus pulled into the inner-city bus terminal in downtown Reading. It was totally unchanged from when he'd left eight years earlier—poor, nondescript, and gritty. Not a place to hang around. He needed to double back somewhat, so he opted for a cab and hailed one that sat idling across the street.

It felt funny to be traveling the streets of this once-familiar town, looking for places he'd known like the back of his hand, only to see they'd gone out of business, replaced by a few trendy little shops, restaurants, and coffeehouses. It couldn't hide what he saw on the side streets—houses boarded up and stores with old for-rent signs hanging in the windows. Apparently, the economic boom hadn't reached this far inside the state.

They'd gotten back on the highway, and he was grateful the cabdriver was silent. He had no desire to make small talk. After a fifteen-minute drive back up Route 222, it was only a short distance from the exit. His stomach churned as they pulled onto the street.

A fog of poverty and disrepair hung over the house. The wooden front steps sagged to the right, and the color had faded to something indeterminate—not brown, not gray. It was as if an artist had finished painting the picture and then smudged it, blurring all the lines.

"This it, buddy?" The cabdriver met his eyes in the rearview mirror.

"Yeah." Brandon paid the fare and got out. The nauseating smell from the chicken coops down the street assailed him. He held his breath and ran up the rickety steps.

From somewhere in the distance, a dog barked. Plastic furniture stood about on the porch. Nausea cramped his stomach, and he wanted to turn around and run again, but this was something he needed to do. He knocked on the door.

From within, he heard shuffled steps. The inner door opened, and a woman peered through the torn outer screen door. "Oh my God."

"Hi, Mom. Can I come in?"

Chapter Twenty-Five

SITTING IN ASH'S office waiting for the phone to ring was torturous. Tash had managed to cancel his patients for the morning as he was in no mental state to treat anyone. Not knowing what had happened to Brandon last night was bad enough, and now to find this morning that he'd taken off the rest of the week for points unknown and wasn't responding to anyone's phone calls was enough to drive Tash to the brink of insanity.

"Where the hell could he have gone?"

"Shh. I'm trying his phone again." Ash put up his hand. "Brandon, is that you? Are you all right?"

Tash jumped out of his chair and ran to Ash's side.

"Please, tell me where you are; don't run away from us."

Tash's heart stuttered in his chest as he watched the light fade from Ash's eyes.

"Brandon, wait." Ash threw the phone onto his desk. "Damn it, he hung up."

"Did he say anything?"

Ash's brow furrowed. "He said he needed to do it on his own and not to worry about him. I'm going to call Jordan. Maybe Keith's old partner, Jerry, can figure out how to track the phone call. Then we might have an idea where he was going."

While Ash put in the call to Jordan, Tash texted Brandon several more times.

I love you. Where are you, and why are you running away?

He received no reply.

Ash slammed down the phone in frustration. "Jordan's in surgery and won't be out for several hours. I'm going to call Luke and speak to him."

Before he had a chance to pick up the phone again, it rang.

"Yes, Laura?"

"Esther is on line one."

Tash watched Ash take a deep breath in an attempt to calm down. No matter how crazy Tash was not knowing where Brandon had run to, he couldn't imagine how Ash felt, having only found his little brother again after so many years.

"Esther, how can I help you? I'm a little busy at the moment—" Ash halted, his eyes growing wide with disbelief. "He did? What did he say?"

Ash listened, and once again, Tash waited with nervous anticipation swirling in his stomach. Ash kept shooting strange looks at him.

"He didn't show up to work today and called in sick for the rest of the week."

Ash listened for several more minutes. "Thank you. I think you're right." For the first time, he smiled. "Very well, Esther. I'm sure you're right. I love you, and I'll call you as soon as we know anything." He was about to hang up when he looked at Tash. "Yes, he is." Ash handed the phone to him. "She wants to talk to you."

Puzzled, Tash took the phone from Ash. "Esther, it's Tash." He waited for her to speak since he had no idea what she had to say to him.

"Sebastian. I had quite a lovely talk with Brandon last night. Do you know why he left your house without seeing you?"

"No, do you? He talked to you?" Not that it would surprise Tash. Esther had a way with everyone she met. There was something about her that made you want to confide every one of your darkest fears and secrets to her.

"He did. He heard you last night. You and your sister. It was so hurtful to him to hear her say those things, and you not stand up and defend him—defend both of you, I should say."

The bottom dropped out of Tash's stomach. "What exactly did he say he heard?"

"That you believed what your sister said: that you're too old for him and he's using you for security." Her voice softened. "You don't believe that, do you?"

"No, no, of course not." The strength of his denial

and anger surprised even him. "He means everything to me. I love him. If he had stayed, he would've heard me wake up from whatever stupid pill I'd taken to tell my sister how wrong she was." He slumped onto the love seat by the window. "My God, how could he think otherwise? I can't imagine my life without him."

"Then find him and tell him that. Don't let him go until you're sure he believes it. He's so fragile now. You may have to persuade him of your truth."

"Thank you, Esther. I will. I promise to bring him back."

He hung up to find Ash staring at him. "What?"

"You really do love him."

"Not you too," said Tash, groaning as he scrubbed his face. "I thought you believed me."

"I didn't realize the strength of your feelings until I saw your face right now."

"Never mind that." Tash pushed up his glasses and rubbed his eyes. "What did she say about where he might have gone?"

Ash was busy checking something on his phone. "She believes—and I tend to agree with her—that Brandon went back to Pennsylvania to try and deal with the issue of Munson's death on his own. She thinks he went home."

"Shit." Tash sat and rested his head on the back of the love seat, staring up at the ceiling. "So, what do we do now?"

"First thing is to find out where the house is and pay her a visit."

Tash bolted upright to a sitting position. "You? You're going to go see Mrs. Munson, your foster mother?"

Lines of anguish etched deep into Ash's face. Tash knew how hard this was on him. But Tash also knew Ash would do anything for Brandon.

"Yeah. And I'm going to call Luke. I'm sure he'll want to come too. We can leave this afternoon and be there by early evening."

Something niggled at the back of Tash's mind, and he checked his calendar. He'd completely overlooked his afternoon court appearance with Connor Halstead. He'd be testifying in Johnny's defense. There was no way he could miss that.

"I can't go until later." After explaining about his appointment, Ash, who was already placing the call to Luke, nodded.

"I'm sure that's fine. Even if we leave around five tonight, we'll still be there before its gets too late."

Tash let out a sigh of relief. As Ash filled Luke in on the details, Tash ran over his last few meetings with Johnny in his head. The young man had made amazing progress and had blossomed in the care of the Ortega family in his home life and at the Clinic and community center for work. Brandon, who'd been working with Johnny the evenings Tash spent at the Clinic, had reported to him that Johnny was a bright kid who showed a real aptitude for computers. He was well on his way to getting his GED, and Brandon had no doubt Johnny would be going to college in the future.

He said good-bye to Ash and headed back to his office. The rest of the morning was spent going over Johnny's file in preparation for the meeting with the judge. At one o'clock, as he was finishing up his lunch, Tash received a call from Valerie.

"Hi, what's up?"

"I'm so sorry, Tash. Please say you'll forgive me." His sister's naturally bubbly voice sounded subdued in his ear, and he had a suspicion she'd been crying.

"What's wrong?"

"It's my fault Brandon left. I said all those things last night, and he heard me, didn't he?" Her hiccupping sobs tore at Tash's heart even though he knew it was the truth.

"I know you were being protective of me, but the truth is, I can't allow you or anyone else to tell me how I should feel." He listened to her sniffle for a few moments. "I love him, Val. Not knowing where he is, if he's in trouble or needs me…it's killing me. It's like a piece of me is missing. Do you understand?"

He held his breath as she remained silent on the other end.

"Yes," she whispered. "I do, and that's why I'm so upset. I'm so sorry I butted in and hurt you and Brandon. Luke is furious with me."

"He is?" Tash was surprised. Though he and Luke had made an uneasy peace, Tash sensed the man was still upset about Brandon's involvement with him.

"He told me I had to leave you both alone to let you work through your relationship. If it was meant to last, it would all work out."

Wise words. "So you know now how much I love him, don't you?"

"Yes." More sniffling. "You know I love you and only want the best for you. I honestly thought I was doing the right thing until we spoke afterward, and I saw it."

"Saw what?"

"I saw you again. The man you were before you retreated into your shell. And I don't ever want to see that other person. If Brandon is the one who brought you back to life, I promise I won't stand in your way."

"Thanks, honey. I have a court date this afternoon, but then Luke, Ash, and I are leaving for Pennsylvania."

"I know. I had to rearrange Luke's meetings."

"Right. So I'll keep you in the loop with what happens tonight, but I have to go now and prepare for this hearing."

After he hung up, Tash showered, dressed for court in a suit and tie, and left to meet Connor Halstead at the offices of Manhattan Legal Aid in Tribeca. He took it as a good sign that the train didn't take too long, and he arrived at the office with time to spare. He received his visitor's pass but still needed to go through metal detectors. The elevators groaned their way up to the space occupied by Legal Aid.

When the doors slid open, he found Connor waiting for him.

"Hey, Tash, good to see you."

They shook hands and proceeded from the elevator banks to enter the offices. Connor swiped them in, and as usual, Tash became overwhelmed by the organized chaos. No matter how many times he'd visited Conner here, Tash had never been able to figure out the maze of offices. After a few twists and turns, they arrived at Connor's office.

"Come on in to the dark side," said Connor with a grin. Tash had a feeling Connor was only half joking. Files were piled in a haphazard manner, looking like a sneeze would send them toppling to the floor. He had two computers and a desk piled with more files and law books. On the desk were pictures of his wife and baby son.

"How do you find anything in here?" Tash walked in and saw Johnny sitting at the small round table squeezed in the corner. "All set for this?"

The young man who sat at the table was hardly recognizable from the street kid he'd met months before. His hair was washed and cut, his skin was clear, and he'd gained some weight. He wore a suit with a tie and kept touching the jacket sleeve and the lapel as if he couldn't believe he was wearing it. When he caught Johnny's eye, the young man flushed. "I never had clothes like this before, but the Ortegas said I needed to look presentable for the judge, so she knows I'm serious." He smoothed his tie. "Mrs. Ortega took me shopping and bought it for me as a present."

"You look great, Johnny." Tash could see the pride Johnny now had in himself in his straight posture and the strong set of his shoulders, but his nerves still broke through in his shaky smile. "Don't worry. You aren't the same person you were when you were brought in on the breaking and entering charge. I've seen it, and I know the judge will as well." Tash tried to speak as reassuringly as possible, but the fear remained in Johnny's eyes.

"Do you think so?" Johnny's expression was doubtful. "She seemed really tough."

Connor sat facing them. "All you need to do is tell the truth. Your foster family already put in their report about how you keep the house rules they set for you and help around the house."

"They're nice to me, and Mrs. Ortega said she wants to see me graduate college. She said she believes I can do it like her son did."

"You can; I know it." Tash squeezed his shoulder. "There's no reason you shouldn't have faith in yourself."

For once the look Johnny gave him wasn't clouded with doubt; instead, hope dawned in his wary eyes along with the realization that maybe Tash was right. Those were the looks Tash had become a doctor for— the knowledge of a person's self-worth. Johnny would make it, and Tash would continue to help others like Johnny in the future.

"Ready, guys?" Connor checked his watch and gathered his files. "Let's go. It'll take us about fifteen to twenty minutes to walk to the courthouse on Centre Street."

Tash and Johnny trailed behind Connor as he led them out of the office and then out of the building. They walked in virtual silence to the court, each with a heavy weight on their mind.

After passing through security, they entered the courthouse, following Connor, who walked through the halls with natural confidence, greeting the other lawyers. They passed by a number of doors, which all looked the same to Tash until they reached one with a sign outside that read COURTROOM. The detective, Jerry Allen, had already arrived, in case the judge wished to speak with him as well and approached Tash with a smile.

"How are you?"

Jerry shook his hand. "Well, thanks. And how is everything here?" He peered over Tash's shoulder. "Johnny looks good. Everything working out okay?"

Tash nodded. "Couldn't be better. Johnny is working, studying for his GED, and the Ortegas have nothing but praise for him. I think it's a win this time."

A tired smile broke out across Jerry's face. "Good to hear. It's nice to finally receive some positive news for a change."

"Things still tough with the investigation?" Tash gazed at him with a sympathetic smile.

"We should be able to make an arrest soon."

He accompanied Jerry to sit with him in one of the courtroom rows while Connor and Johnny sat at the desk in the front reserved for the defendants.

"That's great. I know Jordan will be thrilled."

"I'm putting in for retirement afterward. I'm glad to see Johnny safe, and the community center is a great thing. You guys are to be commended." Jerry patted him on the shoulder. "Luke's brother Brandon is even helping, I hear. He seems like a good kid."

Tash flushed. "He's hardly a kid; he's twenty-five."

"Anyone under the age of forty is a kid to me, Tash."

They shared a laugh; then Jerry sobered up. "Luke told me about his problems."

The smile froze on Tash's lips. "I-I can't talk about it."

"All rise." The bailiff's announcement cut short their conversation.

At that moment, the judge walked in, and they all stood. Tash hadn't even realized the ADA had entered the courtroom while he and Jerry spoke. Tash listened with half an ear to the introductions and the preliminaries.

"Be seated." The judge, Julia Harrison, seemed no-nonsense. She spent quite a bit of time going through the paperwork, and Tash could see Johnny losing confidence as the minutes ticked away. Connor, to his credit, spoke quietly to him, patting him on the back.

"Counselor." The judge directed her attention to Connor, peering at him over her reading glasses. "Your client seems to be abiding by the court-mandated community service. He's in therapy as well; is that correct?"

"Yes, Your Honor." Connor glanced over his

shoulder and waved Tash to join them at the table. "Dr. Sebastian Weber is present today. He is the psychiatrist who's been treating Johnny."

Tash stood beside Connor at the table. "Good afternoon, Your Honor."

"Dr. Weber, nice to see you again. You've been treating Johnny here for a while now. What is your prognosis?"

Before he answered, Tash gave Johnny a reassuring smile. "Your Honor, I am very happy to report that I see Johnny progressing beautifully. He's taken to working at the medical clinic and community center to heart and is learning to handle their computer systems. Additionally, he is studying for his GED and is on track to receive it next June. I have every confidence in him that he won't be re-entering his former life, and I recommend he continue the treatment plan he's been receiving."

The judge took a few moments, then directed her gaze to Johnny. "Young man, you have a lot of people in your corner."

Connor nudged Johnny. "You're allowed to answer her."

"He's right. I don't bite." She smiled for the first time.

"Yes, ma'am, I do."

"I hope you won't let them down." Her smile disappeared as quickly as it had come.

"I won't. I promise." Johnny looked to both Tash and Connor.

"Good." She closed the file. "I'll continue the programs and ask for another report in six months." Once again, she smiled at Johnny. "I'd like to hear that you've received your diploma, young man." She stood and left the courtroom.

"Is that it?" Johnny looked shell-shocked.

Connor, who was putting his files away in his briefcase, laughed. "Yeah. She's a straight-shooter. Keep your nose clean, and do what you've been doing, and you'll be fine."

Tash checked his watch and saw it was close to four o'clock. "I gotta go, guys, but I'll see you later this week, Johnny." He thanked Connor and waved his farewell to Jerry, who stared at him with an unreadable expression. Tash hurried out of the courtroom and strode down the hall, texting Ash that he was ready to leave.

He received an answer almost immediately. *Come to my office, and we'll leave from there.*

"Tash."

He spun around to see Jerry standing behind him.

"I can't hang around. I need to leave."

"I know where you're going, and I'd like to go with you. I'm off duty. I wouldn't be coming in any official capacity except as a friend."

Tash continued to walk, and Jerry matched him stride for stride. "I don't know. Brandon might freak out knowing you're a detective."

"I spoke to Luke, and he's fine with it, but he told me to check with you."

Tash's mind spun as he thought. If the local police showed up, maybe it would be a good idea for Brandon to have someone with him from law enforcement. Between Ash and Jerry, Brandon would have powerful allies on his side.

"All right, let's go. We're meeting Ash at his office."

As he and Jerry hurried out of the courthouse, Tash could only hope Brandon would be coming back with him when this was all over.

Chapter Twenty-Six

"**B**RANDON? OH, MY goodness. It is you. I'm not dreaming, am I?" His mother took a few tottering steps back to clutch at the door frame. Her frightened gaze remained on his face.

Alarmed that she might faint and hurt herself, Brandon put a gentle hand on his mother's shoulder to steady her. "No. It's me." He swallowed hard. "Can I come in?"

"Of course, you can. I can't believe this. God is good. He is merciful. I prayed every night since you left, every single night, and now he's answered my prayers." She kept talking as he slid his arms around her fragile shoulders, wincing at the feel of her bony frame through the threadbare robe and housedress.

He led her to the tiny living room, away from the chill of the front hall. They sat on the lumpy sofa, Brandon amazed that he still remembered to avoid the middle cushion where the springs were close enough to the surface to jab you through your clothes.

Tina Munson had been a pretty young woman

when he came to live with her and Paul Munson so many years ago, but a lifetime of abuse and hopelessness had drained whatever beauty she might have once possessed. Her mental state could only be fragile at best. With sadness, Brandon noticed the webbing of lines crisscrossing her face and the dull gray swathes in her once-luxurious dark hair.

She clutched the tiny cross on the necklace she always wore and mumbled to herself, and he waited, knowing she was praying. When she finished, she opened her eyes and smiled through her tears.

"I waited so long for this day. Why did you leave me? What made you run away?"

This was harder than he'd thought. For years he'd hidden, and now that the time had come for him to confess, the words died in his throat. The disheveled little house reeked of poverty and hopelessness. It was obvious the death of Munson had taken its toll on her physically and mentally. How could he tell her that he was the one who'd killed her husband?

"Brandon, dear. Please talk to me. I've been so lonely here, all by myself. You...you know Paul died, right?" She hugged herself around the waist. "It was such a shock when they found him."

"Who found him?"

"Aaron Masters and Samuel Zinn. He never should've been drinking so much."

Brandon stared at her. "What? What do you mean?" The thump of his pounding heart almost drowned out her words.

"Didn't you know? I thought you must have heard or read it in the newspapers. He'd been drinking at that bar, Imitations, right off Route 61. I warned him so many times not to drink so much because he always got into fights, but"—she pushed back her hair with a trembling hand—"he didn't ever listen to me. He left the bar after the bartender cut him off. All I know is he was found by the side of the road, beaten and bloody."

A fitting end to a monster. It took all of Brandon's strength not to fall apart from the years spent holding himself together.

"He was at a bar?" With the roaring in his ears, Brandon wasn't quite sure if he was awake and speaking or if this whole day was a nightmare suddenly turned dream. "But I thought…" He stopped, unable to continue and process how, with one small sentence, his life had been handed back to him.

"You thought what, dear?"

Brandon shook his head, unable to speak. It was over, all over. All at once he was dizzy with freedom and drunk on life. He wanted to scream from the rooftops and run down the street. But most of all, he wanted Tash. He didn't care anymore what Tash's sister thought. Life was meant for living, and he'd be damned if anyone would tell him whom he could love.

After he finished here, he'd return to that cozy carriage house and refuse to leave until Tash understood that not another day would go by without the two of them spending it together.

"It doesn't matter anymore."

And it didn't. The pain had slipped away like sand through his fingers, leaving nothing behind. He was cleansed, freed from the darkness and secrets he'd lived with for so long like a second skin. He was ten pounds lighter and ready, for the first time, to begin again. Restored, alive, and anxious to take back a life he'd almost given up on.

"How have you been living here?" He looked around at the horrid little house. Even without the frightening presence of Munson, the house huddled within itself, as if preparing for whatever unhappiness might cross its doorstep.

"I have my social security, and the church helps me." She lifted her chin and a spark of some long-ago passion flared, not yet dimmed by her miserable life. "I work in the office. I don't take charity."

Brandon's heart went out to her. This diminutive woman had suffered so much, silently and with dignity. She was as much a victim, if not more, than he and his brothers were, trapped in a never-ending cycle of abuse and pain.

"I prayed for you boys, all three of you. I was happy that you made it out. Because no matter where you ended up, it had to have been better than here. And I'm sorry." Tears poured from her faded eyes. "I'm so sorry I wasn't strong enough to protect you, and poor Luke, and Ash. You deserved so much better than I gave. I wanted children so badly. God was right not to let me be a mother. Look at what I let happen to you boys." She crumbled into herself, crying softly.

Brandon gathered her in his arms, letting her weep. It had to be cathartic for her. "It's going to be okay. We're all fine." He rubbed her back, murmuring to her. "Everything's going to be okay now."

"I'm so glad he's dead." She lifted her head from his shoulder and brushed the hair out of her wet eyes. "I know we shouldn't speak ill of the dead, but God forgive me, he was an evil, cruel man, and he deserved it for everything he did." Her shoulders shook.

"Did you know?" Brandon had to ask.

"I know how he beat you and how he hurt Luke so badly that last night. I called the police and the ambulance to come to the house. That poor child." Her eyes clouded with grief. "I only hope he made it through and could forgive me in his soul."

She didn't mention Ash, and Brandon wouldn't. It wasn't his story to tell, and he doubted Ash would ever bring it up. "I'm a teacher now, Mom. I live in New York City and teach children."

Her face lit up. "Oh, like you always wanted. I'm so proud of you, sweetheart." She hugged him, light as a bird. "Let me make us some tea, and we can sit in the kitchen and talk. I want you to tell me everything."

Brandon stood and helped his mother off the sofa, keeping his arm around her as they walked to the back of the house. There was no family room in the tiny house, only the kitchen where he would sit with his mother after school and do his homework while she gave him a snack. It was the one room that radiated warmth. The only place he'd ever seen his mother relax—whether she was baking, cooking, or praying at the table before their meals.

He sat at the worn wooden table with its faded tablecloth and cheap plastic place mats, feeling like the years had rolled back and he was a child again. She boiled the water and gave him a plain white mug with a store-brand tea bag. She sat across from him with a mug of her own that Brandon could see held only boiled water. It occurred to him then she might not have another tea bag to use.

Like a slap in the face it hit him how far he'd moved ahead with his life, while here in the countryside, time stood still. Everything was as he'd left it eight years earlier—the faded wallpaper with the water spots from the leak in the ceiling when it stormed, down to the kitschy salt and pepper shakers he'd made in school. He, on the other hand, had gotten his education, become a teacher, and fallen in love.

"Tell me, do you have a girlfriend or someone special?" Her hopeful eyes glanced up at him, shy yet curious.

His gaze skittered away. "I do have someone special." Given his mother's religious fervor, Brandon didn't think it was the right time to bring up the fact that his someone special was a man.

"But?" She looked perplexed. "Is something wrong?"

"I'm not sure if they realize how much I care for them."

Her gaze held his. "Are they good to you?"

Remembering Tash's probing kisses and the unfettered joy in his smile, Brandon couldn't hold back his happiness. "Yes. The best. I never thought I'd fall in love, and yet there was never any choice as soon as we met."

She squeezed his hand. "I'm so happy for you. You deserve it." She stood and took away the teacups. Brandon noticed how she saved his used tea bag, and his heart clenched in his chest. "Let me make you something to eat." She opened the ancient refrigerator and frowned. "I remember you boys loved tuna fish sandwiches. Would you like one?"

Although he knew it might be her last can, Brandon couldn't refuse without hurting her pride. "I'd love one, Mom." When she smiled at his endearment, he made a decision. When the time came for him to return home, he'd be bringing her back with him. Ash and Luke would learn to deal with it. He watched her move about the kitchen, opening the can and mixing in the mayonnaise, her happiness increasing with her actions.

She slid a sandwich on plain white bread in front of him, watching him anxiously as he bit into it.

"Wonderful," he said, his mouth full of the sandwich. How many afternoons had he spent sitting here, eating a sandwich exactly like this, while his mother puttered around the kitchen cleaning up, singing hymns? With the space of time and faded memories, he could almost think of his childhood with fondness. Minus the beatings and the verbal abuse.

Back in Georgia he, Ash, and Luke would all fight to help her make cookies, each one grabbing the spoon or the bowl from the other until she would separate the cookie dough into three bowls and give each of them one of their own. If he tried hard enough, he could smell the vanilla and sweet chocolate in the air.

"How long can you stay?" She looked out of the window at the sun, which crept along the bright horizon. "Do you have a car, or did you take the bus?"

When he'd left Esther's this morning, Brandon honestly thought he'd be going to jail. He hadn't planned for anything past tonight. "I took the bus. But I have the rest of the week off if I need to take it."

"It would be wonderful to have you here with me." He grimaced, and she added hurriedly, "But I understand if you don't want to." She braced her arms on the edge of the sink and hung her head. "I'm sure you must hate me for being such a weak woman. I hate myself. If I'd only stood up to him, had more of a backbone, you never would've run away. I could've saved Luke, maybe." A fresh torrent of tears poured down her face. "God only knows what happened to poor Ash."

"Mom, please don't cry." Brandon slipped his arms around her. "They're fine. I promise." He could feel her stiffen in his arms.

"You hardly ever called me that; none of you boys did. I understood although it hurt my heart. I always wanted children. I always wanted to be somebody's mother, but like I said, God was right not to give me a child with what I let you boys go through."

She pulled back to gaze up into his face. "And yet you grew up into a beautiful young man, kind and caring. A teacher." She touched his face with a shaking hand and whispered, "It couldn't have been all bad, right?"

He shook his head.

It wasn't. There were some good memories to offset their past unhappiness. He knew as the youngest they'd all shielded him from most of the misery in the house. His foster mother had even sneaked him some money sometimes so he could get candy. Being with Ash and Luke were the best times of his life, the only times he recalled pure happiness, whether they were fooling around by the creek in the summer or snuggled together watching Saturday morning cartoons. He refused to let the evilness of Munson destroy the patchwork of memories that made up his childhood.

The defeat in his mother's voice broke his heart. "When you leave, will you please let me know how you're doing this time? I understand why you wouldn't want to see me anymore, but a phone call every once in a while to keep in touch would be nice."

He didn't say anything but held her closer. For a second he thought she might resist, but then she settled against his chest.

"Come home with me when I leave. Now that I've seen you, I'd never forgive myself if I left you here."

"This is my home, dear."

"Mom, please. I can help you. I wouldn't be able to live with myself if you stayed here all alone."

"You forget, Brandon dear, I've been alone all my life." The quiet dignity in her voice slayed him. "Even when you boys were here, you didn't need me all that much—you had each other. And Paul..." She stopped and shuddered. "I thought marriage was a sacred thing, but I was as wrong about that as I was with everything else in my life."

His heart broke for her. He and his brothers, by miracle, luck, and sheer strength of will, had managed to climb out and move beyond the fires of their personal hells to create their own lives. Their mother hadn't been so lucky. Trapped by poverty, defeat, and lack of a social structure to help her, she'd believed there was no way out.

"How about if I stay here tonight, and tomorrow we can talk about the future?" He returned to the table to eat his sandwich. While he personally didn't have much in the way of resources, once Ash and Luke learned of their mother's plight, he knew they'd offer her the moon.

Her delighted smile was all the answer he needed. He finished his sandwich and insisted on doing the dishes. Then, despite her protests, he went through the house and fixed what he could. He changed all the burned-out lightbulbs. She confessed they'd been that way for years, but she was afraid to stand on a chair to change them herself. He found Munson's old workbox and tacked down the frayed carpeting where it had bunched up in places or lay torn. The windows in the living room had never opened, so he oiled and then washed them all in both the living room and kitchen.

Sunlight faded into the lavender twilight of early evening, and as Brandon continued to work, his mind busied itself with logistics. He knew he'd be bringing his mother back, but she needed a place to stay. Certainly Ash or Luke would help with that. Both of them had room in their homes for her. He climbed the narrow staircase to the second floor and took a deep breath before entering the room he'd occupied as a teenager.

To his shock, it was almost as he'd left it. Though it was free of dust, nothing had really changed. He walked inside and touched various books on the shelves, then sat on his narrow twin bed, staring out the window at the darkening night sky.

"I waited for you, hoping you'd come back, but deep down I always knew you weren't mine to keep. None of you were." His mother walked into the room and sat on the chair at the narrow desk pushed up against the wall. "I didn't deserve any of you."

Brandon collected his thoughts before he spoke. "After I left, I lived on the streets until the kindness of a stranger made me realize my life was worth something. He also made me think about doing good for others and living a life that had meaning." Even now, so many years later, Brandon missed Gabriel's counsel and guidance. He spoke from his heart, knowing Gabriel would be proud.

"You're the only mother I've ever known, and I love you. I'm sorry for leaving you here with him and not helping when he hurt you. I was too wrapped up in my own misery and uncertainty. I was wrong for running away, knowing how he treated you. I'm surprised you don't hate me."

"I could never hate you. Though you aren't my blood, you'll always be my child. I never stopped worrying about you, any of you boys. And you made more of yourself than if you'd stayed here with me. For that I'm grateful. But what was your uncertainty?"

"Because I'm gay, Mom. I know you don't approve because of the church and everything, but it's who I am." He sneaked a look at her, and to his surprise, her face remained unchanged.

"I knew Ash and Luke were different; people whispered about it to me when we lived back in Georgia. I chose to ignore it. But you too?" She shook her head. "I can't say I understand it, but if that's what you want..." She fingered the cross at her neck.

"Mom, it isn't a choice. It's who we are." He let out a sigh. "I can leave and find somewhere to stay tonight if you're uncomfortable with me in the house."

"Don't be ridiculous." Her eyes flashed. In all the years, he'd never seen her temper rise except for now. "I lived for years with that man who abused me, and if anyone saw my bruises, they did nothing. Many times, I heard people say it's the woman's fault; she should listen to her husband. I listened to him, and he still beat me."

Her small hands clenched into fists, and Brandon thought she might be the strongest person he'd ever met.

"So no one will force me to turn my back on my child."

"I love you, Mom. And I'm sorry for everything we both went through."

"I love you too, Brandon, and I wish…" She stopped and shook her head.

Brandon heard a knock downstairs. "Are you expecting anyone?"

He followed her down the steps and turned the lamps on as they walked through the dark living room.

"Sometimes people from the church stop by to check on me."

"Well, let me see who it is first." He opened the inner door to peer through the torn screen. There was no light on the porch, and the road was dark. "Who's there?"

"Brandon? It's me, Tash. Can we come in?"

Chapter Twenty-Seven

THOUGH THE LIGHT was dim, the surprise on Brandon's face was evident.

"Tash? Is that you?" Brandon's forehead pressed against the torn screen.

"Yes. It's me with Luke, Ash, and Jerry. Please. Can we come in?"

He heard whispering inside and then the door opened to allow their entry. One by one he and the others entered the weathered little house. Six people could barely fit inside the cramped living room. Tash was happy to see Brandon seemed fine, though he couldn't say that for the woman who was next to him. She was deathly white and shaking. Tash was certain she'd pass out if Brandon didn't have a firm grip on her waist.

Ash and Luke both approached her. "Mom?" These two grown men, one a tyrant in the courtroom, the other a financial whiz on Wall Street, were stripped down to the studs, revealing two young, broken men. The raw and naked pain on their faces, along with the trepidation and hesitancy in their voices, hurt Tash's heart. He knew they were wondering if they'd be accepted by their mother. He'd treated people who'd found their relatives after a long search. The fact that this woman was their foster mother didn't lessen their pain. She was the only mother they'd ever known. Treating his patients, Tash had seen so much rejection between family members and the disillusionment that came afterward. He promised himself that he'd give these men whatever support they needed.

The smile that transformed Mrs. Munson's face, however, told Tash that a different story, one with a happy ending, would be the case here.

"My boys. My darling boys. I'm so sorry." Both Ash and Luke embraced her, and her arms came around both men, holding them all together. They remained locked in that private circle for several minutes, shaking with long-held emotions. Tash turned away, pretending to study the lamp in an attempt to give them some sort of privacy. He couldn't imagine the mental toll this reunion took on them all.

When Tash turned back around, both Ash and Luke were wiping their eyes. It seemed full closure on this family's terrible history was about to come to pass. Brandon, however, had to deal with his legal problems before any of them could rest easy.

Before Tash could say anything, though, Brandon spoke. "He died in a bar fight. You were right about the time difference, Tash." His voice rang out, giddy with happiness and relief. "That's why it didn't mesh with what I thought. Munson died three days after I left, exactly like you said."

Heedless of what anyone in the room might think, he grabbed Brandon and hugged him tight enough to combine their DNA, pure unadulterated joy washing over him. If Tash had his way, he'd never let Brandon go. Though it was nighttime and the only light came from the feeble glow of the cheap lamps, Tash's entire world lit up. He was through making excuses or being intimidated by their age difference or any other problems people threw in their path. No one would ever keep him and Brandon apart again.

Unable to hold back any longer, Tash kissed Brandon, deep, hot, and hungry. As always when he touched this man, that magic clicked into place. "This is the best news possible. Your nightmare is over. And not only did you find your brothers, but you have your mother as well."

"I know." Brandon kissed his cheek but didn't move from within the circle of Tash's arms. Their foreheads touched, their lips scant inches apart. "What about us? In your voice mails you said you loved me. But—"

"I do. You left the carriage house last night before I regained my sanity and told Valerie she needed to back off." He brushed the silken strands of Brandon's hair off his face. "I'm sorry for all my doubts. I won't lose you again. Not to my fears or doubts or our family's mistaken belief that they know better than us who we should love."

"I'd never want to be the cause of any problems between you and Valerie."

"You aren't, and she understands now how important you are to me." Tash hugged him again, loving the feel of their bodies together, wishing desperately they could be alone. When he finally let go of Brandon and turned around, Ash and Luke sat talking quietly on the sofa with their mother. Jerry had retreated to an armchair in the corner and was reading a magazine.

"How was it when you first saw each other?" Tash nodded toward Brandon's mother, who was looking at pictures both Ash and Luke were showing her on their phones. "Was it good between the two of you?"

Brandon glowed from the inside. He looked like a kid who'd gotten every present on his Christmas list. "We cried a little but had a good talk. Something we could never have done before. She's so alone, Tash. I can't leave her to live here by herself. I want to bring her back with me. The place is decrepit and hanging together by some nails and glue."

"I agree."

Brandon's attention fixated on his brothers and mother on the sofa. "Look at them sitting there. I never in a million years thought I'd be back in this house again at my own choosing. Add to that Ash and Luke being here?" He shook his head. "It's awesome."

Tash laughed. "You sound like one of your students."

Brandon shrugged. "It is awesome." He leaned into Tash and kissed him softly on the mouth, sending a flood of warmth to pool in Tash's groin. "You're awesome, and when we get home, I'm going to show you how awesome we are together."

Tash could've groaned with frustration. By the teasing light in Brandon's eyes, his lover was well aware of the heated response his kiss caused.

"You're a bit of an evil bastard, aren't you? Last night you promised me a home-cooked meal and some hot and dirty sex, only to disappear. Now you tease me with that mouth of yours. You owe me big-time."

Brandon smirked. "Absence makes the heart grow fonder."

Tash glanced at the others and, seeing they were still involved in their reunion, took Brandon by the forearm and yanked him close. Brandon's eyes darkened, and his breathing increased.

"Your absence makes me hard. And when we get back, I better not find you anywhere but in my bed. Every single night. I don't want to ever be without you again. Understand?"

Brandon curled his fingers around Tash's jacket. "There's nowhere else I want to be. Ever."

Tash held Brandon close, soaking in his scent, loving the way their bodies molded together. Nothing in his life had prepared him for falling in love with Brandon. The man was like a drug; the more Tash saw him, the more he craved him. Their future together now seemed guaranteed, stretching out before them with infinite possibilities. Since meeting Brandon and falling in love with him, he'd moved beyond the prison walls he'd lived behind since Danny's death. Brandon might have been running away from his troubles and in hiding, but Tash had been running from his past and hiding from life and himself as well.

"I'll admit I was scared to death all day, wondering what you were doing and if I was ever going to see you again."

Brandon nodded. "I know, but I had to do it and do it on my own. You have an instinctive need to protect, but you need to let me find my way. If I make mistakes and fall, I can pick myself up."

Tash rubbed Brandon's back. "I don't want you to get hurt."

"It's part of life to try, fail, and get hurt. You can't prevent it unless you lock me away, which is not happening. But I can make you one promise."

"Oh, yeah?" Tash couldn't help the silly grin he knew was plastered on his face, but he was so damn happy it didn't matter. "What's that?"

"I'm done with keeping secrets." Brandon glanced over his shoulder at his mother. "I told her I was gay. I can't say she's happy about it, but I think we'll be okay." A sigh escaped him. "She said she always knew there was something different about Ash and Luke, but she thought I had a girlfriend."

"It'll be fine, sweetheart. And if not, you'll deal with it; *we'll* deal with it together. Right?" He kissed Brandon's cheek, losing himself in Brandon's marvelous warmth.

"Yes. Together. I like the way that sounds. I've

moved so far beyond where I ever thought possible; a job I love, my brothers and I reunited, but none of it would mean as much if I didn't have you." He laughed a little self-consciously. "Yeah, I know, I'm corny."

"Hey, you two, break it up," Ash called out, waving them over. "If you can tear yourselves away from each other, join us."

Tash walked with Brandon over to the sofa. He was yet uncertain how he'd be received by Brandon's foster mother, no matter her smile earlier when he met her.

"Mrs. Munson, I'm Tash Weber."

She looked him up and down, assessing him with a surprisingly fierce gaze. "That's my baby. I know you think I've been a lousy mother, and you're right, but they're all still young enough for me to make it up to them."

"Mrs. Munson—"

She continued on as if he hadn't spoken. "All my life I was told what to do. Listen to your father. Listen to your husband, your minister. They know what's best. No more." The loving looks she gave to Ash, Luke, and then Brandon, standing by Tash's side, said everything. "I'm gonna listen to my heart. And my heart tells me if my boys are happy, then that's all that should matter. It might take me some time to get used to it; I'm not gonna lie."

"I understand." Tash smiled at her fierce earnestness. "I intend to make him happy."

"But if you don't treat him right, I'll make sure you won't ever forget me. Y'hear?"

"Yes, ma'am."

"Mom, please." Brandon's agonized face was bright red, and Ash and Luke chuckled.

Tash understood her protectiveness. "Let her have these times," he said, whispering into Brandon's ear. "She never had the chance when you were young. I don't mind."

"We were talking here, and I think we've come up with a plan that might satisfy everyone." Ash had finished answering a text. He was smiling, and Tash assumed it was from Drew.

"Let's hear it, then." Tash was anxious, knowing it was his future, as well as Brandon's mother's, that they were talking about.

"This is what we're going to do." Ash began outlining his plan, and Tash sneaked a look at Brandon's smiling face, knowing finally, it was all going to work out in the end.

Chapter Twenty-Eight

THE FRONT DOOR slammed shut. "Brandon? Are you home?" Tash's voice reached him in the kitchen as he closed the oven door with a flip of his foot.

"Mmm." Tash gave the air an appreciative sniff from the entrance to the kitchen. "Roast chicken?" He walked in and gave Brandon a kiss hello. Tash tasted like coffee, and his skin brushed against Brandon's, fresh and cool.

"Yep. I got Esther's recipe. And my mom's biscuits are still warm. Want one?" He took one from the basket he'd left on the warming plate on top of the stove, spread a little honey on it, and brought it to Tash for a taste. Tash's eyes closed, a groan of happiness escaping his lips as he chewed and swallowed. If Brandon had anything to say about it, there'd be a lot more happy groans coming from the man tonight.

"Oh God, that was delicious." He licked his lips, and Brandon's cock stiffened. He remembered where those lips had been only last night and was already hard for a repeat performance.

"Glad you like it. She said they were always a big hit, and Esther loves them now."

"They all seem to be settling in well together, don't you think?"

In the month since Tina Munson had moved into Brandon's former apartment in Esther's house, she'd blossomed into a woman who, though cautious, had begun to see all that life had to offer. Being with someone as vibrant as Esther could do that to a person.

Tash had arranged for her to receive therapy from a female psychiatrist who specialized in treating victims of domestic abuse. In addition, she volunteered at the community center and had quickly become one of the children's favorite storytellers.

"She's so happy. She and Esther and Louisa trade recipes and go shopping. I think tomorrow the three of them are going into the city to go shopping and then later on to the hairdresser."

"Look out, New York City," said Tash, laughing as he took another biscuit. "How are you doing with all the changes?"

Brandon sat down and poured a glass of wine for each of them. Since he'd moved into the carriage house, this had become his favorite part of the day—Tash coming home and the two of them sharing their daily stories together. Finally, like a family.

"I'm great. Better than great." He sipped his wine and watched Tash as he did the same. "I love living here, and I still have to pinch myself sometimes to

FELICE STEVENS

believe it all worked out like it did."

"Don't pinch too hard. I wouldn't want you to put a mark on that body of yours. It's much too beautiful." Tash finished off his glass.

Brandon drained his wineglass and stood. "I might have given myself a bruise." He walked past Tash. "Maybe you should give me a physical, being a doctor and all." Tash's chair scraped against the tiled floor, and Brandon took off up the stairs, laughing as he heard Tash's growl of frustration from behind as he pounded up the wooden steps. He entered their bedroom and slammed the door shut.

Everything was as he'd prepared it; the fire had been set earlier and flared behind the grate. He'd found a table at an antique store a week ago and wrestled it up the stairs, placing it in a perfect position before the fireplace. On it now rested a bottle of wine, some cheese, crackers, and chocolate-covered strawberries.

The door burst open, and Tash stalked in. Brandon forgot about the food, forgot everything at the desire flaming in Tash's eyes.

"Come here." Tash held out his hand, and Brandon went to him, mesmerized by Tash's seductive voice and gleaming eyes. "Now take off your clothes."

Impossibly hard from the mere touch of Tash's hand, Brandon managed to find his voice. "Take them off for me." He undid the top button of his shirt. "Here, I'll even start it for you."

Tash quirked his lips in a smile. "You want to tease me? I've been waiting all day to come home and start the weekend with you." With sure, nimble fingers, Tash quickly divested Brandon of his shirt, his hands brushing the soft skin above the top of Brandon's jeans, coming to rest on the waistband for a moment. His thumbs circled Brandon's stomach, and Brandon almost came from that gentle touch alone. A quick pop of the button tab and Tash had the jeans tugged down to Brandon's knees. "Now get these off, so I can give you a proper examination."

Brandon wriggled out of the jeans and glanced down at his boxer briefs, where his cock already strained for release. "I have this swelling I don't know what to do with, Doctor." He stroked himself, cradling both his cock and balls in his hand. "Perhaps you need to take a closer look." Brandon slipped off the underwear and lay on the bed. He continued to stroke his cock and roll his balls. Tash, never taking his eyes off Brandon, removed his clothes in seconds flat, leaving them in a heap on the floor. He crawled up onto the bed to sit between Brandon's widespread legs.

"I think that's an excellent idea." Tash leaned down and kissed Brandon, who slipped his arm around Tash's neck to hold him close. "First, though, I'm going to give you a different kind of oral exam." He plunged his tongue into Brandon's mouth, and Brandon moaned, grabbing on to Tash's shoulders as he stroked Tash's slick tongue with his own. True to his word, Tash nipped and licked his way down Brandon's jaw to his ear.

Brandon cried out, arching off the bed, his cock

jerking and swelling heavily between their bodies. Desperate for some friction, he writhed and humped against Tash, who released his lobe with a wet *plop*.

"Feel good, sweetheart?" He nuzzled Brandon's neck, driving Brandon wild with desire.

"God, yes." Brandon's breath came in pants as he thrashed his head on the pillow. "Fuck, don't stop." He thrust his hips upward, anything to get some vital pressure on his aching cock.

Tash said nothing but continued his teasing licks and kisses down Brandon's body, nibbling at his nipples and swirling around his belly button. Brandon almost screamed with relief as Tash grasped his cock. Tash kissed the head, and his tongue tickled the tiny slit, licking up all the liquid seeping out. "You like that, huh?"

Brandon could barely catch his breath to answer. "Yeah, please."

"You want me to suck you, is that it?"

Oh fuck, the guy was going to kill him if Brandon didn't kill Tash first for making him beg. "Yes, damn it." Then all coherent thought left his mind as Tash's mouth slid over Brandon's cock, engulfing it in heat and wetness.

Tash took him all the way down his throat before drawing tight, then down again, his hands stroking in a steady up-and-down rhythm. One hand reached down and teased Brandon's balls, then slipped farther back to tickle and circle his hole.

Brandon was close to bursting. His painfully hard

cock ached, and the teasing pressure of Tash's lips and tongue had him teetering on the edge. "Oh God, fuck me. Now." He clutched at the sheets, knotting them in his hands as he thrust his hips up, ruthlessly shoving his cock down Tash's throat. His orgasm barreled down on him, and he shattered into a million glittering pieces, his mind wiped clean of anything except the unadulterated pleasure pouring through him.

Tash never faltered and swallowed him to the last drop. Brandon shuddered and lay in a puddle of desire, watching as Tash crawled over to the night table for the condoms and lube, then stopped. With a questioning quirk of his brow, Tash faced him and smiled when Brandon shook his head. Tash left the condoms on the table, returning to kiss him, then pour some lube on his cock. Brandon was far too sated and wrung out from reaching a point of never-before-imagined ecstasy to do anything but hold on to Tash's arms and fall into his kiss.

"We don't need anything else between us, sweetheart. I'm so fucking hot for you; I know I won't last."

Brandon groaned at Tash's words. Tash hadn't entered him, yet Brandon craved to be stretched full and drilled deep.

He lifted his legs, spreading them. "Fuck me. Come on." Tash's slick cock penetrated him, and Brandon couldn't wait. He tilted his hips and pushed up, impaling himself on the thickness, welcoming the sensation of being filled up by the man he loved more than anything.

Tash leaned over and slid his hand through Brandon's hair, holding him down on the pillow while he took his mouth in a scorching kiss. "No one else. Only you and me." He began the delicious pull and drag of his cock, in and out, and Brandon met each thrust with abandon, urging Tash on.

"Only you. Fuck me hard, harder. Yes. Come on. I love you."

Tash plunged into his body, and skin to skin for the first time, Brandon knew they'd never been so connected, so in tune as their bodies moved in perfect synchronicity. With every slide and push, Tash left an indelible mark on Brandon, loving him, claiming him. Brandon welcomed him deep inside, deeper than he'd ever reached before. He tilted his hips so Tash could hit his sweet spot. Tash smoothly pegged it over and over again until Brandon's groans of pleasure mixed with Tash's, and they came together.

Tash collapsed on top of him, and Brandon held him tight, loving the heaviness of Tash's body pinning him to the bed. He buried his face in Tash's damp curls, inhaling his warm scent as he nuzzled into the comforting curve of his neck. The frenzied thump of their hearts settled down into a normal rhythm, yet Brandon was loath to let Tash go.

Tash pulled out of him slowly, then curled his body around Brandon, holding him close. "This was a nice way to start the weekend. I'm thinking, seeing the table by the fire, that this was all a setup?"

Brandon smiled against Tash's chest. "Maybe. But I

made the chicken knowing it would be good cold or hot. It's sort of a celebration for us, don't you think?"

Tash rubbed Brandon's back. "In a way it is; you're right. So I think we need a toast."

They got out of bed and went to the bathroom to shower, then headed over to the warmth of the fire. Brandon uncorked the wine and poured a glass for Tash and one for himself. He stared into the fire for a moment before speaking.

"We've been living here together for one month, and every day it only gets better and better. Because of you, I have my brothers back and my mother here. You gave me back my life. If I'd never stopped running, I would have passed this all right by and missed you, and that would've been the biggest mistake I'd ever made." Brandon kissed Tash, loving the sweet sweep of his tongue and the scratch of evening stubble rubbing against his face. The fact that he had this man every morning and night forever was a gift he planned to never take for granted.

Tash cupped Brandon's jaw, holding his gaze. "I love you more today than the first time I knew it in my heart. Having you here with me, sharing our lives together and creating a home and family is something I'd never expected. I'm glad you stopped running." When he reached out his hand, Brandon took it. "It made you easier to catch."

They clinked their glasses and sipped the wine. Brandon savored the richness on his tongue and then took another sip and kissed Tash, sharing the wine from his mouth. Their kiss deepened, and Brandon knew his days of running were over. There was no place he'd rather be than right here in Tash's arms.

Epilogue

Mike and Rachel

Six months later

MIKE STOOD IN Esther's garden, pulling at the collar around his neck. "Damn, I hate wearing these things. I told Rachel we should've eloped and gone to Vegas or something."

Ash snorted. "And have Esther miss the wedding of her only granddaughter?" He raised a dubious brow. "Surely you aren't that stupid?"

True. Esther was like his grandmother, and he'd never do anything to hurt her. Rachel had told him her childhood dream was to marry in her grandmother's garden, and Mike couldn't refuse her a thing.

"No, you're right." But it didn't make standing in the sun wearing a tie any easier.

"Besides, they're almost ready. Look, here comes Jordan."

Jordan hurried over with Luke a step behind. "I've got the rings right here. Are you ready?" He grinned. "I still can't believe you're the first one to get married."

"And she said yes." Drew slipped his arm around Ash's waist. "That's the one I'm trying to figure out."

Mike crossed his arms. "Very funny, hah fucking hah. Go on, have your fun. Get it all out of your systems now, especially you, D, since you're going to be my brother at the end of the day."

Drew's eyes grew soft. "You've always been my brother, you and Jordan since we were little. I couldn't ask for a better man to marry my sister."

Mike's throat grew tight. "The feeling's mutual, brother." He pulled Drew to him in a bear hug. He knew how lucky he was, marrying Rachel. She made him feel like a whole man again, despite his injury and the nightmares of the attack. There was no one else like her, and he had no problem spending the rest of his life making sure she knew how special she was.

"Drew, it's time." Ash tapped him on the back, and Mike released him. "I see Tina and Louisa waiting in the doorway."

Ever the emotional one in their group, Drew wiped his eyes. "All right, this is it." He turned to Ash and touched his chest. A light brush, nothing more, but Ash's eyes flashed brightly in the sun.

Mike watched them kiss. There was something different about the two of them today. Always deeply connected, they seemed to not even need to speak and could communicate with a glance.

Drew hurried off down the flower-edged path. When Rachel told Esther about their plans, Esther went into full wedding mode. She, Louisa, and Tina planted beautiful impatiens and azalea bushes in the garden, certain to be flowering in time for the wedding. The chuppah, or canopy under which Mike and Rachel would be married, made a perfect arch thick with pink and white roses.

He couldn't have cared less about all the plans and only wanted to marry Rachel and start their lives together.

"Hey, you guys, we aren't late, are we?" Brandon rushed up with Tash. "We got stuck in some stupid traffic." He greeted his brothers and Mike.

"Nope, you're fine." Soft music began to play from the outside patio. Mike saw his parents approach. "As a matter of fact, you should probably take your seats, 'cause it's time."

Jordan kissed Luke. "I'll see you afterward." As best man, Jordan would be the first one to walk up the aisle. Rachel's best friend from college was her maid of honor and would follow him.

Mike took his place in between his parents.

"Ready, Son?" His father smiled at him, and his mother squeezed his arm. "You know, we'd always hoped you would marry Rachel. We couldn't be happier to have her as a daughter."

"Hopefully, you two will be giving us lots of grand-children to spoil." His mother kissed his cheek.

"Carol, really, let the boy get married first."

"I promise we'll work on it as hard as we can, Mom." He kissed her cheek, and she laughed.

"I'm sure you will, sweetheart."

He watched Jordan walk down the aisle to the strains of Pachelbel's "Canon," and then Rachel's friend Jennifer followed, taking her place under the chuppah. The rabbi was next.

"Here we go, Mikey," his mother whispered to him as they walked down the aisle. Mike had always liked the Jewish tradition of both parents walking with their child for the marriage ceremony. He faced the guests sitting in the rows of cushioned gilt chairs they'd all set up this morning.

And suddenly there she was. In between Drew and Esther, Rachel stood out like a princess with her shining dark hair curling around her shoulders and a sparkling tiara in her hair. Her strapless dress showed off her beautiful figure.

She was gorgeous and his, and he couldn't take his eyes off her. They walked up the aisle three-quarters of the way and stopped. Mike went down to meet her and lifted the sheer veil.

"Hi, sweetie." He kissed her cheek.

"Hi." Her green eyes glowed with happiness.

Drew shook his hand, and Esther hugged and kissed him. "You always were like my grandchild; now I get to keep you."

He and Rachel walked up to the rabbi and listened to the age-old words of the ceremony. They sipped the wine and then Jordan gave him the ring. When Mike slipped it on her finger, a feeling of contentment settled over him. Grounding him. Rachel slid his ring on his finger and looked at him.

"I feel it too."

He squeezed her hand and let the rabbi finish speaking. Along with his parents, Drew and Ash stood together, hand in hand under the chuppah with him, Jordan, Esther, and Rachel's friend Jennifer. Everyone dear to him was in this house.

The rabbi placed the glass wrapped in a napkin on the ground. "Go ahead, Mike. You know what to do."

He stomped on it, hearing the satisfying crunch under his feet.

"Mazel tov!"

He and Rachel kissed and faced their guests.

"I love you, Rachel. I always have." He kissed her again, deep and hard, to the delight and whistles of the crowd.

"I love you too, honey."

Forever. It sounded like a damn good plan.

Jordan and Luke

One week later

LUKE PLACED HIS bag in the overhead compartment of the plane. "Do you want the window or the aisle seat?" He glanced over his shoulder at Jordan standing right behind him.

"Aisle is fine. That way I can lean on your shoulder." Jordan winked at him.

"Darlin', you can lean on anything you like. Keep taking me back to Paris, and you can have anything you want." They sat, and Luke relaxed. It had been a hectic day. They'd first had to drop Sasha off at Gage's house, which meant a trip early in the morning to Brooklyn. He'd offered to watch her since everyone else either had cats or wasn't home. Then Luke had wanted to stop at Esther's to see his mother. It still seemed bizarre to Luke for everyone to be together, but strangely comforting in a way. He often found himself reaching for the phone to call Tina during the day to check on her or to say hello.

They'd had her over to dinner several times, and she and Jordan surprisingly hit it off, as Jordan, with his natural charm, made her feel completely at ease and had her laughing at his jokes and cooking with him in the kitchen. He, Ash, and Brandon had all decided to participate in family therapy with her, and after learning more about her brutal life with Munson, Luke slowly let go of the past.

Life, as he knew it, was good.

The flight attendant appeared at their seats.

"Champagne, water, or something else to drink?"

Before Luke could answer, Jordan spoke. "I'll take champagne and so will he."

Luke elbowed him. "What if I didn't want that? Maybe I want something different." The flight attendant smiled at him when he looked to her.

"Do you want something else, sir?"

Luke groused, "No. Champagne is good. Thank

you."

Jordan snickered. "I knew it."

"You're such an ass." He pretended to read the *Wall Street Journal* he'd brought with him.

Jordan kissed his cheek and brushed his fingertips along Luke's jaw. "But you love me, right?"

Luke put the paper down. "Of course I do."

More than ever. He'd never imagined the life he lived now, filled with friends, family, and so much laughter; it sometimes scared him. Finding Brandon was the greatest joy in his life. Now that their mother lived with Esther, he couldn't imagine anything making his life any better than it was at this moment. He was on his way to Paris with the man he loved, flying first class, and staying in a luxury hotel.

And when they arrived, he planned to tell Jordan his surprise. He knew how much Jordan loved the country; some of his favorite weekends were the trips they took to Pennsylvania to go antiquing or fishing. Growing up in the country, Luke had never had a chance to appreciate it, but now he looked forward to their planned getaways from his hectic, soul-draining job. He'd had his eye on a little piece of property in one of the small towns they passed often, with a pond and a garden in the back. Jordan would frequently remark on what a nice weekend retreat it would make.

Two weeks ago, he'd bought it and planned to surprise Jordan with the deed on this vacation.

What more could he want?

They took off on time and within half an hour were already being served their first snack. Jordan had become unusually quiet, accepting the dish of nuts from the attendant. Perhaps it had been a long day for him as well.

The attendant placed his little container on the tray. "Enjoy, sir."

He thanked her and reached in to take a handful of nuts but felt something cold and hard instead. He tipped the dish over, and a ring fell out.

Stunned, he looked over at Jordan, who smiled at him.

"Marry me, Lucas?"

JORDAN HAD SEEN people in shock before, but Lucas seemed paralyzed. Sudden doubt crawled through him as he watched Lucas's reaction. Had he made a mistake about Lucas's feelings for him? They loved each other, didn't they?

"Lucas, if you don't say something soon, I may have to check your breath against a mirror to see if you're still alive. Of course, if you don't want to marry me, I guess I can live with it. I thought—"

"Shut up and kiss me."

Thank God. He could breathe again. Happiness welled up inside him. "Can I take that as a yes?"

"Can't you ever do what I ask?" Lucas sighed and took off his seat belt to face him. "Kiss me. Now. We'll talk later."

The lights had dimmed in the cabin as it was an

overnight flight. Not that Jordan cared in the least. He would kiss Lucas in the middle of the day in Times Square if he decided. Jordan did what he wanted, where he wanted. The only thing that never changed is that he wanted to do it all with Lucas.

He took Lucas's face between his hands and crushed their lips together. His mouth moved over Lucas's, hot and hungry, while their tongues met and tangled. Jordan sank into the kiss, fervently hoping his touch and breath could speak what was in his heart.

When they finally broke apart, both were panting. Lucas had a dazed look in his eyes, his lips so ripe and swollen from Jordan's kisses, it was an effort for Jordan not to grab him again. Jordan took a deep breath and closed his eyes in an effort to slow his racing heart.

"Jordan?" The quiet hesitancy in Lucas's voice scared Jordan.

"Yes?"

"Are you sure? You really want to get married?"

Jordan had spent almost a year with Lucas, and he loved him now as much as when he first fell for the man. They worked hard but always made certain to carve out time where it was the two of them together. Jerry had finally made good on his threat and retired to Florida with his wife, Marie, and he and Lucas planned to fly down to visit them. He'd learned from past mistakes and spent more time at Drew's clinic and had recently thought about teaching at one of the medical schools in the city. It didn't matter any longer to him to be the best and the biggest. What mattered was his volunteer work at the community center and reading to the kids. Or taking long walks with Sasha through the city with Lucas, then coming home to make love. The crushing loneliness he'd suffered from after Keith's death was a thing of the past, but he never forgot how insidious it was and how it had almost destroyed him. Jordan made sure to never keep secrets from Lucas, and Lucas had opened up to him about all the pain he'd had inside since childhood.

It hurt him, then, to think Lucas still had doubts.

"I love you. I want to be a family, have children, grow old with you. Does that sound like I don't want to get married?" Jordan picked up Lucas's hand and stroked it. "I want to be married to you. Only you."

Lucas raised his free hand to Jordan's face and brushed his knuckles along Jordan's cheek. He then took the ring and handed it to Jordan and extended his finger.

Trembling a bit, Jordan slid it on Lucas's finger and held his hand tight. He pushed the Call button for the flight attendant.

"May we each have another glass of champagne, please?" He squeezed Lucas's hand. "We have a wedding to plan."

Drew and Ash

One month later

ASH WAS IN a piss-poor mood when he came home. He threw his briefcase on the chair and headed straight to the bar for an iced vodka. He hated spending Saturdays at the office, but he knew he wasn't good company for his friends right now so better to take his bad mood out on his files. Domino glared at him from the sofa, seemingly disappointed that Ash wasn't Drew.

Ash glared right back at the cat. "I miss him more."

He'd spent almost the entire past week either in court or working late at the office, anything rather than being home by himself. Esther had tried to persuade him to come by, but Ash made excuses about work. Drew had been gone at some damn conference, and Ash missed him horribly. Since they'd first been together, they'd never been separated for even a day. Ash checked his watch, noting that Drew's plane should've landed by now and wondered why he hadn't called.

For all the years before he'd met Drew, Ash had been alone without a second thought. He had work and countless men, and it had all been enough. Until Drew. Once he met Drew, it all changed; Ash shed his skin and became a new person. He assumed falling in love was what did it.

But with Drew gone this week, self-doubt haunted Ash. The nights alone crawled in, bringing with it all his old insecurities about his worthiness to be loved by a man as good as Drew. Phone calls at night and raunchy sex over Skype didn't cut it for Ash. Drew was his home, his center. He needed Drew's touch and calming presence. Without Drew in his bed Ash was rudderless: unsure and alone. After so many years without love, he found it unbearable to breathe without Drew to lean on. Even an extra therapy session hadn't helped.

Ash knew what people thought. They believed his dominance in the courtroom extended to every aspect of his life. He poured himself another drink and stared at the colorless liquid. What a joke that was, a façade. Only Drew knew the scared man Ash was, the man who needed to be held in the middle of the night, the man who couldn't take a deep breath without Drew by his side. The iced vodka slid down Ash's throat, but it was no cure for his loneliness.

The lock clicked, and Drew walked in, smiling at him from the doorway. And like magic, Ash could breathe again. The grayness slid away, and color reentered his life.

"Baby." Ash grabbed Drew to him and crushed their mouths together. They held each other close and rocked. Ash's lips found the curve of Drew's cheek. "I missed you so damn much." He continued to kiss Drew down his neck as he cupped Drew's ass. "Don't go away again. Don't leave me."

"Mmm. Sorry I didn't let you know we landed, but my phone died. Come with me next time?" Drew pulled off his tie and unbuttoned his shirt. "I hated sleeping alone."

"Me too. I couldn't sleep at all without you. That damn cat kept staring at me like I'd done something horrible to you."

Drew chuckled. "You and Domino should be

friends already." He walked into the bedroom, and Ash held his breath.

Several minutes passed, and then Drew walked back into the living room with an odd look on his face. "What is this?" He held out a small box and a red rose.

"Did you open it?" Ash swallowed, more nervous than the first time he'd walked into a courtroom.

"Should I?"

Ash nodded, never taking his eyes off Drew as he opened the box. Drew began to tremble.

"Where did you get this?"

"From Esther. I spoke to her after Mike and Rachel got married, and she gave it to me."

With a shaking hand, Drew took the wide band of gold from the box. "I never knew she had it. I thought it was lost in the accident and only my mother's ring was recovered." He held it in the palm of his hand for a moment, then went to put it on his finger.

"Don't." Ash closed his hand over Drew's.

"Why not?" Drew's green eyes clouded with confusion.

It had never been in Ash's makeup to be with only one man. Before he'd zipped up his pants, he'd been on to the next hot mouth. Until Drew so ensnared him with his purity of heart and sweetness of spirit, Ash couldn't help but lose his own heart. And now he wanted to give his heart to Drew forever.

"Because I want to do it. In front of Esther and Rachel, with whomever you want there when we say our vows."

Drew's eyes shone. "Are you saying what I think?"

Ash held Drew close, letting the peace that only this man had ever been able to give him wash over him like the warm ocean tide. "Yes. Please. Be with me forever. Marry me."

Drew tipped his head back and smiled into Ash's eyes. "That was very poetic and beautiful."

"I have so little to give you; the best I can do is tell you what's in my heart." Ash brushed back Drew's dark hair. "So will you marry me?"

Drew kissed him. "Of course. When and where?"

Ash smiled as he led Drew back into the bedroom. "Leave it up to me and your grandmother."

Drew sighed. "I was afraid you'd say that. My grandmother will be uncontrollable."

Ash laughed as he unbuttoned Drew's shirt.

FOR THE FIRST time since he'd started the Clinic, they closed during the week. Drew had gone in early to do some paperwork, then locked up and hurried over to his grandmother's house.

There was no flower-filled garden or crowds of friends. This time, only his family and Ash's were at Esther's, along with Rabbi Waxman. He opened the front door and was greeted by Jordan and Luke's dog, Sasha. After petting her, Drew heard voices coming from the kitchen and headed to the back of the house.

"Drew, darling." Esther, dressed in a pink suit with

a flower corsage, hurried over to him. "I'm so glad you're here finally."

"Nana." He kissed her cheek and hugged her. "You look beautiful." He scanned the room, his gaze coming to rest first on Louisa in a pretty white suit and then on Tina, also in pink like his grandmother. She stood surrounded by her sons.

"Thank you, sweetheart. I can't tell you how long I've waited for this." She patted his cheek. "I think Asher is more nervous than Rachel was on her wedding day."

They shared a laugh and then Drew left his grandmother to join Ash and his brothers. "Hi."

Ash spun around, that wonderful smile transforming his face. Drew loved seeing him so open and joyful. He loved Ash so much his heart hurt.

"Hey, baby." Ash bent to kiss him, and as always, the pull of his body toward Ash was fundamental to Drew's existence. They had a natural attraction that went beyond the physical; they were in each other's heads, blood, and souls. He couldn't stop loving Ash if he wanted to.

"Ready?"

"I've been ready for forever." Ash cupped the back of Drew's neck and trailed his fingers down Drew's back. "I was waiting for you to find me for years."

Drew held Ash's silvery gaze and knew he'd never grow tired of waking up next to this man. "There's no letting go after today."

Rachel hurried over, the swell of her pregnant belly

beginning to show through her dress. "Come, you two. The rabbi has papers for you to sign."

"Let's do this." Drew slipped his hand into Ash's, and they walked back to his grandmother's living room. It only took a few minutes to sign the English and the Hebrew marriage certificate and then listen to the words that would bind him and Ash together forever.

They'd agreed beforehand that Ash would step on the glass, and he did so, with a large pop.

"Mazel tov!"

Ash kissed him sweetly on the lips. "You're mine now."

Drew tipped his head back and stared into the smiling face of the man he loved more than anything. "I've always been yours."

Tash and Brandon

One week later

TASH CLOSED THE file and stretched out the kinks from his back. It had been a long day, starting with therapy sessions at his office, then meeting Johnny at the Clinic. What a difference believing in someone and giving them the proper resources could have. The scared and angry teenager was a distant memory, and in his place stood a young man of courage, determination, and eagerness.

Johnny burst into the office, waving a sheet of

paper. "I passed, Dr. Weber. I passed my GED!" He literally danced with happiness in front of Tash's desk.

Tash came around and gave the young man a hug. "I'm so proud of you; we all are. You deserve it. I never saw someone as determined as you."

Johnny's dark eyes shone in his face. "I never thought I'd be saying this, but I can't wait to look at colleges. Maybe I'll ask Marly if St. Francis has good computer programs." He raced out of the room.

Tash couldn't help but laugh and marvel at the success story. Johnny had turned his whole life around and gone from street punk to high school graduate in the span of a year. Jordan had no idea how much he'd help Johnny when he pressed for the police to show Johnny a little leniency. To his credit, Johnny had returned the favor in spades. By working here at the Clinic and at the community center, he'd proven himself and given back to other kids. Tash had no doubt Johnny would never go back to a life on the streets.

"Hi."

Tash spun around to see Brandon standing at the door. "Hi. Come on in. I only this minute finished with Johnny."

Brandon walked in and closed the door behind him. "I know, and I heard his great news. I knew he'd graduate." He leaned against the door. "You played such an important part in his accomplishment, and I'm so proud of you and the work you do."

He and Brandon shared much more than a physical

relationship. They talked about how they'd like to expand the help they provided to students to include more teachers from Brandon's school, as well as some of Tash's colleagues. Brandon was also teaching Tash to cook, and they spent many Saturday mornings at the Union Square farmers' market picking up fresh ingredients, then coming home and experimenting with their purchases.

Not that there wasn't passion; every touch from Brandon brought an awareness of how alive Tash was now, and how far removed he was from that broken man he used to be. Tash had imagined Brandon, being so much younger, would have the greater sexual appetite, but Tash had discovered a side of himself he'd never known. Loving Brandon and living with him brought out Tash's passion and desire, and it only seemed to be growing, not diminishing. Perhaps it had to do with love being thrown into the equation.

A small smile played around Brandon's lips. "I'm looking forward to the weekend."

"Do we have any special plans?"

Brandon came up behind Tash and put his arms around Tash's waist. "We do. I arranged a special weekend for us. With all the weddings and celebrations lately, I thought it might be fun for us to get away. Just the two of us."

Tash turned in Brandon's arms, surprised at what he'd said. "Are you upset about your brothers both getting married, and that we aren't?" That was a topic they hadn't spoken of yet. Not because Tash didn't want to marry Brandon, but because Tash didn't want to push him.

"No, I'm not upset. We haven't spoken about the long-term, but you know where I stand." Brandon gazed into Tash's eyes, and Tash winced at the touch of sadness he saw there before Brandon tried to cover it up with a halfhearted smile.

"And you don't know what I want, who I want?" Tash brushed back Brandon's hair. "You know I love you. That's not going to change."

"It won't for me either. Sometimes I think I still have to fight to make you believe that." The sadness disappeared. "Now come on. I have your bag here, and Rachel said she's going to stop by and check on the cats. Our flight leaves at ten."

"Flight?"

Brandon's eyes danced with excitement. "Yeah. I've never been on a plane, so don't make me late and miss it. Let's go."

His questions fell on deaf ears as Brandon dragged him out of the office and down the hallway. Without getting a chance to say good-bye to everyone, he found himself in a car service and on the way to Kennedy Airport before he knew what was happening.

"Do you mind telling me where we're going?" He gazed out the window as they traveled along the highway.

Flashing a mysterious smile, Brandon answered, "You'll see when we get there."

This playful side of Brandon wasn't one he showed

often. Tash guessed there hadn't been much joy or playtime in Brandon's life, and now he was testing his wings and experimenting with happiness. Didn't Brandon see this was what Tash meant? He needed to experience life before making any decisions that might leave him wondering what he'd missed.

"You're doing it again."

Brandon's voice broke into the fog of Tash's musings. "Huh? What am I doing?"

"You're overthinking what's going on, that I need to do this more, to find myself."

Shit, that was scary. "Maybe you do."

To Tash's surprise, Brandon agreed. "You are right. I do need to experience life. But life is meant to be shared and enjoyed, never taken for granted. I don't want to wait around because you fear I might be settling or compromising by loving you." There was an earnestness in Brandon's voice Tash had never heard before.

"All my happiness and joy over the past months since we met was only made better because I had you there with me. There's a special kind of joy in a happiness that's shared between two people. The joy is there because I'm with you. You're my other half, Tash. I don't know how many times I can say it or try and make you understand."

The cab stopped and pulled up in front of the terminal. Brandon took care of everything for curbside check-in, and Tash caught his excitement as they entered the terminal. Only once they'd passed security and were headed toward the gate did Tash look at his boarding pass to see where they were headed.

"Vegas?"

Brandon kissed him. "Why not? It's the city where anything can happen, right?"

BRANDON KNEW HE was ridiculously excited for this trip, but he was entitled, being that it was his first plane ride. Even when Tash fell asleep, Brandon remained wide-awake, reading a book or watching the television monitors, tracking their flight on the on-screen map. Not knowing what to expect, he hadn't realized they'd be flying above the clouds, and he spent some time staring out of the window into the darkness.

"Can't sleep?" the flight attendant asked him with a sympathetic smile.

Brandon shook his head. "No. It's my first time flying, believe it or not."

The attendant's eyes widened with surprise. "Really?" He reached into his jacket pocket and, with a grin, handed Brandon something. "Usually we give these to our kids who are first-time flyers, but keep it as a souvenir." He winked and walked back up the aisle.

Brandon turned the object over and laughed to himself. It was a little miniature airplane, fashioned as a pin. He slipped it into his pocket and, leaning on Tash's shoulder, closed his eyes.

Amazed he'd actually slept a few hours, Brandon

awoke when the plane touched down. He roused Tash, and they deplaned, picked up their luggage and rental car, and were off to their hotel within forty minutes of landing.

Brandon pulled into the parking lot of the Venetian and gave the car over to the valet. He and Tash checked in, and by that time, both of them were hungry. They decided to hunt up some breakfast and soon found an old-fashioned coffee shop, where they ordered their eggs, hash browns, pancakes, and two carafes of coffee.

"Look over there." Tash gestured with his fork at an elderly couple sitting a few booths down from them. "Her hand shakes so much, he's been cutting her food and feeding her. Now he's holding her coffee cup to her so she can sip it. That's true love."

"I think it's sweet. I'd do it for you." Brandon sipped his coffee.

"You might have to."

"That's not funny. You never know what can happen in life from one minute to the next. Look what happened with Jordan's fiancé, Keith. I may be young, but my life experience has taught me to deal with more than most people. Like Johnny and the other kids you help at the Clinic. None of us are immune to what life throws in our paths. It's what we choose to do with our life that makes us who we are."

Tash set his fork down on the table. "You're right. And my path was dark and a dead end until I met you. You're the one who brought me into the light. Sometimes I fall back on my insecurities, but I need you to help pick me back up."

"I'll always be there to catch you. The only falling you're going to do is falling in love with me." Brandon's pulse ratcheted up; his heart pounded madly.

Tash reached across the table to take his hand. "You do know I love you, right? There should never be any doubt in your mind of that. You're my best friend, my lover. You're the one I want in my bed at night. It scares me sometimes to think of where I'd be without you."

"That will never happen." Brandon squeezed Tash's hand, and they finished their meal in silence.

On the way out, they passed the elderly couple. Brandon smiled and stepped aside, letting them pass by, but to his surprise, the woman stopped to speak.

"It's so lovely to see a handsome young couple like you two. You look like my Bernie and me when we first got married. And you were smart to come to Las Vegas to get married. No waiting." She leaned on her cane and walked away.

They walked to the parking lot. It might have been late evening, but crowds of people still strolled along the sidewalk. Brandon leaned on the car. "Where do you want to go now?"

Tash slid his arms around Brandon's waist. "We can go back to the hotel and sleep, or gamble a little and then walk around the Strip." He kissed Brandon's neck, and Brandon shivered. "Or, we can get in the car and go get married."

Brandon kissed him hard, the deep love he had for

this man rivaling the bright lights of the Strip. He opened the car, slid in behind the wheel, and turned up the air conditioning. As they drove onto Las Vegas Boulevard, Tash took his hand and Brandon began whistling "Goin' to the Chapel."

Join my newsletter to get access to get first looks at WIP, exclusive content, contests, deleted scenes and much more! Never any spam.

Newsletter: http://eepurl.com/bExIdr

About the Author

I have always been a romantic at heart. I believe that while life is tough, there is always a happy ending around the corner. My characters have to work for it, however. Like life in NYC, nothing comes easy and that includes love.

I live in New York City with my husband and two children and hopefully soon a cat of my own. My day begins with a lot of caffeine and ends with a glass or two of red wine. I practice law but daydream of a time when I can sit by a beach somewhere and write beautiful stories of men falling in love. Although there are bound to be a few bumps along the way, a Happily Ever After is always guaranteed.

Website:

www.felicestevens.com

Facebook:

facebook.com/felice.stevensauthor

Twitter:

twitter.com/FeliceStevens1

Instagram:

instagram.com/FeliceStevens

Facebook Group-Felice's Fiercest:

facebook.com/groups/1449289332021166

Other titles by Felice Stevens

Through Hell and Back Series:
A Walk Through Fire
After the Fire
Embrace the Fire

The Memories Series:
Memories of the Heart
One Step Further
The Greatest Gift

The Breakfast Club Series:
Beyond the Surface
Betting on Forever
Second to None
What Lies Between Us
A Holiday to Remember

Rescued Hearts Series:
Rescued
Reunited

Other:
Learning to Love
The Way to His Heart—A Learning to Love Novella
The Arrangement
Please Don't Go

CPSIA information can be obtained
at www.ICGtesting.com
Printed in the USA
BVHW040219140219
540281BV00012B/161/P